JIDDY VARDY

Ruth Estevez

Copyright © Ruth Estevez 2018

First published in 2018 by
ZunTold

www.zuntold.com

Cover designed by Isla Bousfield-Donohoe

British Library Cataloguing-in-Publication data
A catalogue record for this book is available from the British Library

ISBN: 978 -1-9998633-0-2

Printed and bound in the UK by Short Run Press

ACKNOWLEDGEMENTS

With thanks to Patricia Labistour for writing about a dark-haired female smuggler in her book, *A Rum Do!* Without finding it in the local history section of a second hand bookshop in Robin Hood's Bay, *Jiddy Vardy* would never have been written. It is loosely based on Patricia's accounts.

To Suzanne, who kindly invited me to stay on numerous occasions at her home in Sunny Place and later at The Homestead. Without her hospitality, I would not have had the opportunity to explore the Bay's hidden nooks and crannies and gain a love of this stretch of Yorkshire coast. Thank you.

At this point, I'd like to point out that the names of these ginnels and pathways are based on how they are signposted now, rather than at the end of the 18th century. This is so that today's visitors can better link Jiddy's footsteps with their own.

My gratitude also goes to my publisher, Elaine Bousfield of Manchester based ZunTold, for her love, faith and commitment to my writing. Without the editorial skills of Elaine and her team, Anna and Debbie, *Jiddy Vardy* would not be the novel it has become. Any novel without good marketing risks going unread, so many thanks to Sarah and particularly Emily at Conker

Communications for their dedication to making sure *Jiddy Vardy* is seen. And the striking cover cannot go without mention, of course. Isla's patience, imagination and design skills make the book visually shine.

And lastly, to all those who have supported me in my writing endeavours, a heartfelt thank you.

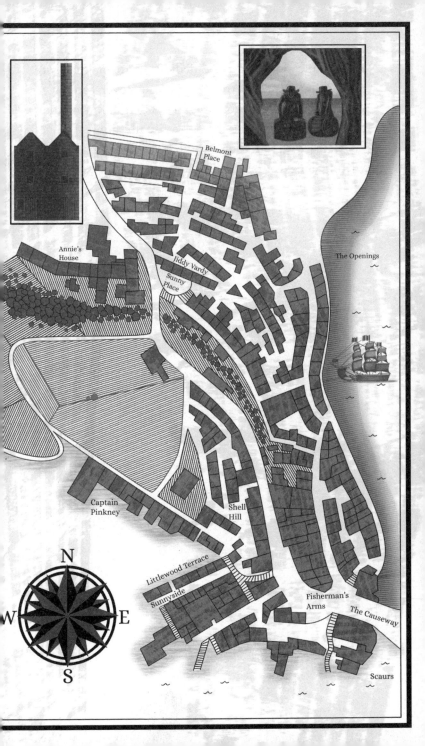

CHAPTER ONE

The North Sea
1779

Maria's dress and underclothes lay in a crumpled pile and she wished someone would take them out of her sight. Gregory looked cross, like a little boy who'd been scolded. His copper brown curls fell over his eyes and his faintly coloured cheeks rounded into the hollow of his wide, voluptuous mouth.

If only the baby had waited until they'd reached land and then a midwife would have taken care of everything. A midwife would have bathed her and the baby and set them right and clean again for when the father re-entered the room, and he'd have been able to lean over and kiss her forehead and the baby's and she might even have wanted to kiss his full, smiling lips, instead of hoping beyond hope that he hadn't been put off by the struggle and mess of it all.

She never wanted to go through anything like it again. The cabin so cramped, Gregory and his friend, Ryethorpe, half kneeling, part lying on the bed then standing. Sheets knotted, her dress, too tight, half on, half off, knees up, legs down, twisting until rigid, then

1

twisting again. Her hair, freed from its tight coils, frizzed dark over her clammy skin. Her teeth, cheek bones, jaw, forehead, all seemed too close to the surface.

'It's all right,' Ryethorpe had said. 'We're here to help.'

'She could have waited until we docked.' Gregory sounded agitated, hands all fingers and yanking jerks.

'She can hear you,' Ryethorpe said.

'Through these shouts? Did Catherine make this much noise? Tell me your son was worth all this.'

'I can hear both of you,' Maria said.

'What do we do?'

'I'm sixteen. Do I look like I've had a baby before?'

'Ryethorpe? What do we do?'

When she screamed, they jumped back like startled cats.

She wished she could sink through the belly of the ship as if it were wool, slide through the hull and plunge into the dark, buoyed by water that would let her drift painlessly into depths where octopus and strange fish would stare at her and the baby, that would slip out of her like butter and she wouldn't have had to move a muscle or pant out a breath.

Maria's dark eyes glittered like polished jet. 'The baby is coming,' she said.

Ryethorpe's high cheekbones seemed to protrude further, his large eyes wider in their deep sockets.

'Go away!' she shouted, gripping the bedsheet.

The men looked at each other then back at Maria, neither moving forward nor away.

The thought flashed through her head: it must look

disgusting. Her bottom felt as though it were full to bursting and she wondered what they'd do if she soiled herself. It was dreadful enough exposing whatever she had exposed – was exposing – in front of her lover.

Her stomach clenched again, pain travelling down, and she pushed and pushed, straining until she thought her eyes would pop out. She sucked in her breath, saliva dissipating through her teeth and she stung as though a huge, heavy cannonball was being fired from between her legs.

'Give me your hands.' She dropped back her head, pressing her skull into the pillow, 'it's here.'

She squeezed Gregory's hand so tight that he shouted louder than she did. She pushed and pushed, hoping only the baby would show itself. Finally, when she'd given up hope of ever giving birth, a baby girl slapped onto the bed followed by a membrane of what looked like a bloody liver.

'Placenta,' Ryethorpe said, 'we need to cut this.'

'Thank God you're here,' said Gregory.

Closing her eyes, she steadied her breathing and concentrated on obliterating the image of herself on the soiled sheets.

'I'll hold the baby, you help Maria into a clean nightdress,' Ryethorpe said. 'Careful.' You mustn't let go of the baby's head.'

'What about the sheet?'

'Pull it back. Use the blanket.'

She didn't care. Let them act like midwives. They'd forget it by tomorrow. She certainly planned to wipe it from her memory.

Ryethorpe sneaked away at some point but Maria didn't notice, only that his voice had gone and the cabin became quiet. She opened her eyes. Gregory stood, holding the baby. Her dress and underclothes made a soiled pile in the corner of the cabin.

'I want to call the baby Jianna,' she said.

Gregory cradled the tiny dark-haired bundle. 'Don't I have a say?'

'Did you give birth?'

He looked down at the baby. 'Jianna it is,' he said.

Maria adjusted her position and twisted her black hair over one shoulder. 'I am looking forward to meeting your family,' she said. 'Your mother and I will arrange a beautiful wedding for us.'

He ran a finger over the baby's round, brown cheek. 'The baby is exactly like you,' he said.

'Where is that friend of yours?'

'Should I call him back in?'

'Was his wife as young as me?'

'She is a few years older, but you'll like her and she will love you.'

Maria closed her eyes again. She didn't have the words in English for the strange cramps in her stomach and tingle in her breasts and she wasn't sure she liked the sensations.

The ship creaked. Maria looked through a port hole at the grey sea and gold-tipped clouds blushing with approaching night. Gregory followed her gaze.

'It's a splendid sunset,' he said.

'What time is it?'

'About nine.'

She caught the whiff of beef stew wafting through the walls. 'Are you hungry?' she said. She knew he would be. Both he and Ryethorpe were always ravenous and would eagerly devour the leaden food that the cook served up.

'Starving,' he said. 'Do you want something to eat?'

'I'll sleep first,' she said.

The bundle in Gregory's arms stirred, making a noise like a hungry kitten.

'It's doing something,' he said, and he held the baby out to her.

'What do you want me to do?'

He brushed the blanket against Maria's arm. 'You're its mother,' he said, 'it will come naturally.'

'You are its father, has it come naturally to you?'

The baby mewed again. Sitting down on the edge of the bed, Gregory waited. 'Why don't you feed her and I'll bring you something to eat and drink?' he said.

Pushing the blanket back from the baby's wrinkled face, she turned dark eyes towards him. 'Giving birth was not so bad,' she said.

Cupping his hand on the back of her head, he drew her closer. The baby pressed between them but his lips touched hers and, amazed she had the energy, she kissed him back.

'You taste of salt,' he said.

'Save it to sprinkle on your beef.'

He laughed. 'I hope she's inherited your wit.'

He kissed her again, the baby a hard shape between them. She wasn't ready for what happened next and, pulling back, clasped one hand to her breast. The tingling she'd felt earlier shot down her breast and a circle of liquid dampened her gown. Something odd was happening. That strange sensation from earlier was growing stronger.

She pulled one side of her nightgown. 'Oh no.'

'What is it?'

'Nothing.'

A prickling rush shot down her breasts again and larger circles of liquid darkened her white gown.

He screwed up his nose. 'Is that milk?'

'Well, it isn't your horrible English custard! Hold her a minute.' She undid the pearl buttons on her gown and held out her arms to take the baby back. 'You go eat,' she said, 'then bring me back something that the cook hasn't boiled to death.'

He paused in the doorway. 'This baby will be the first of many,' he said.

The force of suction made her gasp. For such a tiny creature it had an insatiable thirst. It pulled and swallowed and as it did so, her stomach sucked in and she caught her breath again. She'd never felt anything like the tingling in her breasts or the contracting stomach and as the baby drank, her other breast surged with milk, creating another damp patch on her gown.

'Slow down,' she said.

Touching the baby's long fingers, she traced over the tiny nails and smiled at how firmly it curled its hand around her finger. In a week or so, they'd reach London and she would meet Gregory's parents for the first time. She hoped they'd like her. She hoped she'd have the most beautiful wedding gown in the world. She looked down again at the baby, holding tightly to her finger, and at the mop of black hair. To think she was only sixteen years old and she'd produced this. She couldn't wait to see little Jianna in pretty dresses and with flowers in her hair.

Outside, the sky had turned mauve with a sliver of red resting on the skyline and familiar noises from beyond the cabin door sounded comforting. The crew must have eaten and be back on deck. Gregory and Ryethorpe would soon return and Ryethorpe would want to hold Jianna. He never stopped talking about his little boy, Samuel, about his blond hair and blue eyes. He obviously loved children, but she couldn't let him go on so much about his child now she and Gregory had one of their own. She looked down at the baby again and decided that her baby's darker colouring really did mean she took more after her than Gregory. Shouts made her raise her head. A storm must be brewing after all. She stroked the baby's soft cheek. In a moment, she'd move it to the other breast before all the milk leaked through her nightgown and was wasted.

The door banged open making her startle, and painfully the baby's mouth broke suction.

'Ow!' She glared at Gregory but he ignored her, opening and closing cupboard doors. 'What on earth are you looking for?'

'Have you finished?' he said, pulling a blanket off the bed and making a nest of sorts on the floor of the cupboard.

'I have barely started.' She tried to settle the baby on

the other breast, but it wasn't proving so easy on the right-hand side.

'We need a hiding place,' he said, walking back towards the bed. 'Here, give her to me.'

'What's the matter with you? We are nowhere near done.' Cradling the baby closer, Maria stroked its dark hair. 'And my daughter is not sleeping in a cupboard.'

Gregory slipped his hands underneath the baby. 'You'll regret it if you don't.'

'No,' Maria tightened her hold, 'I am feeding her.'

'Trust me,' he said, 'you will want to hide this baby.'

She loosened her hold and Gregory eased her away.

'What is going on?' she said, 'is it a bad storm?'

He positioned the baby into the hollow of blanket. 'Hush,' he said, and closed the door.

'Why are you telling her to hush? This is madness, she is a baby, give her back to me.'

'Keep calm,' he said. 'We must keep quiet too.' He tried to put his arms around her but Maria slapped him away.

'Get off me!' she said. 'You cannot shut her in there, she will suffocate.'

Banging noises sounded above and they stopped to listen until heavy footsteps and shouts were followed by the solid crack of a gun.

'What is happening?'

Gregory put a finger to his lips. 'There are pirates on board,' he said.

CHAPTER TWO

Shouts and curses punctuated other unidentifiable noises. Maria grabbed Gregory's arm. 'What do we do?' she said.

'Keep quiet and pray.'

'What about the baby? She's still hungry. What if she cries out?'

Gregory looked again at the door. 'She's bound to fall asleep,' he said. 'Stay here, lock the door after me and don't make a sound.'

He tried to disentangle himself from Maria's insistent grasp but footsteps outside the door made them freeze.

'Don't you dare leave me and Jianna,' she said as the door opened.

'Well, well, what have we here?' Standing in the open doorway, a tall man with a triangular hat and a black and grey ragged jacket pointed a pistol directly at them. 'I think I've caught me a pair of lovebirds,' he said, 'and I think I'd like to see if these lovebirds can swim.'

'A gentleman does not enter a lady's cabin,' Gregory said. 'I must ask you to leave.'

'There's no treasure for you here,' Maria said. 'Go away.'

Looking around the room, the tall man walked into the cabin and Maria's heart sank. A man like that had no sensibility about what was right and correct. He was a savage. Men like that ate babies for supper or offered them to the moon. She'd heard about them. They were evil but there was no way she would let a monster like that know she was afraid. Gregory's jacket lay where he'd left it on the bedside chair and his pistol gleamed beneath it. He hadn't seen it though. Cold air breathed through the open doorway and Maria shivered. The man laughed, a filthy sound of grime and soot. 'I have this effect on ladies,' he said.

'Get out,' Gregory said. 'Leave Signorina Vardarelli alone and take what you want from elsewhere on the ship.'

The silence in the room threatened like thunder. Above, boots stamped, crashes and shouts rang out, but none of them moved. It was as if they were waiting for the baby to cry. Maria's stomach clenched and a fine sweat beaded her skin. The damp patches on her gown began to soak through again as her gorged breasts filled to bursting. She felt completely naked. She couldn't wait. Grabbing Gregory's jacket, she scooped up the pistol.

The pirate prodded her pile of discarded clothes with his boot. 'Do you want to put these on as well?' he said.

The pile of cloth was almost unrecognisable as a dress. The white petticoats stained with brown patches looked like they belonged in a farmyard. 'No thank you,' she said, sliding her arms into Gregory's jacket and hiding the pistol beneath her.

'Captain Pinkney? We're almost done up here. Do you need a hand?' A voice from the corridor sounded close.

'You know my name now,' the pirate said, his pockmarked face tinged purple.

'And you know mine,' Maria said. 'Now please leave us.'

'Maria,' Gregory said, 'may I give the man your jewellery? You'll go then won't you?'

She looked at Gregory. 'They are all I have,' she said. 'I will have nothing coming to England without them.'

'A fair trade-off between gentlemen?' Gregory held out his hand to the captain.

'Take them then,' Maria gestured to the trunk near the bed. Her heart beat fast. The baby wouldn't stay quiet for much longer. She didn't know if she could keep quiet either.

Gregory raised the trunk's lid and revealed her best silk dress and a gold box intricately carved with the initials M.V. The captain merely glanced at them.

'I thought pirates loved treasure,' Maria said. 'Please take them and leave us alone.'

Gregory's hands shook as he rattled the key and clicked the box open. 'Here.' He held it out.

With one swipe, Captain Pinkney knocked the box from Gregory's hands and it crashed to the floor, spilling sparkling emeralds, rubies and diamonds.

'No!' Maria tumbled off the bed and sat at Gregory's feet, gathering the jewels together.

Gregory squatted down to help her while another man, thin and scrawny with trails of sandy hair, appeared in the doorway.

'What's happening with these two?' he said.

Captain Pinkney didn't answer at first, but raising his pistol addressed Gregory: 'Move,' he said, 'we want everyone on deck.'

Maria pointed to the pile of soiled clothing. 'You want to know why I don't want to put those clothes on? It's because my baby was stillborn,' she said. 'May God have mercy on your souls if you touch me.'

'Throw the young soul overboard,' the captain ordered, 'and say a small prayer while you're it.'

The sandy-haired man gathered up Maria's dress and hurried with the bundle as best he could from the room. Maria could barely contain from screaming in the silence as they waited for sounds on deck.

'You don't frighten me,' said Gregory, breaking the tension, 'we are not leaving this cabin.'

It happened in a second. The captain punched Gregory in the stomach, sending him reeling backwards. Footsteps were coming back downstairs. Maria couldn't hold the milk in any longer.

'Take my jewels. Take them!' she shouted.

'I didn't make myself clear, Signora Vardyelly,' the captain said, 'we want more than your treasure. We want the entire ship.'

CHAPTER THREE

Hurling himself at the captain, Gregory grappled for a hold of Pinkney's gun and both men fell against the wooden panelling. Maria glanced at the cupboard; her full breasts hurt. She needed to feed the baby as much for its sake as hers. Both men grunted and groaned, boots bashing the bed, thumping against the wall and back again. Noises above erupted. Something splashed into the water outside the porthole. She looked towards it and shivered. A second splash sounded out. Shouts mingled with scuffles and boots thumped the deck. Another splash and spray hit the window.

Gregory and the captain continued to struggle, wheezing and panting like old men. On the bed, Gregory's pistol shone exposed. Maria looked at the men again. Gregory seemed unrecognisable, red in the face and grunting like a hunted pig.

Her hand curled around the handle. The cold metal shot through her fingers, its pattern boring into her palm. She only needed to point it and pull the trigger. Grabbing the gun with both hands, she lifted it up. The weight took her by surprise, and falling forward it banged to the floor.

The pirate's boots were inches from her hands. He could crush them at any moment. He was bending over. She raised the gun. Her hands shook. All she had to do was raise it a little higher. She pulled the trigger. Nothing happened. The captain's face loomed in front of her. Wiry strands curled from his flaxen beard. The wet on his lips glistened. Tired, drooping grey eyes looked at her over purple-threaded cheekbones.

'You need to load it first,' he said.

She let the pistol crash to the floor and, curling over, buried her face. A second later she heard it. The faint mewl of a baby.

'For Christ's sake, Davy, stop messing about.' A voice from the doorway.

Maria looked up. Gregory slumped against the wall. The sandy-haired man who'd taken her clothes stood in the doorway.

She could tell they were listening too. Gregory slouched unconscious and she prayed Ryethorpe would come and save them. Holding onto the bed, she pushed herself to her feet. She couldn't let the baby be heard.

'Leave us alone,' she said. 'Go away.'

Ignoring her, the captain kicked Gregory. 'Get Abe to help you shift him.' They exchanged looks and the other man left.

A moment later, the captain grabbed Maria's wrist and pulled her over his shoulder. The pain as her chest squashed against his shoulder blades made her cry out. Kicking and thumping, she shouted for him to stop, but he seemed to have hands everywhere and he caught her wrists in one giant fist. Face buried into the cloth of his coat, she thought she'd suffocate.

'Jianna!'

He mustn't have heard. How could he with her mouth pressed against his stinking coat and his boots stamping up the narrow stairs? The wind hit like a sheet on a washing line and she gasped in the cold air. Blood rushed to her head, stars pricking her eyes. She hit the deck before she had time to brace her arms.

She should never have left Naples. Her parents had begged her not to but she wanted to see more of the world. If only she'd listened, if only she hadn't thought she knew better. She'd done everything her parents feared and then she'd sinned beyond redemption and now God was making her pay.

'Mother Mary, forgive me.' Hands pulled her to her feet and she saw Gregory standing in front of her, his face distorted by blood and bruises. He opened his eyes, slits in swollen lids. A flicker of recognition. Two men grabbed his arms, dragging him to the ship's starboard. Two others pulled Maria after him. Boxes piled against the side and they forced Gregory to stumble to the top. A lantern swung from the rigging near his head. His beautiful curls blew golden brown in the wind.

'Gregory?' she said.

The deafening crack of gunfire rang out and he fell forwards, toppling over the side of the ship. Splash.

Captain Pinkney stood, smoke dissipating from the pistol in his hand.

'You murderer,' she said. 'You're evil, you're wicked, you'll go to hell!'

Laughter rode on the wind, into the rigging and over the side. There. A face she knew. Long and pale.

Ryethorpe. Thank God. He didn't struggle as Gregory had done and he looked unscathed. Two men shoved him forward and he tripped.

'Where's Jianna?' he said, as they dragged him to his feet. Jianna wouldn't survive this. She was probably dead already, starved and suffocating. She shook her head. She couldn't bear the look of disappointment on his face. 'Find something to hold onto,' he said, 'a barrel, another body. Anything.'

They pushed him up on the box and one of the men hit him between the shoulder blades with a piece of wood and he collapsed overboard with a loud splash.

Struggling as they pulled her up next, she spat in their faces. 'I am Napoletana,' she said. 'I am a lady, you cannot treat me like this. I demand to go home, you cannot do this to me.'

Her bare feet caught the sharp edge of a box and a gust of wind snatched her gown, whipping it around her legs. She smoothed her hands over her stomach.

Grabbing the rigging with one hand, she stopped herself falling. 'I cannot swim.'

A strong hand grabbed her wrist, twisting her arm so that she let go of the ropes.

'You're not going for a swim,' the captain said before pushing her hard. She screamed. The wind caught her, lifting her gown, hair, arms, and after a moment, she fell swiftly.

Hitting the dark water she drew in her breath, before plunging down. Thrashing her arms she rose to the surface again, gulping for air. Waves sloshed in her face and she slapped the surface with her hands, craning her neck to stay afloat. The jacket sucked in water and the pockets weighed heavy. Lanterns glowing on the ship already seemed a long way away. Under she went again, icy water stabbing her skin. She gulped for air once more and, surfacing, she saw orange stars flecking a jagged shoreline.

Coughing, she reached out, fingers breaking the surface for something to hold on to. Ryethorpe's words came back: barrel, a body, anything.

'Away we go,' a voice across the water. We need to be in Robin Hood's Bay before light.'

Lanterns were moving. The ship billowed with canvas. She couldn't see anyone else in the water. She was alone, all alone. Gregory must be dead, the bullet never mind the water would have killed him, and Ryethorpe had been in the freezing water so much longer than she had. Panic flooded her head. She was going to die. Splashing, she reached in every direction until her fingers touched something. It was the curved wood of a barrel and she grappled for a hold. Waves lapped against her chin, covering her shoulders. She dug her fingers into a groove. Her arms ached as she pressed her fingertips down on the smooth, wet wood and clung on.

Resting her forehead against the barrel, she let her legs drift. The baby would have died by now and soon she would be dead too, unused milk leaking for the fishes to drink. Whatever Ryethorpe said, she wouldn't be able to hold on for long, weighed down by Gregory's jacket. Her arms gave way. The water numbed her limbs. She couldn't hold on. Better to let go now. Better to slip away.

CHAPTER FOUR

Robin Hood's Bay, England
1787 – Eight years later

Jiddy sat close to Jonas at the sea's edge. The water glittered for miles and miles and Jiddy flicked the ripples gathering around her wet skirt at Jonas. He didn't notice and she wriggled her toes under his legs, but he continued to peer into the shallow water on his other side. Giving up, she lifted her face upwards to enjoy the early September sun on her skin. She'd turned a deep walnut over the summer, Jonas' skin tinged red-brown and freckly.

She prodded his arm repeatedly with her finger. 'You're covered in sun kisses,' she said.

'You're covered in sand.'

A squawking gull disappeared over the cliff. If she could fly, she'd fly in the other direction, over the green-grey waves to those countries that ships sailed from. She peered sideways at Jonas. She knew he knew she was looking, but he was eleven years old and a farmer's son and he kept telling her, he didn't waste words on eight-year-olds.

'I'm going to swim over there when I'm bigger,' she said.

Jonas ran his hands through the water. 'Why, when you can get a lift on Captain Pinkney's cutter?' he said.

He always had an answer. She wanted to swim though. She'd be strong enough when she was bigger. And besides, she was frightened of the captain's big triangle hat and the huge cloak he wore. Jonas lifted up a cockleshell and held it out. 'Lick it,' he said.

Jiddy touched the ridged surface with her tongue. 'It's rough.'

'What's it taste of?'

'Grit.'

Jonas threw it back into the water. He swirled his hand and brought out a frond of green-brown seaweed.

'What about this?'

She pulled away but Jonas held it out insistently and she leaned towards him. 'It tastes like the sea,' she said.

Jonas hurled the weed into the white surf and strode out up to his knees. Jiddy stood to watch, squinting in the dazzling reflection off the water.

'What you doing?' she said before he plunged his head under the surface. He emerged, chestnut hair a darker shade and cascades of water spouting from his wide mouth.

Running to join him, kicking up spray as she did so, she burst out laughing. 'Can we go out further?'

'Do the same.' He wiped his face and pointed to the water. Jiddy extended her arms until she floated, flat out. After a minute, Jonas dragged her up. 'Did you drink some?' Jiddy spluttered. 'Touch my tongue,' he said. She put out a finger. 'No. With your tongue.'

His tongue looked bumpy with goose pimples. She leaned forward. Her skirt weighed heavy and she concentrated hard on getting her tongue to touch his and not fall over and lick his chin. She always did what Jonas told her to do because he was three years older and always right. Determined not to make a mess of it, she stuck out her tongue as far as it would go.

'It's horrible.' Recoiling, Jiddy wiped her mouth with the back of her hand. 'Why couldn't I use my finger?'

'Because this is about taste not touch,' Jonas said.

Jiddy licked her glistening hand.

'It tastes salty,' she said.

Jonas looked at the mass of water. 'I don't understand how there's salt all around us yet we have to pay for it,' he said.

'That's because the sea's water, not salt.' She didn't look at him as she spoke. She'd never contradicted him before.

'What've you just tasted?'

'Salt.'

'Sea is salt water, Jiddy, how many times? It's not a river, it's not a lake. It's not fresh water. It's salt water.'

'I know.'

'I've told you hundreds of times. Don't you ever listen to what I say?'

'I do listen.' She listened to every word even if she didn't always understand. She was so stupid and Jonas so clever.

'Salt should be cheap when there's this much salt water,' he said. 'We have to work out how to get it.'

'Mr Griggs sells it for a lot of money in his shop so he can afford to buy beer.' Jiddy cheered up. That were a fact Jonas couldn't argue with. Everybody knew the shopkeeper spent all his money on drinking so much he fell asleep. And then the whole of Baytown heard what Mrs Griggs had to say about it.

'I'm not saying it's his fault he has to charge so much,' said Jonas. Jiddy didn't answer. Kneeling down, she twirled her fingers in the water, creating little whirlpools. 'See that?' Jonas pointed.

Along the beach, smoke curled up towards the sky.

'They're burning fish,' said Jiddy.

'Why d'you think they're doing that?'

'You can't eat fish when it's gone off.'

'D'you know why it's gone off?'

Jiddy wound her cold hands together.

'They caught too much.'

'You shouldn't throw it away just because you caught too much.'

'You should,' Jiddy felt pleased with herself. 'You can't eat that much fish in one go. You'd be sick. Are you going to sit down with me?'

Jonas began walking back to the shore. 'We should be eating all the fishermen have caught, that's the point.'

She didn't answer. She was bored of all this talk. She wanted to run and jump and turn cartwheels. She crawled after him, licking the surface of the water every now and then.

'We don't throw nothing away on farm,' Jonas said. 'Of course we can't eat tons of fish all at once, but we should be able to eat it later.'

'The sea tastes good,' she said.

'I don't know why I bother with you, Jiddy Vardy. Come on, you're not thick, why's fish gone rotten?'

'Stop it, Jonas.' Tears welled in her eyes, 'I don't know. It just has.'

'Salt,' he said before striding across the sand in the direction of the bonfire.

Jiddy ran to catch him up.

She tugged his shirt. 'Don't be cross.'

'Why d'you think I'm cross?'

'Because I'm stupid.'

'I'm cross because we need salt, Jiddy. Farmers and fishermen.' He glanced at the children throwing sticks on the flames. 'Listen,' he said, grabbing her shoulders and turning her to face him. 'Don't ever forget this. Government in London puts a tax on salt so folk like you and me can't have it. No salt means no meat or fish in winter. Got it?'

'What's tax?' she said.

Old Silas Biddick was calling out to Jonas from the causeway. Her attention caught by the crackling smoke and boys and girls circling a huge stack of burning fish, Jiddy ran to the fire, putting out her hands, glad of its heat. Others scampered about, throwing sticks of dry wood and seaweed on the flames and watching the fish merge into a smouldering mass.

'It stinks,' shouted Jonas' friend, James, as he threw on a handful of seaweed.

A line of girls giggled at him. Jiddy looked back at the fire; it was much more interesting than James Linskill.

Just as the heat burned through her skirts, a piece of wood struck her across the back. Winded, she only just stopped herself falling into the fire. Tall Nellie Ashner glowered at her, fists clenched. Behind her stood Annie and Betsie, both with their skinny arms folded over their chests. Nellie whacked her again with a piece of driftwood.

'Don't!' Annie exclaimed.

Bending over, she gasped for breath. Nellie's bare feet shifted a step or two closer and Jiddy wondered if she had enough strength to push her away. She peered through her straggling hair to see how close the other girl stood. In the distance, Jonas stood talking to Silas. Scraping the hair off her face, she straightened up.

'You stink more than Alum mine,' Nellie said, pressing her heel on Jiddy's foot and grinding it down. 'Dirty gypsy.'

That was it.

'You stink more than fish guts,' she said.

Jiddy watched closely to see which way Nellie would lash out. Nellie may be bigger and older but Jiddy was more agile and, like all locals in Robin Hood's Bay, everything about Nellie seemed pale; her hair, skin, even her eyes. Nellie took her time, her well-darned apron taut over her skirt and woollen shawl tight across her developing chest. The two other girls, only a pace or two behind, hovered like reluctant henchmen.

'Your skin's darker than rabbit turds,' said Nellie. 'Go back to where you came from.'

'That's not nice, Nellie,' said Annie.

Jiddy daren't take her eyes off Nellie. Her heart thumped so hard she thought it would push out of her chest. She hadn't done anything. This were unjust. It were always unjust.

'You're a wet fish from Whitby,' she said. 'You go back where you came from.'

Jiddy knew she'd hit home by the look on Nellie's face. Other children ignored them, running back and forwards, jumping and shouting when flames spat. Fights were ten a penny, a fire like this happened once in a full moon, whatever Jonas said. Nellie folded her arms and the other two did the same. She was making Jiddy wait. She shivered with cold, angry with herself because that would make her look afraid and to hide the fact, she put her hands on her hips and glowered back. Nellie didn't waste any time. She grabbed Jiddy's arms, swinging the younger girl off her feet and Jiddy kicked, screaming as the bonfire and the girls' faces and the beach blurred into stripes of brown and gold.

Letting go, Jiddy flew, a breath of freedom before hitting the sand, the force jarring through her back. She lay still until, fearing a kick to her side, she rolled over. Her head pounded. She hated Nellie and never understood why she picked on her. But she were tough and getting tougher all the time. Soon she'd be as tall as Nellie, taller and then they'd see who were Queen of Baytown. She jumped up, fists clenched.

Jonas' bare feet padded over the sand, his boots dangling around his neck. 'Stop that,' he said.

'Jonas.' Jiddy held out her hands. 'Let's run away together.

'Shut it, Jiddy.'

'But …'

'She's a weasel, Jonas, always bothering us, weaselling around, snapping at us, isn't she girls?' Nellie said, the evil witch.

Jiddy jumped into his eye line. 'Nellie's a barnacle on a barnacle.'

'She's only little,' Jonas said, looking at Nellie. 'Ignore her.'

But it was Jonas ignoring her. He wasn't looking or talking to her. She could be anyone; an annoying girl being put in her place. Jonas didn't think she could fight her own battles; well, where had he been while she'd been defending herself? She wouldn't cry. Jiddy wouldn't let herself cry even though she could feel bubbles of salty tears surging up her chest. She glared at Jonas before marching off and then, breaking into a run, headed for the causeway. She hated Nellie, hated Jonas even more, hated everyone. She didn't belong here. She'd run away and find her real family, whoever they were. They'd not treat her like this. They'd pet her and cuddle her and treat her like a princess. She'd leave the sea and the beach and all of them behind. She clambered over rocks, scuffing her feet on the rough scaurs.

Jonas didn't even call after her. They weren't friends at all. He used her to carry and do the jobs he didn't want to do and she'd been stupid to do them. And now he'd be sucking up to that Nellie just because she went all giggly and daft around boys. Well, she wouldn't go up to the farm ever again and she wouldn't be nice to him and she wouldn't even talk to him.

Footsteps running behind. Bare feet, like her own, but heavier. She turned. Jonas panted as he came to a stop.

'What are you doing?' he said.

She didn't know. He always confused her.

'You can dry fish, you know,' she said. 'You don't need your horrible salt to keep it for winter. All you need is fresh air. I'm not stupid, you are. Serves you right living on a farm and not in Bay.' She turned swiftly before he could think of an answer that would make her feel stupid all over again.

CHAPTER FIVE

Cutting off Bay Bank, her bare feet slapped paving slabs as she ran along the ginnels. She wanted to put as much space between her and Jonas as quickly as she could. Dodging through lines of drying fish hanging between cottages, she leaped across broken lobster pots left outside cottage doorways. Out of the corner of her eye, she saw faces, blurred by her speed into pale smudges, and heard the odd shout trailing in her wake. She turned a corner. Not far now. She charged into Sunny Place and pushing open a door, bent over, gasping to catch her breath.

Two middle-aged woman, wrapped heavily in thick shawls, sat by a crackling fire.

'What's rush?' Mary, the shorter one, said, her Yorkshire accent scooping deep into the vowels.

Jiddy touched her dimpled cheek where a cut, tinged with the beginning of a large bruise, had begun to sting. 'I hate Nellie Ashner,' she said and, kicking the table leg, flopped onto a chair.

Mary rose slowly. 'Now then,' she said, 'if you did as I told you there'd be none of this nonsense.'

'It ain't nonsense. I were with Jonas when she …'

'You shouldn't be with anyone, least of all up at farm.

You should be helping Mary.' Rebecca said, drawing her green shawl closer around her shoulders.

Jiddy glowered under her thick eyelashes. 'We weren't at farm.'

She knew she was in the wrong but she would never admit that. Mary needed her, she could see that and it made her feel bad, but it was impossible to stay indoors when the moors and the tops beckoned and she certainly didn't need Rebecca pointing it out.

'She said I stink more than Alum mine. Do I stink?' Jiddy said, sniffing her armpit.

'I'm sure Nellie's not so sweet either,' Mary said.

'She said I'm darker than rabbit droppings. She said I should go back where I came from. What does that mean, Mary? Where do I come from?'

'Nellie Ashner's no room to cast any stones,' said Rebecca. 'You take no notice of her.'

'Rebecca's right,' said Mary. 'Nellie's got troubles of her own. From what I hear, her da's none too clever with the bottle. You should feel sorry for her more than anything.'

'I'll never feel sorry for her,' said Jiddy. 'She's a fustylugs!'

'Jiddy, that's not kind.'

Jumping up, she threw her arms around Mary's waist. 'Why can't I call you mam?'

'Do I look like your mam?'

Jiddy put back her head to look at Mary's grey hair and round grey eyes.

'Yes,' she said.

Snatching the ladle from Mary's hand, Rebecca stood up to stir the steaming pot on the fire. A coal spat.

'Why doesn't anyone else in Robin Hood's Bay look like me?' Jiddy said.

Mary peeled Jiddy's hands away. 'Get out spoons,' she said. 'That table won't lay itself and Thomas will be home soon demanding his tea.'

'Jonas says ...' began Jiddy, her eyes on Rebecca and the steam rising from the pot on the fire.

'Jonas Chaplow may be a bright lad, but he don't know everything,' said Rebecca.

Jiddy sighed. 'It's not fair, that's all.'

'You're too old for tantrums,' Rebecca said. 'Get out cutlery like Mary's asked you and think on the folk who put food on this table.'

Rebecca's tone told Jiddy she'd better get on with it, so she pulled open the table drawer and grabbed spoons and forks. She didn't want to talk any more anyway. She wanted to be splashing about in the sea and jumping over waves and never having to smell fish guts and Nellie's hot breath.

Mary put four mugs on the table, and gave Jiddy a gentle shove. 'Dab that cut with a bit of hot water and don't look at table like that, Rebecca's stopping for tea as well.'

'No, it's all right, Mary, you've got Thomas to feed.'

'If I've got a rabbit in pot, you're stopping,' Mary said.

The large pot of stew smelled good and Jiddy realised she was famished. Of course Rebecca should eat with them, she was always round and it would seem odd if she didn't. The heat from the flames made Jiddy's cheek begin to smart and, spitting on a cloth, Rebecca rubbed it, making Jiddy pull away.

Elbowing Jiddy and Rebecca to the side, Mary looked closer at the simmering liquid. 'Like the smell of my cooking, do you?' she said.

'Surprised whole of Fylingthorpe, never mind whole of Bay, hasn't smelled your rabbit stew,' Jiddy said. She was beginning to feel better, with Rebecca bathing her cheek and the thought of a hot dinner.

'This lass is so sharp, she'll cut herself one day,' said Rebecca.

'Don't I know it,' said Mary. 'Now lift me up those plates, I hear our lord and master on steps.'

Jiddy laughed and let Rebecca dab her cheek again. She loved it when Mary called Thomas that. She wanted to joke in the same way with Jonas when they grew up. Right on cue, Thomas came in, carrying his fishing bag and stick.

'Wind is getting up,' he said, leaning the stick behind the door, and before he could put down his bag Jiddy leaped across the room, wrapping her skinny arms around his hips and leaving Rebecca with her hand in mid-air.

He looked pleased even though he pushed Jiddy back so that he could take off his bag. 'Now then, now then, what's this? How do, Rebecca.'

'Jiddy's been fighting with Nellie Ashner again,' Rebecca said.

Thomas took off his heavy jacket and hung it on the

line of pegs, taking a small packet out of one of the pockets.

'I hope you kept your thumbs out of your fists like I told you,' he said.

'Tom,' said Mary, spooning the stew onto a plate.

He winked at Jiddy. 'She won't be able to do much sewing with broken thumbs if she doesn't. Is that rabbit?'

'Don't tell squire,' said Rebecca.

Jiddy walked slowly, careful not to spill any of the stew from the plate Mary gave her. 'What's in packet?' she said.

'Never you mind,' Mary nodded to Thomas to put the packet away and he gave it to Rebecca who took it to the cupboard in the corner by the fireplace.

Jiddy rushed to take another steaming plate. 'What is it?' she said. 'Is it for me?'

'You know what happens to curious folk,' said Mary. 'Now eat your dinner before Thomas eats it for you.'

Jiddy put her plate down, pulling it close and eyeing Thomas as he sat down. He winked at her again.

'You'll know soon enough about packets going from pockets to cupboards,' he said.

'Thomas.'

'She'll have to learn sometime.'

'Eight years old is not old enough,' Mary said. 'Rebecca, come and sit.'

'Old enough for what?' said Jiddy.

'Eat.'

The stew smelled so good and Jiddy was so hungry she soon tucked in and didn't care that Mary gave Thomas that look across the table again. Nellie wouldn't be eating a rabbit stew like this. It didn't matter what Nellie called her. Nobody cooked as well as Mary and she was the only one in the whole of Robin Hood's Bay who had two women running round after them.

When she'd finished and cleared the table, she ran upstairs as fast as she could, hands and feet scrabbling the steps, slamming her room door closed before scampering under the narrow bed. Lying still, she breathed hard. She loved the space under the bed. It was her sanctuary and no-one but she was allowed there, not even Jonas. Closing her eyes, hands on her full tummy, she breathed in the familiar smell of wood and the very faint scent of sea lingering on her clothes. The smell made her think of Jonas. He hadn't come after her and it hurt that he hadn't. Why hadn't he? Because he likes the big girls better, she told herself and rolled over, resting her head in her arms. Things were changing, she could feel it. She'd show them, she were changing too.

She listened. Rebecca still hadn't gone home next door. Mary and Thomas and she would be talking around the fire for another hour or so.

There were no point in talking to Jonas she told herself. She wasn't going to see him anymore anyway, not if he chose Nellie Ashner above her. She'd not help him with anything from now on, not on the farm, not listening to his waffling on about that stupid tax and definitely not teaching him how to swim.

She loved swimming. She loved the sea. She was desperate to swim out and reach a point where her feet no longer touched the ground, drifting with the current. Next time, she decided, when she were alone and the beach empty, she would pull off her dress and petticoat and paddle herself out, one arm over the other, kicking hard, until she could look at the distant shore and feel the pull of the ocean at her back. She'd still not swim out further than that, where currents were dangerous, but one day she would, when she were ready, whether Jonas knew how to swim or not.

She shivered. Mary would kill her if she fell ill, so she crawled out from under the bed. Her skirt had dried stiff with pale swirls of salt making pretty patterns all along the hem, and as she stood up white grains of salt fell on the floorboards.

CHAPTER SIX

T he next morning, Mary handed several chipped dishes to Jiddy without mentioning the day before. She didn't ask anything in fact, what they'd be used for or where Jiddy was going or if she wanted anything to eat. Jiddy didn't say anything either. It was only when she tucked the dishes into her shawl that Mary spoke up.

'Off with Jonas?' she said. Jiddy didn't answer, busy securing her shawl around her waist. 'He's sensible enough, though I hope he's not shirking at farm because of you.'

'I'm not going with Jonas,' Jiddy said.

Mary rested both hands on the table. 'Get yourself some porridge,' she said.

Grabbing a chunk of bread, Jiddy bounded down the steps, nimble as a lamb, determined to be away from everyone that morning, and when she returned they'd be shocked at how clever she'd been.

Grey clouds sky billowed over the wet sand. A couple of figures bent over a small boat by the causeway and the remains of yesterday's fire still smoked. Jiddy jumped past, cradling the dishes in her shawl, seaweed squidging through her toes and popping underfoot.

Bending down at the water's edge, she submerged the first dish. It could take two ticks or all morning, she didn't know. She'd forgotten to find out and Jonas wasn't there to ask. Anyway, she didn't want to ask him, she wanted to show him the salt she'd made when it was all dried and piled high in the dishes. She looked over her shoulder. Only that scary Captain Pinkney and his old mates about.

A good while later and the water in the dishes hadn't changed. She looked up at the sky, willing the sun to come out but it remained cloudy. If she'd done this yesterday, her dishes would be full of salt by now. Maybe it would change by the time the men went off for their dinners.

Looking around for something to do while the water gave up its white granules, she picked her way slowly, looking in rock pools for crabs. That long rise of unblemished sand beckoned now that the sea was at low tide and had left it exposed. Running in a straight line, feet gently sinking, she lifted her arms, hopped and turned a swift cartwheel, palms, one, two, pressing into the sand, then up and running again. To have it to herself made it all the better. No Jonas, no Nellie and her two shadows. She didn't need any of them. And she didn't care where she was from or where she was going because she was here on the sand and she had the sea and she was going to make piles and piles of salt.

She looked back at the indents her feet had made. Sand snuggled into her toes, cool and reassuring.

'Come on, sun!' she shouted.

Pressing her feet down, heel to toe, stepping carefully, she marked out a wide circle that spiralled inwards. She could stay here for hours. Or until she grew hungry.

The water in the dishes still didn't look any different. Murkier, if anything. Maybe there wasn't enough salt in the water near the shore. Maybe you needed to be right out in the middle of an ocean and that's why salt had to come from far away.

She looked at the cliff. It was lonely without Jonas. Jonas had promised to take her into the hidden caves. She could go and stand in the dark entrance of one and smell the chilling damp but it didn't feel very nice on your own. She walked over the pebbles to see. Light seeped into the cave further than she'd imagined but that didn't take away its dank smell. She could see shingle reaching inside. It was dull without the shine of the sea. She knew there were tunnels leading away at the back because Jonas' friend, James had told her so, but she didn't want to explore them on her own. She meandered back to the water and her dishes. Still no salt. Still only dull liquid.

'Jiddy?' Bright-faced, Jonas strode towards her as if she'd never been angry and run off yesterday. 'What are you doing?'

She looked down at the three cracked dishes. He'd caught her out before she were ready and now he'd laugh. She couldn't say she were making salt when she hadn't any to show him.

'What are you doing?' she said.

He gently eased her to one side as he sat beside her on the rock.

'Aren't you cold?'

She shook her head. He studied the grey dishes. She

could almost hear his brain moving, all the thoughts and complicated words shifting around in there, trying to form a sentence that she would understand.

'I thought I'd make us some salt,' she said.

'Thought we didn't need salt because we have fresh air.'

'Thought I'd have a go.' She could be loud and strong when she wanted.

He stuck his finger in one of the broken crocks and licked it. 'Umm, yum,' he said.

She wished she'd done that so she'd have known if salt had started to form, thick and sludgy, the water drying off. His face didn't give anything away.

Silas Biddick, with his ancient old face and gnarled body, came shambling over from the causeway.

'Go away,' Jiddy said, but Jonas shuffled round as if to block her out.

'What are you doing, lad?' The wiry old man looked at them. Jiddy snuggled closer; she liked it when her dark locks mingled with Jonas' lighter brown hair. Them against the world.

'Nothing,' Jonas said.

Jiddy peered around him. Silas prodded one of the dishes.

'What's that then?'

'We're making salt,' Jiddy said before Jonas could open his mouth.

'You're doing what?'

'When the water dries off, it leaves salt behind.'

Jonas looked embarrassed.

Silas took out his pipe. 'It's all right, lad,' he said, 'you might as well get used to your woman talking for you sooner rather than later.'

'She's not my woman.'

'I'm not his woman.'

'Salt, you say?' chuckled Silas.

Jiddy nodded.

'That's what you've been doing with all these different crocks?' Silas said. Jiddy nodded again. 'How much you got?'

She stared at the sea. She didn't have to answer if she didn't want to.

'Just started then?' The old man slipped the words through the gaps in his teeth.

'I've been at it all morning,' Jiddy said.

Silas Biddick's laugh ripped across the rocks.

'Not enough sun round here, is there lad?'

Jiddy jumped up. 'It's me doing it, not him. I'll make salt and I'll show you. Sea's salt water, you see. Water'll go away and these dishes will be packed with salt and then we'll have fish and meat and whatever we want spilling out of cupboards and trunks and boxes and you'll not be laughing one bit.'

'Don't mind her,' said Jonas.

Silas sucked on his pipe, watching her. She didn't like that and she turned her back, pretending she didn't care.

'I'll leave you to it,' Silas said.

That's right, she thought. You go away with your smelly teeth.

'He's rude, I hate him, he always ignores me, why

38

shouldn't I speak back, why should I let him laugh at me?' she said when he was gone.

Jonas scraped the shingle with his feet.

'When will you learn, Jiddy? You're just a lass. Course he's gonna talk to me not you and you'd better learn soon, because I'm not always going to be here to protect you from whoever you pick a fight with.'

'What d'you mean? Where you going?' She could plan to run away, but Jonas couldn't, she wouldn't let him.

'Nowhere,' he said, 'I'm just saying I can't always protect you.'

'You don't need to. I can fight for myself.'

'Jiddy, listen to yourself. It's not you against the world. It's us against government. You are a Baytowner. Damn well act like one.'

He used a bad word at her. That were rare.

'Are you still mad about them burning fish yesterday?'

She thought of the salt on her dress and the line of it on Silas' trousers. Thinking about it made her head hurt. She slipped her arms around Jonas' waist, tucking her face into his jacket. Waves rustled up the shingle. She tightened her grip, but he didn't say anything so she closed her eyes. It struck her like a crack of lightning. She didn't need the sun to dry water and leave salt behind. Water dried up anyway. All she needed was to wet her dress in the sea and collect the salt from it later. They could have sheets of it, hanging in lines all around Baytown. They could call it Salt-town instead. They'd be famous.

But Jonas didn't want to listen. He disentangled

himself and said he had work to do on the farm, and when she asked if she could help he said no.

She watched him scramble up a cliff path and then, pocketing the dishes, she ran back to the causeway. Preventive soldiers were everywhere and she stopped to admire their beautiful red uniforms, even though Thomas told her they weren't good men. Jiddy knew they weren't good men because they carried pistols and they shot people. Locals who had a gun only shot rabbits and animals that were injured. She kept to the wall but she still liked to look at their fancy jackets with shining buttons and their bright white breeches. They take naughty children away, said Thomas. Sometimes, he said, they even take grown-ups.

Sidling past, she cut up to Fisherhead. There was someone important she wanted to see, the only man she knew who sailed to sea not for fishing or whaling. She ran along the row of houses before stopping abruptly. Captain Pinkney sat in the doorway to his cottage, smoking his pipe.

She stared at his pockmarked cheeks, itching to touch them to see if they felt the way they looked. 'Good day, Captain Pinkney,' she said.

When he didn't take any notice of her, she stepped so close to his long legs that he couldn't ignore her.

'You don't have to go out in your boat so much now,' she blurted out. 'I've found a better way to get salt from sea.' She held up the stiffened hem of her skirt.

She held her skirt up higher. 'I found out by accident.'

Staring up at him, she realised that without his big

triangle hat or his long cloak, he wasn't so scary. Sitting in his gansey sweater, smoking a pipe, he was merely a bigger version of Thomas.

'We can use sheets,' she said. 'I don't want to keep getting my skirt wet all the time.'

She thought he'd never answer and then he leaned right up to her face and whispered with tobacco breath.

'You like the sea, do you?'

She nodded, a little too vigorously, trying not to drop the crocks nestling in her shawl.

'Tell me what you see when you look out over water.' He turned his head and she looked with him at the triangle of water shining between Ravenscar and the corner of Cliff House.

What could she see? North Sea. Sky. She shrugged. This was like talking to Jonas, only worse because Captain Pinkney was a grown-up.

'I see money,' he said. 'Lots of it.'

'Oh.' She'd not heard that. Jonas didn't know that, she was sure. If they got the fine nets maybe they could drag the shore and find coins. 'Isn't it full of salt?' she said.

He bent down so close she could have touched his cheek.

'Would you like me to show you how to get salt from sea, Jiddy Vardy?' he said.

Jiddy's black eyes grew bigger. He knew her name. Captain Pinkney knew her name and she'd never spoken to him in her whole life.

'I don't think Mary will let me go out with you on your boat,' she said. She felt a little scared now. She needed to learn to swim in deep water and she needed a bit longer to do that.

'I've seen you watching them preventives,' he said.

'I don't like them,' she said quickly. 'They're bad men, they work for the King and they don't want us to have any food.'

His grey eyes flicked from one of her eyes to the other but she held his gaze. She were right on this, she knew she were, because Jonas had told her and she wouldn't pretend she didn't know.

'So you think you're as good as a lad, do you?' his voice smoky rough. Jiddy nodded. 'If you come down from cliff at Mill Beck onto beach at sunset, you'll see that much salt it'll make your eyes sting.'

CHAPTER SEVEN

U nable to wait for sunset, Jiddy sneaked out of her window and over the coal house roof while the sky still tinged blue. The sound of waves carried in the still air. She wondered if Captain Pinkney would keep his word, but he wouldn't have said he'd show her how to get salt if he didn't mean it. Sliding down, she landed on the flags and waited to hear if anyone had heard. Her neck tingled. This were it. This were what she'd been waiting for all her life. She could feel it in the way her hairs stood up on her arms. Captain Pinkney had chosen her to share his secret with, not Jonas, or James or Nellie or Annie. Creeping around the corner, she looked down into Sunny Place. Not a soul about. Keeping close to the wall, she ducked beneath the window and ran down the steps to Bay Bank. The noise of her shoes terrified her. She stopped. A gull swooped in the thickening sky. Hurrying across to the Bolts, she wondered if Annie would be fast asleep and what she'd think if she knew Jiddy were out at night. Tomorrow she'd be able to tell them. If she made it back alive. She took deep breaths. Reaching the end, she looked up at the dark window of Annie's and her sisters' room before scrambling up the grassy slope into the woods and catching her breath again. Her chest hurt but she was safe. Darker amongst the trees, she crept around the edge of the wood trying not to think what lurked in the undergrowth. Jumping at the sound of every crack and ripple of wind rustling leaves, she kept her eyes straight ahead. There could be foxes and wolves in the woods. What if there were scarier things? What should she do? After what seemed like forever, the trees thinned and she felt her way over the grass towards the cliff edge. Far below, the sea clutched at the shingle and she felt calmer. The dusky sky gave enough light to see. A bird swooped over the cliff. Crouching, trying to see anyone who could be about, she thought about the preventives and their pistols and bigger guns. What if they caught her and threw her into jail? No-one would know and she'd rot there and Mary and Thomas would replace her; they'd take another baby in and forget all about her.

Stop it, she told herself. Preventives won't take any notice of a little girl. The wind blew in her face and she began walking along the clifftop towards Mill Beck. Nearing the cove, she stopped to listen. She couldn't believe it. They were so quiet and yet there they were. In the cliff's shadow, the beach shifted with figures. There seemed to be movement everywhere, from the sea all the way up to the cliff. Captain Pinkney must be showing everyone how to get salt. Watching them, they didn't seem to be carrying water from the sea, but they were carrying something. Scrambling down a narrow winding path, grasping at coarse grass and determined not to be angry that this wasn't a secret only between her and the captain, she jumped onto pebbles. And then she saw the lines. People were passing boxes and packages from the water's edge and men with long poles stood away from everyone else, two nearer the promontory and two or three others, she couldn't quite tell, further along towards the Bay. Keeping close to the cliff, she crept along, stopping at the edge of a cave. A big man strode up the beach, his cloak wafting behind and his hat, a massive triangle, made him look like a mountain. There he was: Captain Pinkney.

'You landers, move it,' he said. 'Got to get this contraband up faster than this to storers.'

She recognised Isaac McCaw and he was pointing to two men. 'You tell carts waiting up top to cross White Moor to Littlebeck,' he said.

'Then what?'

'Then what?' Captain Pinkney sounded scary. 'Tell them to head straight into York and give themselves up to soldiers waiting there, what d'you think, you pillicock?'

Crouching by the cave entrance, Jiddy had never been more afraid in her life. She'd come to the wrong place. Captain Pinkney must have meant to meet him somewhere else. People were moving past without taking any notice of her. She tried to make out the path she'd come down but she couldn't see it. She shouldn't have come. She knew that now. Offshore a ship rocked up and down and rowing boats, laden with various shapes, rowed to the beach. Bags, barrels and crates were being taken from the boats, handed to waiting arms and carried in the semi-darkness, slipping out of sight. No-one spoke a word. And then she noticed how many women trudged past. Somehow, the women made her less afraid. They were lifting their skirts and tying small bags around their waists. She recognised Betty Booth's profile. And there was Rebecca. She wondered if Mary knew. What if Mary and Thomas were there as well? She stood up, trying to see who she recognised. She knew them. There was Abe Storm. Suddenly, Jiddy squealed. Someone had grabbed her shoulder.

'So you made it, Jiddy Vardy. Hold out your hands.' Captain Pinkney dropped a small bag into her open palms. 'Best baptism you'll ever have, now get on home,' he said, 'and then decide which you think is best way to get salt.'

The small bag felt tightly packed and Jiddy cradled it reverently for a moment before someone prodded her to shift inside the cave. Captain Pinkney strode back towards the shore, his cape wafting around him like a jet-black cloud.

Lit by lanterns, Jiddy could see that the cave was full. Women buffeted their hips against her. Men carrying barrels, bags and reams of what looked like oil cloth trudged inside, and all of them were heading towards the rock wall at the back of the cave where one by one they disappeared.

She'd heard of the tunnels, Jonas and James Linskill kept going on about them, but she never thought they'd really exist. She'd have so much to tell Jonas tomorrow. Don't let me be squashed, she thought, as she elbowed and pushed back against the jostling skirts, hurrying forwards with the surge of women. Helen Drake. She recognised the sharp profile as it passed a lamp and disappeared like the rest. Within seconds, Jiddy reached the gap in the wall of rock and stumbled into a line of people moving steadily forwards. She couldn't see anything.

Cold hit her. Noise of feet echoed and the narrow space and uneven floor and walls closed in. Trapped by skirts in front and behind she panted. She couldn't breathe. She'd die. There was no air. Someone prodded her in the back and she fell into the massive padded shape in front.

'What on earth are you doing here?' A woman's voice behind. It sounded like Grace who lived on Bloomswell.

Clutching onto the skirt in front she edged her feet bit by bit. Her head hurt, her arm ached, but she couldn't drop the bag of salt. It went on and on. Her heart beat so fast it hurt. Where were they going? If she didn't keep up, they'd trample over her and she'd be lost forever in the tunnel. She'd never smell fresh air again. She shouldn't have come.

'Night, Jessie.'

A line was filing off to the left with a lantern strung up on the wall, lighting the junction. She didn't know what to do. Jessie lived near the top of the bank and she didn't want to go there. Grace shoved from behind.

'Not that way,' she said. 'Follow Helen.'

They entered an even narrower tunnel. Helen moved faster through a gap in the wall. Jiddy followed her and came out into a cupboard. Helen ducked under a shelf. A moment later, they were stood in a room flickering with firelight. Gulping in air, even stale coal dust air, was better than the tunnel.

Helen Drake's younger sister, Dottie Wright, had her skirt rucked up around her waist. She looked awkward and bigger than usual. Another woman had hold of a strip of material wound around Dottie's hips. Jiddy watched as Dottie rotated in a circle, revealing yards of silk, unravelling into the other woman's arms. As the fabric passed from Dottie to the other woman, Dottie lost the bulging stomach and padded thighs. Mesmerised, Jiddy watched as folds of silk gleamed in the firelight. She'd never seen anything so beautiful.

'What are you doing here?' Helen Drake grabbed her shoulder and Jiddy gawped back, unable to speak.

Helen pulled at the bag of salt but Jiddy held on. 'Give me that.'

'No, it's mine.'

'Not so loud.' Helen glanced at the door. 'Give it here.'

Dottie and the other woman had stopped what they were doing and were watching.

'Captain Pinkney gave it me,' Jiddy said. 'He said it were mine.'

'Oh, leave her, Helen,' said Grace, busy gathering up her own skirt.

Tutting, Helen began shoving several bags behind a false panel in the wall. She pulled a face at Jiddy when she saw her watching.

'Better hide it, you stupid beggar. Looks like you want to give it to preventives holding it out like a slice of bread,' she said.

Jiddy tucked the small sack into the folds of her shawl but Helen tried to take the bag of salt again.

'Get off.' Jiddy struggled but Helen wrestled the bag free.

'Useless.' She tucked it into the pocket under Jiddy's skirt. 'Now will that hold?' she asked. Jiddy nodded. She hated Helen Drake.

Helen then went to the door and listened, before pulling it open a crack. She nodded to Jiddy.

'Git.'

Jiddy looked at the other women but none of them said anything.

'Maybe lass should stay here,' Grace said.

'How did you know about run?' said Helen. 'Does Mary know where you are?'

Jiddy clutched her skirt to her and, stepping outside, waited on the step.

'You know way back?' Helen said, leaning over Jiddy's head and looking around. 'Left, right and keep going and don't stop for a single breath.'

Jiddy nodded and the door closed against her back. She could hardly see it was so dark. She didn't move. The alleyways seemed scarier than the woods. Preventives would definitely be about and she'd not stand a chance against soldiers.

Keeping close to the walls, she scurried to the corner. Her body clenched so tight her teeth hurt. Keeping one hand on the bag, she wished she'd found Rebecca and stuck with her. Rebecca would certainly have told her off, but that would have been better than being on her own.

Soon, soon, she'd be back in bed. She pattered along Sunnyside.

'Stop.'

Pressing to the wall, she waited.

'Please don't see me, please don't see me.'

The boots pounded towards her. Making herself as small as possible, she prayed they'd go another way. Someone was panting hard. Boom. A gun fired. She squealed. She couldn't help it. She slapped one hand over her mouth in case she screamed again. The dark shape of a man ran out of Tommy Baxter Street and down towards Sunny Place. Exactly where she wanted to go.

'Halt.'

Two soldiers ran after the man, carrying big rifle guns. It wasn't her they wanted. Their footsteps faded away. And then another shot made her jump. Trembling, she felt her way along the wall and sidled round the corner. Climbing onto the coal shed roof, she scrambled around to her window. Slipping her fingers under the crack, she edged up the window and tumbled inside, listening harder than she'd listened for anything in her life. Footsteps approached, mingled with that strange noise like a small wagon. Silence. Where had they gone? Then other footsteps, getting louder, stopping outside the front door. They'd come for her this time. She didn't know what to do. Should she call Thomas? No, that would get him in trouble. She waited. The tapping at the door sounded loud. What would Mary and Thomas do? Were they listening too? Would they go downstairs and let the preventives take them away and she'd be left all alone? Go away, she willed, go away.

'Open door.'

The door opened. No, no, don't let them in.

'Mary?'

She knelt up at the window and looked down.

Mary stood in the doorway. 'Thomas is out,' she said. 'Come on, roll it in fast.'

There came that sound again like cart wheels, then the man ran off and the door closed. Looking down from the top of the stairs she saw Mary rolling a small barrel towards the fire. Just as Jiddy was deciding whether to creep down, a loud hammering at the door made her almost fall down the steps. Mary looked up and caught Jiddy's eye.

'Open up.' There was no mistaking the authoritative voice of a preventive soldier.

'Stay upstairs,' Mary ordered.

'I want to be with you.'

'Get in your room. Now.'

Jiddy didn't need telling twice. She leapt into her room, feeling the gust of the front door opening. Thoughts raced through her head. Where were Thomas? What were that noise? She rolled over on her stomach and peered through a crack in the floorboards, the one she always used when she wanted to check who was there.

Mary was sitting down, her skirts ballooned around her. The barrel. Jiddy couldn't believe it, Mary was sitting on the barrel. She looked for the soldier. No, no. It couldn't be worse. The captain of the preventives looked directly up at her. It was Captain Whittaker. She'd seen him strutting about the Bay that afternoon. She didn't move. If she moved, he'd see something change. If she stayed still, maybe he'd think her eye was a button or a dropped piece of coal, anything but an eye. All the moisture in her mouth gathered until she'd have to swallow and the noise could be enough for him to grab Mary's arm, yank her from the barrel and that would be it. Mary would be arrested. They'd wait for Thomas to return and then take them off and hang them both at the Buttercross and she'd be dragged downstairs and thrown into the dark bowels of a ship with hundreds of other orphans and they'd all die of starvation or dark or some horrible rotting illness. She swallowed. The noise sounded like a massive wave hitting rocks.

'We need to look round, ma'am,' said Captain Whittaker.

Jiddy couldn't believe it. He didn't seem to have heard her swallow.

'I would show you,' Mary said, 'but rheumatism's giving me gip.'

So Mary wasn't going to move from barrel. Mary was clever. Jiddy would learn from that.

The boots of several men clomped through the front door and preventives began opening and closing drawers and cupboards, not caring how much noise they made. Next door, Rebecca would be able to hear everything. Jiddy closed her eyes and hoped she wouldn't take it into her head to come round. One of the soldiers pulled open the cupboard by the fire and then one in the far wall. They stamped over the rough floor and dragged up the rug, pushed back the table and opened and closed more drawers. They found nothing. And then came the noise Jiddy dreaded. Someone was coming up the stairs.

'There's nowt up there.'

'We'll see.'

'Sir?' A voice just outside her room.

She didn't move. Let them drag her out from under bed, let them try and take salt from her. She'd kick and scream and bite and punch. Salt were hers, they couldn't have it and she wouldn't be punished for it.

'It's a young girl.'

Damn. She'd left her feet sticking out.

'Bring her down.'

Pressing the bag of salt between the mattress and the bed slats, she crawled out from under the bed. Sturdy on her feet, ready to hit one of them, she pushed past, thud thud down the stairs, heart thudding as loud. Mary hadn't moved from her seat by the fire and Jiddy went and stood behind, her arm around Mary's shoulders. She could grab pan of boiling water from fire if they came close. Scald them all. That would show them.

'She's an odd one,' the captain said. 'Who is she?'

'If you didn't find owt else beside lass,' said Mary, 'I think you'd best be going.'

The captain took a step closer. Jiddy shifted nearer to the fire, her hand grasping Mary's shawl. These men were searching everywhere. Barrel might as well have been singing and dancing. The captain wasn't daft, looking at Jiddy oddly as he walked towards them. Jiddy clenched Mary's shawl tighter.

A fist banging against the outside door made them all jump and Mary reached for Jiddy's hand. One of the soldiers opened the front door.

'Sir. We've caught three men on Low Street.'

The captain marched to the door. 'Are they carrying anything?'

Jiddy didn't move. Mary remained still.

'Plenty.'

It happened fast. The captain gestured the soldiers out and they raised their weapons and disappeared noisily into the dark leaving Mary and Jiddy staring at the open door.

'Shut it.' Mary said.

Jiddy lifted a stool to the door and, standing on it, pulled the top bolt hard. The soldiers' boots were fading. She didn't know what Mary would say now they were on their own. If only she were in bed, under the covers, cradling the bag of salt and falling asleep. What if she'd never gone out in the first place, would this still have happened?

'Jiddy?'

She turned around. Mary straddled the barrel and was straightening her skirts.

'Yes?' If she didn't let on, maybe Mary wouldn't have guessed she'd been out on the beach in the middle of the night with smugglers.

Reaching past plates and cups in the fireside cupboard, Mary pivoted a loose plank and took from behind it a bottle of brandy. The stopper popped, and pouring herself an adequate amount she sat in her chair, raising a toast to the barrel.

'I wish Thomas were home,' Jiddy said.

'Come here and have a nip,' said Mary.

The brandy scorched Jiddy's throat and she coughed.

'Thomas will be right,' Mary said, 'he knows every nook and cranny to hide in. You go on up and get some sleep and we'll see him in the morning.'

Jiddy looked at the barrel, exposed in front of them. 'What about that?'

'I'll see to it. And not a word, mind.'

Jiddy itched to tell Mary about the salt but it was her secret and she wanted to keep it like that a bit longer. Captain Pinkney had been right and there were other ways of getting not only salt from the sea but brandy and tea and reams and reams of that beautiful material.

'Night, Mary,' she said.

Safe in her room, she took out the bag of salt from under the mattress and rolled it over in her palms. The oilskin sack had kept the contents dry and she felt the grains moving between her fingertips. This was only the beginning. Thomas, Mary and she were all smugglers. It didn't matter if she wasn't born in Bay, she belonged there. She was a true Baytowner. She would show Jonas how they could get salt without paying for it and tell him they'd never have to burn fish again. She'd tell him and James how she'd found her way through the caves and tunnels and run home through the lanes that were packed with preventives and how they'd nearly caught her. How brave and clever she were and only eight years old. Think what a smuggler she'd be next year and in all years after. She were very best Baytowner of them all.

CHAPTER EIGHT

C awing gulls woke her far too early and she lay in bed unable to get back to sleep. Inside the house, there wasn't a sound. Or next door. Usually, there would be the noise of a poker rattling coals but today, nothing. A gull landed on the roof, clawing at the tiles and squawking loudly. Shimmering light brightened the square of cloth at the window. Jiddy yawned. Pushing back the blanket, she kneeled at the window and hooked back the curtain. Over the rooftops, a tinge of pink spread to meet pearl grey.

Pulling the bag of salt from under her pillow, she felt its weight. If she hurried, she'd catch Jonas before he were off for the day, up to top meadows or wherever his da sent him. Mary would want her close to home, she knew that, but if she were quick and only stayed long enough to see his shocked face, she'd be back and Thomas and Mary would be none the wiser. She was a smuggler. She could do anything.

Carrying the precious bag of salt, she leapt up the shallow steps of the Openings and along the narrow ginnels to Silver Street. Jonas would be impressed when she showed him and maybe he'd treat her as an equal when he saw it and not like his little assistant. He'd lick the white grains and she'd laugh at surprise on his face that she'd brought him salt after all, and not just a spoonful but a whole sack of it. She, Jiddy Vardy, a smuggler like Captain Pinkney, out at night with grown-ups and bringing back contra-what's it, same as them, even fooling head of preventives. There were no limit to her bravery.

Up and up the hill. She'd fooled everyone. Mary always said she was the nimblest-footed child she'd ever seen and that she had the lightest touch with her slim, long fingers. She'd put them to good use, make Jonas proud, make whole of Robin Hood's Bay proud, make the whole of Yorkshire bow at her feet. She'd be famous, they'd write stories and songs about her.

She started singing to herself, trying to find a rhyme for Vardy. Scampering upwards, she turned the corner onto Bloomswell.

With a sharp intake of breath, she dropped the bag. Her precious bag of salt split on the hard stone, the beautiful white grains staining a darkening pink. A foot length away, a dirty hand stretched out as if to grab hold. An eerie quiet remained over the rooftops until a flapping of wings followed by a gull's call startled her and she looked down at the body. Her heart pounded. Squatting, she studied the milky eyes staring at the sky. They didn't blink.

'Thomas?'

Shaking his arm, she leaned over him but he didn't see her. 'Thomas?' His arm didn't feel like it usually did. It felt stiff.

Her heart beat faster. Reaching out, she gently touched

his cheek. It felt like candle wax. He felt cold as well, like whale blubber left out on a winter night. With a sudden decision, she shot back the way she had come.

Run, run, run, her legs told her. Past the houses, around the corner. Run, run. Past the Square this time, dodging through. Soon be home. Down the slope. But there was someone in the way. She couldn't stop and she crashed into a man dressed in a heavy cloak. She kicked, punched and twisted as he caught her in his arms.

'Steady lass. What's hurry?' It was Captain Pinkney and he held her tight against the rough wool of his cloak, until she calmed down. When he let go, she stood back against the wall, staring at the ground.

'Early for a young 'un to be out,' he said. 'Anything to report?'

Jiddy looked at him. He was as tall as a ship's mast. She should be able to tell him, but she held back.

'I've got to get home,' she said.

Stepping aside, he left just enough room to slither past. She didn't need telling and brushing past him she broke into a run again. Patter, slap of her feet. Round the corner, scraping her shoulder on the wall and into Sunny Place. Shoving open the door, she stood panting. Mary stood in the middle of the room, cup in one hand, spoon in the other.

Mary turned back to the fire and poured water from the cup into a pot over the glowing coals. 'I'm planning on having porridge ready for when Thomas gets back,' she said.

Stumbling across the room, Jiddy flung her arms

around Mary's waist, pressing her face deep into the layers of material.

'Hey, hey,' Mary said, rocking Jiddy against her. 'Think you've found it's not so grand to be up and out so early after all. Where on earth have you been?'

If she started talking, she'd start blubbing good and proper and maybe she wouldn't stop and then there'd be tears all over the flags and she'd sure as anything be the one to have to get out the mop and bucket.

'I saw Thomas,' she said.

'What did you say?'

'I saw him on Bloomswell.'

Jiddy pushed her face into Mary's skirt again but Mary took hold of Jiddy's arms and held her back, studying her face. 'Why didn't he come back with you?'

Mary always knew when something were up but what would she say if she told her Thomas was dead?

'Would they kill a little girl?' she said.

They would, they would kill an eight-year-old and she could be lying in a sea of blood right now.

'Would who kill a little girl, Jiddy?' said Mary.

'Them.' She couldn't hold it in any longer. She hated preventives, hated, hated, hated them.

'What do you mean, them?' Mary bent forward. 'Why were you still awake so late last night, what were you doing?'

Jiddy wanted to shrink away, be tiny, tiny, tiny.

'Nothing.'

'Have you been up to something?'

'I didn't do anything last night,' she said.

'Why were you out so early, Jiddy, tell me truth now?' said Mary.

'I wanted …,' she searched every crevice in her head for an idea. 'Thomas is dead and there's blood and them soldiers killed him. He's dead, he's dead!' Jiddy burst into tears, burrowing her face again into the folds of Mary's apron.

Jiddy listened to the silence as her sobs subsided. She couldn't hide her face forever.

Mary pushed Jiddy away and grasping a cloth, pulled the pan off the fire. 'Damn it.' Her back remained towards Jiddy, moving this way and that, stirring and tapping the spoon against the metal.

'Why do soldiers kill smugglers?' Jiddy said.

'Were there anyone else about?' Mary said.

'I saw Captain Pinkney on Openings.'

The image of Thomas' body, splayed on paving stones, his grey hair matted dark, flashed into Jiddy's head. 'Mary?' she said.

Before Mary could answer the door creaked open and Rebecca stood, blocking out the light.

'Mary, love?' she said.

Jiddy flew across the room and flung her arms around Rebecca as she had with Mary. She wanted to tell her that Thomas had been killed but she didn't dare say it aloud again. Rebecca kissed the top of Jiddy's head, pressing hard with her lips for far too long.

CHAPTER NINE

I t was Rebecca who broke the silence. 'Jiddy,' she said, 'Annie's mam asked if you'd go round and have some porridge with them. Would you do that?'

It was a relief to be let go and she ran along The Bolts until she reached the fourth to last cottage. The door stood open but she couldn't see anyone inside.

She hit the blue door with her knuckles. 'Annie?'

Annie's pinched face leaned out of the upstairs window. 'Up here.'

'Rebecca said I could come,' she said.

Annie began coughing. It took a while until she could speak, but Jiddy waited.' We're all poorly,' she said, her grey eyes watery pink.

'I'm busting to see you.'

'Annie?' A voice shouted from inside, 'are you in bed?'

Annie smiled weakly. Everything about her looked watery. 'Tell me later,' she said.

Annie's mam appeared, taking hold of the window catch and pushing Annie inside. 'Annie's not well,' she said and closed the window.

Jiddy stood for a moment, deciding whether to go back or not. Her belly hurt. Her chest hurt. Everything hurt. She could go back, have some porridge then head to beach or something. Back in Sunny Place, she slowed down. Reverend Cook was going into the house, followed by Helen Drake, Grace and all the other neighbours. Rebecca closed the door. Jiddy stood all alone looking at the empty square that a moment ago had been full of people.

Bobbing her head under lines of fish drying in the pale sunshine, she reminded herself that she was still cross with Jonas so she couldn't go up to the farm. The stone flags, warm under her bare feet, decided her and she meandered down Bay Bank. Kings Beck sounded barely a trickle. Down in the dock, Captain Pinkney and Big Isaac McCaw sat outside the Fisherman's Arms, smoking their big pipes. She watched them, pretending to pick something up by the great stack of lobster pots by the causeway, but they carried on talking. She jumped onto a sandy stretch of beach.

Slipping and squelching her way over the seaweed-covered rocks, she kept her balance until pebbles rounded under her feet and she hobbled over their uneven surface. They'd feel bad for ignoring her when they found out about Thomas. She banged her fist against her leg.

'Don't think about it.'

Her belly rumbled. Clutching to the bank was a mass of brambles. She plucked a couple of blackberries and shoved them into her mouth. In no time, her fingers were stained red and stinging with prickles. Knowing she'd get a belly ache if she ate any more, she wiped her mouth.

The sea was a long way out, so keeping to sandy stretches and picking her way across pebbles, she neared the cave that had hidden them last night. It seemed strange with nobody about. Peering inside, she shivered. It was very dark and smelled damp.

'Anybody there?' Her voice echoed.

Caves were creepy on your own, she decided. No wonder nobody else came back. There was something there. A long shape against the wall. She could barely make it out, but it wasn't a rock. If it moved, she'd be out of there faster than a hare across fields. Maybe the soldiers had killed somebody else. Maybe somebody had decided to sleep there for rest of night. If she screamed it would echo and echo and soldiers all the way from Scarborough would come running.

'Ooh-hoo!' She called. No answer. 'Are you all right?'

It wouldn't be fair to find another dead body. She wondered if Captain Pinkney and Big Isaac had moved Thomas and put him somewhere safe away from preventives. She should go back. Be with Mary and Rebecca. She peered closer into the cave. What if they had hidden Thomas here? She crept closer. The shape looked too small to be an adult and she breathed out, amazed to see her cloudy breath. She'd been the only child out last night, so it couldn't be one of the other children in the Bay. Tentatively, she put one hand on the wall to steady herself, feeling the smooth moss give slightly under pressure. Treading carefully over the uneven ground, she crept closer.

'Are you hurt?' she said.

They didn't look right, covered in a blanket and lying still. She had to do this though, that's what being a smuggler meant, not being afraid of anything. Crouching down, balancing herself against the wall, she put out one hand to touch. There weren't any arms or legs or a head. It couldn't be a person. She lifted the blanket. Underneath lay a slim bale of material.

Dragging it on the blanket, she stepped backwards towards the cave entrance, easing it bit by bit over the floor of the cave. Every so often, she stopped to catch her breath. She was too small and it was too heavy. She should leave it. Let someone else come and find it. She pulled again and then let go. Her fingers ached and her arms hurt. It was too hard but she gave a few more tugs and then a few more. One final pull and she stepped out of the cave's shadow and into the sunlight. Squinting in the sunshine after the dark of the cave, her eyes focused on the exposed material. It burst into life, glowing a luminescent lilac like heather in August. She couldn't take her eyes off it. Alternating colours of yellow and orange hid one moment then shone bright. Slubbed silk, that's what Mary would call it.

Jiddy looked up and down the beach. Maybe someone planned to collect the material when they thought the coast was clear. What would they say when they found it gone? Could she drag it all the way to the causeway? What about Captain Pinkney and Isaac McCaw? They'd claim it for themselves. She thought for a moment. Dottie had had it wound around her body. She could do that. She grabbed one end of the material and pulled. It didn't budge. She yanked again, falling on her backside when the fabric refused to unroll. Dottie must have had help she decided. Drat Annie for being poorly.

Jonas looked at her from the bottom of the cliff path next to the cave entrance. 'What are you doing?'

'Come and help me,' she said, jumping to her feet.

'Where'd you get this?'

She raised her arms above her head. 'I need you to wrap it around me,' she said. 'Pull it out and I'll keep turning round.'

He prodded the silk and she dropped her arms. 'We can't take all day,' she said, 'there'll be others about soon. Might even be preventives along.'

'I heard about Thomas and wanted to find you,' he said. 'I'm sorry, Jiddy.'

She shrugged his hand away. 'I'll do it on my own if you won't help me,' she said. 'I've got to wind it round me. I think it has to go under all my clothes.' She began untying the cord around her waist and letting her skirt collapse around her ankles.

Jonas stared at her. 'Didn't anyone tell you smuggling's a night-time activity?' he said.

She steadied herself. 'Are you going to help me? I were there last night,' she said, 'I were only child in whole of Bay.'

'Hey, hey, slow down.'

She steadied herself again. 'I can't slow down, I've got to get this back home.' With her skirt around her ankles it was not as easy as she thought and she awkwardly kicked herself free.

'Are you serious?' he said.

She nodded. She waited until he picked up the ends of the silk ream.

'Lift your arms,' he said.

He made the fabric taut, gesturing for her to spin around. 'Slowly,' he said when she moved too fast, and he held the material tight as she stepped in a circle, all the time straightening it, round and around so that she soon looked like a bobbin of thread. 'Will your skirt fit over this?' he said.

She nodded. 'Drop it over my head.'

The over dress wouldn't tie properly and it hung half open. Jonas stood back. 'You're mad,' he said, pulling the ties as tight as he could and making a knot.

Clutching her arms around herself, she tottered forward. 'I need you to come with me,' she said.

Jonas caught her from falling. 'Small steps,' he said.

They set off, Jiddy making an odd rotating movement with each step. She couldn't comprehend how older girls did it; there must be a knack but she couldn't find it no matter how she moved.

'Did you coil it tight?' she said.

'We can't change it now.' He put one arm around her shoulders and that felt steadier. 'Maybe you needed to be taller,' he said.

The knot certainly felt tight enough, hurting her belly as it did.

'Do you know how dangerous this is?' Jonas said.

'I don't care.' Thomas was dead. She didn't care about anything anymore. Not preventives. Not nothing.

Slowly, they walked across the beach back towards the causeway. Jonas gestured for her to stay against the cliff while he jumped up. 'Wait here.'

He seemed to be away for ages. What if he were talking to Captain Pinkney and couldn't get away? The tide were coming in. She'd drown if he didn't help her soon and there were no way she could climb up without him. Now she knew what a trussed-up chicken felt like. It weren't good. Where was he? Come on, Jonas. Could she shuffle on her bottom? When she was about to give it a try, Jonas jumped down onto the sand.

'All clear,' he said.

He rolled her up onto the causeway, hauling her back on her feet and then, with his arm around her again, she made small steps forward.

'We're going up King Street,' he said, pressing her to the wall and helping her totter to the right.

She'd never thought King Street that steep before, but with the material wrapped so low down her legs, she could barely make strides. Jonas kept pulling, but she couldn't walk faster.

'Nearly there,' he said. 'Damn.'

'What?' She was sweating and would have collapsed with exhaustion if her knees would bend.

A preventive, his coat standing out like a red poppy, stood at the bend of the street with his back to them. He was looking north, out to sea but he could turn around at any moment.

Hands on her shoulders, his chest against her head, they shuffled like crabs, Jiddy looking at the flags at her feet, relying on Jonas to guide the way along Low Street.

'We could hide in preaching house,' she said. 'I don't want him to kill me.'

'Don't be daft,' Jonas said. 'Will Mary be in?'

Jiddy hadn't thought of that. What would Mary say? What would minister and Helen Drake and Rebecca say?

'House were full when I left,' she said. 'We'll have to hide up tunnel over the beck.'

'We're here now,' said Jonas, lifting her up the steps to the cottage. He opened the door and she fell over the threshold. She daren't look up.

'There's no-one here,' Jonas said, closing the door.

She couldn't believe it. Rocking herself from side to side she tried to gain momentum. One last go. She pushed again and rolled onto her back. The only plus was that now she stared at the ceiling and not the floor. She turned her head. Jonas studied her.

'You baffle me sometimes,' he said.

'Get me up.'

'I think it'll be easier other way,' he said and, crouching down, roughly shoved her onto her belly again.

'I still can't move.' Her words barely audible with her face pressed to the rug.

Grunting and groaning, Jonas grabbed her around the waist and heaved her to her feet. She waited for him to say something but he concentrated on untying the knot before indicating for her to spin around.

'I'm not crazy,' she said.

'Then why are you acting it?'

Jiddy kept spinning, feeling lighter and lighter. She spun faster until the room blurred.

'Slow down,' Jonas said.

'Hurry up.'

The last bit released and she fell against the table. Jonas started folding the silk and, feeling steadier, she walked about.

'I hate preventives,' she said.

Jonas placed the silk at the bottom of the stairs and let out a long sigh. 'We all do.'

'There were blood everywhere, Jonas,' she said. It no longer felt real; it had become a story to tell around the fire at night and she was the one to set the words. 'Minister says killing is a sin.'

He looked weird as if she wasn't Jiddy but somebody else. She didn't like it.

'Why did they kill Thomas? He never hurt anyone,' she said.

'If anyone's caught smuggling that's what happens,' he said. 'There were a bag of salt next to him, it were part dissolved, but they'd be able to tell what it were.'

Jiddy fumbled with the tie on her pinafore.

'It were only a bag of salt,' she said.

'It's contraband Jiddy,' he said. 'Preventives will kill anyone caught with contraband if they put up a fight.'

She stamped her foot. This wasn't fair. She hated, hated preventives and their rules. 'Thomas wouldn't have put up a fight.'

'I'm sorry, Jids.' Jonas reached out to touch her arm but Jiddy stepped back. She felt dizzy and sick and hungry. Her mouth was dry. Her throat hurt. And then her belly let out a loud rumble.

Jonas laughed, standing back. 'Think you need to put something in there,' he said.

'That were my bag of salt,' she said.

'What?'

'I were on my way to see you at farm. I were bringing it to give you but I found Thomas lying on path. He didn't have any salt when preventives killed him. I dropped it.'

'Jiddy, sit down and tell me properly. What've you been up to?' Jonas tried to manoeuvre her but she wouldn't budge.

'I wanted you to be proud of me,' she said.

'Where did you get a bag of salt from?'

She looked at the pile of silk and Jonas followed her gaze. 'Oh, don't tell me,' he said.

'I were right brave and Captain Pinkney asked me special. He didn't ask anyone else, only me.'

'D'you know how dangerous that were? You are eight. Flamin' hell, Jiddy, you're so full of yourself, thinking you can be a smuggler. Why d'you think no-one your age were there? Because we're not stupid,' he said. 'Their mams and das would slay them alive if they thought they'd been out.'

'I don't have a mam and da to slay me,' Jiddy said.

'Did Mary know you were out?'

'I dropped the salt,' she said.

'Didn't you think to pick it up?'

'It's not funny. Bag burst.'

'And you didn't think to scoop it up?'

Tears ran down her face, cleaning a line through the dust on her cheeks. Jonas leaned against the wall by the door.

'Looks like you're making plenty of salt with them tears to make up for dropping that bag. Better fetch some dishes.'

Sniffing, she wiped her face. 'It weren't my fault.'

'Problem is, everyone thinks it were that bag of salt that got Thomas killed and once people believe something, there's no going back.'

'I'll tell them,' Jiddy said, perking up. 'I can tell everyone it were my salt.'

'No-one's going to believe that.'

'Captain Pinkney knows and Helen Drake cos she tried to take it off me. I'll tell Mary, she'll believe me.'

'Mary's got enough on her plate,' Jonas said.

'I could tell minister, everyone has to believe him.'

'Thomas is dead, Jiddy,' Jonas said. 'He were a smuggler. Preventives got to him before you and your salt. Best leave it now.'

'No, I want everyone to know it were my salt!'

Jonas pushed himself away from the wall.

'I'd best be off,' he said, 'and you best wash your face, it's covered in juice.'

She looked at her stained hands. She'd forgotten about the blackberries.

'Can I come with you?' she said.

'No.'

She didn't know how it happened but her voice changed completely. 'Well, I think I've done well,' she said, 'I'd much rather have silk than stupid salt. I can make a pretty dress from this.'

He turned to face her again.

'There is nothing more important than salt,' he said. 'Only vain people would think any different.'

She put her hands on her hips.

'If I look beautiful, people will give me salt without me having to do anything else, so that makes me clever, not vain, Jonas Chaplow. You're one that's stupid, not me.'

He gave her a terrible look, then picked up the blanket from Thomas' chair.

'It's too dangerous to keep this here,' he said, wrapping the blanket around the ream of silk.

'That's mine, what you doing with it?' She grabbed at the roll but he pushed her off.

'I'll keep silk up at farm,' he said. 'Don't want preventives finding it here and Mary getting into trouble. Let's hope this is last time you put others at risk, hey, Jiddy?'

He said her name harshly, sounding out the ds as if they were bullets. She didn't know what to say, it shocked her that much. The blanket now completely camouflaged the silk.

'I hate you as much as preventives,' she said. The anger in his eyes made her look away and he left the door wide open without saying another word. 'You wait until I'm grown,' she shouted after him. 'You won't find it so easy to take things off me then. You wait 'til I'm grown up, Jonas Chaplow. I'll show you.'

She slammed the door. She hated him. She hated smuggling. She hated being a girl. She hated that he was blaming her in some way about Thomas because she'd dropped the bag of salt and most of all she hated that

Thomas were dead and she'd never see him sitting by the fire or smoking his pipe or teasing her or laughing with Mary when she was in bed. She kicked the table, sending a sharp pain up her foot and she fell to the floor cradling it in both hands, determined to get justice for Thomas if she had to die herself in doing so.

CHAPTER TEN

Robin Hood's Bay, England
Eight years later – 1795

Jonas swung a hammer over his bare shoulder then whacked it down on a stone, splitting it in two. His skin, turned ruddy-brown by months of outdoor work, gleamed with a veneer of sweat.

'Stop and have some dinner,' said Jiddy, laying bread, cheese and pieces of meat pie onto a cloth.

Jonas swung the hammer again. His muscles rounded with its weight and his back flexed. He'd changed. Last summer he'd been skinny and now, suddenly, he looked like a man. Jiddy hadn't said anything to him about it. She couldn't. It made her feel funny. He hadn't commented how she had changed either, so if he weren't going to say anything, neither would she. He did look at her weirdly sometimes, though, and she couldn't help studying him through her lowered eyelashes. But she was bored waiting and it looked as if he'd never finish hitting those wooden posts.

'Let's play fight,' she said, standing with her fists raised. 'I need to work up an appetite too.'

'I've taught you all I know,' he said, swinging the hammer again and making his chest look huge.

'Thomas gave me best advice ever,' she said. 'Keep your thumbs out when you clench your fists.'

'Good man,' said Jonas. 'You still miss him, don't you?'

They did still miss him, both she and Mary, even after all this time, but they didn't talk about it.

'Are you going to stop now?' she said.

'All right, if you say so, Lady Manor House.'

'I do say so, Farmer Straw Head.'

Throwing down the hammer, he grabbed her arms, sticking out his leg behind hers and pulling her so close her newly grown breasts pressed against his chest. He looked her straight in the eyes. And then, just when she caught a different look amongst the flecks of grey, he let go and walked back to the scattering of stones around the broken-down wall.

'Don't bother putting on your shirt,' she said, pouring ale into a mug and trying to calm down, 'you'll only get it sweaty.'

He looked up at the sky, then chucking his shirt back down, strolled over and threw himself down on the grass.

She held out the jug. 'Here, you look as if you need it.'

He stuck out his hand and she pulled it out of his reach. Trying again, she shifted it out of his reach again. He looked at her, taking a swipe at the mug. She was quick though and only spilling a drop, moved it out of reach again. He rolled over, hands behind the back of his head.

She shuffled over. 'Here you go, sit up or do I have to feed you like a baby?'

He didn't move. Eyes closed, showing off his bare chest and stomach with its ripples of muscle. It wasn't flabby at all.

'Are you ignoring me?' she said.

Still he didn't say anything.

'I were only teasing.'

Nothing.

'Okay, you baby.'

She took a large swig of beer, carefully balanced the mug on the grass then, sweeping her hair to one side, kneeled over him, trying not to smile. Her shadow fell over his face and torso. He must have felt the change on his skin but he didn't move.

She could squirt it all over his face. She almost laughed. He'd sit up quick at that. Stop smiling, stop it. She held the liquid in her mouth, the aroma of hops rising into her nose. His light brown eyelashes curled over his freckled cheeks. His lips were the giveaway. They weren't relaxed but pressed close together.

She leaned closer. A few strands of hair escaped and dangled black lines across his bare shoulder. Closer. She'd never been this close. Closer. Any second he'd move. Her lips touched his. His mouth opened and out the liquid came from hers to his.

Gulping, he pushed her and she fell back. Wiping a trickle of ale from her chin, she felt his anger scorch between them. He scrambled to his feet then paced in a circle. Stopping, he waved his hand.

'What was that, Jiddy?' he said.

She was on her feet now, legs astride, gesticulating too. 'What was that, yourself, Jonas? I trail all way up here to bring you some dinner and you lay there, ignoring me.'

They glared at each other.

'You've changed,' he said.

'You've noticed, then?'

'You're asking for a fight.'

'I've not time to wait for your army to come and help you.'

'You're asking for it.'

'I'm not asking for anything, I'm taking,' she said.

'You nearly choked me.'

'Wa-wa.' She mocked a baby's cry.

Bending down, he swiped up the mug and drank. She wanted to fight. She wanted to fight him more than anything. She wanted to feel her fingers press into his skin. She needed that tension between their arms, and to feel how it shot down their legs and into the ground, sizzling between them like scones on a griddle. She racked her brain for the biggest insult she could find.

But before she could do so, he strode past, clipping her with his elbow. He wanted a fight too, she could tell. That clip was only the start. He refilled his mug and raised it.

'Thanks for dinner,' he said, drinking it swiftly down.

'Save some for me.'

Picking up a piece of meat pie and taking a bite, he looked down the fields, his eyes on the distant glittering sea. The moment was dissipating. She could feel it. The desire to fight dissolving in him.

Taking another mug, she filled it and drank the ale quickly. It wooshed warm and frothy down her throat, taking tiny bubbles of air and the taste of wheat with it.

She smacked her tongue against the top of her mouth and held out the mug. 'More,' she said.

Mouth full of pie, he stared up at her. She jerked her wrist about to say 'more' again but something other than that rose up her throat. She belched. Putting up her hand to cover her mouth, she let out another.

Spluttering crumbs over the cloth, Jonas burst out laughing. Still laughing, he picked up the flask.

'Certainly you can have more,' he said, 'and would my lady care to sit while she belches again?'

'A gentleman would put on his shirt in the presence of a lady.'

Jonas covered his nipples with the tips of his fingers. 'My apologies, my lady.'

She wanted to smile but she wouldn't, not yet.

'And would my lady like some pie to go with that belch?' he said.

'I've a strong stomach,' she said, tearing a chunk of bread, 'and I've seen that disgusting bare chest of yours more times than I've had fish and potato suppers.'

He held a piece of pie on his knife for her to take. Keeping his eyes fixed on hers, he moved it slightly out of reach. She looked at the pie balanced on the blade and reached out again. He moved it a little further, his eyes on hers.

She could roll over, hands behind head as he had

done. She thought about her lips on his. How quick it had been. How angry he'd seemed.

'You put it in,' she said and she opened her mouth wide.

The piece of meat and pastry spiralled through the air and hit her on the nose. Jonas burst out laughing and she threw it back at him.

'We won't waste it.' He popped the piece in his mouth. 'Go on then, tell me about this job at Thorpe Hall.'

She slumped her shoulders. 'I don't want to go,' she said. 'It's like a competition and Mary's had us all sat round table sewing pillow cases and darning and making tucks and altering seams for months and it's so boring.'

'You might have been doing it since Mary stuck needle and thread in your hands but bet others are glad she's showing them how it's done proper,' said Jonas, taking another bite of pie and chewing as he spoke.

'I don't want to work up at Thorpe Hall.'

'Why not? You'll get your dinner and Mrs Farsyde will love you being there, she'll probably want you to move in.'

'I'm not moving in.'

'Well, you haven't got job yet, so let's not get out of bed before cock crows.'

She threw a piece of cheese at him and he popped it in his mouth along with the meat pie.

'Mmm.'

She laughed. She couldn't help it.

'We've got to go up to hall, tomorrow,' she said, 'all four of us. That will be a joyful afternoon, Nellie trying to act as if she doesn't care and she'll kill any of rest of us if we get taken on and not her.'

'What's likelihood of any of rest of them getting taken on?'

There was a strong possibility, she knew that, but she also knew Nellie and Nellie wouldn't let anyone else be top of the tree.

Jonas lay back, his arms behind his head and closed his eyes. 'Mrs Farsyde might even give you one of her cast-off dresses, think of that, Jiddy. A pretty gown from mistress of Thorpe Hall and her giving it to you.'

A pretty dress. She'd not thought of that. What would be the likelihood of Mrs Farsyde giving away an old gown? Now that would be worth fighting for.

CHAPTER ELEVEN

Jiddy backed through the doorway, carrying a chair between her and Annie. Mary kept out of the way by standing near the table while Rebecca gestured to a place by the fire where Thomas' chair used to sit.

'Don't you want to be at table with rest of us?' said Jiddy.

'I can see well enough from here,' said Rebecca, angling her plump body into the seat.

Nellie, seated already and furthest from the door, looked at Betsie. 'Don't think there's enough room round table anyway,' she said and Betsie giggled.

Mary pushed a stray grey hair off her face. 'Thank you girls,' she said. 'You be grateful I'm letting you in my house at all.'

Jiddy, taller now than Mary, put an arm around the older woman's shoulders. 'Will you be joining us?' she said.

Mary flicked a cloth at her. 'I'm too busy to sit down,' she said, 'but I'll be keeping my eye on you all.'

Jiddy sat on a stool nearest the door as Annie slumped down opposite Betsie, never one to be graceful, and the four of them fell silent as they picked up their needlework. For some reason she couldn't stop thinking about spurting ale into Jonas' mouth.

'Are you going to come back and join us?' Rebecca's voice came sharp. 'You do want a fair crack at this job, don't you?'

Jiddy looked up, flushing hot over her cheeks and down her neck. Rebecca pulled on her pipe, not giving anything away. She glanced at Mary, busying herself as if wiping that plate were the most important thing in the world, and she realised that they were more nervous than any of them. She had to get the job.

'Is anybody else nervous about going up to Thorpe Hall?' Annie said, grabbing a square of cotton then looking around for something else on the table.

Jiddy bent her head again. She'd never understand why Mary had decided to help all of them when it was Jiddy that needed the job so that she could help Mary get through the winter.

Nellie held up Annie's sewing pouch. 'Is this what you're looking for?'

'Thanks Nellie,' Annie said.

Jiddy began a row of kisses, each one precisely the same. She sensed that Nellie kept looking at her but she wasn't going to catch her eye. It had turned out to be such a wonderful day, yesterday. After the pie, she and Jonas had thrown cheese and pieces of bread in air, making them small enough to catch in their mouths and laughing when throws went astray. She loved it when they laughed like that.

'I'm going to wear my Sunday dress to go to hall in,' Betsie said, 'Mam said we have to look our best in front of Mrs Farsyde.'

Nellie put another neatly sewn square onto her pile that was already bigger than everyone else's.

'Quality, not quantity,' said Rebecca from her place by the fire. 'You'd do well to remember that, Nellie Ashner.'

'You'd do well to mind your own business,' said Nellie, only loud enough for those around the table to hear. They were all tense. They all wanted Mrs Farsyde to choose them.

'I was going to go up like this,' said Annie. 'If we're going to need time to change, I don't think I'm going to get anywhere near finished.'

Mary stood behind her. 'Don't panic. It's best to show a few good pieces of work than a pile of shoddily hemmed handkerchiefs. Not casting any aspersions on your work, Nellie. You're a fast worker, we all know that.'

Nellie's face looked like a deranged cat's. This was going to be a difficult afternoon, what with Annie so slow and clumsy with her stitches and Nellie fit to blow. Jiddy looked at Betsie. She seemed oblivious to everything, as usual.

'I think as eldest, I should get position,' said Nellie. 'One of you can take my place when I'm married and too busy for being someone's seamstress.'

'You never told me you're getting married?' said Betsie. 'To who? When? Why didn't you tell me, I tell you everything?'

Nellie did her false smirk and shuffled in her seat. 'I said "when". I've not decided to who yet. I'm just warning you, for future.'

Rebecca did one of her explosive laughs that sounded

like a snort and Mary went back to the fireplace to check on the coals. Jiddy wasn't going to say anything. It wasn't worth it. Let Nellie get married. Get her out of their hair for one thing.

'Did you never think of marrying again, Mrs Waite?' Nellie said.

Jiddy looked swiftly at Mary. Marry again?

'Isn't that illegal?' she said.

Nellie burst out laughing.

'Mary will always be married to Thomas, even after death, won't you Mary?' said Rebecca in a tone that wasn't to be argued with.

They all looked at Mary. Say something, Jiddy prayed. Please say something to shut Nellie up.

'Of course I won't remarry,' Mary said, 'I'm too old for any of that nonsense.' She looked at them all one by one as if weighing them up. Rebecca reached out her hand and touched Mary's arm.

'No-one can fill hole that Thomas left, I know,' she said.

A hole. That was exactly right. There was still, even after eight years, a hole where Thomas had been. It wasn't only an empty chair or his pipe still kept on the mantle shelf. It was smell of him and sound of him walking up steps.

'Were it love at first sight when you met?' said Annie. 'Tell us, Mrs Waite.'

'Annie, don't be nosy,' Jiddy said. She couldn't believe it. 'Can't we talk about something else?'

Betsie giggled again, and this time Rebecca kept

quiet. Jiddy had never thought to wonder what Mary and Thomas had been like when they were young. Annie stared with her innocent eyes.

'No, it weren't love at first sight as you put it, Annie Briggs,' Mary said, 'I were taught better than that.'

Of course it wasn't love at first sight. Mary hadn't a romantic bone in her body but still, Jiddy couldn't bear it. She could feel her ears and eyes and cheeks burning and her fingers, though they looked calm and restrained, itched to lash out.

Nellie nudged Betsie.

'Oh, I'm sure he wooed you with the best Turbot he could catch, Mrs Waite,' Nellie said.

'A good fish isn't to be sneezed at.'

Rebecca sat back in her chair and closed her eyes as if she wasn't listening but Jiddy knew she'd be hanging on every word. Jiddy rethreaded her needle. Quicker she finished, quicker she could say they had to pack up and ready themselves. Ten more kisses.

'Did you pick Mr Waite out? I'm not being cheeky, I just want to know. Some men like that, don't they? Some men are shy,' said Nellie.

Jiddy held her needle still. She sensed everyone waiting. Would Mary say anything now or turf them straight out finished or not?

'I were younger than you are now and I were being courted by two young men.' Mary said.

'Two?' echoed Annie.

'You were fourteen?' said Betsie.

'You're having us on,' said Nellie.

'Are you saying I'm not up to two suitors, Nellie Ashner?' said Mary.

Jiddy didn't want to hear. It could definitely get worse. She looked up at the ceiling, wondering if Thomas was listening from his bed in heaven. Rebecca didn't bat an eyelid.

'How did you pick?' Betsie asked.

Mary crossed to the table and stood over them, her hands holding the back of Annie's chair.

'It weren't easy. One were tall, with them far away sailor's eyes,' Mary said. 'My heart went funny at thought of him.'

'Sounds my type,' said Nellie.

'Anything in breeches is your type,' said Betsie.

Jiddy couldn't believe it. Was this happening? Mary had transformed into another person. She was talking to the others as though she was sixteen herself.

'Thing was, the other did make me laugh,' said Mary.

'A good belly laugh always does trick,' Betsie said, 'James Linskill always has me in stitches.' Nellie made a groaning sound. 'Well, he's funny.' Betsie pulled a face.

'And he's good looking, I mean, was Thomas handsome as well?' Annie blushed. 'I mean, I can't remember, we were…'

'He didn't turn fish off, if that's what you're getting at,' Mary said, patting Annie's shoulder.

'How did you choose?' said Betsie.

Jiddy waited to hear the answer as to why Thomas had won her heart. It seemed important, as if she would release a secret they all needed to hear.

'I took my time,' said Mary, 'I didn't rush but didn't dally either. I didn't want to leave space open for another lass but I were enjoying attention, plus I knew once I picked I wouldn't be able to see t'other again. Not that way.'

'I wouldn't find it hard to choose,' said Nellie.

'You'd pick richest,' said Betsie.

'I'd pick one that loved me best,' Nellie said.

'Give over,' said Betsie. 'You'd go for money.'

Mary eyed Jiddy.

'What about you? What would you go for?'

'Jiddy doesn't count,' said Nellie. 'Nobody round here would marry an incomer, it's only weird inlanders like Jonas spend all their time hanging out with a girl.'

'Better an incomer than a local lass like you,' said Jiddy. 'And Jonas isn't weird.'

'He is an inlander, though,' said Betsie.

'And you, Nellie Ashner, are from Whitby. Seems to me you're an incomer as well,' said Rebecca.

Nellie stuck her needle into her cloth.

Smoothing down Annie's hair, Mary ignored them. 'Either way,' she said, 'it'd be a mistake to pick a husband that loved you if you didn't love him back.'

'Really?' Nellie recovered first. 'I thought it'd be better if he loves you more. He'd always take care of you then and he wouldn't run off with some other lass who wanted her claws in him.'

'What would stop you running off though, if suddenly someone you're better suited to turned up?' Mary said.

'You'd be too busy with bairns and husband and life to have time to notice,' Rebecca said from by the fire.

'Don't listen to bitter old Rebecca,' Mary said.

Rebecca made her weird snorting noise again. Betsie and Nellie exchanged looks.

'Your hands may be busy,' said Mary, 'but there'd be nowt to stop what would be going on up here.' She tapped her forehead.

'I don't believe in any of that,' said Nellie. 'You could be waiting forever.'

'You'd end up an old maid if you were to hang around for someone better,' agreed Betsie. 'I'm sticking to James. I think we'll make a good match.'

'I'm probably going to be an old maid however long I wait,' said Annie.

Nellie and Betsie made cooing sounds.

'My mother gave me a spot of advice,' said Mary, 'that might help you all decide.'

The girls hushed up straight away.

'It were difficult. One lad made my heart soar like a seagull over a catch of fish. But t'other one, well, I think my soul would have broken like a scallop shell smashed on shingle if I turned him down.'

Jiddy wanted to take her hand and cuddle her tight. This was so strange, so odd to be talking about, and she didn't want to think about such things.

'I wouldn't trust someone too handsome,' said Annie, and they all laughed.

'Aye. I'd not choose a man better looking than me,' said Betsie.

'You mean there's any worse?' said Nellie.

'Better than tricking a man into marrying you,' Rebecca said.

'Hard for a decent man to resist a lass who throws herself at him,' Nellie glanced at Jiddy.

Jiddy concentrated on pushing her needle up and down, determined that whatever Nellie said, what any of them said, including Mary, she wouldn't react.

'Tell us what your mam advised you, Mrs Waite,' Nellie said, sitting back in her chair.

'My mam told me that when you kiss your sweetheart, then you will know one way or other. If you know you've come home, that's when you know he's one you must marry,' Mary said.

'When you come home,' Betsie asked, 'what does that mean?'

Annie pulled a face. 'Kiss?'

'When you kiss, you'll know which one's right for you,' said Mary, 'so make sure you kiss him before you say yes. Whatever they look like, however much they make you laugh or however much money they have, that's most important. And if they're poor then so be it, and if they're rich, well, so much better. I'm not saying it won't be hard but that's life. Being with a man you can kiss is a different matter to sticks and stones life can throw at you.'

'When you come home,' Annie repeated.

They all settled down to their sewing after that, thinking about what Mary had said, and Jiddy continued with the row of kisses, trying not to think about Jonas' mouth. Instead, she pictured Mrs Farsyde and the beautiful yellow silk dress she'd worn in church last week, and wondered if she liked kissing the squire. If she got the job as her seamstress, she'd be touching material like that, unpicking seams and tucks and resewing them. She'd maybe embroider an elaborate stomacher with matching sleeves for some ball. Every day, she'd touch silk like that ream Jonas still kept in his barn loft, the one that shone like a rainbow in sunlight. She'd let him sneak in. What would it be like kissing Jonas?

'Gypsy.'

Betsie giggled.

'Wi-t-ccchh.' The word hissed across the table, just loud enough for Jiddy to hear.

'Stop it, Nellie,' said Annie, touching Jiddy's hand.

Nellie was goading her, she knew that but it was so hard not to react.

'Mrs Waite?'

'Yes, Nellie?'

'Did you have a choice of babies or did you have to take Jiddy?'

That was it. Jiddy threw down her sewing. As if in slow motion, Nellie turned her head. Annie froze. Betsie's eyes flitted excitedly. Nellie sat like a waiting toad as Jiddy rose up. A pair of hands lightly touched her shoulders and held her so that she was forced to sit back down.

'Thomas and I wanted Jiddy or we wouldn't have taken her in, Nellie.' Mary's voice was steady and calm over Jiddy's head.

Jiddy twisted around to look at Mary. 'And I'm glad you did,' she said.

'Ow!'

Betsie stared straight ahead while Nellie concentrated on her sewing. Annie cradled her hand, her head bent over so that her light brown hair obscured her face. Mary walked calmly around the chair to stand between Annie and Nellie.

'Let me see,' Mary said.

Annie shook her head vigorously and clutched her hands together.

'What did you do, Annie?' Nellie's voice, sweet as treacle.

'I pricked my finger,' Annie said, holding back the tears that swarmed to her eyes.

Jiddy looked at Betsie then Nellie again. 'What did you do?' she said.

Nellie looked like butter wouldn't melt in her mouth but her needle glinted in the light, its eye empty of thread. Annie trembled slightly against Jiddy.

'Are you girls nearly finished?' said Mary.

'Yes, Mrs Waite.'

'I am.'

'Leave them to it for a bit,' Rebecca said and Mary walked to the front door and stood on the step looking out.

'Annie, did Nellie stick her needle in your hand?' said Jiddy.

Annie clutched her hands together.

'I did it myself,' she said.

Jiddy moved around Annie.

'Get out of my house,' she said.

'It's not your house,' said Nellie.

Jiddy swiped the needle from Nellie's fingers and plunged it into Nellie's rounded palm. Jumping to her feet, Nellie screamed.

'What's going on now?' said Mary.

'For goodness' sake, aren't you lot old enough to be left alone?' Even Rebecca was on her feet.

Grabbing the front of Nellie's gown, Jiddy yanked her down so quickly that Nellie's chin banged hard onto the table.

Nellie scrambled backwards, tears glinting in her steely eyes. 'She's a deranged witch.'

Jiddy didn't care anymore, shoving Nellie hard, she made the bigger girl crash against the wall.

'Jiddy, stop that,' Mary said.

Jiddy dropped her arms and Nellie punched Jiddy in the stomach. Turn the other cheek. That's what minister said. Bunkum to that! If she turned t'other cheek, Nellie would punch harder than first time. She grabbed Nellie's arm.

'Both of you, act your age,' Mary shouted, pulling Jiddy away. 'Nellie Ashner, you should be ashamed, you're two full years older. Go on, get yourself home.'

Jiddy strained and wriggled to escape Mary's hold.

'Betsie, Annie, get your friend out the door.'

'But she's …'

'Do it.'

Rebecca bundled sewing into Nellie's arms and dragged her to the door. Betsie scooped up her own linen squares and pieces of sewing and then they were gone and Jiddy was left shaking with anger. Annie burst into tears and from the doorway, Rebecca burst out laughing.

'What did you expect?' she said, 'Nellie and Jiddy just don't belong in same town let alone room.'

Jiddy couldn't contain herself. It wasn't her, it was Nellie, nasty, evil Nellie.

'Nellie stuck her pin in Annie's hand, you don't expect me to stand by and not do anything, do you?' She picked up the fallen chair and banged it hard on the flags.

'Careful with my furniture if you please,' said Mary, smiling at Rebecca.

'Why didn't you tell truth, Annie?' Jiddy pushed back her hair. She'd had enough of Nellie. She wasn't going to stand for it any longer.

'Sit down and calm yourself,' Mary said, 'more ships sink at sea.' She looked at Jiddy,

'I said sit. Annie, take your sewing and go get yourself sorted for going up to Farsydes'.'

While Annie gathered the handkerchiefs, shirts and petticoats, Rebecca helping her, Mary clattered about, noisy with pans and spoons. Jiddy remained at the table, playing with her hair. It was the only thing that calmed her down. She spiralled it round and around. It couldn't be called brown, even dark brown, the strands gleaming blackest black, curling and thick. They said gypsies had black hair and tempers like hers. Mary was always telling her so. She looked at her long fingers, almost grey in winter, berry brown after a few days of sun. No-one else changed with the seasons like she did. She could tell the weather by her skin. Nellie never changed, always skin like whale blubber.

'Jiddy?' Sleepy head!' Mary raised her voice.

She jumped. 'Yes?'

Rebecca and Annie had gone and she hadn't noticed.

'I've made a pot of tea, come and have some while it's hot.'

If Thomas had been there, he'd have said something to break the atmosphere. He'd say a few words, his eyes would twinkle and Mary would be half cross, half amused. But it would be over. Without him, they didn't know how to make up.

'You've got to learn to control that temper of yours,' Mary said.

Jiddy blew to cool her tea. 'It is in my blood,' she said, 'I can't change.'

'My main question is whether you're going to get spruced up or do you want that Nellie Ashner to be looking after Mrs Farsyde's fancy wardrobe and maybe getting a pretty hand-me-down or two?' she said.

CHAPTER TWELVE

T hat afternoon, in a large, light, airy room at Thorpe Hall, the four of them stood in a line holding their neatly folded items of fabric and clothing. Each of them, even Annie, had managed to put on their cleanest skirts and pinafores wash their hands and faces and neaten their hair. They were all nervous, standing in the grand house in their best clothes, desperate to be employed but trying not to show the others how much they wanted to be chosen. None of them had ever been in such surroundings before and even Nellie seemed on edge. A clock chimed three times and then silence again. Annie grasped Jiddy's hand to stop herself shaking and Jiddy's carefully pressed linen slipped precariously in her arms.

'Annie, let go. Use both your hands to hold your sewing flat so Mrs Farsyde can see it.'

Annie crumpled the handkerchiefs, shirt and petticoat tightly to her chest. Jiddy looked down at her own tidy pile. The clock chimed the quarter hour and their arms were beginning to sag and, losing concentration, Annie finally let her arms relax and the undergarments, shirt and pillowcases dropped to the floor.

They all looked at the door. Any moment, it would open and Mrs Farsyde would sweep in and the girl whose work lay on the rug would be immediately dismissed.

Jiddy bobbed down, pulling Annie with her but so quickly that they fell against each other and Jiddy's neatly folded garments slid on top of Annie's.

Betsie gasped. Nellie smoothed her pile of linen for the umpteenth time. Jiddy looked up. Someone was outside the room. The handle moved. The door opened. Annie grabbed the top layers of clothing and stood, leaving Jiddy kneeling amongst Annie's crumpled linen.

Mrs Farsyde swept into the room, all rustling silk and perfection. 'Good morning, girls.'

'Good morning, Mrs Farsyde.'

Jiddy grabbed the jumbled pile. The other three remained fixed, Annie included, staring ahead like a terrified rabbit. Jiddy nudged her elbow, willing her to change piles but Annie seemed incapable of understanding.

Mrs Farsyde studied them, her small, deep-set eyes taking them in, one at a time. Jiddy tried to flatten the tangled pile into folds instead of creases but it was no use; she'd have had to put them all down and sort them one at a time. She looked sideways at Annie, realising she'd have to snatch her own sewing back rather than rely on Annie giving it back freely.

Mrs Farsyde lifted a shirt from the top of Nellie's tall pile of immaculately folded linen. 'And your name is?'

'Nellie Ashner, ma'am.'

Jiddy couldn't bear it that Mrs Farsyde would think she cared so little as to stand in front of her with badly sewn and carelessly prepared items. She nudged Annie's arm again.

'Very neat,' Mrs Farsyde said, 'and so much. Thank you, Nellie.'

Very neat. Jiddy's ears burned.

'And you are?'

'Betsie Arno, ma'am.'

Mrs Farsyde seemed absorbed in examining Betsie's display of pleats and tucks, hems and seams. Jiddy twitched to grab her sewing. Or should she drop Annie's on the floor, stride over them and leave the room and avoid the humiliation that was bound to occur any moment now? She wanted Mary and Rebecca to be proud of her. Most of all she needed to earn money that had been lacking since Thomas' death. This was her chance to help Mary. She couldn't give up her chance.

She nudged Annie harder. This time, Annie pulled her arm away. Jiddy couldn't believe it. Her chest thumped so hard she thought everyone must hear. Mrs Farsyde would look from the mess in her arms to her face with such disdain. She couldn't bear it. What if she said outright that Annie had her sewing and this pile of badly finished work was Annie's? What would Annie say? Would she admit it? Would Mrs Farsyde discard her as a snitch without even looking at her work? The other two couldn't be relied on to back her up and how unfair and distressing would that be of Annie who was supposed to be her friend?

Mrs Farsyde patted the top of Betsie's exhibits. 'Thank you,' Betsie,' she said, 'you have worked hard.'

Jiddy kicked Annie's foot. Too late. Mrs Farsyde stood in front of her.

She picked up the top item of clothing and turning the shirt inside out, ran her fingertips over the seams. Jiddy couldn't take her eyes off the dainty, pale hands. Annie still didn't move. Betsie looked as if she was itching to turn her head.

Mrs Farsyde touched the uneven stitches. Still she didn't say a word.

It isn't mine, Jiddy willed her to be able to tell.

Mrs Farsyde draped the shirt over her arm and picked up another item, a petticoat with five or six tucks in waving lines above the hem. Jiddy glared at Annie's profile but Annie stared vacantly ahead, her arms making a shelf for Jiddy's neatly folded items. Jiddy cleared her throat. Annie didn't respond. Jiddy looked back at Mrs Farsyde's hands examining Annie's petticoat. They weren't moving. She looked up to see Mrs Farsyde's eyes fixed directly on hers. Fine. Let her think this were her sewing but she weren't going to be ashamed. She knew she were a fine seamstress, let Mrs Farsyde choose one of the others and walk around in substandard clothes. She'd soon realise her mistake. She looked directly at the lady of the house whose eyes sat like small buttons in a cushion, a uniform deep blue giving nothing away.

'You didn't tell me your name,' she said.

'Jiddy Vardy, ma'am.'

Mrs Farsyde nodded. 'Ah, yes.'

Ah, yes? What did that mean? Were that good or bad?

'Thank you.' Mrs Farsyde draped the items on top of the pile in Jiddy's arms and moved to look at Annie's.

'Mrs Farsyde?'

Mrs Farsyde turned back.

'Annie and me,' began Jiddy, 'we...' she hesitated, waiting for Annie to speak.

Mrs Farsyde looked at Annie then back at Jiddy, her intense gaze drying Jiddy's words on her tongue.

'My name is Annie Briggs.' Annie's flat monotone broke the tension.

Betsie bent forward to watch. Nellie turned her head a fraction. This weren't fair. Someone had to say something. Annie was her friend, how could she do this?

Mrs Farsyde looked impressed, her face lighting up. Annie wasn't going to speak up. Mrs Farsyde hadn't guessed the work was Jiddy's and Nellie and Betsie weren't going to say anything. Well, she didn't care. She'd find a job somewhere else. Somewhere better. Bigger. She dropped, half threw the clothes onto the floor, kicking them as she strode out of the line to the door. Betsie gasped. Nellie, for the first time, shifted her feet.

'What's happened?' Mrs Farsyde said, 'what's the matter?'

Jiddy had a plan formed. She'd ask Jane Bell for a job at the Musgrave Inn up at Ravenscar. Bar work, cleaning, she didn't care. She'd find Big Isaac. Ask him what she could do to play a bigger part in a run and get more pay off for it. Her head pounded. She couldn't hear anything but the sound of the sea in her ears.

The door opened. She hadn't reached it yet and someone else was entering. A dark jacket, breeches. Squire Farsyde looked taken aback.

'Have you finished?' he said. 'The minister will be here

soon and I'd like you to join us, my dear.' He eyed Jiddy up and down. 'Is this the one?' he said. 'She certainly looks the part.'

CHAPTER THIRTEEN

Once they were outside, clutching their linen and not caring if it creased or not, Annie couldn't stop saying sorry. Nellie stormed past, refusing to speak to any of them. Torn between who to follow, Betsie started to hum an unrecognisable tune. Jiddy paced in a circle, trying to work out what had happened, and Annie burst into tears.

'Mary needs me,' Jiddy said, and left Annie and Betsie to decide for themselves what they were going to do next.

'I'm not surprised,' Mary said when Jiddy told her that she had been chosen to be Mrs Farsyde's dressmaker and seamstress.

'I think it were squire who really gave it me,' Jiddy said.

'You've not started yet so we can't take anything for granted,' Mary said. 'Go up to farm and see if Mr Chaplow will give you some eggs if I can do some mending for him.'

'Mr Chaplow's good with a needle,' Jiddy said. 'And Mrs Farsyde did say to come up on Monday.'

'No harm in asking.'

Jiddy didn't want to, but when Mary sounded like that Jiddy knew not to cross her. She'd not been up at the farm for ages it seemed, so it was as good an excuse as any to see Jonas. Approaching the farm gate, she felt nervous. Rex barked when she opened the long gate but soon slinked off when he saw who it was. She strolled across the yard before shoving open the barn door. She liked the barn. It smelled of straw and animals and Jonas. He had his back to her, putting all his energy into brushing down Boy, his favourite horse. She loved Boy too, mainly because he had a coat as black as her hair.

'Good afternoon,' she said.

He looked briefly over his shoulder then back at Boy again. Brush, brush.

'What's that on your face?' he said.

How did he always see things and he'd hardly looked at her? She let her hair fall over her cheek. She'd forgotten Nellie's sharp fingernails.

'What you doing?'

Jonas continued wiping the dark flank over and over.

'Boy's sweaty,' he said.

'Did you take wagon to Saltergate?'

'What d'you think?'

He was fed up. She could tell.

'I were only asking,' she said.

'Well, don't.'

'At least Big Isaac makes it worth your while,' she said. 'Mary and I'd love to have amount of tea and extras you get.'

He carried on rubbing. When he didn't want to talk, nothing she said could make him. He could change moods like shadows passing sun to shade over the moors. She sat down on an upturned pail and watched him. She didn't know why he were always in such a bad mood after a run. She always felt high as a sparrow hawk and Mary always said it were worth helping smugglers, even if you weren't out on a run yourself. They were all involved, everyone, even minister, who told them stealing were a sin and so were murder. But he also said it were a sin to starve people on purpose, so there were, what did he call it? Clauses? She gave up trying to understand. But one thing she knew for sure. The sea brought it all; the sea, hushing in all its contraband. Jonas hated her talking about the sea but she couldn't help it, just as he couldn't help talking about how much he distrusted government.

'Them in London think fighting a war is more important than feeding folk like you and me. Sending our army to wipe out other countries' armies. Costs money, so they take it from you and me.' Blah blah.

Talking definitely got him cross. She often ran off so she didn't have to listen sometimes.

But watching him in such a black mood meant she didn't feel like telling him about being picked out of all the girls to be Mrs Farsyde's seamstress, and how she'd be up at Thorpe Hall making dresses and fine things. She'd have to wait a while longer to see look of pride and admiration on his face. Jonas in a bad mood was the worst feeling in the world. Worse than being called names. Betsie had said Jonas and Jiddy were as good as married but what did that mean? Jonas never said anything. He didn't act like a sweetheart. They were friends, the best of friends, but that were all. He'd never tried to even hold her hand let alone snatch a kiss. Spurting ale into his mouth weren't same and he didn't even seem to have liked it. She looked at him, busy with his horse. He were strong and she liked his eyes, like spring sky after rain. He had long fingers and she liked that. She liked finding similarities when there were so few. But they hadn't kissed and Mary said everything hinged on a kiss.

'Give me brush,' she said.

He still didn't take any notice and she'd kept still and quiet for at least a quarter hour. Brush, brush. She could tell he were tired as well as cross.

'Why d'you let other people take him out?' she said. He swept the brush over Boy's back, patting his neck, saying things in a soft voice that he never used on her. 'I'd tell them they couldn't use my horse if I didn't want them to.'

'I almost got caught,' said Jonas.

'What? You've been out? Why didn't you say?'

'I didn't want to tell anyone. It were my fault.'

'How could it be your fault? You shouldn't be on your own. They expect too much. How are you supposed to drive a loaded wagon over moors and be expected to unload at every stop-off point? It's not fair.'

'I get help at stop-offs.'

'That's not enough, you need someone with you to keep look out. I could turn out lantern as soon as we heard anything. You can't be expected to do everything. I'm gonna ask Isaac if I can come with you next time.'

This was exciting. She could help. Riding across moors would beat tunnels and ginnels of Bay any time.

'Don't be daft, you stick to what you know,' he said. He sounded more like himself again.

'Fine. Hope you don't get caught next time.'

'I won't.'

'Good.'

She'd had enough. It had been a long day. Nellie then Annie going weird, and not being able to tell Jonas and now him being like this.

'You don't know things I do, Jonas Chaplow,' she said, 'I'll have you know carrying goods in a cart is nothing to what us landers do. You're not on beach, waiting while there's preventives on look out. You're not passing contraband up line, packing stuff up your skirt...'

'I don't wear a skirt.'

'You haven't got courage to.'

'You lot have batmen to protect you.'

'You could have me.'

He made her so angry when he talked to her like that. Ever since that first bag of salt, she'd been part of the smuggling ring and Jonas never ceased to put her down.

'You're jealous because I started smuggling before you,' she said.

He gave her that look that always made her feel as if she wished she'd never opened her mouth, even though she knew she was right and he was jealous and only put her down because of that.

'It's dangerous for Boy. He's most recognisable horse in county. He's covering rough moorland, at speed sometimes. Could twist a leg, then what'll happen to him? If we're spotted, I'll be strung up on gibbet at Buttercross faster than you can gut a fish.'

'I still have to…' she said, but Jonas was on a roll.

'Boy's got to stand on clifftop, sometimes for hours while we wait for goods to be brought up from beach. It's cold. Damp, windy. It's not good for him standing around then stumbling over rough tracks stopping here there and everywhere dropping off stuff all through night. He's knackered by end of it. And then I've got to scrub him down.'

'You're late doing it today.'

'I've got cows and pigs to sort.'

Jiddy folded her arms. Best not say anything. Brush, brush. She watched his arms moving.

'I worry about you,' she said.

'I worry about you as well.'

She hadn't expected that.

He looked over his shoulder and held out the brush. Jiddy took it and they changed places, Jonas sinking onto the bucket and rubbing his chafed hands. Jiddy liked it like this. In the silence after an argument, she could hear his thoughts. It hurt her that he felt hurt for Boy, pushed to work when he were exhausted, forced to pull a load that weighed too heavy. It weren't fair. None of it were fair. He worried about her as well. That meant something. She threw a blanket over Boy then went over and crouched in front of Jonas.

'Are they sore?' she said, looking at his hands.

He'd have been sat on the cart up on that clifftop waiting for whatever goods they were bringing up. He was right. It were cold up there at night and they did have it hard riding inland when the rest of them were just about done. She leaned forward and kissed his knuckles. The shock of what she'd done made her freeze. She daren't look at him. What would he say? What would he do?

She'd never looked so intently into his eyes. Not even at the picnic. No way so intense. She didn't know whether to stay where she was or move away. His eyes seemed a deeper grey than usual and the black dots, huge. And they were looking at her, really looking, in a way they normally didn't. And so close she could feel his breath on her nose.

'S'pose we've got to get used to it,' he stood and she fell back, looking up at him towering over her.

She scrambled to her feet. 'Yes, no point going on about it.'

But she wanted to ask what he'd felt, looking at her so close.

CHAPTER FOURTEEN

Thorpe Hall looked so grand with its flight of steps leading to a huge front door and so many windows Jiddy couldn't see them all at once. She couldn't believe only two people lived there. They probably wanted a lot of children, she decided, craning her neck to see the mullioned windows reflecting the sky in their tiny panes of glass. They'd need a lot of babies to fill that many rooms. Friday afternoon seemed a long time ago. Nellie's cousin, Abigail, opened the kitchen door this time and Jiddy knew immediately that the smirking girl in the ill-fitting dress would not be friendly. Nellie would have told her all about how she would have been chosen if it had been up to Mrs Farsyde, but that the squire had overruled his wife. There was nothing to say, so after a quick greeting, Jiddy stood waiting outside the kitchen while Abigail shut the back door a little too loudly. Delicious smells of baking bread filled the air and Jiddy saw a massive game pie standing on a board on a long table. She'd never seen a kitchen like it. So big and light and so much food. A tall woman wiped her floury hands on her apron, gave Jiddy a quick up and down then turned to a girl stirring an enormous pan on the big black stove.

'Give sauce chance to stand still and get its bearings,' she said.

Jiddy looked back to see what had happened to Abigail but the girl had disappeared. Great. She stepped into the kitchen.

'I've come to see Mrs Farsyde,' she said.

'Mrs King is person you'll be needing to see first,' the cook said. 'She's right behind you.'

Mrs King looked stern. She took Jiddy to a dark room with a roaring fire in the grate and books on three of the walls. Squire Farsyde stood at a round table. Captain Pinkney was there as well. She stood still. There was movement by the fire. Mrs Farsyde stood up, all yellow and bright. She greeted Jiddy with a smile and rustling silk. The two men didn't bother to look around, but faced each other across the oak table, busy looking at paperwork strewn across the surface. Mrs Farsyde beckoned Jiddy to the table.

'Who'd have believed we'd become the richest place in the whole of England,' the squire chuckled.

'Gentleman,' said Mrs Farsyde, 'before I take my leave, may I introduce Miss Vardy to you?'

Jiddy wanted to pull back. This wasn't what she expected. The squire and Captain Pinkney wouldn't want to be interrupted by a lass from the village who'd come to work as a seamstress in the house. A large map lay on the table. Captain Pinkney gave a quick nod and Jiddy bobbed a curtsey.

'Welcome my dear.' The squire's round red face smiling, 'I hope you will serve my wife well. We're all in this together, isn't that so? Jiddy, isn't it?' Jiddy bobbed another curtsey. What else could she do? 'Have a look at this,' the squire said, gesturing her to the table. 'Look at all the coves where we can land ships. We'll show them in London that they can raise taxes as high as they like, hey, Pinkney? They're not getting a penny out of us. Let the French invade the south coast. What do we care about them when they don't give two hoots whether we live or die up here? What d'you say to that, Jiddy?'

She looked down at the map that traced the ins and outs of the coastline. Small inky ships proudly stood on a few wavy lines. All sails fully blown, set for a journey. Little men rolling barrels on coves she recognised were drawn in and she spotted the causeway at Robin Hood's Bay leading into the sea. There were the chimneys of the Alum mines towering further down the coast, and higher up, the harbour and dockside at Whitby. She didn't need to be able to read, with a map as well drawn with pictures like this following the map was easy.

'Mr Farsyde, I don't think this is quite appropriate. Come with me, Jiddy.' Mrs Farsyde walked towards the library door.

The squire set off laughing again. Leaning on his elbows, the captain looked down at the paper with its lines and drawings. Jiddy didn't want to go. She wanted to look closer at the strings of washing and little faces peeping out of hidden entrances. This was where she lived. There was Jonas' farm and White Moor's marshes and the Salt Road leading all the way to York. She'd never seen anything like it.

'For its size,' the captain said, 'Robin Hood's Bay on

the North Yorkshire coast is the wealthiest spot in the country and it's all ours.'

Mrs Farsyde's skirts swished. She was almost at the door. 'Jiddy?' her voice sounded sharp.

The squire waved a hand. 'Think of your gowns and jewels, my dear and how we don't pay tax on any of them.'

Jiddy couldn't believe it. Jonas would love to be hearing all this and be part of the conversation. It struck her again how natural it was that the squire and his wife would be part of the smuggling ring. So was the minister, Jane Bell up at the Musgrave Inn, farmers, landowners all the way across the moors and as far inland as York. Everyone thought the same as this, even if they didn't say it or know how to say it.

'It's us versus them, isn't it?' said Jiddy.

Captain Pinkney looked at her. She shouldn't have spoken. She wasn't clever like Jonas. She should keep her mouth shut. Squire and captain could say what they wanted, but she obviously couldn't. Fine, leave them to being all manly standing over a map in safety oflibrary. She started for the door.

Mrs Farsyde looked and waited. Jiddy kept walking. She'd not even started working at the hall and already she might have lost her job. What would Mary say?

'Who'd have thought a young lass would come out with something like that,' said the squire, still laughing. 'Told you, you'd picked the cream of the crop, my dear. She's special is our Jiddy Vardy, isn't she Pinkney?'

Jiddy looked over her shoulder at the captain. She wanted his approval. He brought the ships in. He ordered people about when he strode along beach like a warrior. She'd meant what she said. It always felt like she was up against someone else and why not the whole of the north against south?

'Our Jiddy Vardy is right,' Pinkney said. 'We're all dirty thieving blighters according to tax men in London.'

Mrs Farsyde's skirt rustled ferociously. 'Let us leave the gentlemen to their discussions, Jiddy,' she said sharply.

The captain agreed with her. He called her 'Our Jiddy Vardy.' She were quite happy to leave the room now, even though she found that what Squire Farsyde and Captain Pinkney were talking about was many, many more times more interesting than thought of Mrs Farsyde's silks and cottons. Seeing that map, for first time she realised what Robin Hood's Bay stood for. How important their twisting coast was. How their moors cut them off from rest of country. Could she remember what Squire Farsyde said? The outside world knew about them now. They were famous. That were something big and Jonas would want to know that.

'They think all womenfolk here are as broad as a bull's backside and strong as bears.' The captain's guffaw rang out as Jiddy followed Mrs Farsyde. 'They think they're such brave men coming to quell women of Yorkshire.'

Jiddy closed the door. Wait until she told Jonas that southern men were scared of Yorkshire women and that they thought the coast was unforgiving. They didn't know about Mill Beck and North Cliff and all the wonderful coves and inlets and their hidden secret places. So, southerners thought the people of the north were rough and harsh, did they? Cut off from civilisation by marshes hidden in great swathes of moorland to the west and eroding cliffs and unpredictable tides to the east? They didn't think people knew right from wrong. Well, it were wrong to starve people, that's all she knew.

'In future when I tell you to come, you'll come straight away,' Mrs Farsyde said, leading Jiddy up a staircase so wide Jiddy didn't know which balustrade to hold.

She followed Mrs Farsyde up the glowing wooden stairs and, rounding a half landing, faced another, shorter flight. Reaching a room immediately facing them, Mrs Farsyde closed the door and grasped Jiddy's hands.

'I'm going to have a baby,' she said. 'Squire Farsyde doesn't know. Nobody knows, but you have to.' She walked to the window. 'I am three months into my term and...' she laughed, swirling around. 'We have much work to do, my dresses no longer fit me. This is why I need you.'

She stood back, dropping her shawl. The lacing up the front of the bodice stretched revealing the cords and a bulge filling the top of the skirt gathers.

Jiddy noticed a sewing box on the table. 'Should I get straight on with the alterations, ma'am?'

'Yes, yes, and I want new clothes too. Small clothes, tiny dresses and gowns and a special one, a christening gown.'

Mrs Farsyde didn't seem as old as Jiddy had always thought. The girls had got it wrong, looking as she did, she can't have been that much older than Helen Drake's sister, Dottie.

It took all afternoon taking out and choosing unpicked dresses Mrs Farsyde wanted re-sewing. The maps and Squire Farsyde's words faded amongst the braids taken from old gowns to sew on new, and in debates about whether a dark dress suited Mrs Farsyde or a lighter shade.

Jiddy finally left, her head full of colours and fabrics and baby gowns. They seemed the most important and precious things in the world to Mrs Farsyde. Oblivious to her surroundings, she calculated how long it would take to make a new bodice for Mrs Farsyde and how fast her employer's stomach would grow. It wasn't until she reached the end of Thorpe Lane that she realised how quickly she'd reached it. She stopped. What were that noise? Voices and a banging sound. Breaking into a run, she reached the woods and the noise grew louder as she approached the first houses of the Bay. Rounding the final outcrop of trees, she saw a solitary figure standing in the middle of the road facing a crowd of Baytowners. They were all faces she knew but they looked very angry. They held pots and pans, spoons, ladles and stones above their heads. A steady chanting rose up.

'Traitor! Stone the traitor!'

CHAPTER FIFTEEN

Thin, weasel-like, Jack Gobbit turned towards her. His face and hands dripped red and his grey, bulging eyes looked more frog like than usual. The crowd moved in. He scrabbled around in the dust, hands and feet, trying to stand. Helen Drake strode up behind him and whack. He turned. Too late. She smacked him across the face with a massive ladle. Gobbit collapsed sideways. He didn't cry out or shout, but flopped like a rag doll. Jiddy hurried towards him, not sure what she'd do. The crowd of mainly women walked forward, weapons in the air. Nellie appeared from the woods, looking flushed and breathless.

A stone flew through the air and Jiddy jumped sideways to avoid it. Nellie had disappeared in the mass of arms and heads and Jiddy could no longer see Gobbit amongst the skirts and under the battering of kitchen pans and stones.

Standing up on the bank, James Linskill lobbed handfuls of pebbles as if he was having a grand time.

Admiration all over her face, Betsie stood next to him, her fingers twitching with each lobby of stones. He smiled at her and, climbing up the hillock, she opened her palms so that James began pressing handfuls of gravel into her hands.

'Not a pretty sight.' Rebecca stood next to Jiddy.

'How do we stop them?' Jiddy said.

Rebecca shook her head. 'Best wait here until it's over. In this mood, we'd be battered ourselves.'

Jiddy stepped forward but Rebecca grabbed her arm. 'We have to try.'

'If we stand up there,' Rebecca said, 'we might get their attention.'

Rebecca tucked Jiddy's hand under her arm and pulled her up the slope to the right of the road. On the hillock opposite, James and Betsie stood, showering pebbles, while in front of them the crowd of Baytowners swarmed over Gobbit, skirts brushing against skirts, rough boots and powdery soil rising.

Rebecca waved her walking stick. 'Leave him be. Helen, Sam, get everyone to stop it.'

A few faces looked up.

Nellie jumped up onto the mound next to them. 'Go home, Rebecca and sit by fire with your knitting.'

'Don't be rude,' Jiddy said, 'and stop hurling stuff, this is cruel.'

'He's a traitor, this is what we do to traitors.' Nellie ran down the slope and threw herself into the mob.

Jiddy looked at Rebecca. 'They're not going to stop, are they?' she said.

Rebecca shook her head. 'But we're not leaving.'

It wasn't long before people began to disperse, revealing what looked like a pile of rags lying on the ground. Helen Drake picked up a couple of pans, so casually she could have been collecting pebbles on the beach. Betsie looked herself again, smiling and gazing awestruck at James like a shiny, reflecting buttercup. Nellie was laughing, hitting James as if he'd told a rude joke. It was all so normal and yet not. Jiddy wondered what Rebecca was thinking. Had she seen anything like this before and had it ended like this, as if they were leaving Sunday service on any sunny morning?

'What did Gobbit do?' Jiddy said.

Rebecca took a couple of steps forward then stopped. 'Go round by bottom path,' she made a motion with her left hand. 'Tell Mary I'll call by in a bit.'

Jiddy took a step or two closer. The torn jacket and trousers couldn't possibly hold Gobbit's body inside them. One booted foot lay sideways. The other boot stood upright in the grass which looked funny left all on its own. They must have pulled off all his clothes. But what had they done to his scraggly, skinny body?

James, Nellie and Betsie stopped laughing and waited to see if Rebecca or Jiddy would uncover the body. Rebecca shoved past her, raising her stick and Nellie, Betsie and James started making farmyard noises.

'We've done nowt wrong,' Nellie said.

'Get gone,' said Rebecca, shooing them like chickens, 'you've a nasty streak, Nellie Ashner, you and your friends, get out of here and leave poor sod to his maker.'

Nellie gave a look of hatred to both Jiddy and Rebecca, then pulling Betsie's arm marched off down the hill with James following.

'That girl's no good,' said Rebecca, 'you stay clear of her.'

'Is he still alive?' Jiddy said.

Rebecca gestured again, this time more urgently. 'Let's both go and see Mary together.'

Gobbit were there after all. She could see that now. Yellow skin on his face stretched thin over bone. Limbs twisted, body flattened, smears of what must be blood in the dust. His blood reminded her of the pool around Thomas' head when she'd found him lying on the flagstones up along Bloomswell. Preventives weren't only ones to be wary of, she decided.

CHAPTER SIXTEEN

S he walked past the spot the following morning and all that remained were a few smudges on the ground.

'Who took him away?' Jiddy asked, looking from Mary to Rebecca when they sat at the kitchen table that evening.

Mary held up the items one by one, showing them to Rebecca. 'Thank Mrs Farsyde for all this,' she said. 'Is she looking well?'

'She looks fine,' said Jiddy. 'She got some lovely material from run other night. I were going to ask, d'you know why I weren't part of it? Nobody said a word to me until I heard from Jonas day after.'

'You can't be on every run, lass,' said Rebecca.

'But I'm always used,' said Jiddy. 'Were it something to do with Gobbit?'

'It were nothing to do with Gobbit,' said Mary, smelling a piece of cheese, 'I asked you not to be used because you needed to be fresh for going up to see Mrs Farsyde.'

'I could've done both.'

'Jiddy,' Rebecca said, 'Mary needed you to get work with Mrs Farsyde, so that's the end of it.'

Mary took out some carrots and sniffed them before holding them out to Rebecca to do likewise. 'These'll be good in soup,' she said. 'Thank Mrs Farsyde properly, won't you, Jiddy?'

'What did Gobbit do?'

'I want you to stop thinking about him,' said Mary. 'Your job is to look after Mrs Farsyde. Keep her happy. She doesn't have it easy where babies are concerned.'

Mrs Farsyde kept Jiddy busy and soon, the patch on the road where Gobbit had been disappeared and it was as if he'd never been around. Jiddy walked past the spot every day to Thorpe Hall and every time back. Sometimes she cut through the woods because she couldn't bear thinking about how people's faces had looked. That was becoming the worst thing about it and she didn't like that she was thinking more about them and less about Gobbit.

Weeks were passing and leaves crisped on the trees, browning and yellowing and glowing bright red and orange. The air was changing too. You could smell apples and a cooler sun. And one day Mrs Farsyde stayed in bed.

The servants crept around the corridors, hovering in doorways, and waiting until they were back in the kitchen before they gave their opinions about Mrs Farsyde and all the babies she'd lost. Jiddy kept quiet, Nellie's words banging in her head. Maybe Jiddy was a witch or a gypsy and some ancestor had shot curses through her directly to Mrs Farsyde's baby.

'Don't be daft,' Mary said. 'Poor Mrs Farsyde's been losing them babies long before you were anywhere near her.'

'You're not that important,' said Rebecca. 'Only God

decides whether a bairn lives or dies. Don't get above yourself, Jiddy Vardy.'

They'd been so happy the day before, putting the baby clothes Jiddy had made into drawers, deciding what else needed to be done. Planning new dresses for when the baby was born. Maybe they'd been too happy. It made Jiddy think that the map Squire Farsyde and Captain Pinkney had been looking at, that made Robin Hood's Bay sound such a great place to live, wasn't entirely honest. The Bay wasn't a good place for everyone. Not for incomers like Gobbit, who were easy targets for blame, or Mrs Farsyde who only wanted a baby and didn't seem to be able to keep one.

Returning from the hall, Jiddy put down her basket on the table and Rebecca started unpacking it straight away, taking out a pat of butter wrapped in muslin and a small joint of mutton that Mrs King had slipped in.

'It's good of Mrs Farsyde giving us these,' she said. 'Hope you're taking good care of her in return?'

'I do all I can but she lies in bed and cries much of time. What else can I do to help?'

Rebecca looked at Mary. 'Lass said an 'H',' she said.

'A what?'

Two weeks. That's all it had taken. Jiddy tried harder after that. If she could make an 'H' have a sound, she could do that with 'Ts' as well.

'Why's Mrs Farsyde bothering with me?' she said. 'She don't need anything altering anymore.'

Mary sniffed the butter pat before putting it on a plate

and covering it with a cloth. 'She wants to make a lady of you,' she said.

'Why?'

'Don't you want to be a lady?

'It's just one more thing making me stand out,' she said.

'I don't mind how you speak,' Mary said, 'as long as you don't mind how I speak either.'

Jiddy put her arms around the older woman, and bending nuzzled her face into Mary's neck.

'You'll always come first,' Jiddy said, 'you and Rebecca.'

Mary shrugged her off and pushing past gathered up the remaining stalks and peelings on the table. 'Get on with you.'

Tutting, Rebecca began slicing a loaf of bread. 'I don't hold with too much emotion,' she said.

The next day, Jiddy arrived at the hall as arranged. Mrs Farsyde emerged from her bedroom red-eyed and pale. She smiled at Jiddy.

'Come with me, I have something to show you,' she said, leading the way to the sewing room opposite the top of the stairs. A grey linen dress hung in the corner of the room.

'Take a closer look,' Mrs Farsyde said.

The linen felt smooth and the pale grey folds, light.

'I want you to wear it from now on,' Mrs Farsyde said.

'But it's your dress.'

'I'll give you ten minutes.'

Mrs Farsyde left Jiddy alone. The floorboards outside the door creaked as Mrs Farsyde walked up and down. Jiddy didn't really want to be made into a lady if it meant being as idle as Mrs Farsyde seemed to be. She saw how lonely her mistress was, too grand to have a laugh with the servants and too isolated in this big house from all the other ladies like her, isolated in their big houses.

Outside, gulls were squawking over something. It felt very strange in the quiet room, untying her apron and folding it onto a chair, then stepping out of her own thick cotton skirt and looking down at her patched petticoat. It wouldn't do for Mrs Farsyde to see this. Hurrying, she unlaced her bodice, wishing she'd scrubbed her fingers harder to clean her fingernails this morning. She pulled the laces and slid off the brown bodice and laid it on top of her skirt. Mrs Farsyde would be outside the door, waiting. She should put on the dress but she couldn't possibly put it on top of her worn underclothes. She touched the neat alterations someone had made to the bodice. It belonged to a lady. Would putting it on turn her into one?

The door opened. Jiddy skidded across the floor, grabbing her skirt and holding it in front of her. Mrs Farsyde smiled.

'Would you like me to help you?' she said.

She didn't seem to notice Jiddy's underclothes, busying herself with the dress, lifting the skirt over Jiddy's head and letting it slide easily down her arms. The linen ballooned over her, catching the air as it slid down her bare arms, over her chest until it settled on her hips.

'It's beautiful,' she said.

'It's only a day dress, but it looks tidy for when you're here.'

Mrs Farsyde held out the bodice and Jiddy slipped her arms into the sleeves. No-one had ever given her this much attention and this was the lady of the house, fastening her dress and making her feel special.

'I can do that, ma'am.'

Mrs Farsyde pulled the bodice together and finished catching the last hooks. 'Next time,' she said. 'For now, you see how it fits together.'

'Thank you,' said Jiddy, trying to breathe without panting.

'You're turning into quite a young lady, Jiddy,' Mrs Farsyde said. 'No-one will be able to tell you're a fisherman's daughter.'

Jiddy traced her hands over the bodice. She didn't know how Mrs Farsyde could do this every day.

'I'm not their daughter,' she said.

Mrs Farsyde waved her hand. 'You know what I mean. Now, I want you to wear this dress whenever you come to the hall. It will be kept here for you to change into as soon as you arrive.'

Jiddy took a step forward. 'Do you, I mean, do you still need me?' she said.

Mrs Farsyde opened one of the cupboards. 'I'd like you to come up three days, instead of two.'

Once changed into the dress, Jiddy held her ribs as she practised breathing in and out and waited for Mrs Farsyde to tell her what to do.

'I think it's a little tight,' she said.

Mrs Farsyde lifted Jiddy's arms and studied her torso. 'Nonsense,' she said. 'You will get used to it very quickly.'

'I can't bend.'

'Why would you want to bend?'

Jiddy caught her breath. 'To pick things up?'

'Walk around for ten minutes. Bend your knees. It suits you. I want you to wear it. It is yours now.'

'It's yours.' A tingling sensation galloped around her belly. To wear a dress like this and feel it sway as she walked was something she'd only dreamed about. Would it make her become a different type of person? Right at that moment, she hoped so. It would be wonderful to be elegant and refined and looking as though she belonged in a fine, big house. She looked at the pile of brown cotton on the chair and wondered how she could bear putting it on again.

Strolling up and down, she became aware of Mrs Farsyde's sharp eyes on her. This was a test. If she fainted she wouldn't be given a second chance. Her breasts looked huge, pushed up and straining to get out. She took quick shallow breaths but that made her sound like an overheated cow. Her ribs were crushed, she could snap at any moment, but there was something about the tightness that felt thrilling.

'I feel I'm ready to pop.' She laughed and laughed even more at the relief of admitting it until she ran out of breath and started panting again.

'Gently,' Mrs Farsyde led her to the long mirror. 'You certainly look more grown up,' she said.

Jiddy couldn't believe the dark-haired woman with

bosoms and cleavage and a waist pinched in and hips that spread out. The gown glowed in the morning sunlight streaming through the windows. Not as beautiful and rainbow like as the silk she had found in the cave all those years ago, but more beautiful than anything she'd ever worn. It was an elegant, ladylike dress. Jonas wouldn't recognise her either.

Mrs Farsyde pressed Jiddy onto a chair by the table. 'Let's pin your hair up at the sides,' she said.

While Jiddy sat, adjusting to another change in her breathing, Mrs Farsyde brought out a small box. Scooping up Jiddy's dark curls, she used pins to fix them above Jiddy's ears. 'You'll have to make yourself a cap,' she said, 'and we'll see if I can find some white hose.'

Jiddy let Mrs Farsyde lead her back to the mirror.

Mrs Farsyde smiled. 'Just look at you now.'

Jiddy turned her head. Her ears, now revealed, were passable she thought, not big like Betsie's or sticking out like Jonas' da's ears. She liked the way her hair curled into ringlets as they cascaded down her neck, bouncing as she moved her head faster from side to side.

'Look at yourself properly, Jiddy,' Mrs Farsyde said. 'What do you see?'

'Is this me?'

'Should I tell you what I see?' Mrs Farsyde's butterfly voice.

Jiddy nodded. She really shouldn't look at herself any longer.

'A lady.'

A lady. The dress held in her waist making her torso

look like chiselled wood rather than soft flesh. She seemed taller, her shoulders and arms more elegant. The gown hadn't a stain or a darn on it and the pale fabric made her summer tanned skin look a deeper shade of copper than usual. Could a dress do this? She'd never imagined clothes could have magical powers.

'Look how it brings out the darkness of your eyes. The pale grey reflects how they sparkle and you are so lucky with your thick lashes, Jiddy.'

She looked closer, to see if it was true.

Mrs Farsyde adjusted the skirt. 'Stop frowning, Jiddy, your skin is flawless. This colour is so hard to wear as it highlights every blemish and line but your skin glows. Why, it's like smooth gravy, not a flaw in sight and believe me, the sheen of this pale grey is not kind.'

'I think you must look perfect in this dress,' Jiddy said, looking over her shoulder at the coal-black curls cascading down her back.

'Thank you, Jiddy, you are very sweet, but remember, I always wear a lilac shawl around my shoulders when I'm wearing something this pale.' Jiddy did remember.

It seemed strange that she'd forgotten but then everyone wore a shawl. 'From now on, each morning when you arrive, I want you to come straight upstairs and put it on. You don't even have to ask because I won't see you until you are properly dressed and looking like this.'

'I'd wear it all the time if I could,' Jiddy said.

'Well we don't want to cause a riot in Baytown, do we?' she said.

She had so much to learn. If she was ever a rich lady like Mrs Farsyde, she hoped she'd be as wise.

She wondered if Jonas would recognise her dressed like this. He was the only one who didn't seem to notice that she was changing. What would he say if he saw her looking like a lady?

'Thank you,' she said. She couldn't resist it and she kissed Mrs Farsyde's cheek before turning back to the mirror. The sixteen-year-old girl had disappeared and in her place stood an elegant young lady who could pronounce her 'Hs'.

CHAPTER SEVENTEEN

It felt strange walking away from the house in her brown skirt and pinafore. The wool felt rough and the bodice too loose. The September sun felt too warm for a shawl and she tucked it on top of her basket. Shaking her head, she let the curls tickle her bare neck. At least she had this to remember the day. She hadn't thought it would be as hard as it was to get changed and put on her own clothes and she couldn't wait until she could wear the dress again and be a lady. Strolling towards the gates, she slowed down. Some figures were sitting on the wall.

James, Betsie and Annie had their backs to her and she could hear Nellie's voice. After the incident with Gobbit, they'd kept their distance and she wondered what they were doing at the hall. She didn't want them to spoil what had been a wonderful day and she looked around, trying to work out if she could take another way home and so avoid them.

'Jiddy!' Annie ran to meet her.

There was nothing for it. At least Annie was there to make it less awkward.

'Jonas' hen hut is full of chicks,' she said. 'We're on our way up to see them. You'll come, won't you?'

'You're joking,' Jiddy said, 'it's not April, you know.'

Annie tucked her arm under Jiddy's, 'I'm not stupid,

Jonas is trying out a late batch and keeping them in a shed. He's got lanterns strung up. He's crazy is Jonas.'

So that was it. Chicks in September. He certainly was crazy and Annie was always sweet, trying to include her. She glanced at the others, who'd climbed down from the wall and stood in a close group. James beckoned.

'Come on, Jiddy, Jonas wants you to come,' he said.

He was obviously trying to make amends but Nellie looked as if a cow had sat on her face and Betsie stepped closer to James; they'd definitely bonded over the pebble throwing.

They cut across the field as they always did, James first then the rest, scrambling over the wall, all skirts and scuffed overshoes. They laughed at the wind tugging on their scarves and James striding in front. Life felt good again. Jiddy and Annie caught up with the other two girls.

'You'd have thought Mrs Farsyde would have a whole brood of chicks by her age,' Nellie said.

'What's wrong with her, Jiddy?' asked Betsie. 'Why doesn't she have lots of bairns by now? At her age I'll have had a dozen babies.'

'Nothing's wrong with her,' said Jiddy. 'Doctor says it's babies that are problem.'

'I think Mrs Farsyde's too busy going to parties and drinking brandy and ordering people about to have any babies,' said Annie.

'Don't be daft,' Nellie said. 'You're more likely to have a baby if you're going to parties and drinking brandy.'

'You've got a lot to learn, Nellie Ashner,' James said,

cracking a switch through the air and making a whistling sound with it. 'You don't need to go to a party and drink brandy to get with a baby.'

'Stop listening to our conversation,' said Betsie, even though she smiled at him.

'We shouldn't be talking about her,' said Jiddy. 'She's right sad just now.'

Nellie pulled a face. 'Don't go thinking you and Mrs Farsyde are best friends. Soon as she's bored of you, you'll be back emptying lobster pots like rest of us.'

'She won't get bored,' said Jiddy.

'I think she's got too many dresses,' Betsie said. 'How many do you need? She should give some to us.'

Jiddy linked arms with Annie again. The memory of that dress was too special to share.

'She's greedy,' said Nellie, walking through the farm gate that James held open for them.

'Jonas?' shouted Annie, 'we've come to see your chicks.'

Seeing the door open, Jiddy ran to the barn, keen to get away. It felt odd pretending everything was normal and that they hadn't helped kill Gobbit. Even if their stones hadn't hit him, they'd been throwing them and she had stood and watched. She didn't want to be around Nellie and James and Betsie. She didn't want to talk about Mrs Farsyde with them either. It was a relief to get away and in the dim light, she saw Jonas moving straw with a pitch fork.

'You've got visitors,' she said. He took a moment to register. 'Nellie, Betsie and Annie have come up to see chicks. I didn't know you were hatching a second batch this year.'

James stuck his head around the door. 'I'm here as well,' he said. 'Can't miss opportunity like this,' he winked at Jonas before heading back outside.

'You don't mind, do you?' Jiddy said.

'Gives me a break,' Jonas put his arm around her shoulders. 'You lot are only interested in coming up when we've got chicks, aren't you?' he said, leading the way to the hen hut.

James followed, pulling Betsie and Annie, giggling under his arms.

'Jonas? Don't leave Nellie out, get your other arm around her. That way we've got two lasses each.'

Flushing pink under his tawny cheeks, Jonas gathered Nellie up and, delighted, she laughed loudly. Slipping free, Jiddy dodged Jonas' hand when he tried to pull her back and she ran across the rest of the yard, stepping inside the hut and leaving the door swinging open.

Chirping erupted, and lifting her skirts she edged across the floor, the fluffy balls scattering, a constant movement of yellow spheres. The others followed immediately.

'Careless.' Jonas said, lifting escaping chicks back over the threshold.

Damn. Why hadn't they been directly behind? It made Jiddy look as if she'd never been on a farm before.

'Didn't want to slam door in your face,' she said.

Nellie was the last to enter, closing the door behind her and making a show of it.

Betsie squealed. 'They're so sweet.'

'They're my favourites of all animals,' said Annie, scooping one into her hands and petting it.

'They're not animals, you nicky ninny,' said James, 'they're poultry.'

'Why on earth do they have to turn into nasty hens?' said Nellie, drowning out Annie's protest.

'So we can have more eggs,' James said.

'That hatch into more chicks,' Jonas added.

'That grow into more nasty hens,' James slapped Jonas on the back.

'That lay more eggs.' Annie and Betsie joined in.

Nellie didn't look pleased.

'You girls act as if you've never seen any before,' said James, raising one foot at a time to watch chicks fall and then right themselves again.

'It's months ago,' said Betsie.

'I forgot how sweet they are.'

James stood next to Jonas by the door. 'Hear about Gobbit?'

'Nasty,' said Jonas. 'You'd think he'd just be told to leave Bay.'

Jiddy wanted to hear what James had to say about his part. Betsie was completely preoccupied but she could tell Nellie was listening too. Nellie listened to everything.

James folded his arms across his chest. 'You're too soft,' he said. 'Gobbit deserved it for turning informer.'

'I weren't there,' said Jonas, 'but I wouldn't slaughter a pig like that. If you're going to kill anything, you should make it quick.'

'He had to suffer,' Nellie said, 'give a message that you can't snitch on people.'

'How d'you know he were a snitch?' said Jonas.

'It were common knowledge,' said Nellie.

'Ah, common knowledge,' repeated Jonas. 'Yes, he definitely deserved hammering he got.'

'Don't be funny,' said James, 'you can't have informers wandering all over place.'

'Well, don't be so quick to judge,' said Jonas. 'If it were me, I'd want a proper trial.'

'It weren't you,' said Nellie.

'No, I weren't there, but if I had been I'd have done my best to stop anyone battering a poor man,' Jonas said.

'Jiddy tried to stop it, like she were Jesus saving a lost soul,' said Nellie.

Jiddy continued stroking a little chick. 'Rebecca and me are just more human than some,' she said.

'Are you saying I'm not human?'

'I don't think you should charge in like a stampeding bull.'

'Are you calling me a stampeding bull now?'

'Name suits you.'

'Pig shit suits you.'

'Girls, girls,' said James. 'Think we'd better step outside.'

Jonas put his hand on Nellie's shoulder. 'We have to stick together, Nellie,' he said. 'If you were ever in same position as Gobbit I'd protect you, and I hope you'd do same for me.'

Nellie stood as close to Jonas as she could get. Jiddy

knew Nellie was goading her, but she couldn't help it, she was ready to grab Nellie's hair and drag her out of the hut.

James opened the door. 'I can only take so much of this sweetness,' he said. 'Who's coming back to Bay with me?'

Jonas let go of Nellie's shoulder. Betsie and Annie were on their feet, all skirts and foot stomping.

'I'm staying,' Jiddy said.

'Right.' Jonas dropped the chicks he'd been holding and they rolled and scrabbled over other ones to their feet. 'I'll see this lot off, then you can tell me why you're in such a stinking mood.'

CHAPTER EIGHTEEN

So what if she were in a stinking mood? Following Jonas across the yard, she patted her hair. Not one of them had noticed her curls. The wind had tangled them now anyway, so it was pointless. Nothing lasted in this place. If only they'd seen how beautiful she'd looked in the grey dress. It wasn't fair that she had to hide her new life. She was desperate to share this with someone and she had to keep it hidden. It wasn't fair.

Back in the barn Jonas picked up the fork he'd discarded earlier and began filling the already half-full wheelbarrow with sodden straw. Jiddy propped the door open with a bucket. The acid-warm horse smell was as familiar as the whiff of fish on the dock at the Bay but she still couldn't stomach it. She knew Jonas' trick of working like this. He'd carry on until she said something and if she didn't say something, he'd carry on working.

'You didn't notice my hair,' she said.

He lifted another forkful of manure. 'It's different today,' he said. He leaned on the fork. 'Better show me then.'

Turning slowly around, she shook her curls. Without saying a word, he began lifting clods of straw again. Fired burned through her head.

'Aren't you going to say anything?'

'It's all right.'

She glared at him, willing him to look up but he kept shovelling.

'Don't you like it?'

'What's not to like about black and frizzy?'

She looked down at her fingers. She wanted to wrap them round his neck.

'Nellie said there must be something weird about you to hold close friendship with a girl,' she said.

Jonas laughed. 'So what does that say about you?'

Jiddy gave a loud puff. Why, why, when she'd had such a brilliant time with Mrs Farsyde, was it that as soon as she saw the others things went wrong? Jonas wasn't helping either. What were wrong with everybody?

'Betsie and James seem close,' she said.

She sounded so petty and silly, even to herself. All the things Jonas hated but she didn't seem able to stop her stupid mouth rattling on.

'Sorry.'

'What did you say?'

'Sorry.' Louder.

Jonas gave her one of his withering looks and turned back to his shovelling. Folding her arms, she kicked the door before throwing herself to lean on it. Why did they have to be waiting outside Thorpe Hall for her? She'd have been happy to have gone straight home. Mary and Rebecca would have admired her hair. Out of the corner of her eye she watched him lean his fork against the wall and saunter over. Elbowing her to move along, he leaned next to her to look out at the yard.

'You're not to tell anyone this,' he said.

'I won't.'

'You promise. Swear you promise.'

'I swear on silk you're keeping for me in your attic.'

He looked as if he'd decided not to tell her, but then he squared his shoulders.

'I like you because you're different to Nellie, Betsie and Annie,' he said. He cleared his throat as if giving a speech in the pulpit. 'And I'm not weird. I don't think of you as a girl, I think of you as Jiddy. No big deal.' He kicked his way back through the straw and picked up his fork again, shifting soiled clumps of straw and piling them in the barrow. She didn't know whether to shout or cry. He'd said what she'd never expected from him, from anyone else, yes, but not from him. He said it was no big deal.

'If it's no big deal you spend time with me, then it won't be a big deal if we never see each other again.' She stuck out her chest, shoulders back, chin raised, making herself as tall and wide as she could. She wouldn't let him see he'd hurt her. Throwing down his fork, he marched over to her again.

'It's no big deal if anyone knows we spend time together, that's what I meant, so get things straight before you get all spiky with me.'

'I'm not spiky.'

'Don't contradict.'

'I'm not.'

He laughed. 'Come here, give us a hug.' He squeezed

her shoulders. 'Now get off home before I give you a job to do.'

Jiddy stood close, to make the hug last longer. 'Mrs Farsyde chose me to work especially with her,' she said, 'above the others, and she wants me there three days a week. At least.'

'That's grand. Maybe being up at hall will get some of that crosspatch gypsy knocked out of you.' Jonas said, dropping his arm.

'I prefer being with you,' she said. 'I don't like being inside doing Mrs Farsyde's sewing all the time. I don't want to be a lady. I like being out whenever I like.'

Jonas began shaking great armfuls of straw all over the floor and kicking it with his boots. Jiddy sneezed.

'Does Mary let you go out whenever you like?' he said.

'When I've done chores.'

He gathered another armful, looked as if he was about to say something, then threw it down.

'You're earning money, Jiddy, you should be grateful. The others earn barely anything emptying lobster pots and collecting cockles, mussels, winkles, whatever.'

'Crabs,' she said.

'And crabs.'

He wouldn't look at her but she felt his disapproval flood over her. It seemed everything she did was wrong.

She pushed herself away from the door. 'I'm going to be so rich working for Mrs Farsyde,' she said. 'I'll be buying you all salt you need for preserving your pigs and cows through winter and I'll buy both Mary and

Rebecca dresses a hundred times prettier than any of Mrs Farsyde's.'

Spinning her imaginary skirt, she twirled around as if dancing. Swish, swish of her skirt, her hair flying out, she spun so fast. It felt good and she didn't care.

Slipping on the straw, she squealed and he caught her. Holding onto his sleeves, he steadied them both. She stared at his mouth and leaning forward, she kissed him. It only lasted a second, but just for a moment she felt his lips move against hers. And then it was over and the look of surprise on his face made her run outside. She'd kissed him. She'd kissed Jonas. She waited a moment, readying for him to appear. Rex scampered across the yard, barking.

Heading for the gate, she heard Jonas shout. 'Jiddy? Come back.'

She kept running, letting the gate bang behind her. Jumping over bouncing moorland grass, she felt like flying. She'd kissed Jonas. She was flying like a sparrow hawk and Jonas was her eagle. Flying, flying. Flying. This was so exciting. Nellie and the chicks were forgotten. This day was the best, the very best.

Almost home, she slowed, imagining their next kiss. Where should they do it? In the barn again or somewhere fresh? Outside would be nice. If she was wearing her dress, that would be perfect. Maybe she could find an excuse to pop outside and Jonas could happen to be at the hall and her hair would be curled and he'd stare at her, stunned with how ladylike she looked and it would be a very passionate kiss.

'Hey you.' James sat on the wall by the top road. 'Enjoying yourself?'

'What you want?'

Jumping down, James joined her as if they were pals as always.

'It's been kept quiet so as not to give anyone chance for talking, but there's a run on tonight. A big one. You're at Mill Beck end. Get yourself on beach at bottom of cliff path just before dark. Jonas will have Boy and his cart at the top. Your job is to check all ropes and stuff are cleared away. You know spot, don't you?'

He spoke urgently, the teasing tone gone.

She nodded. 'Are you going to tell Jonas?'

'Off up there now.'

'Does Jonas know I'm with him?'

James laughed, turning and walking backwards. 'It were supposed to be Betsie, but I want her with me on Lingers Hill.'

So, this is why Squire Farsyde and Captain Pinkney were poring over the map. She watched James go.

They were changing, all of them, but she wondered what it would mean to the group. James and Betsie pairing off. She and Jonas. Nellie might even cut away from them all, in search of some poor chap she'd snare as a husband, and what about Annie? It felt like all of them were suddenly growing up and heading separate ways.

CHAPTER NINETEEN

Acouple of lanterns, propped up close against the base of the cliff, shone a dim light on the beach. The noise of feet mingled with surf hitting the shingle. An oar splashed. Then silence. Jiddy waited for the sound of the last barrel rolling on the sand as Abe readied it to be hauled to the top of the cliff. A rope fell with a muffled collapse of hemp next to them and grabbing hold of it, Abe shifted it around the barrel.

'You can do it next time,' he said. Jiddy gave the rope a quick tug before the barrel began to rise up the cliff face. 'I'll take these.'

Abe extinguished the lanterns and trudged off towards the cave entrance. More footsteps. Then all was still. The outline of a rowing boat against the fainter sky disappeared into the dark, and the lingering figures of the beaters soon faded behind the others into the cave.

Left alone, Jiddy stood at the base of the cliff, listening as the barrel scraped against the rock. She breathed in the salty air. They were almost done. Tension stiffened her limbs. She waited. Without stars or a moon, the cliff path was too dark to risk. She touched the rope and gave it two sharp tugs, hoping Jonas would understand that she didn't want to risk the path.

It seemed ages waiting and she wished she'd kept a

lantern and taken the path, risking preventives seeing a moving light. It was growing cold. She couldn't hear anything from above. Crunch. The end of the rope landed to her left and she tied it around her waist.

Giving the rope a tug, she hoped Jonas had felt it. A tug back. Putting a boot against the rock, she leaned back, feeling her weight. This was something she'd always wanted to do but would her arms be strong enough to take her to top? The rope jerked. Jonas was pulling her like one of the barrels, only this time she could help. Step by step, she began walking up the cliff. Easy at first, she pressed her feet hard against the face. A few more steps. This were getting harder than she thought but there were no going back now. If she slipped, she mustn't scream. If it could hold weight of a barrel, it could certainly hold her. She listened. The sea hushed against the shore. The rope tugged again.

'Come on.'

She looked up. Grass from the top couldn't be far off. She grabbed out, the soil, sandy now, cascaded in gentle water falls. Her arms began to shake. She wouldn't stop again.

'Jonas?'

'Keep moving.'

Feet. One step, right, left. Heave. Pull. She was sweating. This was awful. She should have risked the path. Almost there, keep going, she could do this. Flinging one arm onto the top, she rested for a moment, breathing hard. Jonas put out his hand to help her up.

'For God's sake, Jiddy, we've not time for you laiking about. What you doing?'

Jiddy waved him away. 'Give me space.' Rolling onto the grass, she lay looking up at the star-crowded sky.

Jonas began untying the knot around her waist.

'Just a minute,' she said.

He didn't say anything, but she heard his breathing, his bending over, his fingers moving quickly against her stomach. The knot loosened and the rope pulled from under her.

'You stupid beggar,' he said. The moon came out, lighting the clifftop.

The ground were lovely and cool and she were so hot. She'd been mad to climb up the cliff. She should have crept up the path but it weren't only thought of doing that in the dark, it were that he'd have been gone by the time she'd edged her way to top and she'd wanted to see him so much. Jonas dropped the rope into her arms.

'Finish this,' he said, 'I've got to be off.'

'I can ride with you.'

'Have you wound that hemp up yet?' he said, rolling the last barrel across the grass.

'It'll take me a minute to hide this away, then I'll come with you.'

'No chance,' Jonas said. 'You hide that rope under tree there and get straight back home. I've a long night and I can't take you back to Bay.'

'You don't need to, I'll stay with you at farm.'

'Yeah, Da would love that. Hide rope and get off.'

'Jonas?' she said. 'Is there something you want to say about this afternoon?'

'I said to get a move on. I for one don't fancy getting caught.'

She couldn't wait any longer. She hadn't been able to stop thinking about kissing him again. Her lips couldn't wait. Her head couldn't. She'd go crazy as a bullock. Dropping the rope, she bounded over the grass and grabbing his jacket, pulled him towards her, kissing him directly on the mouth, nice and hard, smack on as she'd imagined it would be. She remained still, eyes open, lips unmoving. His eyes remained open as well, staring at her so close they merged into one, slap bang in the centre of his forehead. Were they supposed to move their heads sideways or something? Quickly, she pushed out her lips, but his seemed to spread out in a line. His hands tight on her forearms clenched like vices and she wondered what she should do next when he pushed her away. Oh no. She shouldn't have been so stupid. He hated her mouth. If Nellie or the others heard how useless she was at kissing, so useless even her best friend pushed her away, she'd die. Jonas must think her the most un-kissable girl in the entire world. She'd have to run away from Robin Hood's Bay now. She'd have to leave Yorkshire completely.

'What do you think we are, limpets?'

'Shut up, Jonas Chaplow,' she said. 'It were a dare. James dared me. Said it would be a right laugh.'

'Be quiet or you'll bring preventives down on us.' Taking her hand, he pulled her towards him. 'Quit prattling and I'll show you how it's done.' He closed his eyes.

Sweet Lord, how's he going to find my mouth with his eyes shut, he'll kiss my nose or my cheeks, we'll bash heads. Is that what he wants to do? Were I that bad?

She closed her eyes tightly, unable to bear the thought of what was going to happen. When a warm mouth touched hers and a very slight movement began, she tensed up. The mouth touching hers stretched into a line like before. Were he smiling? Were that what it were? Why were he smiling? Were she that funny? The mouth softened again and a tingling sensation coursed through her body.

'Jiddy?'

'Mm.'

He pulled back, no, no, don't do that, she grabbed his sleeves.

'More.' She leaned forward and he put a finger up to caution to be quiet.

'We've got to go,' he said.

'I want to do that again.'

'Tomorrow.'

'Now.'

'Tomorrow, I said.'

Disentangling himself, he climbed onto the seat of the cart, lifting Boy's reins before pausing to look at her. Jiddy stared back, willing him to stay. Tomorrow was too far away. She'd have a whole night to wait and then she had to be up at the hall and she wouldn't sleep thinking about his lips.

'Don't hang about,' as he jerked Boy's reins.

'Do you promise about tomorrow?'

'Yeah, I promise.'

Jiddy picked up the coil of rope at her feet and watched Jonas and the wagon disappear before hurrying over to the tree. Deftly, she pulled the looped rope from around the tree trunk. She couldn't even hear the cart now. It weren't a dream, she told herself. What she and Jonas had was real.

And if that were what a kiss were like, she definitely wanted more. It tasted of earth and the sea and autumn apples and a winter fire combined. It tasted of everything she knew and loved. The sooner she got home, the sooner tomorrow would come. She worked quickly, pushing the rope into the hole at the base of the oak, then stamping down the turf. Crouching, she teased the grass upright to camouflage the cut edges of ground, her fingers moving the blades, so that within moments, the grass appeared untouched. Wiping her hands on her skirt, she headed straight along the tops, following the line of hawthorns and keeping her eye on the North Star.

Another run and they'd fooled preventives. At one time, that would have been enough but not now; now she and Jonas had kisses to look forward to.

CHAPTER TWENTY

Jiddy rested her head in her arms on the table. She wanted to dream about Jonas but her head and body were desperate to sleep. It didn't help that a fire burned noisily, crackling and spitting wet coal, and Mary wouldn't stop moving, knocking dishes and clattering a spoon in a pan.

'Eat your porridge,' Mary said, her voice striking through Jiddy's muddled brain.

She couldn't wake up. She should be allowed to sleep after being out most of the night. Others would be in their beds.

'Let me sleep,' she said.

The scraping of a chair. Mary sitting down.

'Jiddy?'

'What?'

'You're due up at hall.'

'Mrs Farsyde will understand.'

'We have to carry on as normal. Preventives will be about. They'll know summat is up if there's nobody on streets.'

Jiddy looked at Mary through half-open eyes. Mary looked tired too. She never slept properly when Jiddy was out. Preventives. It made her sick every time she thought about them.

'Come on, eat up,' Mary said. 'I've got a basket of goodies ready for Mrs Farsyde.'

The basket was heavier than usual. Tea and coffee, rum and brandy decanted into earthenware jars. Salt in a large bag and a special bottle of perfume.

Instead of cutting up the back lanes, she headed up Bay Bank; even though it was steep at least it was straight. Someone sat on the seat near the top of the bank. Mercifully, it wasn't a red jacket. They did look big though. Stay calm, she told herself, just walk on past. You don't even have to nod. They'll understand. She approached and they didn't move. Now she was closer, she made out who it was. The hat, that massive triangular hat and cape. What on earth was Captain Pinkney doing, sitting there brazen as you like after a run? She forced herself up the last stretch of the sharp incline.

'Make sure you've got that lot properly covered,' he said as she drew level with him.

She tucked the cloth firmly down.

She was desperate to put the basket down and rest for a moment. It was so heavy and Bay Bank steep. She wouldn't stop though, not if it killed her to keep walking.

'Stop being so proud and come and sit down for a minute,' he said.

'I'm due at hall.' She swung the basket to her side, feeling her muscles tug with the strain.

'I'm telling you to. Tell squire you were under my orders if he gives you gip.'

She couldn't argue with Captain Pinkney. No-one argued with Captain Pinkney. Placing the basket at her feet, she sat down on the end of the bench. It was angled towards the Bay, so you could see the water spread all the way to Ravenscar, with the Musgrave Inn perched on top. It was a relief to sit and she stared at the distant cliff, glad of the breeze cooling her face.

'You like sea, don't you, Jiddy Vardy?' he said.

She nodded. Yes, she liked sea, he knew that.

'Nothing better than being in a ship out on water,' he said. 'No land for miles, just the tilt of waves.'

What was she supposed to say? She shuffled to get more comfortable.

'Are you going away again soon?' she said.

She was about to stand up when he put a hand on her shoulder. 'You're not supposed to ask questions like that,' he said.

What did Mary say? 'If in doubt, say nowt.' Why did she never learn?

'Do you ever fancy being out in a ship on North Sea?' he said.

'Me?'

'Anyone else on bench with us?'

She was too tired for tests. She was too tired for anything that morning. Later she hoped to see Jonas, but right now she couldn't face anything more than she had to.

He had an unusual profile. A very long nose and a straight, long chin and his cheeks seemed to hang straight down too. There was no-one else like him in Bay. She'd never thought about it before. Maybe he wasn't from Bay either and that's why he always walked around in his big hat and cloak, to make himself look intimidating.

She looked back at the water. 'I can swim,' she said, 'I wouldn't mind going on a ship.'

He had that staring look in his eyes that many of the sailors had when they came home from months away at sea. She waited but he didn't say anything else, so she picked up the basket. He was the kind of person you felt you should curtsey to, but he wasn't gentry.

'I'm going now,' she said, walking around the bench and heading up the gentler incline before turning along Thorpe Lane towards the hall.

Plodding on, she gave up trying to work out what the conversation had been about or why he had been sat there. The captain was a bit odd, everyone knew that, probably lonely with no family that anyone knew about. Her arm ached. Thank goodness she hadn't met a preventive. Dragging her feet up the tree-lined entrance, dappled with early sun, she fixed her eyes on the hall ahead. She'd soon be putting on the linen dress and maybe Mrs Farsyde would curl her hair. Hopefully Mrs Farsyde wouldn't want to talk too much and would leave her to get on with some sewing and she could take the day slow. Maybe she'd let her off early for delivering these goods. And if Jonas was delivering barrels or some other contraband from last night, he might call at the hall when she was there. Speeding up, she looked for a cart outside the stables, but the yard was empty.

Pushing through the door leading from the servants' quarters into the main house, Mrs Farsyde met her, looking fresh and excited. She wore one of her really good gowns. A pinky brown colour with tiny sprigs of blossom. It was Thursday. Nothing special about Thursday. What was going on?

'I've brought you some things,' she said.

'Wonderful,' Mrs Farsyde said when Jiddy lifted the cloth. 'As soon as you're changed, I have something different planned for today. Today, we're going to have fun.'

'Don't you want to unpack your order?'

'Of course,' said Mrs Farsyde. 'And after we've unpacked it, I'm going to teach you to dance.'

'Ma'am?'

Mrs Farsyde had lost her mind. She looked down the corridor opening into the hall. The house remained quiet.

'I'm sorry, I'm presuming. Do you know the Cotillion and the Quadrille, Jiddy?' Mrs Farsyde said.

Jiddy shook her head.

'We have our work cut out,' said Mrs Farsyde.

Once ensconced in the sewing room, Jiddy put the basket down and rubbed her upper arms. The basket really had been heavy.

'We'll unpack it later,' said Mrs Farsyde, 'I won't have my plans altered. Please change and don't dilly-dally.'

'Don't you want to try the new perfume?'

'What I want is for you to put that dress on,' Mrs Farsyde pointed to a blue striped dress Jiddy had never seen before, 'and then we can go down to the ballroom.' Mrs Farsyde began to bustle around. 'Take your things off,' she said.

This was exactly what put Jiddy on edge about the hall. Always something to trip her up, some word or way of doing something. Even clothes. She was always on the alert for a new way of fastening a jacket or the name of some ruffle or way of tucking, but she'd never dreamed she'd be given another dress, and Mrs Farsyde had already taken it down and was making moves to help Jiddy out of her pinafore.

Untying the pinafore, she folded it onto a chair. Mrs Farsyde remained, pretending to be busy, lifting out packets from the basket and putting them straight into a cupboard without even opening them. Untying the tape around her waist, she let her heavy skirt drop. She didn't care anymore about her underclothes. Mrs Farsyde never said anything. It seemed as if only the top layer mattered.

The bodice slipped on, tight across her chest and, holding in her breath, she looked at the top of Mrs Farsyde's head and it struck her how neat and shiny her hair was.

'Now the top skirt.' Mrs Farsyde busied herself fastening hooks and eyes, tightening the cage around Jiddy's body. This wasn't an every-day dress. It must have cost a great deal of money. It felt heavy and light at the same time. A gathered hem stirred around her ankles. She swayed. It swayed. She rocked her hips and the dress rocked like a boat.

'Good.' Mrs Farsyde looked pleased when Jiddy faced her. 'Now let's sort this mane of yours.'

It was a relief to settle into a chair. Getting dressed was as exhausting as climbing the rope up the cliff or carrying a heavy basket up Bay Bank. She felt Mrs Farsyde tugging a brush through her black tangles, then section by section, pinning little circles creating tamed curls that fell in neat rolls that bounced on her bare neck. Mrs Farsyde concentrated hard as if this was the most important job in the world. Watching her, Jiddy thought how uncomplicated her life must be. She could fall asleep. Curls and pins massaging her head. She began to feel heavy again.

'Jiddy? Jiddy?' Mrs Farsyde's voice brought her back and Jiddy woke with a jerk of her head. 'All done,' Mrs Farsyde said.

Jiddy had never been in the ballroom before. She stared at the large empty space punctuated by chairs and small tables around its edge. Crystal chandeliers sparkled and huge portraits looked at each other across the room. But it was the floor that drew her attention. A golden brown, gleaming expanse of wood that beckoned to be skidded over like a frozen lake. Mrs Farsyde's shoes clicked over the surface and her skirt billowed out as she sped up. Jiddy couldn't believe they were going to dance. What she really wanted was to take off her shoes and glide across the floor.

'Ladies from all over Yorkshire have danced here,' said Mrs Farsyde. She sounded proud. Jiddy had best try her hardest if she was going to learn to dance in the ballroom where ladies from all over Yorkshire had danced.

'First things first,' Mrs Farsyde said, 'let me see you walk up and down the room.'

Jiddy didn't wait. She strode out, chin up, in a massive

circle. Mrs Farsyde watched without saying anything. Jiddy sped up.

Mrs Farsyde smiled as if she knew some secret. 'I can't wait to see you dance a Polonaise. Let's start with some simple steps.'

Jiddy didn't care. She didn't feel tired anymore and she floated around the room doing exactly what Mrs Farsyde said, glad to be kept out of sight from the rest of the house. It could be raining or snowing, in the middle of winter or a thunderstorm, she could dance around the room and no-one would know what she was up to. She twirled, her skirt spinning out. This was bliss. This was heaven. She swirled and swirled. Out of breath, she stopped, holding her ribs. How could she keep breathing wearing something so tight?

'Jiddy? How do you feel?' Mrs Farsyde looked concerned and Jiddy laughed breathlessly.

'I feel wonderful,' Jiddy said, raising her arms and turning slowly. 'I can dance the cod and eel.'

Mrs Farsyde smiled. 'Quadrille, Jiddy. How many times do I have to tell you?'

A knock at the door made them look at each other. Please don't be Abigail, Jiddy thought. Oh no. She suddenly realised. It would be Squire Farsyde and she'd have to dance with him and Mrs Farsyde which would be horribly awkward.

'Come in.'

The door opened. A gentleman wearing a pale blue jacket, matching waistcoat and white breeches walked into the room as if he owned it and not Squire Farsyde.

His fair hair curled around his face and his deep blue eyes looked directly at Mrs Farsyde.

'Jiddy, I'd like you to meet our guest,' she said.

He walked gracefully towards them, his shoes tapping the floor in an even rhythm. Jiddy couldn't take her eyes off the stranger. The curls around his cheeks bobbed with each stride, and his coat tails, cut from a fine cloth, splayed behind him. Mrs Farsyde extended her hand.

He bowed, very quick and small, then again to Jiddy. She curtseyed, then wished she hadn't. As they both straightened up, his piercing eyes flicked across her face. He looked as if he was about to speak when Mrs Farsyde interrupted.

'I do appreciate this favour,' she said. 'Jiddy,' her sprig of blossom dress swaying, 'your dance partner has arrived.'

CHAPTER TWENTY-ONE

The stranger kept looking at her with a strange expression on his face. It was as if he was weighing her up and he couldn't quite join the dots. It made her want to smile. He must be wondering who she was too.

'Are we ready?' Mrs Farsyde stood next to Jiddy. 'We move to the right, Jiddy, while the gentleman moves to the left. I really am very grateful,' she said, smiling at him, 'I don't know what we'd have done without you.'

Jiddy knew. She could be running around the room like a bird, twirling her own circles and making up her own steps. Instead, she would learn to dance like a lady. Mrs Farsyde seemed happy about it and looking at him, she couldn't wait to start the first dance.

Two steps this way, two that way then walk down the room. The gentleman delicately took hold of her hand. It was cool and soft, and closer now she smelled the rose water on his hair. No man she knew smelled of perfume, not even Squire Farsyde. His fingers twitched and she felt a thrill of excitement tickle up her arm. His profile gave nothing away. They stepped forward, then around in a circle. It really was only walking. It was easy, too easy and so boring. Dancing wasn't half as much fun as she'd expected, even holding a stranger's hand.

'Perhaps we should try a Gavotte?' he said.

He had a soft voice and his words sounded different to how she would say them. Mrs Farsyde looked surprised at his suggestion but she quickly hid it. Jiddy looked at Mrs Farsyde. What was a Gavotte?

Before Mrs Farsyde could offer any instruction, he took both her hands and jerked them like a pair of reins. 'Gallop,' he said, and they bounced down the room while Mrs Farsyde stood and watched.

This was definitely more fun. Jumping up and down, skirt bouncing, curls springing, it made her heart race. Slow, slow, gallop down the room again. He was watching her all the time, but she didn't care. She was good at it and this only her first time. Laughing she caught his eye. Yes, he was definitely trying to work her out, but she didn't care. This was fun.

Up and down the shining floor, bouncing and jumping. Mrs Farsyde started laughing. If this was dancing like a lady she could do it easily. He held her hands firmly, his cheeks flushing a light pink. Through the window, a figure caught Jiddy's eye. Someone was watching. Someone standing close to the window. She stopped turning. A crop of copper hair and a brown jacket. And then the figure moved. She'd recognise that tweed jacket anywhere. Jonas. He'd come to see her at the hall and she was in an even more beautiful dress than usual. She had to see him. He had to see her.

'Mrs Farsyde?' She tried to catch her breath when they stood for a rest. 'Let me fetch some refreshment,' she said. 'Would you like something to drink, sir?'

He wiped his neck with a handkerchief and nodded.

'That's an excellent idea,' said Mrs Farsyde, 'have Abigail bring it to the drawing room, we will wait for you there.'

Picking up her skirt, Jiddy hurried through the door and down the corridor.

'Please can Mrs Farsyde have tea in drawing room?' she shouted as she ran past the kitchen.

Outside, the fresh air hit her and she looked about.

'Jonas?'

He and two of the stable hands standing next to the wagon turned around.

'Aye, aye,' said Bill, 'caught yourself a lady, have you?'

The other said something she didn't hear but Jonas walked to meet her, flushed raspberry pink. She beamed.

'Did you see me?' she said. 'Did you see? Mrs Farsyde is teaching me to dance and I'll teach you too. I've learned so much this afternoon. Mrs Farsyde wants me to dance right. It were such fun. I know you saw me. What d'you think?' She twirled on the gravel. 'Do I really look like a lady?'

He looked at her then across at the window to the ballroom. 'You'll be in trouble,' he said, 'best get back inside.'

'No, it's fine,' she said, 'they've gone to the drawing room. Abigail will be ages setting a tea tray.' She held out her arms. 'What do you think? Jonas, look at me,' she grabbed his sleeve and shook it. 'What do you think? Does it suit me? And my hair? See? It can be tamed.'

'I can't let them unload on their own, I've got to help,' Jonas said.

'I thought you'd come to pick me up, treating me like gentry.' She smiled. 'If I change quickly, will you wait?'

'I've got to get up to farm. Da can't manage on his own.'

'Two flicks of a lamb's tail. I'm sure Mrs Farsyde will let me go early, I'm a quick learner, you know.' She picked up her skirts and ran back across the gravel.

He'd turned the cart around but was still waiting when she got back and she heaved herself up beside him.

'Mrs Farsyde didn't mind. I think she was pleased to have tea on her own with her visitor.' She snuggled up to him, smiling and face aglow, happy to see him.

'Come on, Boy.'

She shuffled on the seat to get more comfortable but Jonas remained rigid. She didn't understand it. It couldn't just be tiredness that made him so bad tempered. Leaning her head against his shoulder, she let her curls bounce against his cheek.

'What are you doing?' he said.

'Your shoulder makes a good pillow.'

It didn't though. The wheels over the stones made the cart jolt and she sat up.

He flicked the reins and Boy broke into a trot. 'Where do you want dropping?'

That wasn't what she expected to hear. Normally, she'd have jumped down, cart moving or not and spat some insult at him, but not today; not today when she'd learned to dance, floating like rose bay willow herb and bouncing like cotton grass. His eyelashes curled over his freckled cheeks. His chestnut hair fell down over his collar. She elbowed his arm.

'What's matter, grumpy?' she said, 'and here's me, all riled up to kiss you.'

She felt the tension in his neck spread down his arm. She shuffled closer, her thigh flush against his. The cart rocked.

They'd left the hall, passed through the gates and were on the bend nearing the road up to Fylingthorpe.

'Who's Mrs Farsyde's visitor?' Jonas said, giving the reins another shake.

'I don't know,' Jiddy said, 'Mrs Farsyde didn't say but he seemed polite enough.'

'You were dancing with him.'

'I'd rather have been dancing with you.'

She looked up at the blue sky. She loved weather like this, warming her skin. She loved today. She loved every day. The woods on the left approached and after that they'd see the first houses of Baytown. The feeling in her was overpowering, she couldn't wait; the dancing couldn't have been for nothing. She wanted to hold Jonas close and dance with him.

She looked at the flickering green of the trees then back at Jonas. 'Should we do it here?'

'Do what?'

'Don't say you're going to let me down,' she said. 'You remember last night, don't you? Remember, you promised me?'

Jonas never backed down. Never, not once he'd promised to do something.

'Last night you said you'd kiss me again today.'

That made him look. His mouth all cherry red. She couldn't wait, there was no way she could wait. She leaned forward to kiss his lips, but he turned his face and she kissed his cheek.

Grabbing his chin, she turned it in her direction, forcing him to pull the cart to a standstill.

They looked at each other. His mood was changing, he was coming round, she could tell. He would never resist her again.

'Say you liked me in that dress,' she said.

She watched him study her face, then her hair. She didn't take her eyes from his, willing him to kiss her.

'I think working up at hall has gone to your head,' he said. 'Your hair's different for one and you're talking different. And why aren't you tired? I'm shattered.'

She turned her head to and fro so the curls bounced again. 'You can touch it if you want.'

He raised his hands to jerk the reins but she grabbed his arm.

'Jonas.' She pressed her fingers into his jacket. Her entire body hurt and she couldn't bear it. 'I've got to jump out at corner, Mary's expecting me and you said we'd kiss properly today. You promised and I need you to, please, Jonas, please. You want to too, don't you?'

He pulled up the brake and wound Boy's reins around the wooden post. 'Jump down.'

She couldn't believe it. He was going to do it. Soon they'd be kissing.

'In them trees.' He nodded towards the wood and she jumped down before he'd told Boy to stay.

She leaned against a tree trunk and let him study her face. Hands loose by her sides, she studied him back. She loved his eyes. No-one else in the entire village had eyes as changeable as April skies, like him. She'd noticed them the first time she'd seen him. She'd looked into his eyes more times than she could remember, surreptitiously, in anger, slowly, picking out a speck of straw dust or one of those tiny flies that had no sense where to fly. He had freckles on his nose, faint remains of summer that she adored.

'You're an odd one,' he said.

She never ever, ever wanted that kiss to stop. All the clumsy earlier attempts didn't matter. The rough bark against her back pressing so that she felt every ridge, the uneven ground cradling her feet, sunlight making a fairy glade of green. She could hear birdsong ringing sharp, Boy chomping on his bit, Jonas' breath, his heart against her chest and blood pumping through veins.

Slowly, her lips parted all by themselves, a space opening between their mouths and then she felt the tip of his tongue, warm and gently reaching for hers. If she were honey, she'd have melted right there and then, a delicious mound of happy, golden honey all warm and smooth. It wasn't like before. When had their tongues changed and how was that possible? They were the same tongues that they'd touched as children. Warm and smooth and sending sunbeams through her body.

He held her waist, only tighter, hands splayed so she

could feel his thumb and fingers on her ribs. She liked it, liked that he felt her bones and her tongue and that it meant they couldn't talk. Talk was overrated. Rebecca was right. This was a million times better. And if she were wearing that tighter than tight dress, how much better would it feel? He pressed against her and she could feel him through her wool skirt and oh, heaven forbid, what was that and why was it making her tingle? His tongue filled her mouth, his hand slid up to her chest. What should she do? She had no idea what was happening. She opened her eyes. His eyes were closed, frowning slightly. He was as lost as she was, thank the Lord, she was doing something right.

'I can't take this,' she said. She felt hot and enclosed with his entire body touching some part of hers.

'What?'

'Jonas, this is too good, I, this is...'

There were no words to describe what this felt like. She wanted to keep kissing but she'd probably die if they continued. Her heart would explode, if her head didn't.

'Oh please, kiss me.'

He didn't need asking again. They were like limpets. Her arms around his back, she held him as close as she could. His hands tight, tight, holding her ribs. His feet shuffled against hers, they couldn't get close enough. Putting one hand on his neck he immediately moved one of his hands up her ribs again. This must be what heaven was like.

'Afternoon, Jonas Chaplow, Jiddy.'

What? Who? Jonas turned around without moving his

feet or hands. Breathless, Jiddy looked over his shoulder, still holding him in a tight embrace. Rebecca studied them as if she'd caught them stealing apples. Jiddy didn't move. She couldn't calm the feeling inside and Rebecca would see and oh, heaven's stars, she'd be bound to tell Mary. She wanted to laugh but this wasn't funny, was it?

'Must be something in the air, you're second couple I've seen today acting like you're betrothed,' Rebecca said.

Jiddy wriggled free.

'Please don't tell Mary,' she said.

She sounded sharp, she knew she did but Rebecca had interrupted and Jonas would have to go and they'd never get this moment back. Rebecca gave Jonas a knowing nod.

'You be careful,' she said.

'I'm sorry,' said Jiddy, 'Rebecca?'

Rebecca waved a hand in dismissal as she headed off.

'What does she mean?' she said.

Jonas caught hold of her arm, and pulling her in kissed her warm neck.

'Think she means we should find somewhere more private,' he said.

She put both arms around his waist; she wanted him against her for as long as they could stand.

'Do you feel strange?' she said. He touched her neck with his fingers. 'Tickles.'

He ran his thumb along her collarbone. 'What about this?'

'I like that.'

'And this?'

They looked up. Two figures moved through the undergrowth. A flash of red and they were gone.

'Think that's our cue to go,' Jonas said.

'Not yet.'

'It's all right,' he said, 'I know you're all fired up, I am too, but Rebecca's right, this isn't the place.'

She felt as if her entire body was swirling in the surf. But she wasn't alone; his did too. They were grown up. They could do whatever they wanted. As long as it was well away from Rebecca's prying eyes.

CHAPTER TWENTY-TWO

S he couldn't wait to see Jonas again. There was so much to talk about and so much kissing to be done and there was no room in her head for anything else. When she got home, she ignored Mary's and Rebecca's funny looks and niggling questions, but it didn't last long. It was always like that after a run. Over the next few days, there were packages to disperse. Brandy to decant. Diversions, keep preventives busy, keep contraband moving.

'Aren't you ready yet?' she asked for the umpteenth time, standing on the front door step and looking over her shoulder at Mary and Rebecca.

'Never known you to be so keen to get to preaching house,' said Rebecca. 'Must be someone in congregation and not minister that's giving you such a hankering to offer up your thanks this morning.'

'Ha ha, very funny,' said Jiddy. 'Can we be going now?'

'Yes, yes, I'm ready,' said Mary.

Nodding their heads and shaking neighbours' hands, Jiddy followed Rebecca and Mary inside the large room, all the time looking for Jonas. They were late and most of the pews were already filled, but Rebecca waved her stick and people shuffled along, and the three of them sat a couple of rows from the front. Jiddy stood when she saw Jonas enter and he pushed his way towards them. They sat, sandwiched together with Jonas nearest the central aisle and Jiddy wondering if she dare slip her hand inside his.

Soldiers were entering noisily and people had begun muttering as they stamped their boots on the bare boards.

'Who are they?' Jiddy said.

'I heard they'd sent a group of dragoons in,' he said. 'That must be them.'

'But we've got preventives, are they swapping over?'

'We're lucky beggars,' James said from the row behind. 'We're going to have preventives and dragoons looking after us for a bit.'

'How'd you know?' said Jonas.

James tapped his nose with his index finger. 'In the know, farmer boy, in the know.'

'He's talked to Abe and Silas,' said Betsie.

Frowning, James sat back and Jiddy smiled at Jonas. Already James and Betsie acted like an old married couple.

So what if there were dragoons and preventives in the Bay? It didn't make any difference, double numbers of soldiers didn't mean they'd be any cleverer at finding the tunnels and escape routes that zigzagged through Baytown. Jiddy pushed her hand into Jonas' and his fingers wrapped around hers. Perfect.

The banging down of rifles, and creaking of the front door closing, silenced them all and the congregation grew still, waiting for Reverend Cook to come out of the vestry. Jiddy looked sideways along the pew, still holding Jonas' hand. Red uniforms punctuated the duller clothes of the locals. Silas sat nearby, staring into space. He seemed to do that a lot lately. It was almost funny, all of them pretending to be normal. Nothing more than farmers and fisherfolk pretending they weren't lawbreakers and tax dodgers. And it was so easy because they enjoyed making idiots of these government men. She enjoyed that as much as anyone in the room.

'There's summat wrong,' said Mary. 'Those new dragoons are watching us all like hawks.'

'D'you think they know something about other night? Is that why they're here?'

Rebecca shook her head. 'Hush.'

Isaac McCaw and Captain Pinkney stood at the back, studying the congregation just like the dragoons. Jiddy spotted Annie and Nellie with her cousin Abigail at the back. Behind them stood a row of red-jacketed soldiers. One of the dragoons had curling fair hair and piercing blue eyes, just like the stranger who'd helped Mrs Farsyde teach her to dance. She felt sick. It was him and he was wearing the large black hat and red buttoned-up uniform of an officer. She turned back quickly. What if he recognised her?

People would ask how she knew him. They'd want to know how he knew her. She didn't like this at all. She wriggled her fingers in Jonas' palm and he smiled and she realised he didn't recognise the captain at the back of the room as being the same man who'd been dancing with her in the ballroom the other day. That was one blessing. She kept facing straight ahead.

Reverend Cook climbed the steps to the pulpit. A

hush spread over the room. Jiddy hoped it would be a short service that morning.

'We are here to give thanks for all God has given us,' Reverend Cook said, 'and we also give thanks for each other, because without each other, we would not survive. The carpenter mends our houses, the fishermen bring our food, farmers provide milk and meat.'

Usually she liked Sunday mornings listening to the reverend reminding them why they were all there, but today she urged him to hurry up. Not only because she wanted to be alone with Jonas but because she wanted as much distance between herself and this new soldier. She felt a fool, such an idiot. Mrs Farsyde must have known, and the squire. Why was a captain of the dragoons staying with them? She could not understand that at all. It was awful. Too awful if she met him again.

Reverend Cook called them to the altar. She nudged Jonas with her leg and he stepped out of the pew to let her go first. Mary and Rebecca were joining the aisle on the other side, and those on the pew behind were beginning to stand. Something was wrong. A commotion started. Swords were rattling and boots shifting impatiently. People were still moving forward but there was jostling going on at the back. She kept moving forward. She didn't want to speak to this new captain and definitely not in front of anyone here. From the pew in front, Grace joined the line and Jiddy moved forward again, but she sensed those behind were hesitating. She stopped. Others were making way for someone. The captain, in his red uniform, strode past them and stood in front of her. She didn't know what to do. Surely he wouldn't give her a second glance in what she was wearing, there was no way he'd equate a fisher girl with the lady he'd met at Thorpe Hall.

Jonas gestured for Jiddy to step behind the captain. She looked at his back, his jacket taut across his shoulders and blond hair curling down his neck. He stood so calm and upright. To think she'd had her hand on his shoulder and held his soft hands. To know that he had smiled at her as they danced together around the Farsyde's ballroom was too much to bear.

Jonas dug her in the ribs. 'Come on, you sinner, afraid you'll burst into flames?' he said. She didn't have a choice if she didn't want it to look as if something were the matter so she stepped behind the captain.

Already, Reverend Cook moved along the line by the altar, placing a piece of bread on each tongue.

And then they were at the front and packed so close, Jiddy's arm pressed against the captain's. She tried to pull away, but there wasn't room so she looked down. If she didn't see him, he wouldn't see her she told herself. Luckily, he was staring straight in front. The reverend placed the bread on his tongue, he swallowed and she stuck out her own tongue, the lightness of bread making her mouth dry. How could a cough rise from such a tiny morsel? She couldn't choke, she mustn't spasm with coughing. Jonas shifted, he must have noticed, but captain remained still, waiting for the liquid. Maybe he was very religious. Relax, she told herself, he's not going to recognise likes of you. Reverend held the cup to captain's mouth, it touched his lips, he wiped the rim, held it to Jiddy's mouth.

Bending her head right down, she gulped. She wanted to look at Jonas, her friend Jonas, more than a friend now. The captain was standing. Waiting. Facing away from him, she stood. Jonas wiped his mouth. They only had to walk back to their seats, bend their heads and cup their hands, murmuring thanks for the sins they had committed. Jiddy followed Jonas, watching the ease of his swagger. The captain would be behind her, watching her walk. They reached their pew. Would the captain touch her arm and ask her if she needed him to partner her in a dance tomorrow? Please don't let him speak. Jonas waited to let her in first. She hurried, sitting with relief that she'd made it. Mary and Rebecca were kneeling at the front. And there he was, standing by the pulpit. He hadn't followed her after all.

'You all right?' Jonas said.

'Can we spend all day together after this?' she said.

Before she could say anything else, Mary made her way from the other end of the pew and sat down. Jiddy tucked her arm under Mary's and put her head on her shoulder. She felt safe between the two of them. No-one could get her here.

Something was happening though. Reverend Cook stood at the bottom of the small flight of pulpit steps next to the captain and they were talking. People were growing restless. Isaac McCaw lingered halfway down the side aisle with Abe. People were shuffling in their seats and muttering. Jiddy craned her neck to see around Grace's big bonnet. The captain inclined his head to Reverend Cook so it was hard to see their faces. He made a gesture towards the room before walking up the flight of steps to the pulpit and the reverend stepped to the side. The captain of the dragoons looked as if he were used to standing in pulpits, placing his hands on the wooden lectern as if he were a minister himself. He looked over the room at all the faces gazing up at him and Jiddy's mouth went dry again.

'My apologies for interrupting your Sunday Service,' he said, his voice crisp and light, 'but with the kind permission of Reverend Cook, I'd like to formally introduce myself. I am the new officer in charge of Robin Hood's Bay and my name is Captain Samuel Ryethorpe.' He waited a moment but nobody said a word, so he continued. 'May I also introduce Deputy Andrew Clifton and my team of dragoons.' He swept an arm around the room.

Still nobody said anything. This had never happened before. Of course, the silence didn't last for long. The captain was about to speak again when he was interrupted.

'Right, you've introduced yourselves. How do. Now, Reverend, you're back up.' Big Isaac McCaw who nobody argued with, folded his arms across his great big chest.

Reverend Cook held up a hand. 'I think we should listen to Captain Ryethorpe. Show him what tolerant people we are in Robin Hood's Bay.'

Some wanted none of it. Rumblings. Shifting. Jiddy looked at Jonas. He winked. Jiddy looked back at the captain, who stood tall, calm and clear-eyed. Trustworthy, she'd have thought if she didn't know how he'd hidden his identity on their first meeting.

'This morning, Captain Horseman and his team of preventives are preparing to leave Robin Hood's Bay for an assignment in another part of the country,' he said. All around, people turned to their neighbours. The reverend held up both hands but it didn't quieten anyone. Captain Ryethorpe didn't seem fazed. 'I want you to know that as from today, I have officially taken over Captain Horseman's duties.'

He looked so neat and together and sure of himself. To think she'd danced in those arms.

'I know you regard me as your enemy,' he said, 'but I want this to be the start of a new era. I want us to work together against the smugglers who hide themselves amongst you good folks.'

You good folks? Where did he get a phrase like that? Jiddy looked at Jonas. He didn't flinch. She looked at the pew in front and the row of backs. People had fallen quiet. The tension in the room crackled like a lightning storm but the captain couldn't have looked more relaxed. He leaned on the pulpit, buckles and buttons shining.

'I know these law breakers cause you as much trouble as they do me,' he said. 'You can't want your sons or brothers or fathers rounded up and accused of stealing any more than you want our soldiers in France maimed or killed.' He paused, waiting. Waiting for what? Everyone was poised for the net to be thrown. 'When these thieves are terrorising the streets of Robin Hood's Bay at night, me and my men will be out in the village, working to protect you. When they are forcing you to do things against your will, demanding you hide a barrel under your table, say, or store some contraband in a cupboard, we want you to know that we will protect you from such bullying. If you do give in and say, "yes, all right, what harm can that do?" think about the harm your compliance does. Ask yourself if you have another choice. We all know how persuasive and dangerous these smugglers are, but what if you all said "No. Enough". We will not be threatened by you.' This is why I am here. Why my deputy and men are here. To help you say no and to protect you when you do say no. We are here to say "No" for you if that is what it takes.'

His blue eyes beamed, crystal sharp.

'I say "No" to you!' shouted big Isaac.

Those around him laughed.

Ryethorpe's face flushed with his zeal. 'I ask you to think about how you'd feel if any of your men, your brother, your son or your father, were fighting for England and they didn't have enough food to eat or warm clothes to keep out the bitter winter cold because the government couldn't afford to supply them.'

'They'd know how we feel,' someone shouted from the back.

'If you know how it feels, why would you do it to others?' the captain said. 'Think about it. The government can't send our soldiers ammunition because smugglers have stolen revenue by not paying for goods.'

'He's pushing it,' Jonas said, under his breath.

'Government's more than enough money, they're just greedy beggars.' A voice shouted from the side.

The captain studied the congregation. 'They only have enough money if everyone pays their taxes on luxuries like tea and coffee, silk and other taxable goods.'

Jiddy slipped her hand free and pressed her palms together. The captain was talking like Jonas, about taxes and stuff that usually bored her senseless, but what he said seemed to be making sense. She didn't know what luxury goods were, but she knew about young lads and if they were starving and freezing to death because of what they were doing, then it couldn't be right.

Abe Storm pushed his way forward. 'Reverend? I don't come to preaching house to listen to this. Get back in pulpit.'

'Abe, you should be ashamed talking to Reverend Cook like that.' Grace stood up, 'Reverend Cook, is this your preaching house or isn't it?'

'You tell him, Gracie.'

Isaac McCaw shoved forward. 'Enough of this. Just what exactly are you accusing us good folk of?'

Captain Pinkney watched from the back.

Jonas bent forward to catch James' eye on the row behind. No-one looked happy. Mary squeezed Jiddy's hand. 'It's all right,' she said, 'he's just puffing himself up because he's new.'

But Jiddy didn't believe that. This had a bigger threat behind the smooth words. Red coats dotted the room. These dragoons would make life a lot harder than any of the preventives had done. This lot wouldn't be open to bribes. No way. Reverend Cook had come forward again, standing at the bottom of the pulpit steps.

'All I'm saying is, we are here to protect you,' said Captain Ryethorpe, not moving from his position, above them all. 'And if you do your part and refuse to help these smugglers then we can go back home and leave you in peace. Simple as that.'

Helen Drake was on her feet now. 'Are you accusing us of thieving?' she said. 'Isaac? I think that's what he's getting at, and us honest folk here.'

People near her applauded.

'You've hit nail on head, Helen,' said Isaac.

Women were standing now. The captain shouldn't mess with them, Jiddy thought, watching each of them rise to their feet, stocky frames and stout arms and mouths that wouldn't be stopped.

Reverend Cook tried to hush them. 'Mrs Drake, Mrs Copperthwaite, please.' Too late. Men were on their feet now.

The captain leaned forward. 'I am not accusing you, I am letting you know that me and my men stand with you. While these villains are enjoying their ill-gotten contraband, young men shiver in their tents on the battlefield. These scoundrels are extremely clever at making it sound as if they are in the right, I acknowledge that, but it is my job to show you the effect of what they do. We will keep you safe and law abiding. That is all.' He adjusted his jacket. Jiddy's skin tingled. She didn't feel as if she were listening to the gentleman who had danced the Cotillion and Polonaise. This man seemed a completely different human being.

CHAPTER TWENTY-THREE

As soon as she and Jonas were outside, she felt relieved. Betsie and James stood close together, James talking, standing with his chest out and throwing his arms all over the place. Betsie flushed, giggling. He was funny and capable and Jiddy could see why Betsie and Annie liked him. She looked around for Annie, but she'd disappeared. Jiddy didn't blame her, it must be hard seeing James and Betsie so happy. Nellie and her cousin were hanging around though and that made Jiddy want to get away even more, but James had hooked Jonas into his conversation. She waved her hand at him.

'Be good,' Rebecca said with a glint in her eye, as she and Mary headed back to Sunny Place.

Typical. The captain would be out any minute and what if he recognised her then? Some of the dragoons were trying to chat, but only Nellie spoke back. It hit her in that second. This Captain Ryethorpe wouldn't recognise her. She looked like a Baytowner and that's all he would see. He wasn't the only one who had been in disguise the first time they met. It was a blessing; she'd be able to carry on with her life and he could keep his distance as a high and mighty captain of the dragoons.

Grabbing Jonas' arm, she pulled him away.

James laughed and Betsie laughed too. 'Guess we know who's in charge,' James said.

Jiddy pulled harder.

'What can I say? The lass wants me!' Jonas said.

'Fine, stay,' Jiddy said, striding towards King Street.

He jogged up behind her. 'What's the rush?'

'I'm in a bit of a mood,' she said. 'If you want to go back, go. I'm probably best on my own.'

'Don't be daft. Tide's not in, let's go down to the beach.'

Once on the beach, and walking along the shoreline, Jiddy forgot the tension of the preaching house and that sudden shot in her stomach about Captain Ryethorpe. She wanted her day with Jonas. Looking at the sea, sparkling like the scales of a fish, she breathed in deeply. Here, she felt calm. By the sea, she felt free. Closing her eyes, she smiled as the fresh breeze stroked her face. They had all afternoon together. They could forget everything else.

'Good day,' she said. Should she kiss him now, she wondered.

'What's wrong with you? Good day, back.'

Kicking off her shoes, she pulled off her stockings and threw them on the sand. 'Take yours off,' she said.

'Not likely.'

Grabbing his hands, she tried to pull him but he wouldn't budge. His hands were rough and familiar. She kissed him quickly on the cheek and, taking him off guard, dragged him into the shallows at the water's edge.

'Jiddy, stop laiking about.' He pulled back, stamping about in his shoes.

She yanked him over again. They were here, they had a few hours to themselves to be daft and alone and she felt powerful and strong and brave on the beach.

'Stop it,' he was laughing now, 'it's all right for you, you've got bare feet.'

'Take your shoes off.'

'I'm not coming in.'

She tugged his arm again. 'This is good for you. You need to learn to swim and I want to give you my knowledge of the sea as learned from Captain David Pinkney.'

'Your knowledge of the sea? Why are you talking like that? When does Captain Pinkney talk to the likes of you?' He laughed but he looked nervous.

'Wouldn't you like to know?' she took both his hands. 'We need every escape route we can find. Don't worry, I won't let you go. Come on, take your socks and shoes off, it'll be fun.'

Disentangling himself from her grasp, he strode back towards a line of rocks not far from the water's edge. She sighed. Maybe she'd have to admit defeat and accept that he'd never learn to swim. And then she squealed with delight. He'd taken off his jacket and shoes. Scampering onto the sand, she unfastened her skirt, dropping it to the ground next to her shoes. While he rolled down his stockings, she looked back towards the causeway. Captain Pinkney, Abe, Isaac and Silas sat at the bottom of the dock as they usually did, planning the next run, no doubt. Or more likely, how they'd get rid of Captain Ryethorpe and his dragoons. They'd be so busy with their plotting and planning that they wouldn't take any notice of her and Jonas. She unfastened her chemise to reveal a plain shift. She breathed in, hands on her waist. Jonas was walking back towards the water, his shirt hanging free and his bare feet making impressions in the sand. She sprinted past, splashing in the shallows, and then she kicked, the spray making a rainbow. He put up his hands.

'You'd better be careful, Jiddy Vardy,' he said, slicing up water until she screamed for him to stop.

'Aren't you glad you're giving it a go?'

'Depends if I get swept away or not.'

'This is why you have to learn to swim.'

'What d'you think boats are for?'

'You can fall out of a boat.'

'I'm a farmer, not a fisherman, I don't go out in boats.'

'Well you might go in a ship then, sail off to another country.'

'And sheep and pigs can fly.'

'Here, take my hand.'

He let her lead him, the water tickling their ankles. Even on a hot day, the North Sea wasn't warm.

'That's far enough,' he said after they'd taken a few more steps.

Sinking her feet into the seabed she felt the sand move between her toes. She squeezed his hand and smiled.

'You're doing well,' she said.

'Stop talking like minister.'

They kept walking and the water made Jiddy's petticoat cling to her thighs. Today, she didn't care what he said. She liked the cool nakedness of it and the thrill of cold water. She laughed at Jonas' anxious expression as he let go of her hand to steady himself.

'Solid as a rock, are you?' she said and he nodded, unsure. 'A bit further?'

He nodded again and she realised this was all for her; he was doing this because it made her happy. They were past their thighs now. A step or two and the water, grey green, lapped against their bellies. She paddled her hands in the water to keep her balance. He copied. Brave. And nervous.

'Thank you,' she said.

She moved closer. She wanted to kiss him now. A wave almost lifted them off their feet. She laughed. 'Come here,' she said, reaching out.

Another wave.

'Whoa!' It lifted them, then set them down again.

She was desperate to kiss.

'Jiddy?'

He was looking over her shoulder and she turned to see. Before she could do anything, a huge wave exploded in her face, blinding her. Too late, she clamped her mouth shut. Flung backwards, the force rolled her underwater. Opening her eyes, sand, water and foam were all she could see as the current whipped her around. Was she up, down, which way was she facing? She couldn't swim, couldn't get out of the churning wave. Her hands touched the seabed. Cloudy and rough. She couldn't see anything but swirling water. Her chest hurt. Where was Jonas? And then the wave threw her onto the beach, leaving her exposed, one cheek pressed into the tiny pieces of shell that gave the beach its crunch, and she gasped in air, breathless and grateful.

After several minutes lying still, she dug her fingers into the sand. Her lungs felt heavy. The water pulled on her ankles, trying to drag her back. She kicked then lay still, coughing. She could breathe. Sitting up, she looked around for Jonas. He sat, not far away, by the water's edge. Retching.

Water ran down his chin.

'I'm sorry,' Jiddy said, 'it's stronger than I thought today.'

'You bugger, some swimming lesson.'

'Are you all right?'

He didn't say anything and she looked up at the sky, clouds swiftly moving over the blue, gulls rounding off the cliffs. They sounded sharp, clear.

'That's never happened before,' she said.

'Just my luck,' he said. 'First time in sea and we get a tidal wave.'

'I don't think it was a tidal wave.'

He looked over the sands at Captain Pinkney and the others still sitting at the top end of the causeway. 'Thankfully we weren't relying on them to rescue us,' he said.

'I don't think any of them can swim,' said Jiddy.

'What was it if it wasn't a tidal wave, then?'

'I don't know.'

She shivered. That hadn't been pleasant at all. Her petticoat clung cold to her legs and she waddled towards her discarded clothes. Funny how hard it seemed to walk.

She pulled the cotton away from her thighs and, bending, stepped into the skirt, her hands shaking as she tied it. She jigged it around. It felt comforting, almost disguising her wet legs, and the inside of her thighs rubbing bumpy with salt and sand.

She pushed her straggling hair aside. 'Come on, let's go up on tops before tide cuts us off.'

He meandered to pick up his shoes. He looked pale.

'I said I'm sorry,' she said.

He picked up his shoes and dry clothes. 'Best go by cliff path.'

She looked up. They'd be on the top of the world up there.

Collapsing on the grass as soon as they reached the top, they breathed heavily, lying like stars as they had as children, letting the sun dry their clothes. No-one usually walked on there during the day other than peewits and the odd rabbit. Jonas and she could spend hours and hours looking up at the sky, laughing at shapes clouds made and mimicking birds. Jonas seemed different, still Jonas but a different Jonas, more tender, taller, more exciting. She waited for him to tell her how she had changed but he didn't say anything. What he did do, which was much better, she decided, was to roll on his stomach and slide his hand over her belly. With a quick pull, they lay body to body, she on her back, he on his front, his face so close she could see his nostrils moving. She couldn't believe how quickly he'd gone from being a friend to this.

'What are you smiling at?' he said.

'How can you tell I'm smiling?'

'I can feel you are.'

He eased up on his elbow. The sun shone bright. Would he see the spot on her chin? His face came so close she couldn't see anything but a shady blur. She hoped it would be as good as the other day.

It was. His lips made her feel as if she hadn't a bone in her body and she knew how to kiss now. No banging of teeth or hard dry pressure. It was moistness itself and softness, making everything else in the world disappear.

His throat made a noise.

She wanted to smile and laugh and wriggle all at once. She reached up her arm to touch his shoulder but he pushed himself away and sat back on his haunches, picking at the grass.

'What's wrong?' she sat up. 'I want to carry on kissing.'

He laughed, slightly awkward.

She crept forward but he shifted back further. 'Jonas?'

So he wasn't as keen as her after all.

'Are you worried Rebecca will come walking by?' She mocked horror, looking around.

'No,' he said, 'I get excited, that's all.' He picked at the grass again. 'I don't think we should.'

She shuffled towards him again. 'I get excited as well,'

This was good. They were both excited. They both felt the same. He tried to hold her back, and laughing she pushed away his arms and they batted each other as if they were kids.

She stared at him, widening her eyes and staring, staring; she knew their effect. Hands on his shoulders, using the weight of her whole body, she leaned against him. He gave way, falling on his back, legs twisting, and she pressed on his chest.

'D'you think you could throw me off if you tried right hard?' she said.

'Easy.'

'D'you want to or do you want this?'

She didn't let him answer, kissing him as hard as she could. She couldn't keep that up though, she was running out of breath. She gulped some air, she didn't care how it looked, pressing her lips to his again, touching very, very lightly with her tongue. He held her upper arms and she sensed that he tensed to push her away, so sliding her hands around his neck, she closed her eyes and so the proper kissing began. Soon she thought her head would explode with every flower she had ever seen. Daisies, buttercups and campions bursting all around and inside her skull.

'Open your mouth,' she said and he did as she asked, his lips parting, taking in her tongue so she could taste his delicious tongue.

'Oh lord,' she thought, 'sweet heaven.'

She studied his face, all sunshine and fresh air and familiarity.

'Show me how much you care for me,' she said.

'I'll jump off a cliff for you.'

She stroked his cheek. 'Don't be daft, I'd never ask that.'

She wriggled to lay flat on top of him, laughing at the look of astonishment on his face. She surprised even herself, but it excited her, she felt completely in control, she was the one who forged the way, not Jonas, she was their leader. She was the clever one. She studied his face, every freckle, blemish, hair on it.

Nothing mattered, not Thorpe Hall, not Nellie or being part of the smuggling gang, not swimming in the sea, or even Captain Ryethorpe in his swish clothes and with his fancy words; nothing mattered but being with Jonas. That first clumsy kiss belonged to two different people, and now her and Jonas' mouths fitted perfectly together.

She'd never been surer of anything in her life and soon there would be no going back. She'd felt him harden against her before, felt him press more insistently, so it seemed the only course of action, and this the ideal place. The sound of her precious sea stroking the shoreline, peewits calling overhead, a warm sun in a cloudless sky and no other person around. She dropped her head and kissed him.

It didn't seem real suddenly, after all these years when she'd worshipped him and hated him and cried to him. For a moment she wondered if he'd know what to do when they eventually did it. What if it wasn't natural and you had to have learned from someone? What if he hated her afterwards for making him look a fool?

It must be all right. Cows and sheep and rabbits did it. They didn't listen to an older cow or sheep or rabbit telling them what to do. They just got on with it. Lordy. He'd grown down there again. What would this feel like if they were skin on skin, instead of layers of clothes between them? She wasn't sure. How could it possibly be better than this? Ah. There it was again. That spotting in her head and sliding away into a world of bright colours. It seemed as if her body was slipping, feet first, sideways, backwards, she couldn't tell. If this was what kissing meant, she wondered how anyone ever got any work done.

'Mmm.'

Gulls crying, the sound of soil and clods of earth falling. The earth really was moving.

'Jiddy?'

'Mmm.'

'Jiddy.'

She screamed as the ground at their feet gave way. Grabbing each other, they twisted around, staring at the jagged cliff edge.

Jiddy looked around, flushed and dishevelled. 'What was it? What happened?'

'It's giving way.' Jonas scrambled backwards, dragging her with him as another chunk of earth and rock gave way and rolled down the grassy slope, breaking apart with a loud crack and rumble as it hit the beach.

CHAPTER TWENTY-FOUR

Pressing her hands down hard into the cool grass, Jiddy inched forwards towards the jagged edge.

Jonas pulled her back. 'What are you doing? It could go again.'

'Why did it break off?'

'Because you're a witch, putting spells on the land,' he said, but he looked worried.

'Very funny, is it because you're so heavy?' she said, crawling back.

He pulled her back again. 'Come away. I'm serious.'

'Will it go again?'

She'd not seen Jonas so shaken before and it made her nervous too. There was a trickle of soil but the tremors had stopped.

'Put your things on,' he said, pulling on his shoes. Jiddy strained to look at the broken clumps of soil and turf on the beach.

'Jiddy,' he said, 'come away, it's dangerous.'

Sitting beside him, she pulled on her stockings. It was difficult when everything was slightly damp. Jonas had his shoes on before she'd finished and was stuffing his stockings into his jacket pockets.

Slipping on her shoes, she ran to catch up, shaking

down her skirt as she did so and brushing it clear of grass seeds.

'Don't call me a witch,' she said.

'I'll have to be careful when I've got Boy and the cart up here,' he said, 'their weight won't be good, especially when it's been raining.'

'What difference does rain make?'

'Makes soil heavier.'

'But it's not been raining.'

He strode faster, but she had long strides and kept alongside.

'I'll come with you back to farm,' she said.

'As long as you let me work.'

'Not my fault you're so easily distracted.'

'I'll show you distracted.'

'You'll have to catch me first.'

She ran off, cutting across the field, scattering sheep. She could run forever and never be tired.

'Where the hell have you been?' Jonas' da tramped across the yard with the sheepdog, Rex, trailing low to the ground behind.

'It's Sunday, Mr Chaplow.' Jiddy swung on the gate.

Mr Chaplow gave them a grim look. 'Animals don't care what day of week it is, they allus want seeing to.'

'You'd best go,' Jonas said.

'I want you on bottom field,' Mr Chaplow said, 'take Rex and bring cows up.'

'Why? Thought they were there for summer.'

Mr Chaplow looked as if he'd murder them both. 'It's milking time,' he said.

'Rex! Come on, boy,' Jonas whistled.

Rex sped to the gate and Jonas raised his eyebrows as he passed Jiddy.

'Didn't realise it were that late,' he said.

'Owt you want me to do?' Jiddy shouted across the yard.

Mr Chaplow scowled, making her wish she'd never asked.

'Might as well make yourself useful,' he said, 'someone forgot to collect eggs this morning and you can check water in pig sty while you're at it.'

'Yes, Mr Chaplow.' She closed the gate, pushing so that it clicked properly closed. He'd gone by the time she turned around. He was like that was Mr Chaplow.

'Mister Now-you-see-him-now-you-don't,' as Jonas called him.

It didn't matter. She was happy to help out. Mr Chaplow would let her have a few eggs and that would please Mary. Wondering for a moment whether to peek in at the chicks, she decided against it and finding a pail in the barn, she filled it with straw. If any of the hens had laid in there, it would take an age. She'd start in the usual places. Darting about the yard, the hens avoided her as she bobbed and stretched in all the crannies they liked to use.

She wagged her finger at an old bantam. 'You can't fool me, you know how thorough I am and these eggs are for us, not you.' She picked up another brown speckled egg and placed it in the straw in her bucket.

The sound of horse's hooves made her glance up.

Three red-coated dragoons looked down at her from their horses.

'Open the gate.' The one in the middle stood up in his stirrups to look taller.

She wasn't going to be intimidated. They were new round here, they weren't going to think they could lord it over her. Taking her time, she put the bucket of eggs down by the wall of the house. She rested one hand on her hip. Here we go, let's see if you can do it, she told herself, be all sweetness and delight and let's see what they're up to. Strolling across the yard, swaying her hips, as captivating as possible while swerving to avoid the odd cow pat, she reached the gate. The soldiers pushed their horses forward as she unlatched it and they clattered into the yard, the officer in front bringing his brown gelding around to the farmhouse door.

'Where's the farmer?'

So much for her efforts to distract him. She'd have to practice more.

'In fields,' she said. 'Who should I say called?'

He pulled the reins taut and the gelding's eyes widened.

'Who are you?'

She recognised him from the preaching house. Captain Ryethorpe had pointed him out. Deputy Clint or something. He obviously hadn't given the locals much notice.

'I'm in charge today if you want to tell me your business,' she said. He eyed the buildings. 'You can wait inside until Mr Chaplow gets back,' she said. 'I doubt he'll be long, unless I can help you, that is.'

She slipped one hand up to her waist again and dropped her hip, eyeing him from under her eyelashes. The other two were looking; it must be working. Hopefully, one of them would speak up before long. 'It's Deputy Clifton, isn't it?' she said, 'See? I remember you.'

'We've met?'

'This morning. It's good to know you are God-fearing men, Deputy Clifton, though I wouldn't have taken you for having an interest in farming.' She'd never seen a man look more confused. These soldiers really weren't brightest buttons in the box. 'Would you like to rest your horses if you've got a long ride ahead, or is this a neighbourly visit? I can make some refreshments for you and your men if you want?'

'Are these all the farm buildings or are there any outlying barns?' he asked.

The two soldiers had dismounted and were peering into the stables.

'There are barns all over countryside round here,' she said, 'I'm sure landlady up at Musgrave's will be disappointed to hear you're looking for alternative accommodation.'

The deputy had his eyes on the soldiers, who reappeared shaking their heads.

'You weren't thinking of sleeping in there, were you?' she said.

'No, I were not.'

Jiddy smiled. 'Of course not,' she said. 'You're too smart for bunking down with the animals.'

'Back on your horses,' Deputy Clifton yelled.

This one was a doddle to wind up. Dangerous though. Built like a wild boar and as determined.

'D'you want me to show you our other barns?' she said.

He looked her up and down while the two soldiers mounted up. 'Are you married to this farmer?' he said.

What harm could it do? Better than letting this toad think she was available.

'Betrothed,' she said. 'And you sure look like a happily married man, Deputy Clifton.'

One of the soldiers laughed. And then they were off, through the gate, leaving it swinging behind them, without a thanks or goodbye. Jiddy picked up her skirts and ran.

CHAPTER TWENTY-FIVE

Reaching the first field, she'd already made up her mind. Big Isaac and the others would still be there, sitting around on the causeway, smoking their pipes and telling each other tales. It were only late afternoon if the position of the sun and milking time was anything to go by.

'Jonas?' she shouted when she reached the middle of the field.

Black and white Friesians were heading towards her. They were slow, udders bloated and swinging heavy between their legs. Rex knew not to mither them but tracked around the back of the herd, sticking to Jonas who walked with a large stick up the slope.

'Jonas?'

She bounced towards him, careful of sticky, pungent cow pats.

'Are you off?' he said.

'Yes. That new deputy from the dragoons were at farm, poking around in barn.'

'I knew it. Did they find owt?'

'It's all right, but he asked about outlying barns and I thought you should know.'

'Right. Ta. I need to get on this.'

'I know. I'm off to Bay to tell Isaac. Think you'd best move stuff as soon as you can,' she said.

'Right,' he said again. 'I've gotta sort this lot and then there's swill to make up.'

'Don't worry,' she said, 'I'll sort it. Someone'll be free. You just get on and I'll catch up with you later.'

She ran down the field towards the woods. She'd catch the old men for sure. They'd be there until sundown and they'd run rings round these new dragoons who thought they were so tough and clever.

She scrambled over a wall and dropped into a bunch of willow herb. Rabbit paths crisscrossed through the trees, light glowing lime green and the scent of dry soil rising up. Rowan trees hung heavy with berries and the brambles here had been stripped of their fruits. Her skirt caught on a long swooping branch. Jerking it free, she gauged which way to head, and breaking into a jog wound through the trees. A rabbit bounded, white tail flashing through the undergrowth and Jiddy laughed nervously at herself for jumping at the noise and sudden movement. She stopped. There was a different shifting through the trees. A flash of red that disappeared into the green. There it was again. But there was no noise. Wind caught some leaves and ruffling them made a summer sound that soon dropped. The red flashed again. It was a jacket. A bright red jacket.

You've nothing to be frightened of, she told herself. You have every right to walk through here. No-one's going to hurt you, just keep walking. What on earth were a soldier doing here though? There came a weird sound, half a cry of pain and half she didn't know what. Had he hurt someone? What should she do? Voices broke the spell. A man and a woman. The red jacket moved. Rustling of leaves, feet, shuffling sounds.

She took a step forward, avoiding any twigs that may crack under her feet.

'When are you leaving?' The woman's voice.

'I don't know. Plans have changed but you're not to say anything.'

'With dragoons here, I thought you'd be posted on.'

'We will be but it won't be London, that's for sure.'

It were a preventive.

'I'll go anywhere. Anywhere with you.' Nellie. Oh my, Jiddy thought, that's Nellie's voice.

'We could be posted to Cornwall.'

'I don't care if it's America.'

'Cornwall's opposite end of the country.'

'But that's grand. Everyone knows where London is, who's going to bother traipsing to Cornwall to try and find me?'

Jiddy didn't dare move. She was hearing things she shouldn't hear. Nellie were doing things she shouldn't be doing. What had she done that she didn't want anyone to find her?

More movement. Scrabbling about. What were they doing?

'I'm ready to get out of this hole too,' Nellie said. 'When you go, wherever it is, you have to take me with you.'

'Well, it's not yet.'

Not yet? This was big news. Captain Pinkney and Isaac needed to know that the preventives were hanging around. She looked about. How would she get past them without being heard?

'You did promise, don't forget that. I did things for that promise.' Nellie sounded worried, desperate. Not like the Nellie Jiddy knew.

'It's not so simple,' the preventive said.

'Give over, course it is. Will I have my own horse or ride with you? I think that'd be cosier.'

'You'd best be getting home.'

'As long as you tell me when to be ready, Robbie.'

'I've told you, don't call me that.'

Robbie. Who could she mean? Whoever it was, he wasn't going to take Nellie with him, Jiddy could tell. Could Nellie guess that too? Jiddy wished she didn't have to hear this part.

'I've seen some of the soldiers' wives. I know you take women with you. I'm strong, I work hard and I'm right shape for, you know. I'll be good to you.' Nellie sounded as if she was crying. Nellie would hate anyone to see that.

'I'm not sure you'll fit in, you'd be best off stopping here. That'd be most sensible. You'd miss your friends if you left.' It sounded like Captain Horseman's deputy, only kinder. It was him. Carter. That was the name. Jiddy put her hand against a tree to lean closer.

'I don't care about friends, I can't do this again.' Nellie's voice was far too loud. 'I kept my end of the bargain, you have to keep yours,' she said. 'Put me in a pretty dress, I'll spruce up and learn to talk proper. If Jiddy Vardy can do it so can I. It's only changing clothes and pinning your hair different. You know I'm bright, I couldn't have done what I've done if I didn't have some brains. I'll learn how to fit in. You know I can do it. You have to take me. I know you're going any day. Private Gerrard told me.'

Jiddy rested her forehead against the trunk, wishing she could disappear. Nellie would kill if she thought anyone had heard what she'd admitted. This was dreadful. Awful.

'I've been good to you, haven't I?' he said. 'You're not with child, are you?' There was a silence and Jiddy strained to hear, shifting quickly to stay out of view when he walked into the open.

Silence again. Jiddy peered carefully around the trunk. Nellie had appeared and was holding onto the sleeve of his jacket. They stayed like that for what seemed ages.

Nellie hit him hard across the cheek. 'You putrid sack of dung! I gave you everything.'

'I think you've given everything before and you will again.'

It was definitely Deputy Carter, Jiddy recognised him now. None of them had guessed anything was going on between them. Nellie was a very good liar to have hidden this. She had made Jiddy believe she wanted Jonas. She'd made them all believe that, even Jonas must think that. Nellie really was clever. Cleverer than any of them had given her credit for. But whatever Nellie had done, Jiddy felt sorry for her for this.

Nellie picked up a large stick but Carter grabbed it and easily wrestled it out of her hands. Bending to retrieve it, he pushed her and she staggered against a tree. By the sound Nellie made, Jiddy could tell it hurt. Nellie must have reached for it again and this time, Carter slapped her across the cheek and she fell heavily.

The preventives weren't gentlemen, they were rough and Nellie was no match for him. Could the two of them take him, Jiddy wondered? And then what? Punishment for harming an officer would be harsh no matter what he'd done to deserve it. Nellie would probably attack her anyway, just because Jiddy had seen him hit her and then where would she be, up against both of them?

'Take me to York instead,' Nellie said, sobbing now. 'That's not so far. You can at least do that. I can't stay here. I won't.'

He was moving.

'Is this how you treat your informers?' Nellie said. 'I gave you everything. I made you look good to Captain Horseman.' He kept walking. 'Robbie?' she shouted.

He didn't turn back, pushing his way through bushes and long grass. No-one, not even Nellie should be treated like that. Jiddy held her breath, the bark of the tree pressing into the back of her head as she stared up into the canopy. A ruffle of wind shuffled the leaves. Nellie sniffed. There was the sound of laces being pulled. Another sniff. Movement in the grass. Please don't come this way, Jiddy thought.

The sound of Nellie's movements faded. What should she do? Tell Big Isaac? Captain Pinkney would kill Nellie himself. It were unbelievable to think Nellie could be an informer. She could be with baby as well. She just might. Jiddy stepped from behind the tree. Nellie had completely disappeared.

Jiddy walked quickly along a rabbit path towards the village. How could Nellie? She wanted to confront her, grab her and shake her. She knew something now. Preventives weren't planning on leaving as Captain Ryethorpe had said that morning. They'd stayed to help dragoons, the sneaking weasels. Big Isaac and Captain Pinkney would want to know that. And word needed to be got out. Clear the barns of contraband. Get someone to empty Jonas' and his da's barns. They had to empty every barn and cottage and farmhouse between Bay and the Salt Road.

If she were fast and they could get organised before it was too late, Nellie's informing would come to nothing and she wouldn't have to say anything. Reaching the edge of the wood, she ran down the grass slope. She couldn't bring herself to mention Nellie's name. Not yet.

CHAPTER TWENTY-SIX

The sense of panic was contagious. That morning, to an outsider, Robin Hood's Bay looked the same as on any other morning, washing flapping, sprawling nets ready for mending, but inside the cottages it was a different matter. Women were busy getting stuff ready for travel. Men were passing word to all the farmers to have their carts and horses ready. Packages were being passed through holes in walls, one to another, from bottom up and up to the top of the village. Carts in Fylingthorpe, full of hay and vegetables, already hid skeins of silk and tubs of brandy. The word was out: get contraband away.

Jiddy held up her arms as Rebecca pulled a skirt over her head and arranged it over the dangling pig bladders hanging from the thick woven belt around Jiddy's waist.

'Does it feel tight enough?' Rebecca said, tugging at the skirt to check it held.

'Yes,' said Jiddy, 'I don't think it's going anywhere.'

She rocked from side to side, feeling the weight of her load, determined not to think about Nellie. Not today. Today there was enough to think about. She'd sorted everything too. Captain Pinkney and Big Isaac had got the word out fast as a whippet after she'd told them. Squire Farsyde had said contraband could be stored with him. Dragoons would never dare search his outbuildings.

That was something to laugh about too, with contraband being hidden right under that new Captain Ryethorpe's nose. Someone had been free and leapt at chance to take his cart over White Moor and onto the Salt Road instead of Jonas and Boy. Last night, in the dark, the moor must have been full of carts removing barrels, sacks and all sorts of goods from the scattered barns.

Mary made Annie turn around. 'Let me make sure it's not tucked up anywhere.'

'You've got brandy, gin and rum so you only need to go one place,' said Rebecca. 'Don't take any chances, my heart won't take any more upset.'

Jiddy glanced at Rebecca. She wasn't having a go, she looked worried. Everyone looked worried, in their way, trying to decide whether it was best to hang on to the contraband or not, until this settled down. When it came down to it, everyone listened to Captain Pinkney and Big Isaac so out the contraband went. Dragoons unsettled everyone. They had horses. They'd fought in wars. Dragoons were serious, everyone knew that. More serious than the rough and ready preventives but banded together, they would prove almost impossible to avoid, let alone try and bribe.

'Jiddy,' Rebecca snapped.

'What?'

'Keep your wits about you today, none of your yonderly ways,' she said.

Annie pulled her skirt down, looking pleased with herself. 'She's sharp as any blade in knife drawer when we're doing anything like this, Mrs Crowden.'

Neither Rebecca nor Mary looked convinced.

'Ready?' said Jiddy.

'Basket,' Mary pointed.

Although Annie panted up the lanes and steep steps to the top of the bank, she didn't stop talking and all Jiddy could think about was that she didn't want to bump into anyone. Everything had turned on its head with Nellie yesterday and she didn't trust a soul. Annie, on the other hand, swayed exaggeratedly, enjoying the curves she didn't usually have, seemingly without a care in the world.

'Have you seen that handsome captain what's-his-name when you've been up at Thorpe Hall?' Annie asked. 'I can't believe he's staying there. Has he said anything to you? Have you seen him?'

'I don't think the squire should let him stay with them,' Jiddy said, when they reached the top and began heading towards the clifftop path that led to Whitby.'

'He's too much of a gentleman to stay anywhere else. He's so beautiful. I wish I were a lady and he'd ask me to marry him.'

Jiddy kicked her way through the long grass, holding her skirt a little away from her body, trying to adjust her belt without actually touching it. Should she say anything about Nellie to Annie? She certainly couldn't tell her she'd spent an afternoon holding the captain's hands and dancing the Gavotte.

'I've heard some of soldiers take a shine to local girls,' Annie said.

'Annie,' Jiddy said, 'd'you hear yourself? They're dragoons. You stay well clear, d'you hear me?'

Annie's smile fell. 'I'm sorry, I know. But you've got Jonas and Betsie's got James and I've…'

Jiddy pushed past Annie. 'Nellie's not got anyone and nothing's ever sure until, well, it's sure.'

Annie caught her up. 'I know but she will. She's determined, you've heard her.'

'You're much nicer than Nellie.'

'I do like James but he is sweet on Betsie and she's like a limpet on him whenever anyone else is around.'

'Come on, we're wasting time,' said Jiddy. 'I want to get to Whitby and back before nightfall.'

'It's those uniforms. My favourite colour is red.'

'Shh.'

'What?' Annie, for the first time since leaving the cottage, fell quiet.

The well-worn path seemed deserted. She should be able to see anyone if they were coming. Annie stared inquiringly at Jiddy.

'I thought I heard something,' she said.

The path to Whitby wound around the coastline, plunging where the cliff cut in and steeply up again for another high stretch of exposed grassland with trees growing crooked in the prevailing wind. The sea seemed endless, lapping waves for miles.

'D'you love Jonas?' Annie said.

'Do we have to talk about him? Sounds like you're the one in love with him.'

Annie stopped abruptly. 'Don't jest like that. I'd never

try and take your Jonas from you, not that I could, no-one would look at anyone else when you're around…'

'Annie…'

'It's true. Even Nellie has to admit that.'

'Nellie's no oracle so I wouldn't listen to her.'

'I say it's true, then.'

Jiddy smiled. 'You're very sweet,' she said. 'Any lad will be lucky to be courting you.'

Annie shook her head. 'They don't even notice me when the rest of you are around. Especially you, Jiddy.'

'You're like a forget-me-not,' said Jiddy, 'and though you look delicate you're tough as fish hooks underneath.'

They laughed. At last, Jiddy thought, we can relax. They walked along in silence, struggling with their load as the path wound up and down. Bushes and dips set Jiddy on edge again. Spots like these were where preventives could be hiding. It wouldn't be dragoons, they didn't know the lie of the land yet, but Captain Horseman's lot did. What if they ran into Robbie Carter? She'd have to say something and then where would they be? Annie was panting hard. The steep inclines were even harder, with their belts making it awkward to move easily. When they reached the tops again and saw a long stretch before them, they fell side by side, panting hard.

'Have you and Jonas kissed each other?' Annie said.

'Is that all you've been thinking about?'

Annie looked sheepish and Jiddy couldn't help but laugh. Maybe it were distance from Bay and Jonas and Nellie, she wasn't sure, but Jiddy didn't mind anymore. They had the day ahead, they'd see pretty things in the market. They were free of the Bay and dragoons and it would be nice talking with Annie about Jonas. She could relive bits and Annie really was sweet.

'We've mucked about a bit,' she said.

'Like doing what?'

How did she answer that? They'd come close, very, very close. She'd wanted more, dreamed about it.

'Kissing and that,' she said. 'It's nice. Shall we sit here and have something to eat?'

They opened the packages in the basket, devouring bread and drinking milk, amazed at their hunger. Annie went quiet, as they laid back. It didn't matter. The sun shone warm and there was a gentle breeze. She could think about how they'd arrive in Whitby and work on keeping calm until they got to house to unload goods. Let Annie think about kissing that Captain Ryethorpe if she wanted. Dreaming did no harm. She couldn't rely on Annie thinking about a plan and they'd need to know exactly what they were doing before they got there, because once they hit hustle of market and crowded streets with soldiers and excise men on every corner, there'd be no time for dithering.

'Come on, Annie, time for off,' she said, when she had their route through Whitby's streets in her head.

Annie's pace slowed. They always forgot how long it took to walk to Whitby and Annie was no walker. Luckily Rebecca had insisted on such an early start.

'We can have a look around when we've done business.' Jiddy waited for Annie, who merely nodded as she brushed past, all questions gone now.

Jiddy watched her. She could let Annie set the pace

and walking slower may ease the soreness of her waist as well if she were honest. The belt had really begun to cut in and she couldn't risk exposing the flasks so close to Whitby.

She let her mind wander. Jonas and his da struggled at farm with just two of them, she saw that now. They were behind and autumn slaughter would be coming up faster than they were ready. There'd not been any salt in last haul and winter seas would bring in fewer ships exactly at time when they needed more salt for keeping meat. Jonas wouldn't be a happy rabbit but at least he'd not had to take Boy and cart out. That had let him catch up on farm a bit and she'd get him a treat from market if she could. Something tasty to cheer him up.

'How you doing, Annie?' She was jumping over the tufted grass, swinging the basket, jump, jump, when her foot slipped. She fell heavily, crying out at the impact of hard ground and the painful shapes of the flasks against her hips.

The grass felt cold against her cheek. The soil smelled damp. Lying down actually came as a relief. She had stopped. The world stopped. Her hip hurt and her shoulder but the ground felt comforting. She didn't move. Annie shambled back.

'Will you still be able to walk?' she asked.

It wasn't easy to stand. Jiddy rolled and pushed and came out with all sorts of noises as she awkwardly got to her feet. She looked at Annie, realising how wrong this suddenly seemed. It should have been an adventure; they were young, off to Whitby where anything was possible, stalls and splendid things to look at, a dock full of ships going places and people of all types to talk to. Instead, they were carrying contraband and they could be hanged for it.

Jiddy brushed down her skirts, trying to keep calm before turning slowly for Annie to check she'd covered her underclothes and flasks.

Annie pointed. 'What's that?'

Looking down, Jiddy saw a large dark damp patch on her skirt and smelled the unmistakable aroma of brandy.

'Boilin' fish, Jiddy, what we going to do? You can't go into Whitby reeking like that.'

'I can hiccup and say I'm an alcoholic,' Jiddy said. It wasn't funny. Jiddy wafted her skirt. 'It'll be all right, we've a way to go yet.'

'Well, take that flask off at least, it may still be leaking.'

She lifted her skirts. 'Oh no!'

Three of the pig bladders had split. She untied the sacks from her belt and handed them to Annie, who held them away from her as they dripped onto the grass. Snapping off a twig from a nearby oak, Jiddy scratched away at the dry earth around the tree's base.

Soon the three damaged sacks were buried and they walked on, picking up their pace. As they neared the town, Jiddy spotted lavender growing by a row of cottages and broke off several pieces, hoping the scent would mask the pungent smell of alcohol.

CHAPTER TWENTY-SEVEN

The noise of the market hit them before they saw it. The bustle swamped the streets, crowding pavements and bursting out of openings. There were people everywhere, moving, walking, hurrying, arms gesticulating, heads turning, nodding; earnest faces, laughing faces, thinking faces, bargaining and shouting, whispering and drawing you in.

'Straight to the house and drop off our stuff and straight back here,' Jiddy said. 'Agreed?'

Annie nodded, her eyes bright with all the sights around them.

Jiddy touched Annie's arm to slow her down. 'Careful not to knock anything, we can't afford any more breaks after what I've just done.'

They weaved their way through the stalls, trying not to bump into anyone or anything. Bread and cheeses, herbs, spices, pies and pickles scented the air. Plenty enough to cover the smell of brandy and Jiddy dropped the sprig of lavender. A stall crammed with apple pies sweetened with treacle caught their eye and Annie looked pleadingly at Jiddy.

'We'll come back,' said Jiddy.

Lengths of lace fluttered over her head and Jiddy touched a piece.

'Ow.'

The stall holder slapped her hand. 'Don't touch owt with your grubby mitts,' she said.

'What did you tell me?' Annie said. 'We'll come back?'

'Very funny.'

Jiddy led the way again, swaying through the stalls, and guarding her hips whenever someone pushed too close.

'I'm glad Nellie felt she was above coming today,' Annie said. 'You'd think she'd jump at the chance to come to Whitby and visit her cousins. Look at all this she's missing. And Betsie.'

'Nellie may have to look after her da.' She was beginning to feel sorry for Nellie, but right now they had enough to think about. Also, she didn't trust herself not to say something more.

'Maybe she feels there are too many cousins to visit and she wouldn't know where to start,' said Annie.

'She should be grateful.'

'She's jealous of you and you've not even brothers and sisters, let alone distant cousins.'

Annie stopped, embarrassed.

Jiddy held Annie's hand. 'Come on, let's not spoil our day talking about Nellie. Maybe there'll be a circus parade to see.'

Annie lit up like a buttercup. 'D'you think there'll be jugglers?'

'If we're lucky,' Jiddy said.

A shout from ahead stopped them in their tracks.

'Leave her alone!'

At the stalls on the market's edge, transactions halted. Annie turned her head as if in slow motion. The entire atmosphere of the market shifted and the crowd began to move, taking them with it. Annie squeezed Jiddy's hand tighter as they walked, Jiddy feeling a surge of anxiety as their pace quickened.

'We've got to get rid of this stuff,' she said.

Jiddy knew the danger they as women were in. She had seen the skirt ripped off a woman to reveal packets of tea and skins of brandy and she remembered how they had been slit with a knife and the perfume of the leaves had mingled with fumes of alcohol, and the woman had been hoisted on the spot to some makeshift gallows and hanged before the crowd could react. She'd never forget the black lips and dark tongue and the weird expression on her face. The crush of the crowd swept them forward. Holding Annie tighter, they surged with the current of bodies. The crowd channelled through the narrow street, making it impossible to reach the small back alley with the house at the end that would relieve them of their belts. Jiddy shoved to break out. She could see the incongruous dark ginnel, temptingly near. They had to get there before they were swept onto the dock. She tucked Annie's arm under hers, holding her close and head down, shouldered her way sideways. Annie followed, but the crowd jostled faster all the time and they were packed tight, moving as one.

'Jiddy?' said Annie.

Too late, they were out on the dock where a mass of uniforms surrounded the quay.

'We need to keep to the edge,' Jiddy said, but people behind pushed them forwards. Annie clutched Jiddy's arm, her eyes wild as a rabbit in a snare.

'They're searching people,' she said.

The soldiers on duty were busy searching those nearest them and roughly pushing others on. Maybe they'd be all right, Jiddy thought. We can hide in this crowd. What looked like a navy ship towered over the quayside. They drew closer to the dockside where cows, sheep, crates of chickens and piglets were driven and carried up gangways. The noise was deafening. Farming equipment and all sorts of stuff filled the siding. Several men, shackled and dragging their feet, were being led from a large wagon by soldiers wielding guns.

Unable to escape, they moved with the crowd, which swayed like a nauseous sea. A piercing scream caught their attention. Two soldiers dragged a struggling woman towards the ship.

The crowd surged forward, bringing Jiddy and Annie closer to the front.

'Mam. Maaam!'

A boy of about seven was shouting.

'Leave my mam alone.'

'Get that boy away.'

'Someone help,' the woman said, her voice shriller, filled with panic.

The words tumbled out, from him, her, from soldiers, even the crowd joined in now, trying for a way in through the sticks and batons.

'Frankie!' The woman's voice pierced the air as they

neared the gangway to the ship. 'Put me in prison, hang me. Anything, but don't put me on that ship, don't, no, no, please, have mercy, no! Frank!'

Jiddy stood on her toes, balancing her hands on the shoulders of a woman in front. She didn't seem to mind, she was doing the same to the person in front.

'Mam!'

Soldiers forced the woman onto the gangway. It didn't look easy, even with strong soldiers. She fought and held back and kicked against them. The men from the wagon were being unshackled. As soon as he was free, one of them swung his fist. A soldier smacked him across the face with a rifle butt and blood spurted from his cheek.

The little boy was sobbing.

'She's all the boy's got,' someone shouted, 'let her be.'

A soldier shoved the woman forward. 'She's going on this prison hulk.'

Shouts and screams erupted, Jiddy couldn't tell who was shouting anymore, she could no longer see the figures at the front. She held Annie's hand firmly; she had to hold on to something, make sure they stuck together.

One of them hoisted the woman over his shoulder and carried her to the gangway. People were going mad. The unshackled men were pushing and shoving, one of them was punching his way to reach the woman but the soldiers were having none of it. The entire quay had been surrounded, red uniforms standing out in the sea of brown and grey.

'I don't like the look of that ship,' said Annie.

'Where's it going?' Jiddy asked the man nearest.

'Across Atlantic.'

'More likely Australia', another man said.

'Wicked, them prison ships,' said another.

'Prison?' Jiddy said. 'That ship's a prison?'

A line of men shuffled up to the gangway. One of them looked familiar. Annie pulled Jiddy's sleeve. 'Jiddy, come on, they'll grab anyone now, they don't care. And we've got all this stuff.'

'Can you see that man?' Jiddy said, straining to see, 'I'm sure it's not but…'

'Use your head, Jiddy, you always think for us. I'm scared, we won't be able to do anything, they'll throw us on there too. Jiddy, please.'

'Down with King George!'

The mood was changing, anger underlying. The mob moved like a slick of treacle.

'What are they shouting about?' Annie said.

Jiddy stood on her toes again. 'I don't know.'

People were raising their arms and clenching fists.

'Down with King George!'

'Down with government!'

'Let's go,' Annie said.

Something else was going on. The crowd pushed forward. Annie's hand slid out of Jiddy's and jostled and pushed, Jiddy jolted against a railing at the front of the dock. No-one could move even if they wanted to. She couldn't turn around, let alone see Annie. Cargo was being loaded all around, gulls squawking, dogs barking, the attention of the crowd turning this way and that. Not knowing what to do to get past the soldiers, Jiddy held on tight to the rail. If she let go and fell she'd be trampled on, but the last thing she wanted was to be pushed into the dirty black water lapping below.

'Get back, shift.' Soldiers shoved the crowd, striking to get them to move. The line of unshackled men had begun to plod up the gangway and spaces on the dockside opened up. Jiddy let go of the rail. Free. Something nudged Jiddy's leg and she looked down to see a large dog sniffing her skirts. The soldier holding it hadn't noticed. The brandy. She must still smell of brandy.

The dog barked and the soldier holding him turned around. The last man on the line stepping on to the gangway looked over his shoulder. It was impossible. But she'd been right, she did know him. It was James Linskill from the Bay.

CHAPTER TWENTY-EIGHT

S he pointed to a mound of sacks along the quay. 'Your dog saw a rat,' she said.

Nudging the barking dog away, she forced her way along the railing. Further up the gangway, James held onto the ropes, trying to slow down, but he was being pushed from behind as more and more were wrestled towards the ship's opening.

A young, red-faced soldier lifted her over the lip of wood. 'Seeing as you're so keen, up you go,' he said.

'Get off.' Another soldier grabbed her and together they pushed her forwards. She was blocked in and on her way towards the black hole in the ship's hull with others following close behind. There seemed no way out. She held onto the ropes

Leaning to the side, she looked behind at the quay. It swarmed with people and animals and machinery waiting to be loaded. She looked up towards the ship. James stared back at her.

'Don't go in,' she said.

Shaking his head, he turned away.

'James?' This wasn't like him. James never give in without a fight. She leaned out further, clutching hard to the rope.

He looked back again. His left cheek was darkened

by a bruise and his lip spilt blood onto his chin. 'I were stupid,' he shouted. She just about heard above the noise. 'Thought I were clever. Don't you be. Get yourself out of here.'

He'd almost reached the dark entrance and soldiers were pulling people in.

'No, don't James.'

A soldier struck him and he stumbled inside.

'James!'

She almost toppled off the gangway but the man behind grabbed her. 'Careful,' he said.

The woman in front shook so much that noises came out of her mouth rather than words.

The man behind pushed Jiddy again. They were all pushing forwards, pushing towards the open doorway of the ship. Pushing and shoving up the ramp. Noise from the dock dulled. The ship's noises took over as the darkness of the vessel yawned wide.

Her chest pounded. She couldn't see how they could avoid getting on the ship. The dock was a mass of people. She'd lost Annie and how would Annie manage getting back to Bay? Mary would be alone, she couldn't do that to her. But if she did somehow manage to get back down gangway that dog would rip at her skirts and pull flasks off her belt, its teeth spilling give-away alcohol. And that young lad would knock her out and she'd be back on ship.

'Get yourself out of here,' James had said. 'Get out.'

What could she do? She couldn't go back down gangway. The water heaved far, far below. If she jumped, fall could break her back. The angry soldier had his eyes on her. The man behind shoved her again. The noise filled her head. She couldn't think. The woman in front began leaning back, and they all began to lean. Jiddy gripped the ropes. The man behind began shoving hard. Jiddy leaned sideways, to avoid them both. A channel of water glinted between the hull and the dock. Swinging out, she ducked underneath the thick hemp and let go. Someone shouted, grasped at her arm but she was falling, a rushing of wind in her hair and her skirts rising up. The noise seemed very far away when she hit the water. She plunged down, holding her breath as the weight of her skirts, the belt laden with pig bladders of whisky, rum and gin pulled her deeper. She couldn't see, the grey-green water opaque and dotted with chipped wood, fish bones, debris. This was it. She'd sink to the bottom, body squashed between ship and dockside, lungs filled with murky water and no-one in Robin Hood's Bay would know where she'd gone.

Miraculously, she surfaced and, gulping air, raised her chin to keep above the water. A few strokes and she'd reach the dock wall. She kicked but it didn't help. Her hips pulled down. It was the flasks and her skirt, heavy with water, pulling her under. She gulped and submerged. It turned black as night. Kicking, paddling, feeling herself sinking, she used all her strength. Her lungs were bursting. Keep kicking, keep kicking but her skirts wrapped around her legs, tightening so she could move them less and less.

Stretching out her arms, she touched something hard. She reached out again. It was the hard, sheer drop of the dockside. Fingers slipping against slime and weed, she kicked, grasping for all her might for something on the stone wall to hold onto. She couldn't hold her breath much longer. Her chest hurt. Her throat stung. Her head pounded.

Would they be lowering ropes, would that red-faced lad be remorseful or desperate not to let her escape punishment? Please, please, lower ropes. Nothing happened. She knew they didn't care. One less piece of trouble to bother about. And James? Would any of them ever see each other again? She felt around, shifting sideways and touched a metal girder and what felt like rope. She grappled again. Where was it? Please let it be there, let me find it. Her lungs were bursting.

Her nails scraped through gunge. Then something hard. She grabbed it. One hand, both hands. Her chest ached, throat like a block of wood. Thank God for the strength in her arms. She held on, pulled upwards, but her skirt, weighted by water, dragged her down. Muscles ached. Everything ached.

She didn't know how she did it. Noise erupted, mingling with the pounding in her body as she broke through the surface. Opening her eyes, she gulped in air. In the shadow of the ship, the channel lapped cold and dark. She clung to the ladder bolted to the dockside, catching her breath. Her head hurt. Her throat felt like stone. Her skirts still pulled down but she hung on. All she could see was the slimy wall. She panted noisily. She didn't care, she couldn't do anything else. The ship could crush her. She wasn't safe. One of the soldiers, looking down, could spot her.

She'd be purple soon. Her fingers would be so numb she'd let go of the rungs and sink. It wasn't over yet.

Noises of the ship being loaded. Shouts. Moments of quiet. Sails cracked, shouts rang out, the sea rose and fell, the vast shadow of the ship loomed over her. Waves grew bigger, rounding against the dock wall. The ship was moving. She pressed against the ladder, waiting to be crushed. The hull was taller than any cliff she'd seen. The water grew choppier. She spluttered. Waves lashed over her, pulling her away from the wall. She closed her eyes. Panic, she'd heard Captain Pinkney use that word but it didn't matter if it had a name or not, whatever it was, she had to fight feeling as much as her dwindling strength.

She couldn't get any wetter. She couldn't be any colder. Thoughts filtered in and out. She was merely a criminal cowering from justice, that's how the likes of Captain Ryethorpe and those high-minded officers would think of her. She couldn't pretend to be some brave saviour and the people's deliverer of goods now. She saw smuggling for what it was, cowardly skulking in the dark.

She shook herself. Not yet. Keep your eyes open. She wouldn't give in yet. The cold rose up through the water and out of the stone, reaching through her bodice, through her skin and seeping into her muscles. Sludge and slime gathered under her nails. She'd never look Mrs Farsyde, let alone the likes of Captain Ryethorpe, in the face again. She didn't even know why she was thinking about them. The likes of captain would never steal anything and smuggling was stealing.

She was ready to let go. Darkness was her friend. She

heard music. Mrs Farsyde singing. Dancing. She was dancing.

Let go. Let it be over. She didn't belong here, not anywhere. Nellie's voice was telling her she was an odd one who didn't belong anywhere. The Bay would be better off. Let go, let your fingers and hands and arms slip. Lean back, it will be easy, dissolving into the sea, your hair like tendrils, all feeling gone. She loved the sea. What could be better? Her belt would pull her down. The sea would help her sleep. Jonas would be better off too, marry Annie maybe. A peaceful, easy life. Let go. Her fingers slipped.

CHAPTER TWENTY-NINE

Plunging underwater, the shock jolted her senses and she grasped for the ladder. Trembling, she heaved herself up, the rusty iron grazing her hands and the weight of her skirt dragging around her legs. Resting her forehead against the hard, cold rung, she began to shake. The ladder stretched never-ending up the grimy wall, all the way to the top. Her limbs already exhausted, she balanced her feet on a rung under the water, hunching close to the metal, arms locked firmly through higher rungs. She'd not lose her grip again. Voices trickled down from above but they could have been in a different country. She looked up again. It would be like climbing to the clouds.

She forced her fingers to unclench. It took so much concentration to lift one hand off the worn, rusting rung, raise a leaden arm and grasp a higher rung. The weight of her skirt seemed determined to hold her in the water. Her arms ached. Linking them around a rung, she pulled herself up. She must have made a noise but she didn't care. Water poured from her dress as she used all her strength to clear the waves lapping at the quay wall. Up another rung, her hands so sore now with scraping the rusty, rough metal. Breathe. She was out of the sea. The noise was quietening down now ship had gone. James would be somewhere over North Sea. She breathed out slowly. She could wait a little longer.

Dusk came and she willed her limbs to move. They ached. They were stiff but step by step she moved higher up the ladder. She waited again, watching the sludge on the wall until she knew every wrinkle and spot and shade of grey, green and brown. She must have closed her eyes at some point because jerking awake, she saw that the sky had turned black. She couldn't hear a sound. She put her foot on the next rung. It slipped on her skirt. No, no, she couldn't fall! She pulled herself in, kicking her foot free. At the top, her head on a level with the open quay, she waited. She was scared to move this last bit. She might put a hand on some shiny boot, be hauled up, stabbed, shot, perhaps strangled. She could even be strung up on the gallows but she couldn't cling to the ladder on any longer.

One last effort and she rolled on her back. The hard dock, solid under her body, felt like the best thing she'd felt in a long time. High, high above, white stars peppered the black sky. A cusp of moon slithering out of its dark blanket gave the quay a whisper of light. The sound of breathing filled her head. She had never in her entire life been so exhausted. Sleep. That's what she craved. A bed, a barn full of sleep. Cold no longer mattered, she couldn't feel anything, not fingers, or feet, nor the ground anymore. If she lay there, morning would come and the sun would warm her again.

Her body stiffened, her heart slowed, her wet clothes couldn't protect her from the bitter night air. If only she could stop the breeze off the water. She imagined rats sniffing her hands, foxes nuzzling the strange smell of her skirt. If only a fire roared to keep her heart beating. If only someone would come to find her. If only someone would come.

Dragging herself to her feet, she looked around. To think that the quay had been packed with people a few hours ago. The noise had been overwhelming. Now the quiet was too much to bear. The sea licked the dock wall. She took a step or two. A few more steps. It was like sleep walking. One foot in front of the other, arms heavy by her sides, skirt clinging to make her stride difficult, the hard shapes of the flasks bruising her hips. She'd forgotten that they were there.

One foot in front of the other. Drifting across space towards the dark alley they should have gone to first. She touched the walls, ran her fingers over doors, all the way to the end of the alley. The door was locked. She tapped. No-one came. Resting her forehead against the grooves, jolting upright as the door opened. Her knees buckled.

'Quick, get her in.'

'What the hell?'

'That girl said, didn't she? Said there'd been another one.'

'Said she'd gone off on that ship.'

'Obviously not.'

'How'd we know it's her?'

'Look under her skirt.'

'You kidding, woman?'

'She said she were dark. She's dark, isn't she?'

'Get her inside.'

'Shut door then, you pillock.'

The light of the fire blinded. The air smelled different. She must be in a cave, a small cave with no gusty tunnels. A cave with a sandy floor and a rug and chairs to sit on. Strange cave, with two people in it and no sea churning shingle or lapping against her, rising and falling, lap, lap, lapping.

'She's sodden.'

'You all right, dear? She's not all right. What do we do?'

'I don't know. Get her closer to fire. Thaw her out.'

Warmth, heat, life started to seep into her tingling hands.

'Am I here?' she said.

'Bugger off for a minute, Seth, I'm going to get her out of her wet clothes.'

Noises, groans, muttering and footsteps. Jiddy let the woman untie her skirt, let it fall, stepping out and her underskirt, tight sleeves, awkward, peeling the skin. A weight lifted. Weights as the woman removed the belt and the bruising flasks.

'Seth, she's the one.'

A blanket around her shoulders.

'Sit here. Take this.'

A bowl of hot broth, trickling down her throat like a lifeline. She drank it all.

She must have slept in the chair. Even though the surface of her skin felt warm, she felt cold beneath, cold in her bones and joints and blood. But she was here, alive, making her delivery, safe in this cave of a house.

She stared at the flames, at the orange heat and ashen wood. Thud. The other two had gone quiet.

'Listen.'

'Shut up.'

Someone knocked at the door, quiet but persistent.

'Take those clothes down. Get her in cupboard.'

The woman raised Jiddy up. The man pulled back a shelving unit, pushed her inside, an armful of hot, damp clothes to hold and darkness again with strips of flickering light through cracks in the wood.

'Ready.'

The woman made a sound.

Jiddy's heart beat fast. She hated it. Hated that she felt fear again.

The stranger spoke quietly and Jiddy couldn't quite hear what he said. The old man sounded relieved. The door closed.

'It's a long way on foot,' said the woman.

'I left my horse on the edge of town.'

The old man made a noise of agreement.

'D'you want to warm yourself?' The sound of a dragging chair.

'Open cupboard woman, he's not here on a Sunday visit.'

'Are you sure it's her?'

'See for yourself.'

Jiddy clutched the pile of clothes in her arms and didn't move. Familiar eyes stared at her. Grey eyes she'd recognise in her sleep.

'Thank God, Jiddy.' Jonas pushed the damp clothes

sideways, grabbing her arms and pulling her into his embrace. He squeezed her so tight it hurt, and she tried to hug him back but her arms, stiff and cold, merely rested against him. Instead, she rested her cheek on his shoulder, feeling the thick, comforting wool against her skin. The ordeal was over and he'd come for her. He hadn't given up on her; he hadn't given her up for dead. Tears pricked her eyes but she held them in, her throat tightening.

Gently relaxing his hold, he leaned back to study her face. 'Are you all right?' he said. 'Do you want to rest here until tomorrow?'

She couldn't speak and she squeezed her eyes tight to hold in the mounting tears. As if he knew, he hugged her again, his fingers pressing hard and she rested her forehead on his shoulder.

'Think young lady should get dressed,' the woman spoke.

'Might be best if you got going while it's still dark,' the man said.

Jiddy felt the tension in Jonas' body change.

The woman helped her dress while Jonas and the man stood in the doorway, the man smoking a pipe and both of them checking on the passageway outside. Jiddy kept close to the fire. She felt she'd never be warm again.

'Ready,' the woman said.

Jonas' face softened as he walked back into the room and looked at her. 'Thank you,' he said to the woman.

After a minute or so, the man handed Jonas a bag with the empty flasks in and the payment for their contents.

'I don't know where Annie is,' Jiddy said.

'She's safe,' said Jonas, 'and so are you.'

She could barely walk and Jonas supported her through the streets. In the dark, the town remained quiet but stars lit their way. It was good to feel Jonas' arm around her and his thick coat warming her. When they reached they edge of town, Jiddy saw Jonas' horse tied to a tree at the edge of some woods, his breath steaming the cool air. Jonas cupped his hands and she lifted one foot into his palms. He did all the work, springing her up, and she held on to Boy's saddle and settled into her seat. Jonas eased into the saddle behind her, cradling her in the captain's chair of his arms as they rode out of Whitby. She felt safe in this chair, Boy's flanks rounded below her legs, Jonas protecting her back and preventing her exhausted body from falling. She rested one hand on top of his, feeling his knuckles below her fingers.

'I wish we were children again,' she said.

He leaned closer. 'Did you say something?'

She swore to herself that she'd never leave Baytown again. Never wish herself on a boat on another shore. Thoughts disappeared. The gentle motion of Boy's walk lulled her to sleep.

Jonas nudged her awake.

A pale line along the horizon gave the moor a grey sheen. The Buttercross rose up ahead of them.

'I'm taking you to farm,' Jonas said.

'No. Take me home. Mary will be worried.'

'She'll be asleep.'

'She won't.'

He turned Boy east and they headed downhill, past quiet houses, and when they reached the woods where they'd first proper kissed all those hundreds of years ago, Jonas pulled Boy to a standstill.

'Why've you stopped?'

'I don't want to take Boy further and wake anyone,' he said, swinging his leg over and jumping onto the grass.

'Did you talk to Annie?' she said.

It was coming back. Everything was coming back.

Jonas put his hands around her waist and lifted her down.

'You're still damp,' he said.

'D'you know if she told Mary?'

'I guess so.'

'Can I see you tomorrow?' she said.

'It's tomorrow already.'

The sky had turned yellow. It was already another day. They walked to the top of the bank and she put her hand on his sleeve.

'Don't walk me down,' she said.

'You don't make it easy.'

'It isn't easy though, is it?'

'Let me walk you down,' he said.

'No, just in case there's soldiers about. You get off.'

'I thought you were gone on that ship or that you were dead,' he said. 'Either way, I thought I'd never see you again.' She couldn't bear it. Talking about it brought it closer. All she wanted was to be home, feeling safe and warm. 'Boy will be fine in woods, he's got grass to eat. I'm coming with you.'

As they dropped down the bank and rounded the steps up to Sunny Place, Jiddy wondered how Mary would react. She would have stayed up, that was certain, and some of the neighbours might be waiting with her as well. Annie might be there too, worn out and scared. She pushed open the door. Two figures snored gently by the fire.

Jonas walked past Jiddy to the fireside. 'Mary? Rebecca?'

Mary jumped awake immediately. 'Come, sit down,' she said, rushing to take Jiddy's arm. 'Oh, my, let's get you out of those clothes.'

Rebecca held up a blanket and Jiddy dragged her feet to the fire. Her limbs ached. She couldn't stand. She curled around Mary, holding tight and stretching out an arm to Rebecca.

'I know love, I know.' Tears streamed down Mary's lined cheeks. 'Jonas give us a minute.' He stepped outside while Mary peeled the clothes off her and Rebecca wrapped her in a nightgown warming by the fire.

'Oh love, we've been worried sick, haven't we Rebecca?'

'We have. Now, sit.'

Kneeling on the rug, Mary pulled thick socks on Jiddy's cold feet and Jiddy looked down at the older woman's greying hair.

'Jonas, come and get some soup,' Rebecca said. 'You both need something hot.'

They didn't say much more as they sat by the fire. Her second bowl that night. She would drink ten if they'd let her. She could tell that Mary, Rebecca and Jonas exchanged glances but she was too tired to say anything.

Even her heart ached and she still felt cold. Cold forever like those iron rungs plunging down into the dark water. Tears welled up. She couldn't stop them. Maybe the sea had got inside and filled her up and the warmth of the fire drew them out and she'd leak salt tears until the day she died.

'I'll be off to my bed,' Rebecca said, getting up to leave. 'Thank you Jonas for bringing back our girl. Mary, I'll see you in morning.'

'Think you'd best get you up to bed as well, Jiddy,' Mary said. They were both watching her, their faces glowing in the light of the flames. She didn't want to leave them or the heat. She didn't want to be alone. 'I've put a hot stone in your bed,' Mary said. 'Night Rebecca.'

'Night.'

'You can sleep down here, Jonas,' said Mary taking Jiddy's arm. 'Come on you, we all need some rest.'

Jiddy wrapped her arms around Mary's shoulders. 'Thank you,' she said.

'Think it's lad here you should be thanking.'

Jonas looked flustered. 'No, it's, I'm...'

'Thank you,' Jiddy said.

'That's what happens when you get over tired,' Mary said. 'Now are you going up first or am I? Jonas? Stand at bottom of stairs and I'll chuck you some blankets down.'

It was as if they were children again and the fire and cottage and Mary and Rebecca would protect them from all the dangers out there on the streets.

CHAPTER THIRTY

G ulls scratched at the tiles on the roof outside. The
cloth hanging over the window made the light in
the room dim. Jiddy listened for noises downstairs but
the cottage remained quiet. Mary must be up and out.
Jonas would be back at the farm. She couldn't stay in bed
though, it wasn't fair.

Jiddy stood on the top step. It felt like weeks since
she'd stood there, not a day. She touched the wall. It was
real. The noises were real. She had made it back home.

It was a bright day. She cut across to the Bolts. Annie's
mam answered the door.

'She's on causeway with Nellie and Betsie,' said Mrs
Briggs before closing the door again. Annie's mam had
never been the talkative type.

The woods spread out from the end of the Bolts. She
could head up to the farm that way but Mr Chaplow
wouldn't be best pleased to see her if she took Jonas from
his work. She could cut up to the cliffs and spend the
afternoon sleeping in the long grass or scramble down
to the beach. No. She had to see Annie. Check for sure
if James really had sailed off.

Girls' voices drifted up from the causeway and Jiddy
quickened her step. The smell of sea hit her. She was home
and she couldn't help but be relieved. Four barrels stood

at the top of the causeway a few feet away. Nellie, Betsie and Annie carried lobster pots in both hands towards a pile that cluttered the area near the barrels. Annie saw her first.

Dropping the pots with a clatter, she picked her way through the stacks.

'I'd have called in,' she said, 'but Mary said to let you sleep. I'm so glad you're safe, I were scared and I didn't know what to do. I didn't leave you on purpose but the man at the house said to come back home and I thought you'd been thrown on that ship.'

'You did the right thing,' Jiddy said, 'I could have been half way to America and you'd have been stuck alone in Whitby.' Jiddy looked up at Nellie and Betsie approaching. 'I'm sorry, Betsie, are you all right?'

'Course she's not all right,' Nellie said, folding her arms. 'How would you feel if Jonas had been on that ship?'

Betsie had obviously been crying for hours her face was that puffed up and red.

'Does Jonas know?' Jiddy said. She hadn't told Jonas. How could she not have told him?

'Of course he knows,' said Nellie, 'everyone knows.'

'It weren't Jiddy's fault,' said Annie. 'James were on ship and there were nowt anyone could do.'

'I thought you said Jiddy tried,' said Nellie, 'charged up gangway then jumped into water when she lost her nerve.'

'It were crowded,' said Annie, 'Jiddy were pushed off.'

'Jumped.'

'Pushed.'

'You weren't there, Nellie,' said Jiddy, 'how would you know if I jumped or were pushed.'

Betsie wiped her face with her sleeve. 'Did you talk to him?' she said.

'James were right at top, near door,' said Jiddy.

'Didn't he say anything?'

'Jiddy just told you, he were too far away,' said Annie, 'I've told you everything, Betsie. Jiddy could have been taken away on ship as well.'

Nellie stood back, arms across her big chest. Betsie's eyes looked sore and watery.

'I were hoping he'd said something.' Betsie sniffed. 'Were he on his own or were he with a load of others? If he were chained up to others, he might have been shy to say summat nice to pass on to me.'

Jiddy tried to remember. It has been noisy and crowded. There'd been a line of men that had been shackled but their chains had been undone before they'd gone up to the ship.

'It were difficult,' she said, 'there were soldiers everywhere.'

'I told you,' said Annie. 'I told them everything, Jiddy.'

'Not how James happened to be there,' said Nellie. 'What I don't understand is why James was caught, one time he helps out when he never takes contraband on his wagon. That's Jonas' job. Why weren't Jonas doing it, Jiddy? Did you know something and warn him not to go so you could keep your sweetheart safe?'

'How would I know anything? Jonas were behind with work at farm, that's why he didn't go,' said Jiddy.

'Funny how he's always behind with farm work but this is first time he ducks out of shifting stuff from barns,' said Nellie.

Annie took hold of Jiddy's hand. 'Jonas would have gone if he could,' she said. 'Don't listen to Nellie. James were right brave and he went because he's a good friend of Jonas and nobody knew anything bad were going to happen.'

'I know what happened,' Jiddy said. 'James took over deliveries because he were there when I were telling Captain Pinkney and Isaac about the new dragoons searching all barns and farm buildings. It weren't anything to do with Jonas,' Jiddy squared up to Nellie. 'James were caught because preventives and dragoons are working together and knew where to look. Preventives haven't left Robin Hood's Bay yet, isn't that right Nellie?'

A smile flitted over Nellie's face. 'I wonder where Jonas is today?' she said.

Jiddy's mouth went dry. 'What d'you mean?'

Annie squeezed Jiddy's hand. 'He's in bottom field,' she said, before turning to Nellie. 'He's busy helping his da. And he'll be sick to his stomach about James and I bet he's real sorry too that it weren't him caught but there it is, it's one of them things and it isn't anybody's fault.'

The girls were quiet for a moment. Jiddy wondered if it had occurred to Jonas that he could be the one on that ship. Poor James, the one time he took to delivering contraband he was caught.

'Forgotten how to talk?' said Nellie.

Jiddy let go of Annie's hand and turned to Betsie.

'James is strong, he will be all right,' she said.

Betsie's eyes drew the tears back in. 'I don't care if he'll be all right,' she said. 'I care that he's gone and I'll never see him again.'

'But you must…'

'There's no must about it,' Nellie said, 'Betsie will never see James again and it's your fault.'

'He were my only chance,' Betsie said. The sound of her voice made them look at her. 'No-one will look at me now and I'll never have anyone and I'll be an old maid like Annie'.

'What do you mean, an old maid like me? Who says I'm going to be an old maid, that's a horrid thing to say Betsie. I know you're upset, but that's really spiteful,' Annie said.

'Oh, you know what I mean, Annie,' said Betsie. 'You say it yourself but I had James. I had James.'

Nellie bashed her shoulder into Jiddy's, edging forward so close that Jiddy stepped back.

'Stop it,' Jiddy said, pushing back. She'd stuck up for James, she'd tried so hard and she'd nearly died in the process. Nellie was the informer. She itched to say something but she wasn't going to snitch. Betsie was upset enough. She didn't need to learn at that moment that her closest friend, Nellie, had got James exiled on a prison ship by informing on entire Bay.

'Betsie, I'm right sorry about James,' she said, 'but I can't go back and try all over again and even if I did, we'd probably both be on that ship or one or both of us would be dead. I'm sorry, Betsie, I'm so sorry.'

Bursting into tears, Betsie pulled her skirt up to hide her face.

'Seems to me, that's what should have happened,' said Nellie.

'It's informer we should be pointing finger at,' Jiddy said. 'I think we all want to know exactly how they knew that somebody were going to be driving a wagon full of contraband across moors, hey Nellie? Do you want to tell Betsie and Annie how they knew?'

'All right,' said Nellie, smoothing down her apron and looking at Jiddy. 'I'll tell you all how soldiers knew James were driving a wagon full of contraband across moors.'

Jiddy waited, relieved she wouldn't have to put her friendship with Annie and Betsie to the test. She hated herself for being a coward but there was always that lurking doubt that they wouldn't believe her because she wasn't really one of them.

Nellie took her time, making them wait. She smoothed down her apron again. 'I'm sorry I couldn't keep this from you, Betsie,' she said, 'but I suppose Jiddy's right. You do need to hear.'

'What do I need to hear?' said Betsie.

'It weren't no mistake James were put on that ship.'

'What?' said Jiddy.

'I don't understand.'

'James is informer, Betsie,' Nellie said, 'I bet he chose to go on ship rather than stay here and risk anyone finding out.'

'That's not true,' said Jiddy. 'Don't believe her. Nellie? You know that's not true. He were thrown on that ship. You're a liar.'

'I'm not lying,' Nellie interrupted, folding her arms and squaring up to Jiddy. 'I heard couple of preventives bragging about how they'd turned James Linskill into informing on rest of Bay. I weren't in Whitby and you weren't here but if you've got something else you want to tell us, go ahead. You had a right lucky escape from what Annie's said…'

'I've not said owt.' Annie stepped forward, her pale face paler than usual.

'You didn't end up on ship. That's all I know,' said Nellie. 'Strikes me, soldiers wouldn't let anyone get away if they didn't want them to.'

'You don't know what you're talking about,' said Jiddy.

'Jiddy, take no notice, it doesn't matter,' Annie touched her arm.

'Shut up!' Betsie shouted, silencing them all. They all looked at the ground, not wanting to look at each other. The sea sounded distant, lapping way out on the scours. 'Didn't James say anything at all to you?' she said.

Jiddy looked at Nellie who continued to look at her feet as if she wasn't interested.

'I don't believe he'd turn informer,' she said.

Betsie didn't say anything, nor did Nellie. The silence between them became unbearable.

'I hate him,' said Betsie, breaking the unbearable tension. 'Nellie's right. Why else would he run away? He's a coward.'

'They all are' said Nellie, 'I hate men, they're all wishy-washy cowards!'

Annie clenched her hands together.

'They're not all,' Jiddy said. 'He didn't run away. They took him.'

'So you don't agree with us?' said Nellie. 'You're not sticking with Betsie when James turns out to be a right Molly.'

'Of course I'm with Betsie.'

'Then say it, all men are right fussocks!'

Betsie looked as if she'd kill the first person who disagreed. Annie looked frightened. Nellie, triumphant. Jiddy pictured the ship, the noise, the pushing and shoving. James had told her to get out of there.

'Think we should get on with this lot,' Jiddy said, eyeing Nellie. 'Can't leave all these lobsters drying out in their cages.'

She couldn't bear to be near any of them. They hadn't asked about how she'd fallen into the sea or how she'd got back on the dock. They didn't care that she'd almost died. She walked towards the causeway.

'I'm sorry, Betsie, but you needed to know that, so you can forget about James.' Nellie's voice sounded smooth and oily. 'He wanted a new life; well, let him sail off to Australia with a few shillings in his pocket and get on with it. Big coward that he is. He's on his own, at least we've got each other.'

Jiddy turned around. Nellie had an arm around Betsie's shoulders and Annie stood on the other side, quietly watching. Betsie was crying again.

That was exactly what Nellie wanted. The three of them together and she standing at a distance, on her own. Her belly hurt. She hadn't eaten. The breeze made her shiver.

CHAPTER THIRTY-ONE

T he next morning, Mary made Jiddy promise to go up to the hall.

'Folk in Bay believe what they want to believe and you have to get on with it,' she said. 'There's still fire to keep fed, pennies to be earned.' She gave Jiddy a knowing look. 'You have to learn which battles to fight and which to walk away from.'

'Where's Jonas?' said Jiddy.

'Jonas has work to do same as everyone else and farmers can't come keeping you company whenever you fancy.'

She knew that, of course she knew, but sometimes, special times, like today when she'd come through the worst ordeal of her life, she thought he'd make an effort. Maybe he'd heard about James being an informer. Maybe he was waiting for her to go to see him.

'They've caught James Linskill's accomplice.' A man's voice greeted her as soon as she stepped out of the door.

People were hurrying up the bank, some carrying buckets filled with pebbles, others had pots, pans, ladles, whatever they could lay their hands on.

'But we don't know James has done anything wrong,' she said.

'He were a snitch and we've caught his friend. At least we can make him pay.'

'Nasty, two-faced snitch,' said Helen Drake, wielding an empty cooking pot.

People were pushing and shoving. Nellie worked fast. What if she'd said it was Jonas just to get her own back? James' friend. Jonas was James' friend. She'd kill her, she'd absolutely kill her if that's who she'd named.

Behind, in front, coming out of doorways and ginnels, people were everywhere.

'This lad isn't going to know what's hit him,' an old woman said as she pushed Jiddy along.

Jiddy caught hold of Grace. 'Who is it?'

'Some farmhand from the tops. Come on, get a move on. I want to see.' Grace slipped free. 'See if you can find Rebecca. She was off fetching wood earlier.'

Grace swept along up the steep incline. Pressing close to the wall, Jiddy spotted Helen Drake again and this time she was with Dottie. Buffeted by shoulders and arms as the crowd surged up hill.

Annie caught hold of her arm. 'Come on, Jiddy. Nellie and Betsie are saving us a spot.'

Jiddy dragged her back. 'Nellie's accusing anyone she wants and it's not right. It could be Jonas.'

The din was so loud and people were talking all around them, shoving them forward. It was impossible to stand still.

'James Linskill may think he's got away with it, but we'll get this bugger. '

Jiddy pushed forward. Not a stoning. Not another

stoning. This crowd was bigger than the one that had brought Jack Gobbit down. It seemed like everyone had gathered, from the dockside, farms, shops, even the Alum mines along the coast. Everything was getting shaky. It didn't seem as if you could rely on anything anymore. The noise was overpowering and people knocked each other as if they were strangers. There was an excitement to the angry edge. It didn't seem right. The noise jolted her nerves. Women banged pots, their faces livid and yet eager. She'd never seen this many all-together, old and young and in between, wide-eyed bairns being carried, dogs barking and all with a speed unheard of on the steep street. It was even more crowded at the top. People so close you could hardly breathe.

Annie swept to the right towards Nellie and Betsie, who were wielding rocks, and Jiddy remained caught tight by the figures around her. She made out distinct voices, one sounding like that Captain Ryethorpe and other shouts telling the crowd to hold back and then the crack of a gunshot. The dragoons must be in charge. The crack of another shot rang over their heads.

Everyone halted. This wasn't exciting, it was out of hand. Gunshots meant it was serious. She couldn't see. Pushing and shoving, elbowed and sworn at, Jiddy tripped over feet, twisting to slide through, and eventually she scrambled up the mound on the left and clambered onto a wall.

It was unbelievable. The entire population of Robin Hood's Bay had gathered and the racket they made would be heard at Raw it was so loud. At the very top of the hill, higher than the crowd and with a gap in between, Captain Ryethorpe sat on a white and black mottled horse. He held his arm high in the air and fired his gun. The crowd quietened. At least a dozen men made a semi-circle that sheltered a petrified figure. It wasn't Jonas. Thank God, it wasn't Jonas. The man cowering in front of the crowd seemed an odd-looking informer, lean and spindly and petrified. How on earth could James know him?

'Give him to us.'

'Birch him.'

A flurry of pans and utensils flew through the air. This was worse than with Jack Gobbit. Jiddy remembered the blood though. The people near the front had begun throwing stones, ladles and sticks and were shouting. She couldn't make out the words. Their anger unnerved her. Those further back raised whatever they'd brought, waving them and crying out. There was an anger in the air she'd never felt before. People she'd known all her life seemed unrecognisable, as if they'd turn on anyone. This was about more than one informer. This was anger that one too many had turned on them and they wanted someone to pay for it in a big way.

More hammers, sticks and metal pots thudded and crashed. Preventives were there too. Private Gerrard and a couple of others she recognised. Dragoons on their own would never be able to cope with this crowd. Horses, wild-eyed and frisky, stepped backwards. The soldiers on the ground bladed up muskets and readied themselves as the crowd pressed closer. Jiddy had never seen faces she knew so transfigured by hatred. They shouted terrible things at the man, who risked being trampled by horses rather than face the mob. Everybody shouted and yelled and the smell of the horses and sweat was overwhelming.

Balancing against a tree trunk, she strained to see. There he was. A scrawny figure with a bloodied forehead, dirt-ingrained hands and shabby, ripped clothes. He was no fisherman or sailor. It was so obvious he was a jobbing farmhand that it seemed ludicrous he could know anything about the smuggling rings. Stranger still that someone like James would hang around with such a lad. They couldn't be serious accusing a weed like him of being a traitor. Someone needed to say something, bring some logic back into the day. She edged sideways along the wall.

Captain Ryethorpe raised himself in his saddle. 'Settle everyone,' he said.

Voices swelled. Shouting, yelling, chanting. No-one listened, no-one wanted to know. People had gone mad. She had to shout louder to get Captain Ryethorpe's attention. She had to get him to stop it somehow. The noise rose deafeningly. She jumped down, pushed into the crowd, staggered, pushing back, shoving more and more roughly. She didn't feel safe and if she didn't and she knew these people and they knew her, there was no hope for an outsider. She could imagine the soldiers giving him up just to save themselves.

She spotted Betsie and Annie again. As she reached them, Betsie threw stones, but Annie looked scared, chucking a couple of sticks half-heartedly.

'Annie,' Jiddy said, 'are you all right? Where's Nellie?'

Annie dropping her hands by her sides. 'I dunno.'

'We've got to stop this,' said Jiddy, touching Betsie's arm.

Betsie turned, her face changed by a lust for blood. So this was it. She couldn't hurt James but she could hurt this poor lad. Annie's eyes seemed paler and bigger than ever.

'Traitor.'

The word unleashed all the pent-up anger of the mob. Jiddy forced her way up onto the mound. No-one seemed to care who was hit. Dottie was crying and a boy sat with his head in his hands.

The din was so overpowering it hurt. The crowd didn't really care who it was as long as they had someone to blame.

'Steady on, everyone, calm down.'

Jiddy strained to see who had spoken. It sounded like Rebecca but she couldn't see. Typical of Rebecca though. She'd probably grab one of horses and mount up if she could.

'Stop that. Put those down girls.'

She must be nearby.

'Rebecca?'

Captain Ryethorpe didn't stand a chance with a crowd so angry. He had no experience of Baytowners. He wouldn't be able to protect the man for much longer. Jiddy wondered what Captain Horseman was up to. He would have been better dealing with this situation. What could a new captain do? He held up his hand again, pistol ready to fire. The crowd jeered.

'Go back to your homes,' he shouted. 'We're taking John Barrow into custody. Be peaceable and let my soldiers get on with their job.'

Nellie stood at the edge of the clearing, raising a pan. 'I'll throw things at traitor if I want.'

'Too right. He's going nowhere,' shouted Helen Drake.

'Put those down.' That was definitely Rebecca.

'This is between him and us,' said big Isaac McCaw. 'Hand him over.'

The crowd urged Isaac on, goading each other forward. Jiddy spotted Betsie and Annie again, further round. And Rebecca. Thank God. She stood near the soldiers, not far from Nellie.

Captain Ryethorpe leaned down to say something to this John Barrow but the man hesitated and the deputy gave him a shove, nodding to two soldiers to get him away. Ryethorpe signalled for the preventives to move forward. Jiddy hoped that John Barrow would slink away unnoticed and, with no focus, the crowd would tire of their anger and head off home. She'd tell Nellie she knew about Robbie Carter. Tell her she'd heard everything. Then she'd have to decide if she told anyone else.

Hurling abuse, the crowd moved forwards instead of back, grabbing at nervous-looking preventives and reaching out towards the terrified John Barrow, picking up thrown pans, objects, sticks, stones, anything they could pick up. Out-numbered preventives held them back as well as they could. The mounted dragoons steadied their horses and raised their muskets. The villagers were in no mood to give in. They aimed a barrage of pebbles and kitchen ware at the soldiers.

'Move forward together,' Ryethorpe instructed, his gun raised again.

He seemed so different from the aloof gentleman Jiddy had danced with or the passionate man in the preaching house. Here, he looked like a real soldier. A man who could kill. Stones struck metal. Metal struck metal. Fists struck skin.

'Hold your ground,' he ordered.

The Baytowners were too numerous. Several preventives sidled off. One of them deflected a large black kettle. It bounced heavily off the side of his gun and struck a young woman whose bared teeth gleamed against her reddened face. It was out of hand. The captain raised his arm and fired a gun shot. Before the crack of sound had finished its echo, rocks and pans, every object imaginable flew through the air. Jiddy cried out, she couldn't stop herself. Isaac McCaw shouted, his fists raised. The farmhand would be a pulverised pile of clothes like Jack Gobbit if he didn't get out of there. Jiddy looked for Rebecca, hoping someone was keeping her steady on her feet.

'Load your weapons,' Captain Ryethorpe shouted.

Several soldiers fumbled with their guns. A volley of shots were fired. Stones, pots and pans were flying again. People shouted. Some were screaming. Smoke filled the air. Shots hurt her ears. A tiny pebble spun past Jiddy and embedded in a trunk behind her head. She ducked down. Not bullets. This couldn't be happening.

The crowd thinned. Soldiers were lowering their rifles. Smoke settled. A silence rippled out through the crowd until even those right at the back quietened. Jiddy stood up.

People were stepping back, clearing a space. A preventive said something. Skirts were shifting, men shuffling. A clearing opened. Jiddy joined those on the road. Someone cried out. Grace was shouting. Next to her, Dottie clasped her hands to her mouth.

Jiddy shoved her way through, reaching the cleared space as Grace sank to her knees. A large basket lay upturned. Sticks scattered around people's feet and a woman splayed out on the ground.

'Rebecca's been shot,' someone said.

Jiddy ran forward, her eyes on the skirt rucked up around the woman's knees showing thick darned stockings. Kneeling next to Grace, she lifted the woman's wrinkled hand.

'Jiddy's here, Rebecca,' she said.

'Who is it?' someone pushed through, Helen Drake, by the sound of it.

'Rebecca?' Grace said.

'Is she hurt?'

Annie crumpled down, her bare arm touching Jiddy's. Wisps of mousy hair brushing Jiddy's cheek.

'Someone fetch doctor.'

Cries of 'doctor' went up and news that Rebecca had been hurt.

'Is she alive?'

Jiddy couldn't let go of Rebecca's hand. It was too

much. This was too much to bear. She rested her head on Rebecca's chest.

'Come on, Jiddy love, come away,' said Grace, putting a hand on Jiddy's shoulder.

Sitting up, Jiddy looked at Rebecca's face. She knew it so well. That mouth that always had a pithy retort. The high cheekbones and deep-set eyes. They stared, unblinking. She laid a hand on Rebecca's hair. They needed to keep her warm. Pulling off her shawl, she lay it over Rebecca, tucking it underneath her body.

'Annie, do same,' she said. She looked up at the figures standing at a short distance. 'What?' she said, 'can't you spare your shawls? You'll get them back.'

Grace untied hers straight away. Helen and Dottie and others gathered close, laying their shawls over Rebecca's inert body until a soldier pushed through.

'Company doctor,' he said. 'D'you want him or not?'

She'd seen it before, the colour draining from cheeks and tiny red kisses splattering the ground. She wanted sarcastic words and sharp-toned remarks. She wanted Rebecca up and talking and making it difficult. The doctor shook his head and gestured to the preventives waiting near.

Jiddy grabbed Rebecca's body. 'No, you're not taking her.' She couldn't see anything but the muted woollen shawls, greys, brown, russet, black. 'Leave her alone.'

Someone pulled her. Helen Drake and Dottie, hauling her up. 'No. No. I want to stay with Rebecca. Let me go.'

She clutched Rebecca's arm as a soldier lifted her. Silently, people parted to make way.

'Where's Mary?' Helen Drake's voice.

'I'll go.' Must have been Dottie speaking.

'Everyone go back home.'

Captain Ryethorpe stood up in his stirrups. 'They're like animals,' he said.

CHAPTER THIRTY-TWO

Tears streamed down Mary's cheeks. Jiddy didn't even remember her crying at Thomas' funeral. An old woman crying wasn't nice to watch. It wasn't like a child's tears that dried quickly. These quiet tears poured from deep down inside.

'Rebecca were like a sister, weren't she?' said Jiddy, helping Mary sit in a chair by the fire.

'And like a mam to you. I don't know how we'll manage without her,' said Mary.

They sat for a bit, watching the fire engulf the coals.

'If you had to go out early, she was always here to look after me,' said Jiddy.

'And if you weren't up, she'd have something to say about it.'

They fell quiet again.

Later, when she had left Mary in bed, Jiddy looked at the stars through the little window in her room and although exhausted, couldn't sleep. Too much had happened since she and Annie went to Whitby. And she still hadn't seen Jonas. Why hadn't he come to find her? At some point she must have fallen asleep because the next thing she knew, daylight shone through the curtain and Mary shouted that she was heading off to Gracie's to help prepare Rebecca's body for the burial.

'Don't sit and mope,' Mary said when Jiddy sat on the bottom stair watching Mary tie her shawl. 'Think what we always say.'

'Pennies have to be earned,' Jiddy said.

'Yes,' said Mary, 'pennies have to be earned.'

Fastening her skirt and tying her bodice, she repeated the phrase. Every step, on the way up Bay Bank and along Thorpe Road, she said it. 'Pennies have to be earned, pennies have to be earned.'

The stables stood quiet. It was eerie. Here she was, going to darn sheets or begin to alter one of Mrs Farsyde's gowns or maybe a bonnet and Mary was laying out Rebecca's body. It seemed wrong to be here. Clutching her basket, she looked in the kitchen. Cook, kitchen and scullery maids quietly busy at their jobs. The news of traitors in the village and Rebecca's death must have affected everyone. Low voices coming from the library made her pause to listen, wondering if it were Captain Ryethorpe telling the squire about yesterday's riot and Rebecca's death. With the door standing ajar, Jiddy crept closer. The squire seemed to be doing most of the talking.

'It's getting too dangerous for you,' he said. 'You should get out of the country as soon as possible.'

'Not on your life.'

The squire sighed. 'You've been lucky,' he said. 'You've had a good run here and you can always set something up in Holland, say.'

Who was he talking to? It wasn't Captain Ryethorpe. Jiddy put her eye to the crack in the door. The other man stood out of her eye-line. She recognised the voice, though she only needed him to say something else to be sure.

'What do you say, man? You'll go?' said the squire.

Jiddy looked down the corridor towards the kitchens. Someone could come along at any moment and she'd be caught earwigging. Mrs Farsyde would also be wondering where she was. One of them cleared his throat. It sounded rough. Movement. The squire came into view and then the other man. It was Captain Pinkney and they headed towards the door. She shot towards the stairs, stumbling on the first step.

'Jiddy?' Squire Farsyde said.

Holding the balustrade she stepped back down, straightening her skirt. 'Good morning, sir,' she said. 'Morning Captain Pinkney.'

They were shaking hands. 'So who do we have here?' the captain said. 'Been spying on us Jiddy Vardy?'

'No,' Jiddy said, stepping down.

The captain looked at the squire. 'Think she's caught us out, Farsyde,' he said.

Captain Pinkney walked back into the library. 'Come on in, if you are so curious,' he said.

Jiddy didn't need asking again. The captain walked directly to Squire Farsyde's big desk and opening the top drawer, took out a wooden box. The squire remained by the door.

Opening the box, the captain took out a pistol. Jiddy stared. She'd never seen one close up before. The squire didn't say anything, which was unlike him. Everything felt too quiet. No Mrs Farsyde, silence in the kitchen and her in the library looking at a gun. She looked at the squire again.

'D'you want a gander or what?' Captain Pinkney said.

She wasn't sure. It was the squire's pistol but Captain Pinkney handled it as if it belonged to him.

'Yes please,' she said.

'Right. Watch carefully, you never know when you might have to use one of these.'

'Pinkney.' The squire didn't look pleased at all, but the captain took no notice, beckoning Jiddy to stand near him.

She couldn't believe it. She wanted to touch it herself but she didn't dare and she waited for what he'd do next. She didn't wait long. He drew out a thin stick from the side of the barrel and put it down on the table.

'The ramrod,' he said. 'Flints, balls, black powder. Cloth.' He laid a dirty pouch and a box on the table.

He pointed to each in turn. Lifting the pistol, he pointed again, touching the parts this time. 'Barrel, small amount of powder first. Bullet wrapped in a bit of cloth. Tear pieces in advance. Ram down with this.' Lifting the stick, he looked at Jiddy then traced his fingers down the gun. 'Hammer, the flint,' he tapped a small, sharp piece, 'fixed slightly downwards, like this. When you pull trigger, mainspring will release hammer, which powers down flint onto this,' he pointed again, 'the frizzen. You want flint to strike nice and hard so it sparks and sparks should fall into gunpowder which you put here in pan after you've sorted barrel.' He looked at her again. Was she supposed to remember this? It was far too much but she had to look as if she'd understood. There was always a point to whatever the captain told her. 'When you pull trigger, that shifts cover from pan and sparks should drop in from flint, striking frizzen, and boom, off goes your bullet and hits your target. Dead with an hole in him bigger than a rat's head.'

'Simple,' said Squire Farsyde. 'Thank you captain.'

'Jiddy ain't your average young lass, are you my dear?'

Dying to tell Jonas all about it, she nodded. 'Can I have a go?' she said.

Squire Farsyde shook his head and this time, Captain Pinkney listened. 'Watch me go through it again,' he said.

Deftly, he wrapped one of the bullets in a small amount of cloth, poured a little black powder down the gun's barrel and using the rod, pressed them in. Dropping the rod, so the clatter made Jiddy jump, he half-cocked the trigger and dribbled powder into the pan. 'Loaded,' he said.

'Pinkney, man, be careful, Mrs Farsyde will jump into tomorrow if that goes off.'

The captain winked at Jiddy. 'Got it?' he said.

She looked at the gun, eyes moving over each part and mentally repeating the actions. 'I think so,' she said.

'Good. Here, pull again and it's fully cocked and ready to fire,' Pinkney walked to an open window and legs splayed, held out his arm. 'Keep your eye on the target – I've got that tree in sight – and pull slowly on the trigger.'

'Not one of my horse chestnuts.' The squire marched to the window. From behind, Jiddy couldn't see what the captain did next but the wait was excruciating before a loud bang scattered cawing birds out of the wood.

'Goodness, man,' the squire said.

Screams erupted from the back of the house and the squire shook his head. 'I wish you'd take your schooner off to France and leave us in peace,' he said.

'You like a jest,' the captain said, but he was looking at Jiddy.

She didn't take her eyes off his hands as he cleaned out the pistol. 'Flint's still good,' he said to the squire, 'I'll leave it in.'

'If you want me to remember that,' Jiddy said, 'I don't think I will.'

Pointing, the captain repeated the procedure. 'And whatever you do, don't take your eyes off target and don't move while you're waiting for powder to spark.'

'It's a hanging offence if you shoot anyone,' the squire said. 'Jiddy, thought you came here to help your mistress?'

She'd completely forgotten that she was supposed to be upstairs and sewing something together for Mrs Farsyde. The thought of threading a needle after the sound of that pistol seemed so mundane. Captain Pinkney sailed a schooner over the rough North Sea, what was swanning around in a pretty gown compared to that? Looking at the captain's tough, blackened hands putting the pistol and accessories back into the box, she realised she'd much prefer to be his helper than Mrs Farsyde's.

'Run along, Jiddy.' The squire's voice was stern.

'Take note of what I said,' said the captain. 'Learn all

you can from mistress as well, at least that should come easier to you than most.'

'I will,' Jiddy said. She didn't know what he meant but she was definitely going to take any advice he had to offer.

Closing the desk drawer, he tapped the rim of his hat and strode towards the door.

'I hope I don't see you here again,' the squire called after him, and the captain raised one hand.

'Not ready to go yet, Farsyde,' he said before disappearing through the door.

The squire headed after the captain and she was left alone. The big grandfather clock ticked.

Through the open window, she watched a rusty brown fox trot across the grass and wondered if the captain really had put a big hole in one of the squire's trees. How quickly things changed, she thought, how quickly she changed.

The pieces of a dress she'd unpicked only a few days ago lay on the table in the sewing room. She'd been excited about resizing and re-pinning it for her frame instead of Mrs Farsyde's. Today, it all seemed silly. Mrs Farsyde had given her two dresses already, what on earth would she do with a third? She picked up her needle and drew the thread through. Sewing kept her calm and stopped her from thinking usually and that had to be a good thing. She pulled the needle along the seam, up and down, up and down. Her mind filled with all sorts of voices.

'It's your fault.'

'Get yourself out of here.'

'Get back, gerroff, keep moving.'

'I wish we were children again.'

She jumped on hearing Mrs Farsyde enter the room.

'Jiddy, thank goodness. Where on earth have you been? Did you hear that gun go off? The squire will be the death of me one day.' Mrs Farsyde's excited voice filled the room. 'I have an important job for you. My, you're quiet.' She remained silent for a moment. 'I'm sorry, I should have asked, how is Mrs Waite? Such a dreadful accident to have happened. She is no doubt most upset.'

'We're all keeping busy,' Jiddy said.

'That's perhaps best in these circumstances,' said Mrs Farsyde. 'Now let's cheer you up.'

Jiddy gaped at her. They'd just been talking about Mary being upset. Fair enough, Mrs Farsyde might not know about James or that Jiddy nearly drowned, but wasn't Rebecca's death enough? It was as if she hadn't heard or didn't care. If it had been squire Farsyde thrown on a ship that would have been a different matter. What should she say, 'yes, please, cheer me up?'

Mrs Farsyde looked at the pieces of cloth on the table. 'Dresses must wait today,' she said. 'You really must humour me on this. I want to give you something.'

Mrs Farsyde took a gold box out of a cupboard and placing it on the table, unlocked it. What could be inside this one? Mrs Farsyde held up a long gold chain. Dangling from it was a gleaming red droplet like a bloody tear. Walking behind Jiddy, she reached over Jiddy's head and let the droplet fall cold against her skin. Jiddy put her hand over the dark red stone.

'What are you doing, Mrs Farsyde?' she said.

'Sit still while I fasten it.'

Jiddy sat still. The jewel felt heavy and alien against her breastbone.

'It's a garnet,' Mrs Farsyde said, standing back and looking pleased with herself.

'I can't wear this,' said Jiddy. 'Please Mrs Farsyde, don't make me. It's not right I wear your jewellery as well as this dress.'

She couldn't explain it. The necklace was beautiful, but it wasn't for her to wear.

'Please, this is yours,' she said. 'I can't wear it, please take it off.'

'No, Jiddy,' Mrs Farsyde said, 'this necklace is yours to keep and you're going to wear it.'

'Oh no, ma'am,' Jiddy said, filling with panic, 'I can't, it wouldn't be right. Mary would kill me. She'd think I'd stolen it, everyone would think me a thief.'

'Well, you haven't stolen it. I'm giving it to you.'

'Why,' Jiddy said, 'you pay me my wages? Please take it back. It's too kind.'

She couldn't understand. This must be worth so much money. It would pay for food for ten years. It would pay for the cottage. Everything.

Mrs Farsyde stopped Jiddy's hands from unfastening the chain.

'It's a gift and it's not in place of your wage,' she said. 'The red suits you. Honestly, it doesn't suit me at all and

I never wear it. Please. Take it. Have pleasure from it. It will give me pleasure too.'

'Please Mrs Farsyde, people really will think I've stolen it from you.' Jiddy managed to unfasten it and stepped towards the box on the table. Looking down to place it inside, she saw the contents and stopped. Diamonds flashed, sparkling like stars, pearls glowed luminous pale creamy white. Green twinkled and a deep ochre string of glistening beads flashed. She'd never imagined any woman having so much treasure.

'These are beautiful,' Jiddy said.

Mrs Farsyde caught hold of Jiddy's hand, holding the garnet as she closed the box. 'I said I'm giving you this necklace and I don't want to hear another word.'

Jiddy touched the smooth stone. 'Thank you,' she said.

Relocking the box, Mrs Farsyde carried it to the cupboard and placed it on a shelf. She turned the cupboard door key and pocketed it.

'Now we've sorted that,' she said, 'I want you to bring your sewing basket down to the library. Captain Ryethorpe has arrived and he is waiting for you.'

CHAPTER THIRTY-THREE

The last time she had seen Captain Ryethorpe was when Rebecca had been killed, and every time she saw him he did something unexpected, like dancing without hardly saying a word, then making a long speech at the preaching house in front of the whole of the Bay and calling Baytowners animals. She wasn't sure she wanted to find out what he'd be like next.

'Can't I work up here today, ma'am?' Jiddy said.

'Certainly not,' said Mrs Farsyde. She no longer looked friendly. 'Captain Ryethorpe's uniform was torn in the skirmish yesterday, you must have seen, I heard from Abigail that you were there. I still can't believe this and he's only just arrived. I'm ashamed, honestly I am Jiddy, that he comes here and sees people from Robin Hood's Bay behaving like this. You'll soon mend it, you needn't worry. I have full confidence and when you're done, you can work on this gown up here.'

One of his men had shot Rebecca. She wasn't sure she'd be able to control her anger if she saw him.

'Will you be with me?' Jiddy said.

'I don't think that is appropriate,' Mrs Farsyde said, opening the door, 'I'm not a seamstress.'

'It will be easier to mend his jacket up here,' Jiddy said. 'Maybe Abigail could fetch it?'

'I told him you'd do it in the library.' Mrs Farsyde had completely lost her usual friendly air. 'The fire has been lit. He is waiting.'

There was no way out. Mrs Farsyde may pretend they were friends but they weren't. Mrs Farsyde was gentry and she was a commoner. The captain of the dragoons thought the same. He wanted her to mend his jacket and that was that. Simple. That's the role he'd be playing today. The customer. And she was the seamstress. Picking up her sewing basket, she walked past Mrs Farsyde and into the hall.

Mrs Farsyde walked ahead and as they descended the stairs, Jiddy watching Mrs Farsyde's stiff back. Mrs Farsyde didn't want Baytown Jiddy at the hall, she wanted a Jiddy dressed in fine clothes and jewels, like her.

'Jiddy,' Mrs Farsyde said, 'Captain Ryethorpe doesn't have all day.'

He stood by the long window overlooking the garden. Despite her intentions, her hands trembled as she placed the sewing basket on the table by the window.

'Thank you for doing this,' the captain said when Mrs Farsyde closed the door behind her. 'We may have managed to contain the riot yesterday but I didn't come away unscathed.'

Jiddy opened the basket. If she kept her hands busy she wouldn't have to look at him. 'Mrs Farsyde said you've torn something.'

'I take pride in my uniform,' he said. 'A small tear can quickly become an irreparable hole.'

Jiddy took out her needles and a pair of scissors. 'I'll soon have it mended.'

'I was talking with my deputy about the woman that was killed,' he said. 'We were surprised that she tried to stop those young women from hurting Mr Barrow. I noticed you with her. Did you know her?'

Jiddy nodded. If she opened her mouth she wasn't sure what she'd say. She hadn't expected him to mention anything about yesterday but of course he would, his jacket had been ripped during the uproar.

'What happened to Mr Barrow?' she said.

'The poor fellow got away. He's a lucky man.'

'Isn't he an informer?'

'Not to my knowledge, it was a complete distraction. It's a pity that old woman got caught up in the sorry affair.'

'Her name is Rebecca Crowden.' Jiddy looked down at her sewing basket. All the threads in her basket stood out like a bright rainbow. If she concentrated on them she wouldn't have to speak again. Captain Ryethorpe had admitted he didn't think this John Barrow was an informer. It was for nothing that Rebecca had died. It was so unfair she had died for nothing.

He stood next to the table, holding up the hem, so she had to take notice, splaying it to reveal a waistcoat as taut as her bodice across his body. 'As you can see,' he said.

'At least a jacket can be mended,' she said.

She raised her eyes and found he was watching her. She looked down again. She could do this, she'd altered a jacket for Squire Farsyde, letting it out, like his wife's dresses. Rebecca didn't matter to him, nor did John Barrow. Not really. None of them did. It was his clothes that mattered. Play the seamstress, not the Baytowner or the lady.

She looked at the tear. It was merely a seam, pinned in a second. Don't look at his face, that's all, concentrate.

'Can you mend it?' he said.

She nodded, eyes fixed on the red fabric.

'What should I call you?' he said.

'Sir?'

'You don't look like a Miss Vardy.'

'Jiddy.' Putting her in her place. Well, that were fine with her; make life easier.

'Jiddy,' he repeated, as if to brand her.

'Should I call you Captain Ryethorpe or something else?' she said, before she could stop herself. Under the jacket she could feel him straighten. He was taken aback. If she got too carried away, she'd soon be dropping all her 'Ts' and 'Hs' and 'Thes' and calling him a murderer and Mrs Farsyde would shoot through the door and hoy her out of there. Could be the best thing if she were honest.

She took her pins out of the cushion.

'I didn't kill her, you know,' he said.

She waited, trying hard to stay calm. 'I didn't say you did.'

'But you're angry.'

'If you hadn't been firing your guns, she wouldn't be dead.' There she'd said it.

'She wasn't shot,' he said. 'Is that what the village

thinks? Some women came for the body. They know. I'm afraid she was hit by a stone to the head.'

Her hands were shaking.

'You need to take off your coat and turn it inside out,' she said.

He did as she asked, turning the sleeves in on themselves then slipping it back on, seams exposed. She pinned it, a line of silver holding the tear together from neck to waist.

He kept still. A black ribbon held his hair in a softly curling ponytail that reached just below his collar. His shoulders weren't as wide as Jonas' but his slimmer frame felt taut as a newly skinned drum under the palm of her hand as she smoothed out the jacket. She picked up the last pin and slid it into the seam.

'You can take it off now,' she said.

Before she could help him, he jigged the jacket off his shoulders and it slipped down his arms. Catching it before it dropped to the ground, she folded the pinned garment over her arm.

He adjusted his waistcoat. 'Have you ever been to London?'

'I've not even been to York.'

'You're going to mend it here while I wait, aren't you?' he said, sitting on the window seat and crossing his legs as if it was the most casual thing in the world to do. 'Maybe you could tell me what you know about the area, where to visit, what places to avoid? I'm sure they'll be different from Squire Farsyde's anecdotes.'

He was relaxing, making himself comfortable. He'd

completely put aside about Rebecca and was talking almost as if they knew each other. Well, you're no friend of mine.

'I think Captain Horseman will be best telling you what you need to know, if the preventives are going to be staying.' She sat on the window seat, keeping a distance between them and spreading the jacket over her knees, 'Apart from yesterday, Robin Hood's Bay is usually a very quiet place for us locals.'

'And you like that?'

He hadn't picked up on what she'd said about the preventives staying. 'Yes, I like that,' she said.

'The capital, where I am from, is very different from Robin Hood's Bay.'

'No riots there then?'

He didn't answer and she wondered if he was testing her. She'd have to try and listen and be careful what she said. She sounded rude, she knew that, but she couldn't help herself.

'Were you actually born here?' he said.

She stopped mid-stitch. She hadn't expected him to bother to ask her personal questions, only details about the Bay that would help him catch smugglers.

She completed the stitch and stuck the needle through again. 'Why?'

'You don't look like anyone else I've met in the area.'

She forced a laugh, 'I think the gypsies or the fairies left me here.' He was looking at her again as if he didn't understand. 'I'm joking,' she said, 'I've lived here all my life.'

'I'm surprised,' he said. He looked out of the window at the area of grass bordered by trees. She sewed a few more stitches and he continued to look at the garden. She'd soon be finished and the thought of leaving the quiet room didn't make her feel as pleased as she thought she'd be.

'Do you like living in London?' she said.

'Yes,' he said, 'when I'm there. It's a grand, bustling place. I've been to York, but there is no comparison. You say you haven't been?'

She shook her head.

'Do you think there will be a chance of you visiting York or London?' he said. 'Perhaps with Squire Farsyde and his wife?'

'I don't think so,' said Jiddy. 'I don't know if they've ever been to London and I'm not Mrs Farsyde's maid. She'd take Cassie with her if she were to travel.'

'I see,' he said.

He moved gracefully as if nothing took any effort. She smoothed the back of his jacket. To think he'd soon be putting it back on.

'Will you be having another dancing lesson with Mrs Farsyde?' His voice clear. Perfectly pitched.

'I don't know, sir,' she said, 'she didn't say.'

'I wasn't much help,' he said. 'I'm not a good dancer at all.'

He was smiling, actually smiling at her. Was he making a joke? 'Maybe you're the one needing the lessons then?' she said.

'Ah-ah,' he wagged his finger. 'Careful. I may have

to ask Mrs Farsyde's permission to have you act as my practice partner.'

She could feel the heat flare in her cheeks. Was he threatening or flirting? He was certainly waiting for her response.

'I don't think so, Captain Ryethorpe,' she said. 'I don't have much call for dancing and you're a better dancer than you say.'

'You think I'm modest?'

She tried to remember if she'd heard that word before. She had, surely she had, but she couldn't remember.

'I think all captains know how to dance,' she said.

He made a noise. Could have been a laugh and then silence so she continued to sew. Finally, when she thought she must have said the wrong thing, he spoke again.

'What do young ladies do here, if they don't dance?' he said.

What she'd give to dance every night she thought. Dance with a partner who knew how to dance and not jig around like a trapped bee. What did she do? Played around on the beach. Helped out at the farm. Messed around on the clifftop with Jonas, the sound of curlews flying in the sky. Lying in the long grass with Jonas. Kissing Jonas. Kissing. Her whole body felt on fire. Would he notice? Had her cheeks gone red? He was smiling, his long, thin lips making a curvy line.

She held up the jacket. 'I'm a seamstress,' she said. 'I sew.'

'Ah yes,' he said, 'but when you are not sewing?'

She was a smuggler and he wouldn't understand. In his

eyes, she was a thief. She pulled the red cotton through. He cleared his throat.

'In London, for example, the young ladies go shopping, so my father's friend tells me. They spend hours and hours at it. Every day if they could.'

'We don't have many shops here, certainly nothing young ladies from London would like,' she said.

'They learn to play the harp or the keyboard as well. Drawing is a regular pastime, though I suspect most young ladies are making sketches of the latest fashions. You like pretty things, don't you?' he said.

She held the needle still, a tiny pin prick on the fabric. How did he know that? Had Mrs Farsyde been talking about her? She didn't think so. It must be written on her face. She wanted to say something, she was going to, but the way he looked at her stopped her. He was serious. He really wanted to know. Did she like pretty things?

'I'm sure you would like to wear a dress made from fabric you'd picked out yourself in a draper's shop,' he said. 'I know a shop I am certain you would like.'

Fabric. Reams and reams of fabric on a shop's shelves stretching from floor to ceiling. Cottons and silks and frills and bonnets. A pattern she had chosen herself, not passed down to her or loaned for the day. Pinks and blues, yellows and lilac and all she could see at that moment was Captain Pinkney showing her how to use a pistol.

He came into focus. He was smiling. She looked down quickly. Next to the red jacket, her grey skirt shone in the sunlight. One time, that would have made her happy, but not today. She'd almost finished stitching. Two more. What should she ask? She knew so little about what young ladies did.

'Do ladies dance every night?' she said.

'Depends,' he said. So she hadn't said the wrong thing; that was a relief. 'It changes how often balls are held with the time of year and how wealthy the hosts are and if they want to celebrate an occasion on that scale or not.'

She'd finished and soon she'd be upstairs again, piecing together Mrs Farsyde's gown, and she'd never get to ask questions like this again.

'I don't understand,' she said.

'What don't you understand?' He was watching her fingers. Her heart began to race.

'I wish I could wear a beautiful gown and go to a ball,' she blurted out.

'I knew it,' he said. 'You will have to get the Farsydes to bring you to London.'

'Sometimes I do wonder if I was born there,' she said. 'Sometimes, I feel I don't fit in and I'm like a cuckoo in a sparrow's nest.'

She stopped. He wasn't laughing anymore. It had come out in a jumble, all wrong and tied up and he wouldn't understand. How could he when she didn't understand herself? She'd admitted something she had never admitted to anyone. She held out the jacket. She should help him put it on but she wanted to be out of the room as quickly as possible, upstairs, closing the door and alone to hide her embarrassment.

He took the jacket. She sounded like an idiot, babbling about dresses and balls and where she'd been born and birds, for goodness' sake.

'Thank you,' he said, putting on the jacket slowly. He did everything slowly, as if he never had to be anywhere other than where he was. He pulled the jacket straight then rounded his back. The stitches held.

She put the thread and needles back in the box and picked up the scissors.

'I knew you weren't born here,' he said.

'Pardon me?'

He pulled his cuffs straight.

'Please don't tell Mrs Farsyde what I said.' She bobbed a curtsey before heading towards the door.

'Jiddy? Wait a moment. I may call you that?'

'Yes, of course, sir. Everyone calls me Jiddy.'

'You'd suit London, you know,' he said. 'In fact, you put the other young ladies in the shade.'

She clutched the sewing box. It sounded like a trick. Maybe he was going to ask her to be an informer for him and flattery was his way in. Well, she was having none of that.

'Thank you, sir,' she said.

She stood in the doorway, ready to leave. She had one more question.

'Why are you here, sir, if it is so wonderful in London?'

He didn't take his eyes from hers. He was going to say something important, she sensed that. For the first time in the hour or so she'd spent with him, she felt the garnet warm against her collarbone.

'You tell me first, Jiddy,' he said. 'Why do you stay in Robin Hood's Bay when you obviously don't belong here?'

S he didn't know the answer. She was here in the Bay and that was that. How on earth could she go anywhere else? In dreams maybe, but not in real life. Trouble was, the question went round and around in her head.

Why have you stayed here? Why have you stayed when you don't belong here?

Of course the answer was simple. Mary. She could never leave Mary. And now she couldn't leave Jonas. And people from Yorkshire didn't go to London anyway. And people from Robin Hood's Bay certainly didn't go any further than Scarborough. But still the question niggled: why, when you don't belong here?

She should have asked him more about London. She should have asked if there were people who looked like her there. Where did he think she was from? Oh, why hadn't she taken longer to mend his jacket? Now she'd never have another chance. Stupid, stupid, stupid.

At the end of the afternoon, when she'd tacked the pieces of gown together and Mrs Farsyde had approved, Jiddy stood outside Thorpe Hall, wondering where to go. She looked back at the hall's mullioned windows reflecting late afternoon sunshine and she wondered what it would be like to wake up there. Not a breeze stirred. Not even the birds were singing. She looked across the fields that bordered the garden. She couldn't face the jostle of houses or the Bay hemming her in, not after yesterday. It seemed natural to go up to the farm, what with Mary's neighbours sitting in to keep her company, talking about their hatred of the preventives and dragoons and how hard done by they were.

Sitting at the table in the Chaplow's dark kitchen, she watched Jonas eat. For some reason, his silence irritated her. He'd obviously come in, poured himself a bowlful of soup and sat straight down to eat it. No washing his hands or face, no combing his wind-tangled hair. And even though she had arrived, he continued to ladle soup from his bowl to his mouth and then another dripping spoonful and slurp it in again.

She pushed the basket, laden with offcuts and leftovers, to one side. He supped another spoonful. She hadn't seen him since the night he'd brought her back from Whitby and now he sat there ignoring her.

'Are you mad at me?' she said.

'Why would I be mad at you?'

'I don't know. You seem it.'

'I'm tired, that's all.'

He did look tired, but he often did and usually that didn't stop him talking.

'Are you mad at dragoons?' she said, pulling her chair closer. 'If it weren't for them James wouldn't be headed off in that ship somewhere and…' She stopped. It seemed hard suddenly to say Rebecca's name.

'It's government I hate,' he said. 'Officers like that

new captain, trying to wheedle themselves into our good books by making fancy speeches.'

She tucked the cloth neater around the packets inside the basket.

'They may only want to be friends,' she said. 'The captain must be lonely, so far from his family.'

'Don't be daft. Men like that don't want friends. They're only out for the-selves and will stamp on anyone to get further up ladder and then pull it up so no-one can follow.'

'Here.' She pushed back the cloth and took out half a loaf of bread, 'have some of this with your soup.'

Picking up a knife, she cut a piece.

'James were a stupid beggar to get caught,' he said.

'He shouldn't have been out.' She stopped. Every subject now seemed full of pitfalls.

'I don't blame myself, if that's what you're bothered about,' he said, slurping another spoonful, 'I couldn't do trip and he could. End of.'

'Have some bread.'

Jonas shook his head and drank the thin soup. His face was hidden between the bowl and his wavy hair.

'Are you sad that James has gone?'

'Course I'm sad,' he said, 'but there's nowt to be done about it. James'll be all right. He can look after himself. But if you ask me, it's a bit of an extreme way to get out of Betsie's clutches. I suppose a lad's got to do what he must though, hey?'

'Betsie is heartbroken.'

'I'm jesting with you.'

'No you're not.'

'I just mean good luck to him. May be a better life where he's going.'

'He weren't an informer,' Jiddy said.

'I know. Nellie will say anything to get attention.'

'If you know, why are you so flippant?'

'It's done,' he said.

Rex spread out on the rug, head on his paws. It was a big fire in the grate and the room was warm.

'I didn't tell you, but I saw Nellie, you know, in woods with Captain Horseman's deputy,' she said. There. It was out. She put down the knife.

Jonas closed his eyes for a moment. 'I'm tired Jiddy,' he said. 'I just want to eat, get some sleep and not think about anything. I'm not interested in who Nellie is favouring now.'

'It were more than that,' Jiddy said, 'she wants to leave Bay.'

'Great. Let her go.'

'She were doing things for him, telling him things so he'd take her with him when they go.'

'No business of mine, Jiddy, or yours. You hate her. You should be glad she wants to go.'

'She's telling people James were informer when he wasn't. It's her, you know, she's informer. I even think she could have killed Rebecca.'

'Oh give over.'

'I think she threw a stone and hit Rebecca on purpose.'

He slurped his soup again. Took another spoonful. 'Stones were being lobbed all over place from what I hear,' he said. 'I know Rebecca were dear to you, Jiddy, and you'd like to blame someone, but it were a miracle there weren't more people struck with stones people were flinging.'

'That's what Captain Ryethorpe said.'

He paused again and she knew she shouldn't have said that. Reaching forward, he took a piece of bread and wiped out the bowl.

'Rebecca were sticking up for the farmhand they'd accused and she'd also told Nellie and Betsie to stop throwing things, Nellie wouldn't have liked that.'

'When were you talking to Captain Ryethorpe about it?'

'I haven't been.' She took a deep breath. 'Mrs Farsyde made me mend his jacket and because I were there at riot yesterday, he said something about me knowing Rebecca. I guess he'd seen me with her when she were carried off and asked if we were close.'

'And you said?'

'I said we were. And Mary was and that we'd all thought dragoons had shot her with gunfire going off, but he said they weren't going to be blamed for it. Someone in crowd, one of Baytowners, had done it. Typical southerners, trying to wheedle out of it. But it makes sense, Nellie were close and…'

Her words petered out. She was waffling, saying things she didn't mean.

'Jonas?'

He carried on wiping the bowl, though it was now so clean it wouldn't need washing.

'What do you think?' she said.

'I think you should talk to your new friends about it, they seem to know what's what.'

'What new friends?'

He threw the last morsel of bread into the bowl and pushed it away. 'You're spending a lot of time up at hall,' he said.

'You're one that said what a good job it is.'

'Aye, you get well paid for idling about in fancy frocks with that new captain.'

'Is that why you're sulking?'

'Is that why you're having a go when I've told you I'm exhausted?'

Jiddy looked at the door. Mr Chaplow should have come in by now. There really must be more to farming some days than others. Jonas' hands were dark with soil. Two chairs stood near the fire. Dreaming, Rex kicked out a back leg. Buckets and sticks clustered around the door. It was another world at the farm compared to the hall. She shouldn't have come, neither were in the mood for talking. She should have gone straight home to Mary no matter how many neighbours were there.

'Would you like to live somewhere else rather than here?' she said.

His eyes looked tired. His hair more matted than usual.

'I don't think about things that can't happen,' he said.

'I'd go where nobody were poor.'

'Poor are everywhere, Jiddy.'

'I just want out of here, Jonas, can't you understand that? I want a better life.'

'You don't know what you want.' Folding his arms on the table, he buried his face.

'Oh, for goodness' sake, what about you?' she said. 'Jonas? What about London? You could make your fortune there?'

'I'm fine here.'

'Stop it, Jonas. I think London would be a fine place to be, don't you?' she said. 'Jonas? Where would you pick if you could pick anywhere in the whole world?'

'Bed.' His voice came out muffled.

She pushed back her chair. He didn't move. She knew by his shoulders he was in a stubborn mood. 'I wish I lived up at Thorpe Hall, at least there I get decent conversation,' she said.

He lifted his head. 'Why don't you then? Ask Squire Farsyde if you can be a lady up at hall and have a fine old time with Mrs Farsyde and that captain of yours. Better still, why don't you go off to London with him and have a better life.'

'He's not my captain,' she said, 'and I don't want to go to London with him.'

'You looked happy enough dancing with him.'

She couldn't believe it. This wasn't what she wanted, this was so far from what she meant.

'I nearly drowned,' she said. 'James has been shipped off, Rebecca is dead and I'm only saying I want something better.'

'You've never danced with me.'

'Don't be such a pudding head!' she shouted. 'Get up, come on, get off that lazy backside and let's dance.' She grabbed his arm, pulling him. 'Come on, get up. Let's dance, if it's more important than all the horrible things that have happened.'

He pulled his arm free, sitting back in his chair. 'I'm sorry about Rebecca,' he said.

'So you should be. Mary's heartbroken. So am I. It's not right. It may not have been Nellie, I don't know, but I hate all this. I hate Robin Hood's Bay.'

'Saying you hate Bay is like saying you hate me,' he said.

'Well, right now, I do! And for your information, Mrs Farsyde made me dance with Captain Ryethorpe. I didn't want to but I have to do everything she says and I hate having to do things other people tell me all the time. Look, she even said I have to wear this.' She pulled the chain out from under her dress and held out the garnet.

He tipped his head sideways, his eyes dark in shadow.

'Jonas, Jonas.' Sitting herself back down, she dragged his hands towards her. 'Can't you make some effort? I'm here, aren't I?' she said. 'And God knows why when you didn't come and see me like you said you would. You came all the way to Whitby to find me and bring me back to Bay and Mary lets you sleep night and then you vanish. What's that about? Did you think you'd done your bit, you'd got me safely back and all's fine now?'

'It's a nice necklace.'

'Agh.' She pushed his hands away.

'I told you I'm shattered,' he said.

'Yes, you have a ton of work to do on farm, you always do, and I got caught up with Baytowners out to get that poor so-called informer's blood and he got away and Rebecca were killed and I do think Nellie did it.' She stopped. Her heart caught. Someone had killed Rebecca. Her Rebecca. Rebecca who gave her cuddles and reprimands all in a bundle. She looked down. Her heart might burst. 'Say something Jonas, say something to make it better,' she said.

'Nellie's a pain in the backside,' he said, 'but I've known her all my life, so have you. Her da worked for my da on farm before he fell to drink. You shouldn't go accusing fellow Baytowners, Jiddy. Whatever her faults, she's loyal.'

What could she say? She sounded petty. She didn't want to sound petty.

'Nellie would go to London if she could and have a different life,' she said.

'Stop it Jiddy, this isn't you and I don't like it. Don't talk about our friends like that.'

His hair was matted and dusty from the hay. His eyes half closing he was so tired. It wasn't the same. It really wasn't the same as it had been when they were young.

'We hardly see each other anymore,' she said, 'and when we do have a chance, you don't believe anything I say.'

She looked at his dirty hands flat on the table. He'd known Nellie all his life. His family knew Nellie's family. She were a local lass, he were a local lad. No matter how close they got, she would always be an outsider.

Captain Ryethorpe's words rang in her head. 'Why do you stay when you don't belong here?'

She picked up her shawl, making a big gesture of shaking it out. 'I'll be off then, seeing as you need to get to your bed.' She couldn't look at him. She hated herself for this change, this great foaming storm. A mist shimmered behind his eyes. He was exhausted what with farm and then nights on the Salt Road dropping contraband off to keep innkeepers and farmers happy, and the one time he hadn't done it, James got himself arrested and thrown on a ship. He just wanted some quiet and here she was demanding that he give her some attention and accusing him of not knowing what was going on.

'It doesn't matter,' she said. 'Let's not argue. Go call your da. He must be starving. I'll see you tomorrow.'

She watched him pull on his jacket and walk outside. Rex lifted his head, scrambling to his feet and padding across the rug. Picking up the basket, she looked around the room before stepping into the yard. The faint tendrils of a sea fret drifted through the air.

'Jonas?' she said.

The yard stood empty. Mister Now-you-see-him-now-you-don't.

CHAPTER THIRTY-FIVE

T he fret soon uncurled, quickly thickening to a heavy mist, and by the time she reached Lingers Hill it had drawn white cloud up from the sea, settling its cold breath over the countryside. Jiddy stood still. A noise tapped behind. She didn't like it. The mist, as wafts of breeze made it shift, closed in again, exposing her to who knew what. She shivered. The Lingers Ghost could be real and not a myth they used to keep the road clear of preventives when a run was on. Don't think about it, she told herself, there were no such things as ghosts, only people dressed up as them. Inching sideways, she reached out tentatively until she touched a tree trunk. Thank goodness. Slipping between the trees, she waited. A breeze blew and the mist parted again, revealing the shape of a rider made grey by the moist cloud. She pressed herself against the tree trunk, thankful for something real and solid against her back. She should have gone straight home after leaving Thorpe Hall, not up to the farm. Her heart beat harder. What if the rider heard her? Or sensed her? Ghosts picked up vibrations, didn't they? It could be a ghost. She pressed close to the tree trunk and screwed her eyes up tight. Nothing happened. Opening her eyes, she stepped away from the trees. The mist cleared further and a horse revealed itself, large and mottled black and white. The red uniform of a dragoon rose out of its saddle.

'Who is there?' The voice sounded nervous. She recognised it. It was Captain Ryethorpe. He lifted something. A rifle.

'It's me.' Putting down the basket she walked forward. 'Jiddy Vardy.' She pushed the shawl off her head so he could see her. He kept the rifle raised. 'From Thorpe Hall,' she said. 'I mended your jacket today.'

'Jiddy?' She heard the relief in his voice and she stepped by the horse's flank.

'Are you lost?' she said. 'Sea frets are terrible for making you lose your way.'

He slotted away the rifle, his black hat disappearing as the cloud sank again. The horse nudged against her. The captain's face, shoulders then torso shrouded in white. His thighs faded, then the black boots until she only knew he was there because his horse rested against her and its breath warmed her face.

'Are you still there?' his voice, less sure again.

She touched his leg, the smooth boot of his calf a reminder. 'I'm here.'

He didn't respond. The horse snorted. There was a creak of leather and movement. And then there he was, sliding through the mist and landing beside her, so close there wasn't a gap of air between them.

'Where are you going?' she said.

'Thorpe Hall.'

She pointed a finger over her right shoulder.

'Am I far off?' he said. He swallowed. He was afraid.

To think, a captain of the dragoons was scared by a little bit of mist and she could either help him find his way or send him completely off track.

Her heart beat fast.

'Keep woods on your left after the bend and follow the road. It's a little way. When you reach a sort of rough crossroads, you head left, downhill, but you'll have to watch you don't miss the entrance otherwise, well, you'll end up in sea if you keep on going.'

It was off putting, but she held his gaze. Up at the hall, or at Musgrave Inn, he might be in charge, but here, out in the open, she had the upper hand.

'We wouldn't want to lose a new captain to the North Sea,' she said.

The look of concern on his face made her wish she'd never said it. Her words sounded crude, like a sledge hammer hitting an apple. Soldiers were usually tough, rough men. Captain Ryethorpe was a gentleman.

'Are you out here on your own?' he said, looking past her as if he'd be able to make out an entire army of cutthroats.

The mist grew thicker. He was disappearing again. He stepped in, one hand still holding the reins that looped next to her. She held his gaze. Even in the mist, his eyes pierced blue. She'd never seen any so even coloured before. Blue from the edge to centre, paler than a cornflower, deeper than a forget-me-not. A long, narrow nose like a real gentleman's nose and a mouth, narrow and fine. She wondered what his lips would taste like. Stop it, she corrected herself. Stop it. He's a dragoon. He's a captain and a gentleman; he's the enemy. And then in an awful moment, she realised that she was the same as Nellie. Both of them wanted a better life, a different life from the one they had. He knew it too. He knew she liked pretty things and she would love to dance at a ball. That's what Nellie wanted too and Jiddy hated the thought of them being the same. Slip away, run, she urged herself. You're nothing like Nellie.

'It's dangerous out here for a lady alone,' he said. 'Please allow me to escort you wherever you are going.'

She choked back a nervous laugh. If he realised what she really got up to, he wouldn't hesitate in arresting her on the spot. 'I'd not call being with the captain of the dragoons, alone,' she said.

His eyes hid behind blond lashes. 'Where are you heading?'

Jiddy nodded behind him. 'Home,' she said.

Blue eyes fixed on hers, holding her to the spot. A gust of wind parted the mist and her hair lifted, brushing her face. She pulled it back and his breath wrapped around her ear. Noses almost touching. Breath passing between them.

Her eyes held his attention now, she could see that. She knew their power. She could lower her thick lashes and look up again. She could step closer. She could hold him to the spot too. They were both trapped by the thickening mist, their senses tingling and no-one around to see.

'You really shouldn't be out.' His voice caught in his throat. 'There are dangerous men on the roads.'

She must keep up this facade. She stood even closer to him. It felt as if they were caught in a web, made all the more tantalising by the beads of sea fret that shone a gossamer of diamonds on their hair. The horse breathed heavily next to them. There was no-one but them, no-one to see. They could do anything, she could be anyone and tomorrow it wouldn't be real. At that moment, she wanted to feel his lips against hers and taste whatever he tasted like. He wanted to, she could tell by the way his eyes strayed to her mouth. Her hair blew across her face again and she lifted it away. There was only one thing stopping her: Jonas. If Jonas saw them, he'd be hurt and he'd show it by being angry. She knew him inside out. His lips that kissed with the pull of a whirlpool and his taste of moorland grass and summer days. She'd let him touch her and she wanted him to do that again. It couldn't be this captain she wanted, it was Jonas. The mist was tricking her. She pulled back.

'It's that way to Thorpe Hall.' Her hand shook as she pointed left.

'I can't leave you here alone,' he said, his face showing signs of worry.

'I know a short cut,' she said. 'And besides, smugglers won't be bothered about me. They're more likely to slit the throat of a dragoon than a woman any day.'

He wasn't buying it, peering into the shapes of the trees as if he'd spy a murderer there. She had to do something and, feeling the ground with her foot, she touched the horse's hoof. Tracing up its leg, she tapped its knee with the toe of her shoe. It shifted back, pulling the captain with it. As soon as he looked away to see what had spooked the horse, she picked up her skirts and ran.

CHAPTER THIRTY-SIX

I t seemed as if she'd dreamt about Captain Ryethorpe all night, but opening her eyes to the morning light, she thought of Jonas. He had always been the one who grounded her, making any dilemma go away, but this was something she could never tell him about. She couldn't tell him or anyone about last night. Pushing back the bed cover, she crawled to the window. Gulls cawed out. The sky was pale, but clear. Morning really had come too soon.

Voices rose up from downstairs and Jiddy sagged back on the bed. Already, women from the village had called in to see Mary and she didn't know how Mary stood it. Surely she would want to be just the two of them by now? Jiddy looked out of the window again at the rooftops.

'What time does Jiddy call this?' Helen Drake's mean voice. 'Are you going to let her sleep all day, Mary?'

That was it. Scrambling out of the window, hips scraping against the window frame, Jiddy wriggled out, sliding down the shed roof and landing on the flags at the back. Sunny Place was empty but Jiddy could still hear the women talking inside. She opened the door.

Grace clasped her large soft chest. 'Oh my.'

Mary stood up. 'What's going on?' she said.

'Nowt,' said Jiddy, 'just letting you know I'm heading out.'

'Haven't you heard of stairs?' said Grace.

'Haven't you heard of knocking?' said Helen Drake.

Mary hushed them with one hand. 'Where are you going?'

'Not sure,' said Jiddy. 'Annie's maybe. Tide's in, so I may head to preaching house and pester Reverend Cook.'

She pulled back, shutting the door quickly. That was it. The reverend would tell her what to do. She could tell him about Nellie and he wouldn't admonish her like Jonas. He'd be calm and weigh it up. He'd tell her to leave it with him.

She hurried down the slope and left towards the preaching house. Carefully closing the heavy door behind her, she looked to see if the reverend was there. The room was always so different without a congregation. Long empty benches, plain walls rising high to dark beams, demanding silence. Sunlight filtered through windows, highlighting spots on the floorboards. It was early. Reverend Cook was probably finishing his breakfast but even if he didn't come, she could stay all day and no-one would know and that may give her the peace she needed to get her head straight. She wondered if he would have left any bread in the vestry.

Sitting on the front pew she looked at where she'd knelt at the Sunday service. It seemed an age ago. She clasped her hands together; maybe she should pray? Someone knelt in the shadow at the far end of the alter. How come she hadn't noticed them? They were so quiet.

She'd been so quiet. They obviously wanted to be alone, maybe she should come back another time? The person stood up and Jiddy's heart sank.

'What are you doing here?' Nellie said, her blotched face showing she'd been crying.

'It can wait,' Jiddy said, standing to go.

Nellie came forward, her watery eyes hardening. 'Stop right there.'

'It's all right, Nellie,' said Jiddy, 'I'll leave you to it.'

'Why are you really here? Reverend Cook isn't about.'

Jiddy grasped the end of a pew. 'Why are you here so early?' she said.

Nellie took a step closer. 'Shouldn't you be up at hall leaving your slime around Mrs Farsyde?'

'Not my day,' Jiddy said.

'Then you should be with Mary.'

Jiddy folded her arms. 'I know you're upset about Deputy Carter,' she said.

'Shut up,' Nellie said, 'you don't know anything.'

'It's all right, Nellie,' said Jiddy, 'I understand why you like him.'

'Shut your gob, Jiddy Vardy. You don't know anything about me.'

'I know you want to get out of here.'

Nellie's eyes filled watery grey and she struggled to reply. 'You don't know,' Nellie said, her words shaky. 'Everything always goes right for you.'

Jiddy put her hand on the end of a pew, wanting to pat Nellie's arm, touch her hand, or something. 'It doesn't, honestly, it doesn't.'

Nellie was desperately trying to hold back her tears and her face contorted with the effort.

'He promised,' Nellie said. 'And then he said he wouldn't take me with him. He lied and I don't know what to do.'

She was on the edge of breaking down completely. It was hard to watch and Jiddy racked her brain trying to think what to say.

'I won't tell anyone,' she said.

Wham. Nellie slapped Jiddy hard across the cheek. Her skin seared red and hot and she raised her fist. Catching her wrist, Nellie twisted Jiddy's arm and she ended up with her back to Nellie. Struggling to break free, she bumped her backside into Nellie's pelvis, but Nellie held on, tightening her hold until Jiddy thought her arm would snap.

Their breaths punctuated the creak of floorboards. Jiddy stumbled backwards and losing balance, she pulled Nellie with her. Scraping between the pews, they fell, Nellie slumping down hard on top. Trapped and bruised, Jiddy lay still. The back of her skull hurt. Everything hurt.

'I've wanted to do this for a long time,' Nellie said, spittle dripping onto Jiddy's face.

Unable to free her hands, Jiddy shook her head from side to side and, catching a whiff of Nellie's acid breath, she angled her face towards the wooden seat.

Nellie lowered her face. 'Too right, you're not going to tell anyone,' she said.

Jiddy jolted her body, pressing both hands wherever

she could, until she kneed Nellie in the thigh. Nellie punched Jiddy's ribs and the pain caught her breath.

Trying to back out, Nellie couldn't find leverage. Struggling against each other, the chain slipped free, twisting around Jiddy's neck and the garnet clunked against the floor. Nellie's body came crushing down. Heavy thighs and larger breasts pressing the air from Jiddy's lungs.

They remained like that for some minutes, both exhausted. Neither of them could move. Hot, struggling to breathe, Jiddy panted into Nellie's face, trying not to panic that her breath grew increasingly shallow.

Shoulders, then hands pressing on Jiddy's chest, Nellie groaned as she sat up, wriggling to sit on Jiddy's pelvis.

'Not so clever now, are we?' said Nellie.

'So it's clever to sit on me all day, is it? Well, I don't have to be anywhere.'

Nellie looked as if she'd been slapped by a giant cod. Her eyes glazed cold and the high colour in her cheeks faded.

'I can sit on you for days until you promise to keep your fat mouth shut,' Nellie said.

'Why don't you make a promise if you're so keen? Why don't you promise to tell everyone you're a … ow!'

Nellie bounced down hard on Jiddy's pelvis.

Leaning over so that her nose almost touched Jiddy's, Nellie pressed her hands down on Jiddy's black curls and slowly licked Jiddy's cheek. It was the most disgusting sensation Jiddy had ever felt. Rough and sticky with a lingering fish smell. It came again, thick and sludgy.

If this were the torture that witches were given, Jiddy guessed how they'd yearn to die. Stones would weigh less than Nellie's bulk, pressing heavy, her mouth open, breathing hard, the rottenness of old meat spilling out.

Jiddy wondered how long it took to stop breathing and for how long she could stomach taking in Nellie's pungent breath. She lifted her head, but unable to sustain it, she soon dropped down again and closed her eyes. She couldn't bear Nellie's face so close, breathing hot breaths. She'd be sick. Nellie's groin leaden against hers, their breasts squashed, thighs pressing. She was suffocating. And then Nellie's face moved. What was she doing?

Nellie held the chain in her teeth and the garnet dangled cold against Jiddy's face.

The latch on the front door clicked open. A moment later, the door closed. Footsteps. Jiddy raised her head.

'Help! Jiddy said as loud as she could.

The chain slipped back over her cheek, the garnet hitting the floor by her ear. Nellie's head brushed down the side of her face, wiry hair brushing skin. As Nellie bit hard into her neck, Jiddy screamed. The sound filled the chapel, echoing down the pews and up to the roof. Reverend Cook or whoever had come in was too slow. She was going to die. She turned her head. The pain tore through her skin. Strands of Nellie's hair blurred in front of her eyes, turning from brown to grey to black as she lost consciousness.

CHAPTER THIRTY-SEVEN

Jiddy sensed rather than saw Nellie prise herself up. Footsteps echoed and the big door slammed. And then the room became so still, she could hear dust spiralling in the air and the vein in her neck pulse. Footsteps broke the quiet, moving towards her, measured and slow until they stopped at the end of the pew.

'Good Lord.' The words sounded surprised, spoken low. It was a man's voice.

There were some awkward noises.

'Jiddy?' She recognised the voice but still didn't open her eyes. She couldn't. This was too dreadful. She didn't want to look at anyone and now she recognised who it was, she certainly didn't want someone like him seeing her as a rough Baytowner caught in a scrap. Although she knew he'd be studying her, if she didn't actually see his eyes react to her rucked-up skirt, tangled hair and the bite on her neck, she could pretend this wasn't happening.

'Are you able to move?' he said. 'Can you give me your hands and I'll help you up?'

He wasn't going to go away but could she raise her hands? Did she even want to? It would be so much easier to lay still. She cradled her arms across her belly and turned her head so that her bleeding neck was hidden against the floor. The vein throbbed and the wound stung like a cut on a winter's day. She swallowed. Go away, leave me in peace.

There was that shuffling noise again. His feet edged against her legs then her hips. His hands slid under her shoulders, his fingers tightening into the flesh of her upper arms. He groaned. She must be heavy. As she rose off the floor, his hands moved behind her back and she scrambled with her feet, like running on the spot. Woosh. She stood, bashing straight into his chest, the embossed buttons pressing into her cheek. He held her tight, shuffling back and then they were out of the pew and she felt the revealing space of the room. Stepping away, he released her shoulders then arms, until all that touched were their hands. She opened her eyes.

He was bending forwards, concern in every feature on his face, and he was swaying. How fuzzy he was, his uniform not crisp and neat at all. And then she realised he wasn't swaying, she was. Her knees gave way. He was catching her and the room went black.

She was floating, up and down, rising and falling, a lullaby of warmth, with something, a pain, jabbing her neck. She was a baby, held in someone's arms, cradled and rocked. Something touched her neck, a splash of surf, a feather stroking, cleaning, soothing.

She felt wood beneath her. Solid floorboards. Dry wood and dust. The wound stung sharp. Her vein pulsated. Raw skin and globules of blood bursting into rivers. She rocked. Was the preaching house afloat? Had the sea washed all the way up Bay Bank from the causeway and borne them away? Hair brushed her cheek.

Soft hair, unlike Nellie's. Something warm touched her neck, moving up and down, so gently and then round in a soothing whirlpool. Her head lolled sideways, she wanted its comfort to continue. Sleepy, so sleepy, like a kitten being taken care of by a tabby cat. The movement reached through her skin, into her sinews and down the muscle in her neck. There was suction now, a pain tinged with a hypnotic pull. The softness of a tongue, a gentle scrape of teeth and lips holding the wound together. It almost felt like a mouth. She turned her head slowly, her eyes still closed. She didn't want to see, she only wanted to feel. Moving like a blind kitten, nuzzling under his chin, searching, pushing, she found what she was looking for. Her lips met the mouth that had been soothing her wound and her tongue tasted blood. It was her own blood. Slipping her arms around his neck, bringing him closer, feeling his heart pump against hers, she tasted more. His kiss was comforting. He was tasting her and she wasn't alone.

A brush of cold air wafted in. He pulled back. No. She wouldn't let him, she clung on, stay with me, stay. His arms tightened around her back. Thank God, thank God. Footsteps bumped heavily. Go away, go away.

'Jiddy?' A familiar voice. 'I thought Nellie were stirring it when she said you were only biding your time with me until something better came along.' There was a catch in the voice. Damage. 'I see she were right.'

'Jonas?'

Pushing against the bright red uniform, Jiddy rolled onto her knees. Her neck throbbed painfully. She felt hot, cold, fire. Wiping her mouth, she rubbed blood onto the back of her hand. Next thing, the captain took her arm and helped her to her feet and she held onto a pew to steady herself.

'Who are you, sir?' the captain said.

'None of your business.'

'Jonas, please, take my hand,' Jiddy said, reaching out, 'Come home with me.'

Jonas' eyes gleamed cold and he turned abruptly back to the door. Stumbling forwards, she almost fell. 'Don't go.' Stamping, crashing footsteps. 'No, stay!' Bang. The door slammed.

She ran, hands splaying against the door to stop herself. She grabbed the door handle. It wouldn't fully turn. Rattling it back and forth, she kicked the door. 'Open! Open!' she shouted.

The captain strode after her, his boots cracking their heels on the floor. He edged her aside, but she elbowed him back, 'I can do it,' she said, grabbing the handle with both hands and twisting.

'You're not well enough,' he said. 'Let me find a dressing for your wound in the vestry. I'll bathe and bandage it properly.'

She pushed and pulled the handle but the door wouldn't open.

'Please, let me escort you.'

'Why won't the door open?' She kicked it again.

'You're not steady. I'll walk you home when you're fully yourself,' Captain Ryethorpe said again, touching her arm.

She felt dizzy, sick, confused. Blood smeared dry on her fingers. 'No, you can't come with me,' she said.

'Who is that man? Is he somebody close to you?' he said, standing back. 'I can explain you were bleeding and I did the best I could without a medical kit. Saliva does heal. I apologise if I hurt you, but on the battlefield if we have nothing else we use spit.' He reached out but she slapped his hand away. Spit. She felt cold and shaken. She had to get out.

Another twist and the door opened. Fresh air snapped her face. Gulls cried as they usually did. Noises, voices, everyday sounds filled the fuzziness in her head. Jonas. She had to find Jonas.

Low Street stretched out empty. As she reached the end, she heard the captain behind her.

'Go away,' she said, 'I cannot be seen with you.'

Hand on the wall, she looked up at Mary's cottage in Sunny Place. A crowd of people filled the square all the way to Mary's door and more people were coming from Bay Bank and turning up the shallow steps.

Nellie pointed towards Jiddy and Captain Ryethorpe who stood at her side, his hand around her waist. 'There she is, the traitor.'

CHAPTER THIRTY-EIGHT

Jiddy pushed through the crowd as people jostled against her, elbows and shoulders bashing and shoving, but she kept going. Some stepped back to watch and she kept her head down, she had to get to Mary. Reaching the steps, she looked straight at Helen Drake.

'Have you seen Jonas?' Jiddy said.

Helen filled her mouth with saliva and spat.

Betsie and Annie huddled together, staring in disbelief next to Nellie, who stood in front of her now, hands on hips, fully recovered from the tussle in the preaching house.

'Let me past,' said Jiddy.

'I told you,' Nellie shouted at the crowd, 'turning up with her fancy man, bold as brass, thinking she's above suspicion. Have you see love mark on her neck?'

People mumbled. One or two shouted out agreement. Jiddy tried to push Nellie aside but quick as a bullet, Nellie shoved back and losing her balance, Jiddy stumbled into the crowd. Hands caught her.

'Is Jonas here?' Jiddy said to Annie. But, paler than ever, Annie shook her head, before looking at Nellie.

'Betsie?' Jiddy said.

Betsie shrugged and glanced at Nellie. Someone tugged Jiddy's skirt from behind. It was Helen Drake.

She spat again.

The word came from the crowd, whispered again, and repeated into a chant. She spun around. Danger sparked the air. Boots began stamping. The quickening beat in her chest began to hurt. She couldn't see the captain.

'Traitor.' Someone prodded her in the back. 'Traitor.' The word was taken up.

To her right, she saw a pan raised in the air. More and more pressed into the space. Jiddy's heart pumped harder. Nellie looked triumphant.

'Jonas found you with captain of dragoons,' she said. 'You've lost him, Jiddy Vardy, he hates you now; he hates you because you betrayed him like you've betrayed all of us.'

Jiddy leapt up the steps, banging Nellie against the door. 'You sent him. You set me up.'

The crowd drowned out her voice. She saw blood and anger and she shook Nellie as hard as she could. Nellie grabbed Jiddy's hair and yanking it upwards revealed Jiddy's neck and the smarting bite.

'There,' shouted Nellie, and those nearest pulled Jiddy around, 'see the love bite Captain Ryethorpe gave her.'

A rolling pin struck her across the back. She crumpled, knees bashing the top step, her hands slapping the flags. Tensing for the next blow, she closed her eyes, but it didn't come. A black pair of shiny knee-length boots stepped next to her. She looked up. Captain Ryethorpe stood where Nellie had been and he was facing the crowd.

He held up two hands as if in surrender.

Jiddy faced the crowd next to him. Surrounding faces

hovered on the edge of anger. 'You all know me,' she said. 'You know I'm no traitor.'

'You're his informer.' Nellie jabbed Jiddy's shoulder. 'She's an outsider as well, you can never trust an outsider.'

'But you're from Whitby, Nellie.'

Captain Ryethorpe stopped Nellie's fist from striking just in time and he held her arm while she struggled to break free.

'Tell everyone,' Jiddy said, 'tell them who the informer is.'

Nellie glared, struggling, clamping her mouth tight shut.

'Miss Vardy is not an informer, now please go about your business,' the captain said.

'This is our business,' said Abe Storm.

'Isn't this proof?' Nellie shouted. 'She's never been one of us, she's chosen him over us.'

A stone shot through the air.

It was like being a child all over again and that feeling of loneliness surged back. People were screaming, shouting, no-one could hear anyone else. She had to get out of there and fast but the crowd wouldn't let her, she knew that. It was too late for talk. The captain certainly wouldn't be listened to.

There was nothing he could do without his dragoons and a backup of preventives. People were raising pans and sticks. Nellie had been organised, Jiddy couldn't believe the speed she must have gone around, whipping people up that quickly.

'I say we make an example of Jiddy Vardy. I say, she's

not from here, she's not one of us, I say we deal with informers like we dealt with Jack Gobbit.'

'Jiddy?' Annie was crying.

'Traitor.'

'Stone her.'

'Jiddy!' Annie's voice.

They surged forwards. She had to get out. Someone tugged her skirt again. It ripped with a ragged tear. She slapped away someone's hands. Someone else tried to grab her wrist but she wrenched herself free.

Everyone closed in. Her head hurt, her hands and arms ached. Spoons began to beat against pans. She couldn't see straight. Her heart was beating so fast it would explode.

The door opened. Faces changed. Hands released her. Voices quietened. Mary stood on the threshold.

CHAPTER THIRTY-NINE

Jiddy rammed bolts in place while the captain leaned against the door. Every time someone shouldered against it from outside, he shook under the vibration.

'Done,' said Jiddy, and he dragged the kitchen table across the floor, barricading them in. The anger in the villagers' voices battered into the room and Jiddy stood further back, praying it would hold while the captain leaned up the stairs, looking to left and right at the bedroom doors. Hands clasped, Mary stood by the fire, her eyes jittering with fear. Jiddy looked around. Jonas wasn't there. He wasn't there. Mary's eyes flickered to Ryethorpe and back to Jiddy, her face trembling with shock. Voices outside rose. Shouts spat into the room.

'Traitor!'

'Informer!'

A flurry of stones beat the door and Jiddy leapt further back. The bolts shook. Fists, sticks, and pans struck the wood. Jiddy put her hand up to her neck. The wound pulsed painfully and her head felt as if it would burst.

Walking back to the door, Ryethorpe pulled out his pistol and began opening it to load. 'I'm not cowering in here,' he said. 'They will not dare touch me.' His hand shook as he emptied out the bag of bullets on the table.

'You've seen how they are,' Jiddy said. 'We can't go back out there.'

'A captain of the dragoons does not hide,' he said. 'I have no choice but to go back out.'

'One shot against that mob?' Mary said. 'Go away!' she shouted, thumping the door. 'This is my house and I'm not sending anyone out until you send a proper request with someone I'll listen to. Get away from my door!'

Voices outside continued to shout but the beating against the door stopped. Ryethorpe slotted his pistol into its holster while Jiddy flung her arms around Mary.

'Jonas were looking for you,' Mary said. 'I said you might be at preaching house. What happened?'

Before Jiddy could answer, a resounding bang at the door made them all jump and Ryethorpe headed straight for the stairs. The sound of his boots marching from room to room kept them silent.

'Do these windows open?' he shouted.

'You're too big to get out that way,' Mary said.

Jiddy pulled back to look at Mary. 'I'm not a traitor, Jonas knows that, doesn't he? You know that?' Mary's pale eyes had confusion flitting through. 'Nellie and I had a fight,' Jiddy said. 'She were desperate and it got messed up...' Even now, she couldn't bring herself to say it. 'Captain Ryethorpe saw I were in a bad way,' she said. He tried to help, I guess Jonas thought there were more to it but he's got it wrong and I need to find him.'

'Weren't Reverend Cook in preaching house?' Mary said. 'Couldn't he have helped?'

The captain's footsteps thumped over the floor again.

'We didn't see him,' said Jiddy, 'I didn't expect to find Nellie there.'

The captain jogged down the steps. 'Most of them are leaving,' he said.

He walked to the window and pulling back the curtain, looked out.

'What happened?' said Mary, wiping back the hair from Jiddy's face. 'Tell me why everyone's turned so angry. Oh my goodness, what's this?'

Mary turned Jiddy to face the window, pushing back her hair further. 'Sit,' she said, 'let me look.'

Tilting her head, she let Mary look at the wound on her neck. After a moment, Mary glanced at the captain then back at Jiddy.

'Stay there while I get some hot water.' Mary opened the cupboard and taking a bowl, went back to the fire and ladled water from a pot.

'Is this what Jonas saw?' Mary said. She was angry, Jiddy knew every tone in Mary's voice.

'Nellie bit me.'

Without saying a word, Mary dabbed the wound. It stung and Jiddy drew in her breath but Mary didn't take any notice, moistening the dried blood so that the water ran pink. Jiddy held her hands tightly in her lap. She didn't want to look at Mary's disapproving face or see the captain moving about. Bang. Something hit the door and she jumped, knocking Mary's hand and spilling the water down her skirt.

'They're still here,' said the captain, 'I have to go out.'

'No,' Mary said, 'neither of you go out there.'

'I've had enough,' said Jiddy, standing so that Mary had to step back. 'I'm not skulking in here either,' she said. 'Let them kill me, I'll fight back, I won't let them have it easy.'

'What have you done?' Mary said.

Bang. The door shook under a battering of pans and heavy spoons.

'Let her out, Mary, she's no kin to you.'

'And that coward of a dragoon.'

He began pulling the table away from the door. 'Lock the door after me.'

'No.' Jiddy grabbed his arm. For the first time in her life she was afraid of her own people. In the preaching house, she'd wanted Captain Ryethorpe to touch her neck. She'd wanted to kiss him and she'd wanted him to kiss her. How could she explain that? She'd liked it? She'd wanted more? Jiddy looked at Mary's lined face, the eyes that were both clear and childlike and deep at the same time. The button of a nose, small mouth. Everything about Mary seemed small at that point.

'Let me come in, Mary.' It was Captain Pinkney's voice.

There was no getting away from it now. Not if he wanted her blood. No-one would stop him, not even Captain Ryethorpe.

Mary clutched Jiddy's hands. 'Nothing you or I say will appease him,' she said. 'You have to go.'

'I have to try,' Jiddy said.

'No.' Mary's voice was firm. Her grip tightened. 'Not that way. For me, Jiddy. I don't know why they want your blood, but they're not having it. Not if I have anything to do with it. You,' she jolted her thumb at the captain, 'you have to go with her. I won't have you causing even more trouble.'

He nodded at Mary.

'Use the tunnel,' she said.

The bolts shook. The door bounced.

'Mary Waite, it is Captain Pinkney, open the door.'

Mary opened the cupboard door at the side of the fireplace. A gust from the narrow passageway wafted in.

'Get yourself up to Thorpe Hall,' she said. 'Squire Farsyde will know what to do. He'll get you out of here.'

'What? No. I'm not leaving you.' Jiddy looked at the door, then Mary, 'I can't leave you here. You come too. We'll all go.'

'Yes, Mrs Waite,' said Captain Ryethorpe, ushering them both. 'It's the only safe option.'

'I'll slow you down,' said Mary, 'and besides, they'll not harm me. They know I wouldn't be able to stop you if you wanted to go.'

Bang, bang, bang. The table bounced. The door wouldn't hold.

'I'm not going without you,' Jiddy said.

Mary patted her cheek. 'Jiddy, love,' she said, 'I belong here. You don't. The squire knows. Let Captain Ryethorpe take you.'

'What d'you mean, I don't belong? Course I do, I'm not going anywhere without you.'

'Go,' Mary said, pushing Jiddy towards the false entrance. 'You,' she prodded Ryethorpe's arm, 'take her.'

'No, no.'

'He'll take you to London,' Mary said. 'He knows where you belong. Don't you?'

Jiddy held onto the cupboard door. 'I don't understand.'

She looked at the captain then Mary again. The door creaked. People were kicking and bashing.

'If you don't try, you'll regret it,' Mary said. 'I will regret it.'

'We must go,' said Captain Ryethorpe.

'Jiddy Vardy? You're no coward, open this door.' Captain Pinkney was not going to let it go. The door shook under the beating.

Mary pushed her into the tunnel. 'Go while you can.'

Jiddy caught Mary's arms. 'Come with us.'

Mary shook her head, peeling Jiddy's fingers from her arm.

'Your real mam is out there, Jiddy,' she said. 'He knows, now go and find her. Go before it's too late.'

'No,' Jiddy tried to shove him out of the way, but he blocked her in and then the door was closing. 'No!' Tearing at his jacket, Jiddy tried to haul him aside, but Mary closed the door and they were enveloped in darkness.

CHAPTER FORTY

U nable to see anything, Jiddy and Ryethorpe didn't move. All Jiddy could hear was her own breathing. She wondered what to do. She had a real mam out there and the captain knew. Mary knew as well. Questions jumbled in her head. What should she do? Force her way back to Mary and ask her to tell her more or go with the captain? Damp and stale air filled her nostrils. Turning around, she reached out and touched cold stone. He was close behind, shifting his feet. She could lose him if she wanted, take him in the wrong direction then double back in a different tunnel that he'd never find.

'I think we should be going.' His voice sounded strange in the dark.

'You know my real mam?' she said.

'Yes.' His voice a quiet hiss.

She had a mam. A real one and the captain knew where she lived. She took a step. And then another. Running her fingers over the uneven surface, she edged forwards. Another step. Her foot caught on an uneven stone and he caught her elbow when she stumbled. He was there. Right behind.

'I'm fine.' She had to keep moving otherwise she'd think too much about what they'd said. Another step. There. The air turned colder and her arm slipped into the tunnel leading down to the beach. A moment later, her hand touched rock again.

'Careful of the gap,' she said, 'don't go that way.'

'I won't, I'm following you.'

It was eerie not being able to see him but knowing he was there. She wanted to ask him about Mary, get reassurance that she'd be all right, but how would he know? He didn't know Captain Pinkney. She didn't really know what Captain Pinkney was capable of but Mary had seemed sure. And that had to be enough. They had to think about getting out before Captain Pinkney decided to follow.

Holding the walls, she walked faster, gaining momentum. Abe and Silas and others could be waiting at Thorpe Hall. If they were, this struggle of an escape had only been postponing the inevitable. Stop it, stop it. She couldn't think like that. She had to try and she wasn't going to let on to Captain Ryethorpe that she was afraid. She had to keep moving and lead them to the hall and hope Captain Pinkney would think she'd gone down to the beach, planning to escape overland.

She sped up, hands moving quickly, ignoring the grazes and knocks as her fingers caught on rough snags in the walls. Sweating, her neck a dull ache, she thought she heard numerous feet behind but when she stopped, forcing Ryethorpe to stop too, so did the noise. Her breathing took over, so loud it dragged out behind her. She blundered on and he followed.

She could hear his breathing now and his feet. It was impossible to talk, even to think coherently. Her chest thumped. Anger consumed her. That's what it was. She was red hot angry.

All those years trying to see land on the other side of the North Sea. Stupidly thinking that could be her home. To think she'd thought being a gypsy would be exciting and exotic and she could have been snatched from a nomadic life. Instead, they'd known. Mary and Thomas had known. How could they have done it, with his playful insults about the colour of her skin and knowing all the time who her mam was? Choice? They hadn't given her a choice then. No-one had so what was the point now?

She knocked against the rock again, grazing her knuckles. She didn't care. What was one more graze, one more drop of her blood smeared in Robin Hood's Bay? Did Jonas know too? He couldn't. Jonas couldn't tell a lie even if Boy's life depended on it. What should she do? This was crazy, running away up the tunnel, away from everyone as if she was guilty. She couldn't have that. She couldn't leave. This was her home, it was all she knew. If she cut up to the farm she could talk to Jonas and tell him what had really happened. Let this Ryethorpe go to the hall without her.

She stumbled again.

'Do you want me to go first?'

'No.'

Sweat trickled down her back. He must be feeling the heat too. She could hardly breathe. The air was too heavy, too close. He was panting hard. The rock walls turned softer. Soil, damp and peaty. Scrambling up an incline, she pushed her hands in front. There. The slab of stone. She pushed hard. It wouldn't budge.

'Do you want me?'

'No.'

Groaning, she pushed hard, shoulder against the stone. She had to move it somehow. She had to. The stone scraped.

'Got it,' she said. Bright sunlight pierced her eyes and she climbed out, levering herself up. A light wind cooled her cheeks. Watching him climb out, she realised that he knew about the tunnel now, and that did make her a traitor. She couldn't go back.

The house towered over the slope of grass, mullioned windows flickering in the sunshine, and she looked to see if anyone was watching. Wind buffeted the trees, crows gathering in the top branches. She couldn't see anyone. No Captain Pinkney, or Abe Storm or Big Isaac. Breathe, she told herself, breathe and don't think about what happens next. The sea sparkled way behind them, a line of flashing fish scales and a mirage of spray. Would the mob come up here? Mary's words wouldn't go away. Her real mam. Real family. She'd wanted this her entire life.

He took her arm, leading her across the lawn. 'Let's go,' he said.

She followed the captain into the house, seeing the cook and other hazy figures as they hurried past the kitchen. Captain Ryethorpe went straight to the drawing room, swinging open the door and marching inside. Squire and Mrs Farsyde stood up, unable to hide their surprise.

'I've got to take Jiddy away from here,' he announced. 'Will you order my horse to be brought round and is there one she can use?'

'What's going on?' said the squire. 'Are all the dragoons leaving? Jiddy?'

'There's no time for explanations,' said the captain. 'Jiddy and I are the only ones departing right now. Please, we must hurry.'

The squire rang a bell and Abigail came, surly faced as he gave her the orders.

Mrs Farsyde knocked over her tea cup as her skirt brushed the low table. 'You have to tell us something about what's going on,' she said.

'Jiddy's been accused of being an informer and the locals will be heading up here,' the captain strode to the window and looked out.

'Oh my goodness. They're coming here?' Mrs Farsyde said. 'Can't you call your men to stop them?'

'I'm not an informer,' said Jiddy. 'It's a mistake and I don't want to go.'

'I agree,' said the squire. 'I'll not have injustices happening without sorting them out.'

'Jiddy was seen talking to me,' Captain Ryethorpe said, striding back to the group. 'A young woman obviously angry about something has stirred people up and right now, there's no going against it. I'm taking Jiddy to London.'

'London? Why so far?' Mrs Farsyde said.

'You know why,' said the captain. 'It's for the best for both our sakes.'

'I'm not going,' Jiddy said. 'You can't make me.' She turned to the squire. 'I'll not go, I want to stay here. If you step in, you can put my side of things.'

'Jiddy,' Captain Ryethorpe said, 'you have family in London and you belong with them, not here. Remember? We talked of you belonging there,' he said, 'of dancing all night and wearing the latest fashions.'

'Don't you dare you use that against me,' Jiddy said. 'You were talking about fancy things, you were tempting me.' She couldn't believe how he turned her words for his own use.

Mrs Farsyde stepped forward. 'Jiddy, it's all right. It's natural for a young girl to want to do those things. You must go to London and see what is there for you.'

Jiddy pulled the chain clear and twisted to unclasp it. 'It's all the fault of this necklace, if you hadn't given it to me Nellie wouldn't have used it to say I'd been giving him information.'

'Why didn't you tell people I'd given it to you?' Mrs Farsyde looked confused.

'Because with everyone yelling and grabbing at me I didn't get a chance,' said Jiddy. 'Argh, I can't do it, please will you unfasten it?' She turned her back to Mrs Farsyde.

Mrs Farsyde backed away. 'No, no, it's yours.'

'Which necklace is that?' the squire said.

'It's Jiddy's,' Mrs Farsyde said. 'It's only the garnet, I thought Jiddy should have something.'

'Yes, keep it my dear,' the squire was swift to answer. 'Now let's get those horses sorted.' He walked quickly out of the room and they heard his footsteps striding down the hall.

'What about Mary?'

'We'll send word,' Mrs Farsyde said. 'It'll be all right, you'll see. You're a very lucky girl going to a big city like London. This is your chance to meet your real parents and to find out where you came from.'

'Right. That's settled. Let's prepare the horses,' said Captain Ryethorpe, walking towards the door.

'One moment,' said Mrs Farsyde. 'Jiddy can't go to London dressed like this.'

'There's no time, Mrs Farsyde, thank you, but we're going. Now.'

'No.' Mrs Farsyde said. 'I will not have Jiddy leaving like this. She will get changed while you prepare your horses and we will be down by the time you're ready.' Taking Jiddy's hand, Mrs Farsyde led her to the door.

'Mrs Farsyde, we haven't time. I believe they will be coming up from the village,' said the captain.

Mrs Farsyde smiled. 'I don't have much say in anything, but I do know about this,' she said. 'Jiddy will not go to London looking like a peasant. I will not have gentry in London thinking we don't know how to dress and look after ourselves.'

'Five minutes,' said Ryethorpe, 'and we'll see you outside with the horses saddled up to leave.'

As soon as they reached the dressing room Mrs Farsyde opened her closet doors.

'Take everything off,' she said, pushing aside dress

after dress. Jiddy had never seen so many clothes and she stared. 'Jiddy, now. We have no time to waste.'

Jiddy untied her skirt and let it drop to the ground revealing her underskirt. Stepping out of it, she unfastened her bodice while Mrs Farsyde made a pile of undergarments on the table.

'Underskirt and chemise too, please,' said Mrs Farsyde.

Mrs Farsyde helped Jiddy step into a pleated underskirt and to slip her arms into a white embroidered chemise. Making Jiddy sit, she bent down to roll white stockings up her legs.

'What have you done to your hands?' Mrs Farsyde turned them over, touching the rough grazed skin.

'It's all right,' Jiddy said. 'If I could wear some gloves?'

'I think this for travelling,' she said, 'I'll pack the other.'

Mrs Farsyde deftly helped Jiddy into a dark red and green dress and within fifteen minutes she was completely transformed.

'Best put your shoes on for the ride and I'll pack the slippers in here,' said Mrs Farsyde, folding a yellow dress into a brown leather bag.

'I don't think I can leave Mary after all,' Jiddy said.

Mrs Farsyde draped a bright red cloak around Jiddy's shoulders, her hands shaking as she tied the ribbons.

'There's no looking back now,' she said. 'Remember the first time you saw yourself? Here, look again.' She led Jiddy to stand in front of the long mirror. 'Look. You belong with people who are like you, not here, Jiddy. You have to go. Mary wouldn't have sent you here if she didn't want you to go with Captain Ryethorpe.'

CHAPTER FORTY-ONE

Two horses stood saddled up and ready to go. When she appeared through the back door of the house, Captain Ryethorpe strode to meet her and taking the bag gave it to a stable hand.

'Strap it to the back,' he said.

Panic bubbled up her chest. It was too much. Mary would be at home trying to calm Captain Pinkney. Annie and Betsie would be listening to Nellie telling them all sorts of evil nonsense and more likely than not, believing her. What seemed worst of all was that she didn't know where Jonas had gone and she wanted to see him.

'Squire Farsyde?' The grey-haired stable hand holding the horses pointed.

Across the fields and silhouetted against the sea, three men headed towards the hall.

'It's Pinkney,' said the squire, 'I'd recognise that hat anywhere.'

Jiddy looked at Captain Ryethorpe. The thought of the sea captain angrily banging on the cottage door and now coming to find them with two others in tow made her realise that they wouldn't let her get away. She was dressed up like a lady and he'd not take kindly to that transformation. It made her look as if she really had sold them out.

'I should never have changed,' she said.

'That's the decision made,' Captain Ryethorpe said. 'I'll be in touch with my deputy, Squire Farsyde, and if you can keep me abreast of news. Miss Vardy?' Stepping towards the horses, he held out his hand.

'Can't we talk to them?' she said.

'We have to go.'

Squire Farsyde gestured for the younger stable hand to bring the horses closer. 'Jiddy, you need to mount up,' he said.

'Take good care of her.' Mrs Farsyde wrapped her arms around Jiddy and gave her a long hug. 'She's like a daughter to me.'

The squire gently eased Mrs Farsyde away. 'Don't upset yourself, my dear,' he said.

'I'm not.' She gulped back tears. 'Jiddy, go. For me, please, you need to meet your mother. I'd be heartbroken if I found out my daughter didn't want to see me. It would break my heart. Please don't do that to her.' Overwhelmed with tears, she turned into Squire Farsyde's embrace.

Jiddy looked across the fields. The three men looked determined, striding out, Captain Pinkney's distinctive cape catching the wind and flying out behind him, the other two tall and stocky in their fisherman's sweaters and hats.

'You'll soon be out of this, Jiddy,' the squire said, 'your family can offer you a good life.' Everyone was waiting. The squire kept his eyes on the captain. 'She'll not have any worries, will she?' he said.

Clutching the squire, Mrs Farsyde spoke up: 'You're a lady, Jiddy, you belong with your family,' she said.

'Remember lass,' the squire said. 'There's more than one happy ending for all of us.'

'What do you mean?' She didn't expect the squire to say something so meaningful but this felt important and she had to hear.

The squire glanced at his wife. 'Not everything goes as planned but it's the ending that counts,' he said.

'I don't understand.'

The squire waved his hand. 'Go.'

It was too much. The captain stood by the horses, checking over his shoulder to see how close Captain Pinkney and the two others had come.

'Sir?' The stable hand pointed again.

Captain Pinkney stood out, his big tricorn hat and cloak, distinctive as always, and on either side were Big Isaac and Abe Storm. The biggest, hardest men in Baytown.

Mrs Farsyde tried not to cry. Squire Farsyde had his eye on the figures approaching the near field. Captain Ryethorpe took Jiddy's arm and led her swiftly to the copper gelding.

'Help her up,' he ordered one of the stable hands, taking the reins from the older man and leading the horse forward.

This couldn't be happening. The stable hand bent down, cupping his hand and waiting for her to raise her foot.

'Jiddy, you have to mount up.'

'Take care of her,' said Mrs Farsyde.

Jiddy's eyes sparkled with tears as she settled into the saddle, the leather bag containing the yellow dress and heeled shoes resting against the horse's flank. 'You'll tell Mary,' she said, 'and Jonas Chaplow?' She had to say his name, she couldn't bear to think that he'd think she didn't care.

Mrs Farsyde looked in confusion at her husband. 'Jonas Chaplow?'

The squire raised a hand. 'I know who he is and don't you worry about Mary, I'll see she doesn't go short.'

'Thank you, Squire Farsyde,' Captain Ryethorpe said, moving his horse forward. 'And please don't worry Mrs Farsyde, I will take good care of Miss Vardy.'

The stable hand stepped back. A jolt and her horse moved. The stones under their hooves crunched loudly. The captain's horse broke into a trot and Jiddy tapped the gelding's flanks. There was a shout from the field. Captain Pinkney raised his arm. A gun shot fired into the air and they broke into a canter, the wind catching her face and the sound of horses' hooves drumming hard. They were through the gates and away into the dusk, heading straight for the moors and the South.

CHAPTER FORTY-TWO

Maria – London

Maria Vardarelli touched her black coil of hair and looked at Lord Ryethorpe through dark eyelashes. 'I don't like it when you call unannounced,' she said, turning to look at the rain teeming down the drawing room window.

'You know that Samuel was put in charge of a group of dragoons and assigned to the north of the country?' he said, as soon as the man servant closed the drawing room doors. 'Well, he has sent news.'

Maria sipped her morning tea, letting its sweetness tickle her tongue. She'd only seen his son, Samuel, once or twice since he'd returned from France and she had only been to the North once in her entire life. She certainly never wanted to go there again.

'Are you going to tell me that he has found my diamonds and the rest of my jewels?' she said.

'He found one jewel,' Lord Ryethorpe said, straightening his jacket. 'Your daughter.'

Putting down the cup with a chink against the saucer she dabbed her mouth with a napkin. 'I don't have a daughter,' she said.

Her mouth had gone dry. She didn't like this, she didn't like it at all. 'You're ruining my day,' she said. 'Tell me some other news. Who is playing at the Queen's Concert Rooms? I want to hear some music.'

'Jianna has been found,' he said.

She had not heard that name spoken aloud for over sixteen years. At the beginning she'd said it many times to herself of course, lying in bed or walking around the park, but not aloud. Never aloud.

'That's impossible,' she said.

'Nevertheless, Samuel insists that it is your daughter and he has brought her to London.'

'I don't believe you. She's dead. Does your son know how hurtful he is being by declaring something like this?'

'He is positive it is Jianna and he has proof.'

'Nonsense. How does he know she ever existed? No-one knows except you and I, and I told you never to talk about it. You promised me, you said you hadn't even told your wife.'

'I didn't, and I didn't speak of it to Samuel. He sent me a letter saying he had met a local girl who looked exactly like you. Exactly like you, he said. Now how could that be? In a fishing village in Yorkshire? I had to tell him.'

'He is mistaken. She could not have survived.'

'She's the right age. Samuel said he had to pinch himself as a reminder that you were here in London.'

'There are plenty of girls the same age. This is lunacy.'

'I very much doubt there are any Neopolitan-looking girls living exactly where we crawled ashore.'

'I don't want to talk about it.'

'He said the local people are pale, mousy haired, fair, with light-coloured eyes mostly, but this young woman was browner skinned, jet-black hair and eyes. He could have been describing you, Maria. And her name is Jiddy, Jiddy Vardy. What kind of a name is that if it is not a pieced together version of the name you gave her? He must have heard you say it. You must have said it out loud for him to come up with that. Do you remember?'

Maria threw down her napkin, knocking over her cup and saucer. 'I said I don't want to talk about it.' Pushing the table, she sent the tray sliding to the floor, the teapot and china crashing and soaking the rug.

'I'll call for Robert,' Ryethorpe said, walking to the bell by the fireplace.

'No, leave it, I don't want to see anyone.'

The clock ticked. A piece of coal in the fire spat.

'Oh, say something,' Maria said. 'Why did Samuel go to that God-forsaken place?' Maria strode up and down, skirt crackling as she turned swiftly. 'How did she survive? I cannot believe this. She cannot be that baby.'

Clutching her hands tightly together helped prevent her breaking other things in the room. She wanted to, she wanted badly to break everything in sight. And she was shouting. She heard the fear in her voice.

Ryethorpe took her hands and led her to a seat by the window. 'Let's sit down, Maria,' he said.

She could smell coffee on his breath. Even now, even after all this time, it reminded her of home. She leaned away from him.

'Why is she here?' she said.

He shook his head and smiled. He was making fun of her, she knew it, patronising her as if she was a child.

'You're bound to be nervous,' he said, 'but you needn't worry. I'll be here with you. We will send word and Samuel will bring her here when you are ready.'

Maria tucked a few stray hairs behind her ears. 'Have you seen her?'

'No. They arrived late last night and I came here first thing.'

Sitting so close and with the light on her face, she hoped he wouldn't see the faint lines that traced from her eyes to her temples. She turned her head away from the window.

'What's wrong,' he said, 'what are you so afraid of?'

'I don't know.' She pulled away her hands. 'Do I have to see her?'

'She is your daughter,' he said. 'Somehow, that little baby survived.'

'But how?' Maria stood. She couldn't bear being so close to him that he could read her thoughts. She walked to the fireplace.

'She must have inherited your survival instinct,' he said.

'Survival instinct?' she said. 'I was an adult and we're talking about a few hours' old baby. I want proper answers. I want facts.'

'You were barely an adult yourself, Maria, you were only sixteen years of age.'

'I know how old I was, you don't need to remind me.'

Ryethorpe looked down. Not for the first time, he

wished Gregory was there to take responsibility for what he'd done.

'I think you're uncommonly strong,' he said, 'and I'm guessing that she must be too.'

'She would have suffocated in that cupboard and in any case, a baby dies if it's not fed,' Maria said. 'I wasn't there to feed her, she couldn't have survived and no-one knew she was hidden away. And they were all men. Uncivilised, savage men.'

'She must have cried out to be heard,' Ryethorpe said. 'They can't have been completely evil if they rescued her and found her a nursemaid.'

Ryethorpe's voice was always soothing, but today it grated on her nerves. She had survived being thrown into that cold dark sea. Off that horrible, horrible ship by those ruthless, disgusting pirates. Ryethorpe had somehow survived too. They hadn't drowned although they were supposed to. The impossible had happened.

'I don't want to talk about it,' she said.

She looked at the long blue drapes at the windows, the flowers on the round polished table and the padded cream seats. She loved this room, it was a beautiful room. And she had worked hard to get it.

'She's come a long way to see you,' he said, 'I really think you should meet her this afternoon.'

They had never spoken about that night. Ever. It had been their pact over the years. Don't talk about how they escaped that black sea. Don't talk about how they abandoned that baby. Don't talk about how Gregory's family had wanted nothing to do with her.

She smoothed out her light green skirt and put her hands on her waist. She was proud of her tiny waist that she'd retained over the years. No-one would ever guess she'd ever given birth. For that matter, what decent woman in London society gave birth out of wedlock? No, it couldn't possibly be happening.

'What does she know about me?' she said.

'That she wants to meet you.'

'It's impossible.'

'It's a miracle.'

'Does she want money? Is that what this is about?' she said.

She could give this girl money, enough to take back to that cold, horrible place and make her go away for ever.

Ryethorpe touched her hands and, startled, she brushed them away.

She couldn't help how she felt, could she? Anyone would react like this at such news. At least she hadn't taken herself to bed like some delicate flower. At least she was dealing with the revelation, trying to make sense of it and find a solution.

'I take it Samuel didn't find my jewellery box along with this girl?' she said.

Anger bubbled inside her. She'd had to rely on Ryethorpe when they had returned to London. She'd had to curtsey and be nice to people and she'd hated it. Hated it now, even though she didn't need his help anymore. Didn't need anyone's help. And now this, why?

'You don't need to worry Maria,' he said. 'You can say whatever you want to people, explain her existence in any way you want. I am here for you, I will support any decision you make.'

She didn't answer. Her head hurt. This was going in circles and she hated circles. She mustn't panic. If she stayed calm it might all go away. Jianna might not want to stay in London. She might want to pay her respects and then go home again.

'Jianna was brought up by a local couple who didn't have any children of their own,' Ryethorpe said. 'The man was a fisherman but he's dead now. They weren't well off. They're mainly fishermen, whalers, that sort of thing, in a village like Robin Hood's Bay.'

'Is that the name of the place?'

'There's more to it than I'm making it sound. There is mining in the area that draws in tourists and the usual farming, I suppose. And smuggling. It's a centre for it.'

'It sounds worse the more you tell me.'

'The local woman who took Jianna in is still alive.'

'She'll be the one wanting compensation for raising the child,' Maria said, clutching her hands together again.

'I don't think so,' he said. 'No-one has asked for anything as far as I can make out. The girl wants to see you that is all. It's only natural she should want to meet her mother.'

'None of this is natural,' she said. 'What kind of pirates give anything away? In fact, why would they give anyone a baby? They could have used her for ransom. I'm not stupid. Explain it to me. What am I not understanding about this? They were pirates, weren't they? They told us they were, I'm sure of it. Did they say they were something else? It's so long ago. Pirates don't give things away, they take. They took our ship and they intended to take our lives.' She looked at Ryethorpe for an explanation but she couldn't wait. He hadn't a clue. 'Don't tell me,' she said, 'I know. I've heard of this place. I remember now. Robin Hood's Bay. I do listen to conversations. It's the richest place in the country thanks to those pirates and smugglers, isn't it?'

'The wealthiest place outside of London, I believe, but these aren't wealthy people, Maria.'

'But they could afford to buy a baby?'

'Please, Maria, calm yourself. I didn't mean to cause you anxiety. You need time, of course you do. This is so unexpected and I'm sorry, truly, if I broke the news too abruptly.'

'Oh, don't give me that.' She slapped away his hands again. Hands, hands, why was he wanting to hold her hands every second? He looked shocked but she couldn't help it. All her gold and pearls and diamonds gone and Jianna turning up empty handed. When there were such jewels. Such sparkling bracelets and rings. She should have guessed.

Ryethorpe hadn't fought to protect her. He'd gone along meekly letting those vicious men push her overboard and he hadn't given her a thought except to say, 'save yourself'. Save yourself? She had stood in her nightgown, just having given birth to a baby, and he had said 'save yourself'. If she hadn't had the foresight to put on Gregory's jacket and fill her pockets with what jewels she could she would have been destitute. No wonder she'd never seriously flirted with him after that. No fire in his belly. No fight in him like Gregory had had. For a moment, looking at his worn face, she wondered why he had survived and not the man she loved.

'All right,' she said, 'bring her here. Let's see what a fine young lady she has turned out to be.'

They looked down on the busy street below, taking in the noise of passing horses and carriages.

'What's wrong with me?' Maria said.

'Nothing. It's a shock, that's all.'

She could tell by his shadow that he'd moved to face her but she couldn't look at him. He'd see the fear in her eyes that the pleasant life she'd built for herself would be changed.

'You're right,' she said. 'I have a daughter. I must meet her and see what she has become. Have Samuel bring her here at four o'clock.'

Carriages continued to rattle by. She spread her hands over her silk skirt.

'It is not my fault,' she said. 'It was Gregory who hid her.'

'It isn't anyone's fault,' Ryethorpe said. 'We were in the wrong place at the wrong time. That is all.'

It is your fault, another voice said. You should never have left Naples.

CHAPTER FORTY-THREE

Jiddy – London

I f anyone had asked, Jiddy wouldn't have known how to describe the journey. Thrilling, scary, tiring. Yes, she wanted to go back home but she was also strangely excited by the changing scenery as she looked out of the carriage window. Captain Ryethorpe said it took six days to reach London but she couldn't put that number into reality. They slept in an inn sometimes and sometimes in the carriage, and her back hurt from sitting down for so long by the end that she never wanted to go in a carriage again. Arriving in London late in the evening, she thought she'd come to a different country. There were huge buildings, massive domes and towers silhouetted against the sky, and it was quiet when she'd imagined it full of people and noise.

'Wait until day time,' Captain Ryethorpe said, 'then you'll see.'

The carriage stopped outside a tall building in a row of other tall buildings and they walked up the longest flight of steps she'd ever seen leading to a house. Inside, a tired-looking woman met them.

'Would you like me to fetch you and the young lady something to eat, sir?'

The captain looked at Jiddy. 'Are you hungry?'

What she really wanted was a bed and to be alone. After six days and nights crammed in with other people she yearned for solitude.

Captain Ryethorpe said something to the woman and next thing Jiddy knew, she was walking up a huge flight of stairs and standing in a grand room with a bed so high you'd need a stool to climb in.

'May I help you undress?' the woman said.

'I can do it myself, thank you,' Jiddy said, looking at the room flickering with candlelight. When the door closed, she dragged a chair across the floor to climb onto the bed. Sleep. Soon she'd be sleeping under these wonderful covers.

And sleep she did, waking the next morning to find a young girl of about twelve looking at her.

'My name's Dora,' the girl said. She held a tray with a pot of tea and two slices of toasted bread on it. 'I've come to help you with your clothes, miss,' Dora bobbed a curtsey, tipping the tray and making the pots slide precariously.

'There's a table there.' Jiddy pointed and Dora managed to put the tray down without anything crashing to the floor. 'Please call me Jiddy,' she said, 'I'm not "miss".'

'Oh, I couldn't miss, I mean, I couldn't.'

Jiddy didn't know what to do. It had been strange enough having Mrs Farsyde fasten her skirt and help with her with her bodice but a maid was going to help her? And she was going to call her, 'miss'? She watched

Dora open the heavy curtains and the light spill into the room. It was even grander than it had seemed last night. A pale rug covered the entire floor, gleaming wooden furniture stood around the walls and a dressing table with mirrors reflected the white sky outside.

'You don't need to stay, I can dress myself,' Jiddy said.

Dora had already laid out the yellow striped gown that Mrs Farsyde had packed all those days ago on the end of the bed. It looked like there'd be no escape.

'I'll pour you some tea and you can eat this while I straighten your covers. If that's alright, miss?'

Jiddy was starving and the toasted bread smelled good. She slid her feet onto the floor.

She ate the bread quickly, almost choking when she swallowed a mouthful of tea too quickly. Coughing, her eyes filled with moisture. Luckily, Dora, busy pulling the bed covers taut and plumping up the pillows, didn't notice.

There was no getting around Dora helping her dress. She raised her arms and turned around, all the time avoiding eye contact and remaining quiet. She laughed only once, when Dora's cold fingers touched her arm pits as she straightened the bodice.

'Tickles,' Jiddy said, with a quick grin.

Dora's hair had fallen across her pink cheeks. 'Sorry,' she mumbled.

'Do I look as if I'll fit in?' Jiddy said when she sat at the dressing table and caught her reflection in the mirror.

'You look the spit of Signora Vardarelli,' Dora said, tugging at the knots that had gathered in Jiddy's hair.

Signora Vardarelli. Such an exotic name. Watching Dora trying to tame her unruly hair, questions jumbled around in her head. Would she be called Jiddy Vardarelli from now on? And what should she call her mother? Should she curtsey or kiss her? She wished Mrs Farsyde was there to tell her the proper thing to do. She should have asked, there were so many things she didn't feel she could ask the captain and now it was too late and she'd make a fool of herself and do the wrong thing.

'I really look like her?

'Yes, miss,' Dora said, 'we're all talking about you.'

Jiddy hadn't expected that, London sounded exactly like Bay for gossip.

'Does everyone in London know who I am?'

Dora laughed. 'London's a big place, miss,' she said, 'I think it's only people who know Lord Ryethorpe and Signora Vardarelli, but they do have a lot of friends.'

'Do I look like Mr Vardarelli as well?'

'I don't know, miss. I didn't know Signora Vardarelli was married.'

'What about Lady Ryethorpe?' No-one had said a word about her and the amount of questions that rattled through Jiddy's brain seemed overwhelming.

'Lady Ryethorpe is dead, miss, I do know that. It's only Lord Ryethorpe and the captain here and the captain's away a lot. I don't know where Signora Vardarelli lives but I don't think it's far from here. The master spends a lot of time there so I'm glad you've come as it's dreadful quiet in the house. Hopefully you'll liven the place up a bit.'

She had so much to learn and so many questions to ask. They'd had five days – or was it six – why hadn't she asked more? In fact, why hadn't the captain told her what to expect? He should have told her they'd be living at his father's house and she'd have a maid. For a moment, the image of Abigail came into her head.

A bell rang from somewhere far away in the house.

'I'm needed downstairs,' said Dora, putting down the comb.

Dora had a strange way of talking but she was kind. At the doorway, she hesitated.

'I'll be back in a bit to finish you off,' she said.

Jiddy poured another cup of the tea, spooning in more sugar than she normally could. This might be her only meal and she was going to make the most of it.

Later, standing at the window, watching a light drizzle cast a silver sheen over a well-cared for garden, she wondered what Jonas would be doing. If she'd stayed in Bay, she could have forced him to listen to her. That was her home, Squire Farsyde would have calmed people down and then they'd have understood that she wasn't a traitor and it would all have gone back to normal. She'd meet Signora Vardarelli and then go back. That's what she'd do.

Turning her back on the velvet lawns and carefully planted borders, she looked around the room. The high bed, with its thick covers and drapes, rose from the floor, so different from the narrow bed she hid under at home.

It was a beautiful room. If she hadn't been given away as a baby, she'd have grown up in a house like this. She'd have had soft hands and would have spoken nicely like Mrs Farsyde. Her hands. She studied them, wishing she had gloves to cover the grazes and that Mrs Farsyde's gloves had fitted. Samuel had said he'd known who she was the first time he'd seen her but would her mother agree? She'd never been scared of anything in her life and now it seemed she was scared of everything. It didn't feel good. She looked at herself in the mirror. Mrs Farsyde's yellow dress was pretty, with its tiny flowers winding up the stripes. The garnet didn't look right though. Opening drawers and cupboards, she decided to hide it in the pocket of her red cape. If she needed to leave in a hurry she wouldn't forget it there.

It seemed ages, waiting. Pacing up and down, she wondered if Dora had forgotten about her and it would be best to go downstairs. What should she say? Good morning? How do you do, as Mrs Farsyde had taught her. It was turning into a nightmare. She peeked outside. Rooms opened off a central staircase. Voices came from a room nearby. Leaving her door open, she crept to look into the hall below. There was no-one about. Voices chattered away and she tiptoed to a door that stood ajar.

'Is she rough?' a woman's voice said. 'I heard all northerners are rough.'

'Not really.' It was Dora's voice. 'She speaks funny, it were awkward not making out what she were saying but I don't think she guessed, I covered it well.'

'She's probably stupid,' said the other voice, 'they're all thick up North.'

Dora giggled. 'She's pretty though.'

'Does she look like Signora Vardarelli?'

There was a pause. Jiddy strained to hear. Maybe Dora had been pretending and she didn't look anything like her mother.

'Yes,' Dora said, 'only bigger.'

Tiptoeing back, embarrassed though she wasn't sure why, she carefully shut her bedroom door. She'd never go out again. If only Thomas and Mary had told her she was their child and that sometimes children don't look like their mam and da. If they'd given her their name of Waite and not some stupid patched up name like Vardy, she'd have believed them. Adults were supposed to know what was best. How on earth had they thought it a good idea to tell her they were merely looking after her, allowing all sorts of dreams and fantasies into her head that could only end in some girl she didn't know calling her stupid? If she'd been Jiddy Waite Mrs Farsyde would never have tried to treat her like a daughter, dressing her up in fancy clothes, and if she hadn't been wearing Mrs Farsyde's dress Captain Ryethorpe would never have noticed her. And if it wasn't for that necklace no-one would have believed Nellie Ashner and she'd be in Bay right now, probably with Jonas, and she'd never have known this horrible place and these horrible people existed.

She would go home. Now. Opening the closet door, she reached for her red cape.

A knock on the door made her drop it. Someone tapped again.

'Are you ready, miss?'

Dora was less talkative this time, leading Jiddy down

the wide staircase, and Jiddy didn't feel like talking to her. They crossed a tiled hallway to another room with long windows and drapes and a fireplace so big you could walk inside it. Captain Ryethorpe came striding across the carpet to meet her and the relief she felt took her by surprise. Instead of his uniform he wore a deep-blue coat and a long, lighter blue waistcoat with curls of silver thread as a border, similar to the one he'd worn when they first met.

'Did you sleep well?' he said.

'Do you think I'm rough and thick?' she blurted out.

'Excuse me?' The look of shock on his face made her look away and she marched to the window.

'I heard some servants talking and...' she stopped.

'What were they saying?' The look of shock had changed more to anger.

What could she say? She'd charged into the room, acting without any manners. Of course she must seem rough to them.

'Dora said I look like my mother. She said everyone thinks so,' she said, determining she would be calmer and show them that she was cleverer than they thought. She'd show them how brilliant she was at embroidery too. She'd been a smuggler. How many of them could say that?

He was smiling, even his eyes crinkled. 'Have you slept?' he said again, 'and have you eaten?'

She nodded. To think that they'd spent so many days together travelling. Now it seemed as if she'd clicked her fingers and here they were.

'You're to meet Signora Vardarelli this afternoon,' he said. 'We will go to her house at four o'clock. Do you have any questions?'

Rain lashed against the windows.

'What do I need to do?' she said.

'Nothing. My father will be present as well. You will like him.'

He was so polite and calm. The room was perfect, he was perfect. Blood raced to her head.

'First things first, don't be scared,' he said. 'This is where you belong even if it feels a bit daunting. That's natural but your place is in London, Jiddy, be certain of that, you are Signora Vardarelli's sole heir.'

He was using words she didn't understand but he seemed sure of what he was saying, so she nodded. As long as she could go home afterwards she'd do whatever they wanted.

Strolling to the fire she looked at the flames, feeling the heat rise to her cheeks.

'I wish I'd asked you more questions,' she said, looking around the room for something to do, something to occupy her hands, some piece of mending, sewing, cooking, fixing, anything but this idleness that concentrated her anxieties.

'What do you want to know?'

He made it sound simple and she was trying to be as calm as he was but feeling the opposite inside. She stroked the smooth wood of a table.

'I'm not used to this,' she said.

'We're rushing you,' he said. 'Perhaps you'd like to delay until tomorrow?'

She sat down. This waiting was torture but she wasn't sure. He sat next to her and the panic bubbling in her stomach pounded up into her chest.

He touched her hands with his soft ones. 'You don't need to worry about anything. You can relax this morning, we'll have something to eat before we go and give Signora Vardarelli time to prepare herself as well.'

'You think she needs time?' She hadn't thought that her mother may be nervous too.

'Of course. It is sixteen years since you were taken from her. She is bound to worry about how your meeting will go.'

'I shouldn't have come,' she said.

'Jiddy. Jianna,' he said, 'listen to me. You agreed on this. Yes, don't shake your head, yes, you did. You remember that, don't you?'

Yes, she remembered. She remembered everything.

'Your mother is a wealthy woman,' he said. 'She will want to make it up to you.'

He sat close to her, his blue eyes piercing. He didn't really know her, not like Jonas.

'I don't understand why it's taken so many years,' she said. 'Didn't she want to find me?'

'She thought you were dead,' he said. 'That's what my father told me. And why wouldn't she? The men that took over their ship killed all the crew and threw the rest overboard. You were a few hours old. She didn't come looking for you because she didn't think you were alive.'

'You found me.'

'Fate, Jiddy. You look exactly like her.'

She looked exactly like her mother and that's why she was here. It did sound like a fairy tale.

'She calls me Samuel, maybe you should too.'

'Oh, no, I don't think...'

'You said I could call you Jiddy, I think it's only fair.'

'What do I call Signora Vardarelli?'

He looked surprised but he quickly hid it. 'Mama, I suppose.'

'Mama. I suppose mam won't do?'

'I am sure she will tell you which.'

He was kind and he was laughing with her.

'Do you think she'll like me?'

'She cannot fail to.'

Ever since that kiss in the preaching house he'd acted differently, and if she was really honest with herself that was the thing that scared her the most.

Taking hold of his hands, she pulled him to his feet. 'If I'm going to be a lady in London, I'm going to go to a ball, aren't I, so I'll need to practice,' she said, 'I don't want anyone thinking a lass from Yorkshire doesn't know how to dance.'

During the morning, they danced the Cotillion and all the other dances she had learned with Mrs Farsyde, and Jiddy didn't give any thought to what Dora and the other servants had said until one of the man servants came in to announce luncheon was served.

CHAPTER FORTY-FIVE

T he noise of the street was overwhelming. Bells ringing all the time, carriages, carts, horses, and people shouting. Looking out of the carriage window, Jiddy watched street sellers with baskets of gingerbread and oranges ringing hand bells and shouting their sales and men with wheelbarrows cutting shells open whilst yelling 'Oysters!' A man in bright clothes made an announcement but she couldn't tell what he said as he had a funny accent, a bit like Dora's. It was so much noise all at once. And strange smells. Coal dust, which she didn't expect, and horse manure and odours like rotting apples and wet leather and flowers. People dodged between carriages and wagons to cross the road. Huge buildings looked so grand, Jiddy thought that nearly all the people must be wealthy in London. She didn't know if it was the bells, or shouting, or the bumpy ride that gave her a headache and changed her excitement to dread, but it altered somewhere between leaving Samuel's house and arriving at Signora Vardarelli's. By the time the carriage came to a standstill, she sensed a storm brewing in her chest.

'Samuel?' she said, looking up at a tall house in a row of other tall houses, all with steps leading up to grand front doors, similar to where they had just come from. 'What if she really doesn't like me?'

'She will, you're from the same family,' he said, stepping onto the pavement and holding out his hand.

She looked at the white front door.

'Maybe this is a bad idea. Maybe I can wait here and you go in,' she said.

He lifted his hand for her to take and looked at her earnestly. 'They will be watching from the window,' he said, 'it would be best if we went straight in. Together.'

Jiddy looked up at the windows but she couldn't see anyone.

'You don't need to be nervous,' he said. 'I am right here.'

'I'm not nervous.'

'Do you remember what Mrs Farsyde told you,' he said, 'about how she'd feel if her daughter didn't want to see her?'

That wasn't fair, Jiddy thought. Mrs Farsyde had been on the edge of tears when she'd said that. Mrs Farsyde had lost baby after baby before they were born. Jiddy stepped down from the carriage, taking his outstretched hand. The front door opened as they mounted the steps and a smartly dressed servant welcomed them inside.

Signora Vardarelli greeted them in a tall ceilinged, pale green drawing room. Samuel's father stood by one of the long windows but Jiddy only noticed him as a grey figure in the background. It was the black-haired, petite, dark-eyed woman who drew all her attention. It was like looking in a mirror, only the reflection was a beautifully finished painting. This woman was too perfect to be her mother. She stood completely still, her hair glossy without a strand out of place. A green brooch glittered in the centre of her dress. Her large, dark eyes sparkled bright and alert, observing Jiddy from top to toe.

It was unnerving. The yellow dress she'd thought so elegant seemed shabby and brash compared to the dark green and purple striped frock that her mother wore. How could she have thought she could turn up in London and fit in? They had all tricked her. She wasn't a lady. She would never be a lady like the figure standing beside the delicate chair and table in the centre of the elegant room.

She tried to smile, bobbed to make a curtsey but straightened again. That was wrong. So wrong. She was this woman's daughter, not a servant. The door behind closed. She squeezed her hands together.

Samuel touched her elbow and led her forward towards the beautiful lady, closer, closer. The man by the window moved. They were closing in on her, pulling her towards a spider camouflaged in green and purple who was going to gobble her up. She pulled against Samuel but he held her firmly; closer and closer, they moved forward. His hand rested on her back and there was nothing between her and the black-haired lady and all she could think of was how darkly sweet the woman smelled, like ripe blackberries and polished wood.

'Signora Vardarelli, may I present your daughter, Jiddy … Jianna.'

He was nervous too. But that was who she was, he wasn't mistaken. She was Jiddy, not Jianna.

'Welcome.' Signora Vardarelli's voice sounded like a

sharp tinkle, adding to the hundreds of other bells in the city.

'I am very pleased to finally meet you.' The man who had stood by the window came forward holding out a hand.

'May I introduce my father, Lord Ryethorpe?' Samuel said, stepping in. 'Father, Jianna.'

'Lord Ryethorpe,' Jiddy repeated.

This was the most nerve-wracking thing she had ever done. Far more frightening than meeting a new officer and trying to get information out of him. More terrifying than the dog and soldiers in Whitby and falling into the water and thinking she'd die. Here, she had no control and she couldn't see an escape route. Every sound was over loud and she didn't know if she wanted to laugh or shout or hide. She held out her hand and the older gentleman took it in his, cupping his left over them both and shaking her hand as if he treasured it. Bending forwards as he did so, he looked kindly into her eyes.

'How do you do?' she said, as Mrs Farsyde had taught her.

'I am very well, thank you,' he said, still holding her hand, 'and how are you after your long journey?'

He had a kind voice, like his face, and Jiddy relaxed. 'I slept well,' she said. 'The bed was very soft.'

'Ah.' He released her hand, smiling more broadly and looking at Samuel. 'That is good to hear, my dear,' he said, 'very good to hear.'

He looked at the dark-haired woman as if it was her turn to speak. Samuel and his father averted their eyes and they all stood waiting. Waiting for what, Jiddy thought? Was she supposed to ask how Signora Vardarelli was? Should she shake her hand? If only she'd listened more closely to Mrs Farsyde. She really should have asked more questions.

Samuel's father gestured towards two spindly legged settees facing each other with an equally spindly table between them. Signora Vardarelli moved to sit, her stiff skirt rustling louder than a pile of autumn leaves. Samuel moved as well but Jiddy hesitated. Surely they weren't all going to sit on the settees all at once. They looked as if they'd collapse with the weight of two people but Samuel's father was indicating for her to sit next to Signora Vardarelli, which meant the two men would be sitting opposite. That couldn't be wise, surely.

If she said anything it would sound rude. She sat, hoping she wouldn't laugh when they ended up on the floor.

'Your mother received a letter from Squire Farsyde this morning,' said Samuel's father. 'So now we know what happened,' he said, his eyes flitting to Signora Vardarelli and back.

'Yes,' Signora Vardarilli became animated. 'This squire,' The words hissed with foreign pronunciation, 'he tells me that you were saved from the ship and brought to him, and that his wife gave you to another woman who lived in the village.'

'Mary,' Jiddy said, 'and Thomas.'

'It sounds like you were very helpful to Mrs Farsyde as well,' Samuel's father said.

They were confusing people, Jiddy decided, making statements sound like questions. Was she supposed to answer? They were looking at her as if she should. Her mother wasn't behaving at all the way she'd expected. Samuel had told her she probably wouldn't get a word in, Signora Vardarelli spoke so much and so quickly, but she had hardly said a word. Thank goodness for Lord Ryethorpe, at least he was trying.

'Mrs Farsyde taught me to dance the Cotillion,' Jiddy said.

Lord Ryethorpe was looking at Signora Vardarelli again. It really was too much, all this looking at each other and then pretending not to.

'I have a new pianoforte, you must play for us,' said Signora Vardarelli. 'Do you sing as well?'

Jiddy didn't know what to answer. She'd never touched a musical instrument in her life and the songs she knew might not go down so well here.

'Jianna is an excellent horsewoman,' said Samuel quickly, 'and she is a graceful dancer. May I suggest we organise a ball, father?'

'A ball?' Signora Vardarelli's eyes lit up like wet coals. 'I will hold a ball.' She looked at Jiddy's dress. 'But first we must make sure she has a suitable gown. You gentlemen, shoo! We want to be alone to talk about clothes.'

Jiddy didn't mind that they left. A ball. She had a ball to think about.

'We'll go tomorrow. You are tall, aren't you? We will need a lot of material.'

'Must be all the fish I eat,' said Jiddy.

'You eat a great deal of fish?'

'Bread and porridge and,' she could feel Signora Vardarelli's attention drifting, 'eggs. We're lucky we know the farmer.'

'We will feed you with more exciting foods here and tomorrow we will pick out material,' said Signora Vardarelli, her small hands darting in the air like birds.

Tomorrow. Shopping. All Jiddy had ever dreamed about was coming true. She would see inside a shop, gaze at shelves of material, maybe touch reams and reams of fabric, and it would be out in the open not hidden away like her precious silk stashed in Jonas' dusty attic under hessian sacks and straw. There would be so much choice too, she'd have to be really careful to make sure she picked something to suit her skin tone. Mrs Farsyde said that was very important but she must also choose something that would make her fit in with the other young ladies in London.

Signora Vardarelli's skirt rattled as she stood, making Jiddy jump to her feet. 'Come, Jianna,' she said, 'we will have your belongings sent for. I won't have my daughter staying elsewhere. Let me see, I think Kitty will be the best one to take care of you here.'

Signora Vardarelli's green and purple striped skirt brushed past her and Jiddy breathed in the musky, slightly sour scent of her perfume and hoped Kitty would be easier to get along with than Dora.

CHAPTER FORTY-FIVE

The gold sign over the entrance read, 'Vardarelli.' Inside, every glass panel, chair back and mirror had a gold 'V' carved into it.

'Yes, it is mine,' said Signora Vardarelli. 'How else do you think I survived in this city?'

Jiddy gazed at the sparkling sight before her eyes. In her entire life, she had never imagined a shop could look like a giant jewellery box. Everything shimmered and glittered and it went on and on into the distance. And this enormous emporium belonged to her mother.

'Come along, Jianna.' Signora Vardarelli walked between stands holding white, brown and black furs of varying shades and sizes and every shop assistant they passed curtseyed and said, 'Good afternoon, Signora Vardarelli.'

Long tippets of ermine, mink and fox draped from pegs. Jiddy ran her hand over a line of huge ermine muffs. The air, heavy with animal pelts, rose water and musk, filled her nostrils. A cacophony of voices asked questions and gave demands that made grey-dressed assistants scatter away and come back again. And everything – furs, people, assistants and chandeliers – was duplicated in gleaming mirrors.

Without pausing to look, Signora Vardarelli brushed

past the array of furs, through a glazed partition where ladies, both seated and standing, tried on gloves under more glittering chandeliers so bright they hurt Jiddy's eyes. The ladies fluttered fans, wafting the air as though with birds' wings. Mesmerised, Jiddy watched the swishing of lace fans, delicate fretwork fans, ones with painted scenes and others with sparkling with gems. It was like being in a garden filled with exotic birds. Voices, bouncing off marble and glass, chirped and tinkled.

'Good afternoon, Signora Vardarelli,' over and over.

Rainbows of threads, spools of trimmings and buttons drew Jiddy's eye. It really was like a garden or a feast filled with goodies to touch and see. She didn't know where to look. It was a fairground, a field of wild flowers only grander, brighter, better.

'We'll come back here after we decide on your gowns,' said Signora Vardarelli.

Jiddy couldn't think what to say. She'd never have guessed in a hundred years that this was how some people acquired their clothes and that her mother owned such a grand shop. Mrs Farsyde had never spoken about anywhere like this, but then she couldn't imagine Mrs Farsyde in such a palace. The wealth of the Farsyde's faded in comparison to the opulence of the Vardarelli emporium. This was completely another world, where a different type of female existed, where money quadrupled in ways unimaginable in the North.

Tick, tick, tick. To their right, clocks of all shapes and sizes stood on tables, covering walls, their faces shining at each other, lights reflecting on and on. Ladies meandered slowly in a room to their left where the air choked with scent and bottles shone on glass shelves.

'This is my favourite section,' said Signora Vardarelli, waving her white-gloved hands around the vast central area at the diamond brooches, clips, clasps and rings. Here, the light shone brightest of all, the chandeliers firing life into emeralds, rubies and best of all, diamonds.

'It's beautiful,' said Jiddy, her eyes widening.

There was more. Passing through another glazed partition, they entered a room filled with sumptuous silks, deep jewelled in colour, cottons printed and painted with birds, flowers and paisley . Embroidered shawls, half-made gowns with ruffles and frills marked their way as reams of fabrics, stacked on shelves from floor to ceiling, rose higher than apple trees.

'Good afternoon, Signora Vardarelli,' a woman in a plain grey gown bobbed a curtsey.

'This is my daughter,' Signora Vardarelli said. 'Bring me the blue silks and dark greens. You will suit green, Jianna,' she said, 'it suits our skin tone perfectly and we'll have leather shoes made to match.'

Jiddy couldn't believe it. Signora Vardarelli had said 'my daughter' and in public. It was official. She was Signora Vardarelli's daughter.

'Would you like a contrasting material for the panel or trim, ma'am?' said the draper's assistant.

'Of course, now bring me a chair, this is going to take some time. I want three dresses.'

Three dresses? Could that be possible? Jiddy looked down at the sharply pointed blue shoes peeping out from below Signora Vardarelli's blue paisley dress. To think she'd have a pair of shoes like that as well. The wooden overshoes she wore in Robin Hood's Bay and her plain wool skirt and cotton jacket belonged to another person. She couldn't imagine that person here, not even as a servant, and the thought of how she'd looked made her ashamed. No wonder Mrs Farsyde insisted she wear one of her cast-offs when she went up to the hall, but if she were honest, even the red and green and the yellow striped seemed common here and she pulled the bright red cloak that Mrs Farsyde had given her closer together and clutched the necklace in its pocket.

'I want gold thread for the embroidery,' Signora Vardarelli said, 'Jianna, let me look at you.'

Lifting her chin, Jiddy faced Signora Vardarelli's scrutiny. It was impossible to tell what she was thinking, her dark eyes sweeping over Jiddy's frame.

'Definitely the green,' she said. 'There is lilac, I suppose, but it doesn't seem, I don't know, strong enough.'

'I like that.' Jiddy pointed to a deep red and ochre patterned fabric.

'Your daughter has excellent taste,' said the draper's assistant, 'that is a new design.'

'Twenty yards,' Signora Vardarelli said, 'and show me plain matching fabrics and we'll want braiding for this.'

Twenty yards of completely new fabric to be made into a gown specifically for her, it made her heart race. What would Mary say? What would Betsie and Annie's faces look like seeing this place? What would they say when she told them it belonged to her mother?

Jonas' voice popped into her head. 'You're a vain, spoilt brat,' he'd say. Well, he knew nothing and she didn't care. He wasn't here and she wasn't there and she had to dress well in London. She was Signora Vardarelli's daughter and she had to dress like it. A farmer's lad would never understand that in a million years, not like Samuel. Samuel knew how to dress and how to treat a lady.

'What about this, ma'am?' The assistant opened a ream of glowing gold.

It was still raining when they stepped outside but Lord Ryethorpe and Samuel had returned in the carriage and with the footman's help, Jiddy climbed in quickly after Signora Vardarelli. Looking at her mother and Lord Ryethorpe sitting opposite, and Samuel by her side, Jiddy wondered if this was what being part of a real family felt like. Samuel and his father looked alike, she and her mother were like twins, and together they made a handsome group. The Ryethorpes and Signora Vardarelli were comfortable and relaxed in each other's company and now she was one of them too. They'd ordered her first ball gown; she'd been measured and treated like the lady everyone kept telling her she was and now they were riding home in a carriage and they'd have tea and cakes and whatever else she desired.

Funny how you could go from thinking about food when it was sparse to thinking about it all the time when there was so much of it. She couldn't work out why she felt hungry all the time either, when she ate so much. What did it mean? Maybe that was why Signora

Vardarelli always carried sweets in her little bag because the more you ate, the more you wanted to eat.

'So, Jianna,' said Lord Ryethorpe, waking her out of her daydream, 'what would you think of going to a concert?'

'You will like Mozart, I think,' said Samuel. 'The Hanover Square Rooms are the place to be. When shall we go father? There is nowhere like this concert hall in the North, Jianna, you are in for a treat.'

'I think York must have concert halls,' said Jiddy, 'and Scarborough.'

'Yes, yes, but nothing like this. Prepare to be dazzled.' Samuel's eyes sparkled like the chandeliers in the draper's shop, 'Haydn himself was here last year. It's a pity he went back to Germany.'

'Mrs Farsyde told me there is a theatre in Richmond but it is a long way from us in the Bay,' said Jiddy, 'but she and the squire have been there and she said she saw a play there, Rory and Julia, though she didn't like the ending. She said it made her cry.'

'I've not heard of that,' said Lord Ryethorpe, 'who is the playwright?'

'I don't know,' Jiddy said, 'but she did say they were tightly packed together.'

'But the Hanover Square Rooms, Jianna,' said Samuel, 'a little theatre in a place like Richmond is nothing in comparison.'

'It is the music that we go for of course,' said Lord Ryethorpe.

'Well, there is no point in planning anything until

Jianna has suitable gowns, now is there?' Signora Vardarelli said, 'and that will be at least another week.'

Jiddy drew her cloak over her knees. 'I can't thank you enough,' she said.

'It will be worth the wait,' said Lord Ryethorpe.

'We'll practice dancing for the ball in the meantime,' Samuel said. 'We have plenty to occupy us.'

'Fittings.'

'Writing invitations.'

Yes, thought Jiddy, looking through the rain splattered glass, misted with condensation. There was much to look forward to and a ball, her very first ball, was to be held in her honour.

'If only this dreadful rain would stop,' Signora Vardarelli looked out of the window, 'it has not ceased since you arrived.'

A crashing sound made the horses whinny and Jiddy grasped Samuel's arm.

'What can that possibly be?' said Signora Vardarelli.

'I don't know.'

'I hope it isn't…'

'Isn't what?' said Jiddy.

The carriage slowed. Jiddy let go of Samuel's arm and rubbed the condensation clear on the window.

'Don't do that, you'll dirty your sleeve,' said Signora Vardarelli, but her words petered away when the carriage came to an abrupt standstill and the noise of horses' hooves and carriage wheels turning on cobbles was replaced by the louder sound of a horse's squeal.

Samuel opened the carriage door. 'I'll see what has happened,' he said. 'Driver!'

'I'll come too,' Jiddy said.

'My dear, I don't think that's suitable,' said Lord Ryethorpe, but Jiddy was already half way out of the carriage.

'Jianna, stay here,' ordered Signora Vardareill, 'it is pouring down and you will be soaked.'

Lifting her hood, Jiddy jumped onto the road, making Samuel turn around with surprise.

'I want to see,' she said, closing the carriage door and watching men running down the street past them. Walking at first, she soon broke into a jog, and her hood fell back. She didn't care about the rain, she didn't care if she was soaked to the skin, it was so good to be outside.

She was amongst people, shoes and boots tapping on the road like a crowd hurrying to greet a whaling boat that had returned after months at sea. She shook her head, her dark hair already a gossamer net of wet beads.

'Jianna.' Samuel appeared at her side.

Slowing, they joined a ring of by-standers gathered around an upturned cart, its wheels spinning in the air, and all across the ground were wooden crates spewing out carrots and turnips, green beans and potatoes. They moved closer. A large brown horse thrashed about, its eyes wild and frantic and its back legs trapped between the poles of the cart. Frantically scrabbling, hooves scraping cobbles, it twisted its neck and bared its teeth. No-one seemed to know what to do. There was no-one taking charge, no driver to be seen, no official to issue orders, everyone stood around growing wetter in the rain. Puddles shimmered with movement and the sky pressed deep slate but Jiddy couldn't take her eyes off the horse. Baring its teeth, it scraped at the rough ground, grunting out misty breath. The noise of its hooves and the grating sound rising from its throat was becoming unbearable. Jiddy tried to edge closer, she wanted to stroke its brown coat and push back its mane sticking black to its neck, and make it calm.

'Who's looking after the horse?' she said to Samuel. She pushed through the crowd, but he caught her arm.

'We can't do anything,' he said.

'Yes, we must.'

Samuel pointed. 'It's all right.'

A bare-headed man edged around the panicked horse, trying to grasp its harness but the horse was too frightened to let anyone near.

'Come away,' said Samuel, 'we'll wait in the carriage until this has been cleared. You'll be ill if you stay out in this weather.'

Jiddy edged closer. A couple more men, shirt sleeves and jackets dark with rain, were circling.

'Where's the driver?'

'He were going too fast.'

'Should know better in this weather.'

'There, by them crates. Don't think he's too good.'

'Jiddy, come away,' Samuel took her arm again but she pulled herself free. She had to see. The figure reminded her of something.

The driver slumped into the ground, a red circle of

blood around his head turning to a watery pink. Jiddy's hair dripped into her eyes and she wiped her face. One of the driver's arms stretched out, the other twisted over his back. She'd seen a body like that before. She'd seen a pool of blood spilt around a man's head before.

Crack. The snap of a gun made everyone startle. A soldier, his red coat a stab of colour in the crowd, held a pistol that smoked the remains of gunpowder. The big brown horse lay still, a hole glowing in its head just below the ear. She couldn't bear to see, and turning found Samuel's shoulder to burrow her face into. He put an arm around her and held her close and the damp wool of his jacket filled her nostrils.

'Jianna?' Samuel said.

His eyes looked grey, not blue any more. Her sodden hair stuck to her cheeks and he gently lifted the strands off her face.

'I wish you hadn't seen that,' he said.

He tucked her arm under his and they headed back towards their carriage. The noises around them muffled in her ears. Shadowy figures hurried in the wet. Buildings were different to the tall houses she'd seen, these were low and dark with dark windows and shabby doorways. Samuel held one hand to his hat, manoeuvring her though the crowd.

A little boy stared at them. He only had a shirt and some half-length trousers on and although he was soaking wet and getting wetter, he held out his hands as people brushed past.

They were walking past him themselves. His sunken

eyes stared blankly and he didn't flinch when people knocked him, but stuck out his hands again. Breaking away from Samuel, Jiddy hurried back.

'What's your name?' she said.

The boy looked up at Samuel and he threw a coin into the boy's hand. 'Come on, Jiddy,' he said, 'the boy has what he wants now.'

Jiddy held back. 'Where's your mam and da?' she said.

The boy's scrawny arm shot out and he pointed towards the upturned cart.

'That was your father?' Samuel said.

The boy nodded and Samuel put another coin in his hand.

'We can't leave him,' Jiddy said. She turned to the boy. 'Come with us.'

The boy stepped back, shaking his head.

'I think we're scaring him,' said Samuel.

The boy had already turned to others walking by, cupping his hands and looking up with his solemn, pleading face.

'You can help him, can't you, so he doesn't have to do that?' she said, 'Samuel, tell him he can back with us. Please? Look at him, he's all alone.'

Carriages were beginning to move, blinkered horses cowing their heads to the rain. The boy moved down the street.

'He's not alone, Jiddy,' Samuel said. 'Come on, there's plenty like him.'

It was irrational, she knew that, but there was something about him that reminded her of the boy on the dockside crying for his mother. Somebody gave him a coin and he dodged further down the road. Samuel shook the rain from his face. They were drenched, everyone and everything was dripping cold grey rain that seeped through to their bones and the base of the buildings. People pushed past, nudging and knocking them off balance. Samuel took her arm.

'The cart owner isn't the boy's father,' he said.

'You're soaking,' Signora Vardarelli said as soon as they were back inside the carriage. 'What took you so long?'

'They shot the horse,' Samuel said.

Lord Ryethorpe tapped his cane against the window and they started moving. The day had grown darker and it seemed as if the time in the sparkling bright Vardarelli shop had never existed and that this was the real London. Jiddy looked out of the window to see the little boy again but he'd already disappeared into the crowd.

CHAPTER FORTY-SIX

J iddy pushed the needle into the deep-blue fabric and drew a straight blue line. Sewing kept her calm, kept her from thinking about the rain and the horse and the driver with his pink halo. Most of all, it stopped her thinking about the little boy who reminded her of the boy on the dock in Whitby, crying for his mam. And remembering that this boy had lied.

Samuel had tried to cheer her up. Dripping wet, he had looked dreadful, his skin a pinky mauve colour and his fair hair flattened like wet sand. She pierced the fabric again with the needle.

'How are you today, Jianna?' Samuel's voice startled her and she pricked her finger.

'I am sorry,' he said, closing the drawing room door. 'I didn't mean to startle you.'

Sucking the globule of blood, she watched him walk towards her, perfectly groomed once again.

'Let me have a look,' he said. 'Here, show me.'

'I'm fine,' she said, 'I don't damage easily.'

He remained on his knees looking at her.

'I didn't expect London to be like this,' she said, leaning as far back as she could in the hard-backed chair.

'London is an exciting city,' he said. 'When the sun shines we will go for walks in the parks and we'll visit St

Paul's and call on people I know. This rain isn't normal, you're not seeing the city at its best. I promise you, you will grow to love it here.' He smiled, a rippling beam. 'Should we practice again for the ball?' he said. He was trying so hard, she could see that in his face. When the sun shone, she would feel better. Rain always got her down, in Bay, up at Farsyde's, or farm. Once she started to explore London, she would see the great things about London that Samuel talked about.

'Do we have stay in the house until my dresses are ready?' she said, and he laughed. She hadn't expected that and it made her smile. 'I'm not being me at all,' she said. 'I don't usually care about dresses and what I look like.'

'I don't believe that.' Standing, he held out his hands for her to take. She looked at them, fingers, clean and smooth, nails, pink and shining. 'Let's practice,' he said.

'I'm sewing.'

'One practice isn't enough if you're going to want to do justice to those dresses you say you don't care about.'

He was funny. She hadn't expected that either. Taking his hands, she jumped to her feet. 'Ooh,' she said, the surprise of his face so close to her own.

He dropped her hands. 'Do you remember the Allemande?' he said.

'What about music?'

'Where you are there is always music,' he said, but his mouth twitched.

'Agh,' she groaned, 'that's terrible.'

He shook her hand. 'Ready?'

She heard the music in her head, the sound of Mary's voice and the shanties they sang when mending nets. Jumping to the right and then the left, they began. She spun under his arm then he under hers. Holding both hands now, they turned together, inside out, arms outstretched, their bodies opened to each other, then back to back and turning again. His shoulder blades touched hers and then, facing each other, they stared solemnly. It was good to move and exciting to be dancing, and with Samuel who knew when to look at her and when to look away. Jumping and turning, the feeling of sadness disappeared. She was going to a ball where she'd dance for an entire night with an orchestra playing and chandeliers sparkling in their eyes. They turned again, it seemed a little too close.

'Do you think we need more light?' Samuel said.

The room had gone dark, with only the orange of the fire offering a glow.

'I like a challenge,' she said.

Lifting her arms, he took her in hold ready to move. None of the lads at home danced like this, not so slowly and elegantly. He was watching her, smiling.

'The Cotillion,' she said.

They stepped right, then left and then he turned her, their hands above her head. Mrs Farsyde had said to look at your partner as you turn under their arm, keep your chin down and your eyes up. She remembered and she did as she had been told and she looked into his eyes. At first, all those ages and ages ago, she'd thought them cold like clear spring water, but today they seemed different.

Maybe it was because of yesterday, when his eyes had looked grey, he'd reminded her for a second of Jonas whose eyes differed like storm clouds from one moment to the next. But here, the bright blue had returned to Samuel's eyes and he flushed a light fresh pink. She turned into his hold again so that they repeated the side steps right and left and another turn, so slow they looked at each other for what seemed a very long time.

'Now walking,' he prompted when she forgot to stand by his side, 'forward, two, and cross steps side. Forward, two and cross steps side.'

She nodded and they repeated it again and again, their hands held up between them, his gently nudging her in the right direction.

'Will you help me if I forget?' she said.

'I will if I'm dancing with you, otherwise you're on your own to remember I'm afraid. Let's hope that you have a discreet partner.'

He was teasing her again, so gently that she couldn't help but smile and that made him watch her even closer which made her smile more.

'One more and then tea,' Samuel said.

'All right. Not the Gavotte, I know that well enough, but we could try the current, it's only walking really, isn't it?'

'Courante,' Samuel corrected. 'And I think there's a little more to it than walking.'

She laughed. 'The courrrrornttttt it is then.'

Samuel took her hands and she tilted back her head, her curls brushing her neck.

'Jianna?'

He was close, closer than they'd stand in a ballroom. All she would have to do was lean slightly forward and he would know she wanted to kiss him. She knew he wanted to kiss her. She tried to remember what his lips had felt like in the preaching house and what he'd tasted of. It hadn't been salty or moorland grass and fresh sea airy like Jonas at all. And then she remembered. Blood. She had tasted blood and it had been her blood she'd tasted. He'd tried to stop the flow on her neck from the bite Nellie had given and when they'd kissed, his mouth had tasted of her blood. She remembered the sensation of his mouth on her neck, dragging and stinging. He wanted to kiss right now, she could tell. What would happen if they did, what would it mean in this London world full of etiquette and rules that she knew nothing about? He released one of her hands and began leading her around to stand at his side. They had been so close, almost kissing, he'd wanted to, and she'd wanted to too. She had almost made a mistake and shown herself as the peasant girl she was. She looked down at the carpet. There was so much to learn.

'I'm happy I can remember all the dances,' she said. 'I didn't think I would.'

CHAPTER FORTY-SEVEN

T he next morning, as if he never left the house, Samuel stood in the morning room, seemingly waiting for her. Seeing him in his bright red uniform, shining buttons, white breeches and black boots, sword and pistol in their holsters, she couldn't help but stare.

'Are we going to war?' she said.

'Not this morning,' he said. 'I'll explain later.'

Deep in conversation by the window, Lord Ryethorpe and Signora Vardarelli didn't seem to think it any different from the clothes he'd been wearing since they'd arrived in London, but to Jiddy it was like looking at two different people: an enemy and a friend. She didn't know what to say and sat down on one of the two sofas, placing her hands on her lap.

'Are you all right?' he mouthed at her as he sat opposite. His blond hair suited the bright red. He looked as clean and new as he always did. It were only a uniform, she told herself. He was still Samuel. He wasn't Captain Ryethorpe of the dragoons. Heads close together, his father and her mother were still deep in conversation.

'When we first met, why didn't you say you were a captain?' Jiddy said.

'When was that exactly?'

He didn't remember. 'In the ballroom at Thorpe Hall,' she said, 'Mrs Farsyde …'

'Ah yes,' he said. 'I was incognito at that point.'

'Is that what you call normal clothes in London?'

'My uniform was being cleaned,' he said, 'otherwise I would have been wearing it.'

'Mrs Farsyde didn't say your name at the time, either.'

'Good morning, my dear,' Signorelli Vardarelli interrupted.

'Good morning,' said Lord Ryethorpe.

They'd walked up without Jiddy hearing. Samuel rose to his feet. Between the two sofas, a large tea tray stood on the low table. The prettiest tea service Jiddy had seen filled the tray; green cups and saucers, plates and teapot, all with gold scrolls and swirls and bright red, yellow, orange and blue flowers decorating the outside and inside as well. A large ginger and lemon cake stood in the centre, the sharpness of both flavours making her mouth water. She waited for Signora Vardarelli to start. This was much more important than Samuel in his officer's uniform.

'If you would serve the tea, Jianna, that would be very helpful,' Signora Vardarelli said, 'I will only have a sliver of cake.'

'Me?'

'Yes, Jianna, you.'

She remembered the last disastrous attempt in front of Mrs Farsyde. Pouring tea so it stopped before the edge of the cup and didn't flow into the saucer. Cutting that very first slice so it slid out in one piece and didn't crumble to pieces. And then eating the cake without crumbs flying everywhere and drinking the tea without slurping or spilling from such ridiculously small cups.

She wanted to melt into the sofa. The cups were positioned in a row and the teapot on the far end. She'd have to reach across and it would be hot. There was no cloth so should she use her skirt to lift it? Samuel handed her one of the white napkins. Taking it, she shuffled forwards. She mustn't let the cups rattle on the saucers. Could she remember everything that Mrs Farsyde had taught her? Luckily, only Samuel seemed to notice her nervousness as Signora Vardarelli began talking immediately, claiming Lord Ryethrope's attention.

She managed it. No spillage. Signora Vardarelli took the offered cup of steaming tea. 'Thank you, Jianna.'

She really must concentrate. Cut the cake. What was a slither? Sounded mean and tight. It must be a small slice. The knife hid near the plate. Samuel was watching, he wasn't even pretending to listen to the conversation. A paper-thin slice. Napkin.

Signora Vardarelli balanced the pretty plate on her knee. Lord Ryethorpe was watching her. Hand him some cake, she urged herself, a bigger slice, on the plate, napkin, no shaking, get it right.

He held up a hand. He didn't want any. How dare he refuse when she'd done it right? Samuel was looking at her. Why were they all staring? She smiled gormlessly. I'm just going to sip my tea, she thought, eat my cake, drop crumbs everywhere if that's what happens and let them talk. This is exhausting.

'What do you think of London?' said Signora Vardarelli.

They were all of them looking at her. She couldn't ask about the little boy and how many there were like him in the city.

'I liked your shop,' she said.

'Ah, my shop.'

This wasn't easy at all. She didn't think it appropriate to mention her gowns, it would seem rude to ask again when they'd be ready, and a dead horse wasn't what you talked about over pretty china. She didn't know where to ask about that she could visit. Concert halls and whatever St Paul's was.

'I'd like to visit a park,' she said.

Signora Vardarelli looked at the window. Rain continued to stream down the glass.

'A museum might be a good idea,' said Lord Ryethorpe.

'What's a museum?' Jiddy said, and the silence crackled louder than the fire.

'Have you decided on a date for the ball?' Samuel said, dropping crumbs onto the rug.

Signora Vardarelli turned to face Jiddy.

'You have a fitting tomorrow,' she said 'and the ball will be on Friday next.'

'We've been practising the dance steps, haven't we, Jianna?' Samuel said, putting down his plate and standing. 'We'll show you.'

'If you don't mind, I have a thousand things I must do before next week,' Signora Vardareill said, 'Jianna, you won't mind, will you?' Jiddy shook her head. 'Good. I want everything to be perfect for you, with all the right people here, and I want savouries and sweets looking and tasting the very best. I have a new gown myself and I must go for a fitting. Lord Ryethorpe, I am going to need your help.'

He was on his feet and they both moved to the door, leaving Samuel and Jiddy looking at the tea tray and the ginger and lemon cake.

'Are you going to tell me why you are wearing your uniform?' she said.

Pulling down the hem of his jacket, he became the officer that she'd first met and not the relaxed Samuel she had come to know over the past few days, and who only minutes before had spilt crumbs on his breeches.

'I still have to report, Jianna,' he said. 'But it is only today and I will be back in my civilian clothes tomorrow.'

She walked to the window. The garden dripped its shades of green. She felt like a caged animal. Picking up a cushion from the window seat, she threw it down hard. Grabbing another, she clutched it in both hands. Where should she throw it next? She spun around. Samuel stood, a patch of red in the dull room, his sword handle gleaming.

If only she was an officer, she'd hack her way outside.

'Show me,' she said, throwing down the cushion and striding towards him.

He stepped back, a look of surprise on his face. 'Show you what?'

'Your pistol.' She held out her hand decisively, 'I know how to use one, show it to me.'

'Jianna,' his voice softened, 'I know you must be frustrated, I know Signora Vardarelli isn't easy to get to know, but give her time, she is as in shock about discovering you as you are about meeting her.'

'That doesn't bother me,' Jiddy said, 'but I am bored with nothing to do. Give me the pistol and I'll show you what a good soldier I would make if I was a man.'

That made him smile. 'I don't think so, Jianna, come, show me the embroidery you were doing yesterday. I could never do anything so intricate. Why don't you build a nest in the window seat and continue with it? I'll come back later and you can show me.'

'Will you stop talking to me as if I'm a simpleton?' she said, reaching for the pistol. Taking him by surprise, she wrapped her hand around the handle. A moment later, his hand wrapped around hers and held it down. They stared at each other. It was different. They were challenging each other.

'I have all day to stand here like this,' she said. 'Don't you have to be somewhere else or don't you care about being a soldier?'

Releasing her hand, he let her lift the pistol out of its holster and she walked back towards the window, turning it over in her hands.

'Sit next to me and I'll show you,' she said.

He sat beside her and she turned the pistol on its side, withdrawing a rod from a channel down the side of the barrel.

'Wrap a bullet in a bit of cloth,' she said, 'and pour a small amount of gunpowder down here.' She tapped the end of the barrel, 'then I'd push the bullet ...' She mocked dropping something down the barrel followed by the rod which she moved up and down a few times. 'You have to do this gently,' she looked at him while she did it, 'you don't want to press the powder too hard and make it solid because it won't catch so easy if you do and you want it to catch fire quickly so that you're not an open target for someone quicker and more skilled than you.'

'Really?'

'Really,' she said. 'And then you put some powder in here,' she tapped the hollow on the top of the gun with the rod. Holding the pistol in both hands, she aimed at the door and pulled back the cocking arm. 'And now I'm ready to shoot.'

Her arms straight out, her eye on the door, the pistol in her sight, she felt strong and she wanted Samuel to know it.

'Where did you learn to do that?' he said.

He looked like a confused and vulnerable five-year-old. What could she say? I'm a smuggler? I'm a thief and I break the law that you try so hard to uphold. Standing, she placed the pistol back in his hands.

'I'd like to make it against the law to have guns,' she said. 'Then soldiers wouldn't have to go to war and all the money spent on fighting could be used to feed little children like the boy we saw in the street.'

S amuel never asked what she meant, and during the next few days they talked of little else but the weather and the ball. The sound of cups clinking saucers and spoons and swallowing cake had never sounded so loud. When the week turned into a whirlwind without a moment alone to think, she stopped thinking about it as well. She had fittings and shopping excursions and one day someone came and she had to sit very still while they trimmed her hair. She'd never known there was such a thing unless you were selling your hair or you had ringworm or were sick and had to have your head shaved. Samuel seemed busy too, always rushing to the house to see her or his father, because Lord Ryethorpe spent all his time with Signora Vardarelli as well. All this rushing about, meaning they never talked about what she'd said or what she had meant.

She tasted ice cream and blancmange and cakes and all sorts of delicacies for the ball and she practised dance steps over and over. The excitement was contagious. A ball. For her. What would Annie say?

In addition, the rain stopped. It was hard to believe. After so many days of rain, one morning it ceased and the sun came out. In the garden, trees sprinkled their load and leaves blew colourfully across the grass.

Through the window, it looked like a framed painting, not something she could step into. Signora Vardarelli, Lord Ryethorpe and Samuel seemed happy to remain indoors but she itched to be outside. Outside, trees and clouds and leaves danced, but inside the furniture sat rigid and unmoveable and the air grew stale. She began to wonder if the air was actually poisoned with some form of sleeping potion but it couldn't be because everyone else seemed fine. Maybe only people like her were affected. Maybe fisher folk were too wild to breathe with the restrained breaths required. She couldn't face asking someone to teach her how to fill only half her lungs and be able to survive on that. They'd think her a simpleton for sure. She put her hand on the glass. All the way up the country, all the way across the moors, Jonas would be breathing for her.

Jonas. Her Jonas. She missed his teasing and his bad moods. She missed kissing. If only he'd come to London and fill her lungs with a fresh snatch of cold off the sea.

'May I join you?' Lord Ryethorpe stood in the doorway. 'I thought we could take a stroll in the garden?'

Jiddy breathed in the autumnal air and felt the breeze on her face. They walked in silence but she didn't mind. She didn't know him very well, but if he was willing to open the door she wasn't going to quibble about walking through it. Her skin already felt fresher and her head clearer.

'Samuel seems to think I am more qualified than him to give you certain information,' he said when they'd reached the bottom wall and turned to look back at the house. A gust sent leaves swirling across the grass. 'It's been remiss of us but I want to rectify that.'

Jiddy remained quiet. She didn't know what half those words meant but he did sound nervous and that seemed odd. They walked back towards the house. It loomed high over the garden with flat stone walls and windows full of squares.

'Please can we walk around again?' Jiddy said.

They turned along another path and already Jiddy could see how it curved around and back to the house. High walls bordered them in so that they couldn't see beyond the garden, only up to the grey clouds blowing quickly above.

Lord Ryethorpe tapped his cane on a tree trunk as they walked past. 'Your father and I were good friends,' he said. 'Our families knew each other. We were always close.'

'I didn't think about family,' she said. 'Do I have aunts and uncles? And cousins?' She thought of all Nellie's cousins in Whitby and Betsie's mam always having another toddler clinging to her skirt. 'Are we going to go to Naples to meet them? Is this what you want to tell me?'

Lord Ryethorpe didn't look as happy as she felt. 'It's a long way to Naples,' he said.

'I would love to meet my father's family. And my mother's too of course. I never dreamed I'd meet them, let alone travel in a ship to another country.'

Every day something new, something better as her family grew. Naples. It was supposed to be hot there,

376

not bitter and grey like a winter in the Bay. Sunshine. She lifted up her face. She could definitely fit in there.

Reaching a bench, Lord Ryethorpe pointed with his stick and they sat down. He seemed tired.

'I don't know about Signora Vardarelli's family,' he said. 'She hasn't mentioned them in all the years I have known her and she has never shown an inclination to return. Your father's parents are old now, but please Jianna, please don't be too optimistic. Your mother and father met in Naples, you see, and then there was the long voyage back to England.'

'I was born at sea? I knew it. I knew there was a reason I love the sea so much.'

'Yes, you were born at sea,' he said. He spoke so slowly, she wished she could say the words for him. 'You were a beautiful baby, with thick black hair and huge dark eyes.' He paused as if remembering.

'Why were they leaving Naples?' Jiddy said.

He looked confused for a moment. 'Your father was not Neopolitan,' he said. 'He was English. He was sailing home.'

'But if he was English, what about Signora Vardarelli's name?' It was Jiddy's turn to look confused.

Lord Ryethorpe turned up the collar of his cloak. 'Vardarelli is your mother's name. They weren't married you see and your father's family, well, they'd never met your mother and you,' he paused. 'They refused to meet Maria. And we thought you had perished, so she never did meet them or feel she had the right to take his name.'

Jiddy looked at the holly bush directly ahead and tried to put his words in order.

'That means Signora Vardarelli is the only family I have,' she said.

'Samuel told me you were a bright young woman,' he said. 'You take after your mother.'

'I wish you'd married her,' she blurted out.

He smiled and his eyes crinkled. 'I have asked her,' he said, 'several times, but she always refuses.'

'I suppose she thinks you loved your wife so much, she doesn't want to spoil that memory.'

'I think it is more because she doesn't need anyone,' said Lord Ryethorpe, 'I mean, apart from you. A daughter is different. She doesn't need mine or anyone else's fortune, is what I meant.'

'I will help her now,' said Jiddy. 'I know about fabric and cloth. I can help her run her shop.'

Lord Ryethorpe studied her and she stared back. 'I can,' she said. 'I do know what I'm doing when it comes to dressmaking. I was a seamstress, you know.'

'Yes, Samuel told me.'

Jiddy jumped to her feet. 'I don't care about knowing my father's family,' she said. 'I know you and Samuel and the more I learn about my mother, the more I see we are alike. I'm so glad you told me this.'

'That's not quite how it works,' Lord Ryethorpe said, but Jiddy was already spinning across the grass, leaves swirling around her feet. She wouldn't have to sit around doing nothing, her hands would be occupied, touching beautiful fabrics every day, making dresses, sewing on jewels and lace and being there; it would be enough to be in that place every day. Her mother would want that. They had much to share and she couldn't wait a moment longer.

'Thank you, Lord Ryethorpe,' she shouted, 'thank you so much!'

CHAPTER FORTY-NINE

J iddy studied her black hair hanging in thick,
gleaming ringlets. Her eyes looked even darker if
that were possible, larger and sparkling. She was a lady
now, going to her first ball and to be publicly introduced
as Jianna Vardarelli, the daughter of the wealthy and
beautiful Signora Vardarelli. Every night, she rubbed
her hands and arms with a sweet-smelling cream and
her skin had softened so that she felt she'd always
been a lady. She thought it a shame to cover them in
gloves, but Signora Vardarelli had been insistent on a
white pair in tight kid skin. She had been right about
the dress too. The green suited her perfectly, the deep
emerald coat gleaming over the intricately gold and
paler green embroidered underskirt with its matching
ruffled edging. The frill on the sleeves tickled her arms
but that made it even more exciting to wear. She turned
around again. The material weighed heavier than any
she'd ever worn, heavier than any of Mrs Farsyde's best
dresses. But the final touch had been her own. The dark
red garnet stood out beautifully against the emerald
green. She straightened the droplet and looked at her
transformation.

'I found this at the bottom of the bag you brought with
you.' Kitty laid the velvet case on the dressing table and

lifted out an ornate diamond necklace. 'Surely you want to wear this for your first ball?' she said.

Jiddy unfastened the garnet with shaking fingers and put it in the box while Kitty stepped behind and fastened the diamonds. They lay flat against her breastbone, sparkling in the candlelight.

'Beautiful,' said Kitty. 'You're going to cause quite a stir.'

Thinking of Mrs Farsyde's box of jewels, Jiddy touched the glittering stones. Mrs Farsyde must have worried about her to have given her such a necklace. 'It was a gift,' she said.

'Signora Vardarelli is going to be very proud of you,' said Kitty.

'Would you like to go to a ball, Kitty?' she said.

'Pardon, miss?'

'D'you like to dance?'

Kitty, like Dora, had that confused look when she didn't understand what Jiddy was saying. They weren't the only ones. Many of the people Jiddy met had as much trouble understanding her as she did them at times. She must remember: sound your 'Ts' and pronounce your 'Hs'. And don't gabble.

'You're almost there,' Kitty said. 'One last check on your dress and then you'd best be going down. Most of the guests have already arrived, they are so keen to see you.'

'Will you come with me?' said Jiddy.

'Oh no, miss, I can't be seen down there.' For a second Kitty looked as if she knew Jiddy wasn't quite one of the gentry, even if Signora Vardarelli was her mother, and for a moment a cold sweat swept over her body. What if they did all know? Upstairs and down and what if no-one asked her to dance because they could tell by looking at her that she wasn't one of them, despite the expensive gown and heavy diamond necklace?

But she had to go. This was what she had been preparing for all day. Kitty had already begun tidying away. Jiddy took one last look at her reflection.

Standing at the top of the stairway, she listened to the orchestra, the chattering voices and the tinkle of glass. Shadows were in constant movement and she smelled the mixture of perfumes. Holding up her green and gold skirt to see the emerald slippers, peeking out with each step, she descended slowly, her mind racing. Practising the Polonaise and Cotillion in her room the moves had flowed easily, but she could easily forget once surrounded by strangers in all their finery, and what if none of the gentlemen were as kind as Samuel? She hoped they would be, she desperately hoped that she remembered everything and stunned them all. Almost there. The shadows had taken on colour and a rainbow of figures floated across the hall and into a brightly lit room beyond. Reaching the bottom step, she took a deep breath. What should she do? She didn't know anyone except Samuel and his father and Signora Vardarelli. Should she go into one of the rooms alone? All doors had been opened and she glimpsed chandeliers and flickering candles, silk gowns and suits of black, blues and greys. The music made her tingle. As soon as she was inside the room, she'd ask someone to dance. Yes, that's what she'd do. A hand touched her elbow.

'You look beautiful, Signorina Vardarelli,' a voice said.

It was Samuel. Of course it was. He looked beautiful too, in a pale blue coat and embroidered waistcoat and not the red uniform. His face looked clear and slightly flushed.

'Are you nervous?' he said.

'I'm excited.' She held his arm tightly.

The air smelled of deep-red-coloured aromas, rich heavy wine and citrus and sugar and the bright mix of flowers and musk. Samuel's mouth curled into a familiar smile.

'Shall we go in?' he said.

She didn't expect dancing to be so noisy, with shoes tapping, hands clapping and many chattering while dancing. They didn't seem to mind puffing and panting, often it seemed louder than the music. Skirts swirled, men's tail coats flaring out and lights blazing so bright she thought they'd set fire to the room. Faces glowed with exertion and punch, and those not dancing clustered around the edges, drinking from pretty glasses.

'Would you like a glass?' Samuel said.

'I'd like to dance.'

He took her right hand, slid an arm around her back, his palm pressing below her shoulder blades. He flicked his eyes sideways to his shoulder.

'What?' she said.

'Have you forgotten already?' His eyes flicked again and she rested her left hand on his right shoulder. His coat felt expensive to touch, her dress looked expensive too. Even to her, they looked like a young couple who fitted perfectly together. She glanced about the room. Ladies glittered with sparkling jewels and she was glad that Mrs Farsyde had slipped the diamond necklace in her bag. One day she'd need to give it back, but not tonight; tonight the necklace was hers.

'Let's dance then,' he said.

She caught snatches of conversation but she didn't want to talk. She wanted to hear the orchestra, so big with two clavichords and an array of large and small stringed instruments, the players moving bows quickly, and long clarinets making sounds she'd never heard before. Turning again, she liked the blurred effect of the room and how Samuel's face and arm kept her balanced. They were so in tune, dancing the steps smoothly, bouncing joyfully, turning exactly in time with one another. He smelled subtly aromatic of rose water. The ringlets Kitty had taken such care over bobbed against her neck. They were equals, he a captain, she a lady. His hand tightened around hers, pulling her closer to him. She could do this forever. Jonas couldn't dance like this, she doubted even Squire Farsyde could; she was so lucky to have a dance partner like Samuel and a mother like Signora Vardarelli. She was Jianna not Jiddy, such a silly name to hang on to, such a childish name, when she looked so elegant. A woman like that deserved a name like Jianna Vardarelli.

When the music stopped, he tucked her hand under his arm and led her to the side of the room.

'Would you like a glass of punch now?' he said.

'I don't want to leave this room,' she said, watching people reassemble on the dance floor.

'I can see there are others who want to ask you to dance,' he said, 'so you might get your wish and end up staying in here all evening if you're not careful.'

He was smiling and behind him she saw other gentlemen looking in their direction.

'I don't know them,' she said.

'That doesn't matter,' he said, 'they will introduce themselves. See? Here comes Mr Copley.'

Jiddy held tighter onto Samuel's arm and he looked at her in surprise. It was obviously not the correct thing to do but she didn't care. She didn't want to dance with Mr Copley.

'Dance with me again,' she said, staring so hard that he was in no doubt what she wanted.

'I would love nothing more,' he said, 'but etiquette dictates that you dance with others. Later, though, when you have had other partners.'

The noise of the room crammed out everything else. She wanted to dance and she wanted to dance with Samuel. They danced so well together, she remembered the steps, people looked with admiration at her gown and grace. Pulling Samuel so he had no choice but to follow, she dragged him back into a dance hold.

'This isn't right, Jianna,' he said as they stood close together, poised to begin the next dance.

'You should feel honoured,' she said, their faces so close she could speak in a whisper.

'I do,' he said, 'but we must follow the rules.'

They spun around. She touched hands with another partner and then back to Samuel, turning with another then back to him, always returning to each other. They danced a Minuet and then a Courante and another and she didn't care that it wasn't good etiquette.

'That's it,' he said, after a Gavotte. 'I need a glass of punch even if you don't.'

He seemed to know everyone, nodding and bowing, and she noticed people looking at her as well as him, both men and women, running their eyes up and down, admiring her gown and the curls in her hair and diamonds around her throat.

'You're charming everyone,' Samuel whispered.

'Well, they've not spoken two words to me, so how would I know?' she said. Samuel smiled that strange secretive smile again. 'What?' she said. 'And besides, when I open my mouth they can't tell a word I'm saying.'

'It's such a pretty mouth, I don't think they care,' he said.

'Careful, Captain Ryethorpe, you're turning so sweet you may end up drowning in a bag of sugar by the end of the night,' she said, angling through the crowded corridor.

'It's Captain Jenkins,' he said. 'Now you'll get your chance for conversation. Mrs Jenkins,' he bowed his head. 'Captain Jenkins, may I introduce Miss Jianna Vardarelli? Captain and Mrs Jenkins.'

'So you're the long-lost daughter?' said Captain Jenkins, taking her hand. 'We had no idea that you existed until today.'

'Pleased to meet you,' said Mrs Jenkins.

'Pleased to meet you,' copied Jiddy, her eyes caught by the older woman's emerald brooch.

Her husband, seeing Jiddy distracted, turned to Samuel.

'This isn't what we'd been led to expect,' he said. 'No wonder you've kept her under lock and key. Quite the image of her mother, isn't she? Those Northern women must have thought she'd dropped into their laps from another world.'

Mrs Jenkins was talking about a card game or a board game, some sort of activity for the next day, but Jiddy had heard Captain Jenkins' last comment and she wanted to hear the rest.

'I was very well received by the local squire and his wife,' said Samuel. 'They are more refined than you would think.'

'Lord preserve us from country squires and their tedious wives,' Jenkins said.

Jiddy couldn't ignore that. 'Excuse me, sir,' she said, 'but I don't believe you have met Squire Farsyde or his wife. They are good people, so I don't think it fair you speak badly of them.'

He bowed. 'My apologies, Miss Vardarelli,' he said. 'There are always exceptions to every rule.'

Jiddy pressed Samuel's arm. 'I'm thirsty,' she said, 'can we get some punch?'

'A young lady who knows what she wants,' Captain Jenkins said.

'We have been dancing and we are desperate with thirst,' Samuel said. 'If you will excuse us?'

He bowed and before the couple could answer, she and Samuel weaved towards another room.

'Signora Vardarelli knows a lot of people,' Jiddy said. 'Are you sure we won't suffocate?'

He laughed. Funny how she could make people laugh so easily. She looked about. Shoulders and heads and faces all too close, blocking her view. Samuel's blond head in front. She mustn't lose sight of it. Air thickened with heat. She needed air, she needed space. The urge to shout rose up her throat. She could feel herself panicking and at the moment she thought she'd pass out, they emerged through a doorway. The long table that usually stood in the centre of the room had been positioned along one of the walls and chairs graced the perimeter. Guests milled in and out, carrying glasses of punch and wine. Delicacies and desserts and ices were being served and the chatter of voices obliterated the strings of the dance room.

'Captain Jenkins won't be pleased at my snubbing him,' said Samuel. 'You are a bad influence.'

'How am I a bad influence? He was rude talking about Squire and Mrs Farsyde like that. I'd say he is the bad influence and you are best well away from him,' said Jiddy, looking around the room for the source of the punch until she saw the table laden with refreshments. 'Are we going to get some?' she said.

He smiled, as he seemed to be doing a lot that evening. 'Yes, let's have a glass of punch,' he said, 'and we'll take it outside where it's less crowded. I want to ask you something.'

CHAPTER FIFTY

The evening air cooled her cheeks. They were the only ones outside on the terrace but the windows had been opened and the voices of those inside drifted out and lights cast squares across the stone floor. Jiddy cupped the glass to her lips, tasting the warmth of punch.

'I am so thirsty,' she said.

Samuel put down his cup on one of the many round tables set along the terrace wall took her empty one and settled it next to his. Taking hold of her hands, he raised them to his lips.

'You like kissing gloves?' she said.

'I think it's time,' he said.

'Time for kissing gloves?'

He looked very serious, not a smile in sight.

'Jianna Vardarelli,' he said, 'will you do me the honour of becoming my wife?'

'Your wife?'

'I can take that as a yes?'

The delicate perfume of his hair caught her breath. He meant it, she could tell by the look on his face. They danced so well together. They looked perfect. People had looked at them as if they belonged. Her stomach bubbled with the drink she'd swallowed so quickly.

'Yes,' she said.

He slid his hands around her back. Puckering his lips, he leaned towards her. This was it. It couldn't be more romantic. His lips brushed hers.

At last, she thought, we're going to kiss. She was aware only of shadowy figures on the other side of the window and his lips.

It was the most delicate of kisses. Completely different from Jonas. It was so polite, so careful, as if he was afraid he'd hurt her. So unlike how he'd been in the preaching house.

He stroked her hair again, lingering his fingers over the curls around her neck. She watched him as his eyes followed his hand, taking in her neck and the diamonds shrouding her collar bone. She kept still, trying to steady her breathing.

'I love you, Jianna,' he said.

She brushed her lips over his cheek. He cupped her head with one hand. This was it. Opening her lips slightly, she felt him relax. Her tongue touched his bottom lip. Voices came clearer through the open window. Words filtered through.

'I didn't expect it,' a woman said. 'I've always been the one that was unique, the only one. And I've loved it, I've always loved being the one who was different from everyone else.'

Samuel's hand tightened around her waist.

'Kiss me,' she urged.

The woman's voice grew stronger. 'Of course, I was broken after what happened but then I blocked it out. You know how ill I was, I would have died without you. Are you angry with me?'

Jiddy froze. She knew that voice.

'No.' The male voice came out slow, there was a pause before he added, 'I understand.'

Jiddy and Samuel turned their faces to the window at the same time. Signora Vardarelli and Lord Ryethorpe stood with their backs to the window.

'It's absurd,' said Signora Vardarelli. 'I can't believe it. I've never felt jealous of anyone in my entire life, not even of families in the park or mothers, plump with child.'

Jiddy couldn't move. It was as if they were watching a play and it would be rude to interrupt.

'Maria,' Lord Ryethorpe said, 'I know how hard it was. I was there. You don't have to hide anything from me.'

'A sixteen-year-old is not the same as a baby,' she said.

'Let's go to the library, somewhere quiet.'

'No, no, I can't, I have to be seen,' she said. She put a hand to her forehead. 'Where is she?'

Jiddy realised in that instant that this grand ball wasn't for her at all. It was for her mother. She had to be seen, she'd said. She was jealous. Jealous of a sixteen-year-old. Of her.

'She's looking for you,' said Samuel. 'Come, let's go back inside and tell them our news.'

Putting a finger to her lips, Jiddy led him to the side of the window so they were out of sight.

'She doesn't sound as if she wants to see me,' Jiddy said.

'You are the reason for this ball,' he said. 'We must go inside.'

He took her hand but she pulled back. She couldn't

explain why but the ball had become more frightening than dodging preventives in Robin Hood's Bay back streets.

'She's getting all the attention.' Signora Vardarelli's clipped voice, 'I don't want to share the people I know. I don't want her here.'

'Maria, she's a child.'

'Don't look at me like that.'

'She's your daughter, you can't be jealous of her.'

Jealous. Her mother really was jealous of her. That's why she hadn't come to her room to check she was all right, that she wasn't scared or that the dress didn't look right after all, or for a hundred reasons. They should have walked into the ballroom together. Her mother should have introduced her to the room, not left it to Samuel.

'Everyone looks at her.' The words kept coming. 'No-one even wants to talk to me except to ask where she is. It's as if I'm invisible. What about me? Don't they care how I am?' She began to mimic other voices. 'Where is she? Are you hiding her? Hiding her? If only they knew. I wish she'd never been found.'

'You don't mean that, it's because she is newly arrived, that's all,' Samuel's father said. 'If she wasn't your daughter, they wouldn't be interested ...'

Jiddy looked at Samuel.

'People want to meet her because she is beautiful and young.'

'You are beautiful, Maria, and you are still young.'

'She is sixteen and she is taking my place!'

It sounded like the very worst thing someone could do.

Samuel caught Jiddy's arm, but she brushed him off. Her mother hated her. Well, she'd had enough of playing a part for them. Let them hear the anger she felt in return. Let them all hear her Yorkshire accent and witness the fire in her belly.

'Let go.'

Hitching up her skirts, she ran inside, her heels ringing on the stone flags then loud on the wooden floor as people one by one stopped talking and turned to look.

Each step brought her closer. Her gown swished. Everyone said how alike they were with their jet black hair and shining dark eyes; her mother should have been proud of her tonight. She should love and cherish her and stand by her side.

A tinkle of glass brought Signora Vardarelli into focus. She stood with one hand pointed and a look of horror on her face. The glass she had been holding spread its shards across the floor. Jiddy slowed; she only had to pick her way through the pieces of glass and stand face to face with her mother, but something was wrong. She slid to a standstill.

'She's wearing my necklace,' Signora Vardarelli cried out. 'That girl has stolen my diamonds!'

CHAPTER FIFTY-ONE

Jiddy didn't know how they removed her from the room. She didn't know if it was Lord Ryethorpe or Samuel, footmen or soldiers. Somehow, she'd been transported from under the diamond-bright lights and her mother's horrified eyes to the shroud of her bed.

She must have slept, but she didn't remember falling asleep. She didn't remember changing from the green ball gown into a nightgown either.

The curtains were open. Rain smattered the window as it had almost every day for the last couple of weeks. It seemed appropriate, that's all London had been, so why should today be any different? But it was. Today was entirely different. Pushing back the covers and clambering out of bed, she walked over the rug to the window and looked out. Heavy clouds filled the sky. Tracing a rivulet down the glass, she shivered. Rain teemed down, pattering hard on the pane. A movement below caught her eye. A thin-looking girl lifted her arms and threw a handful of crumbs into the air that fell in tiny specks onto the ground. A moment later, she'd gone and a sparrow or two flew down to peck at the ground.

The fire crackled, catching her attention. Someone had built it up to keep the cold at bay, but the cold was inside her, seeping out, not the other way around. Nellie's taunts were nothing to this. They were laughable, childish. What Signora Vardarelli had said last night belonged to a grown-up world, a world where truths sliced like a blade.

This wasn't how she wanted to live, tucked away in a room far away from everyone else. She was disappearing in this grand house but she wasn't becoming Jianna, whoever that was; she was disappearing and if she stayed in London she'd disappear altogether.

Crossing to the cupboard, she looked at the green dress she'd worn last night.

'I'll never wear you again,' she said, pushing it aside and pulling out the red and ochre gown instead.

On the dressing table lay the velvet box containing the diamond necklace, which glinted dully in the grey light. Before closing it again, she wound in the chain and garnet until the two intertwined.

'Sorry.' She touched the red stone gently before closing the lid.

Kitty didn't appear. There was no-one about outside her room, or as she walked down the wide staircase. In the large hall, she looked at the closed doors that had stood open last night and wondered if she had dreamed it all, but the velvet box in her hand reminded her it was real. She couldn't hear any noises in the house. Maybe they were all still asleep. It could be six o'clock or noon, she had no way of knowing. Tiptoeing across the hall, her heels making a faint tapping on the wood, she opened a door that she'd never been through before. The floor there was of stone flags and the walls of painted plaster. Closing the door behind her, she walked cautiously towards sounds emanating from a room at the end of the corridor.

She couldn't help but stare at the sight. The room's heat met her full on. The noise of crockery and glass being washed jangled from a further room beyond the main one. Here, in the main space, a large table stood, cluttered at one end by piles of vegetables and a large gleaming pot. A girl looked up, her knife raised. She turned to an older woman standing at the side of the table, her sleeves rolled to her elbows and bare arms covered in white flour. The older woman turned her head towards Jiddy, and after a moment she stood up straight.

'Can I help you?' she said.

The kitchen and smells were so familiar, Jiddy could imagine it was Mary stood there, though she'd have said, 'Come and help me' not 'Can I help you?' And of course she would have helped. At home, Jiddy would be chopping carrots and turnip or potatoes.

'Can I sit for a minute?' Jiddy said. 'It's cold upstairs.'

The woman gestured to a chair.

The sounds at the back of the room continued. Something splattered on the stove, hissing into steam as liquid hit the hot black surface. The girl kept glancing up as she continued chopping vegetables but she didn't say anything, and the older woman thumped and kneaded dough, sprinkling flour from a bag every now and then. Sitting quietly, they soon ignored her and, placing the velvet box on her knee, Jiddy began to relax. It was easy there. She didn't have to talk or pretend. Flour spread over the table and she made a line through it with a finger. The cook – that must be who the older woman was – didn't take any notice, so Jiddy traced a curve. She'd done this before, many times at home, until Mary told her to stop messing about. The memory made her smile. She looked down to see she'd made a 'J' and a 'V'. She smoothed more flour towards herself and made more letters, forming a triangle with the initials: 'R S' and further across 'J C'. The reverend would be proud she'd remembered her letters.

A noise of feet made the cook and girl look up. Jiddy turned around to see Samuel standing behind her in the doorway.

'What are you doing in the kitchens?' he said.

Lord Ryethorpe and her mother looked as if they'd been waiting for her. Walking directly to Signora Vardarelli, Jiddy placed the velvet box on the table.

'I'm not a thief,' she said. 'These were gifts from Mrs Farsyde but I think they mean more to you than they do to me.'

Signora Vardarelli opened the box and lifted up the red stone.

'This garnet is mine too,' she said. 'It must be Mrs Farsyde who is the thief.'

'Maria, I don't think Mrs Farsyde personally stole those jewels from the ship,' said Lord Ryethorpe.

All the calm Jiddy had felt in the kitchen flew away.

'You think I'm a thief and now Mrs Farsyde is a thief as well? You must have a high opinion of us Northerners,' said Jiddy, 'I think I had best be off before you accuse me of ransacking the whole house.'

The 'Ts' were stripping away, the 'Hs' were well gone but it felt liberating, freeing; Jiddy was coming back.

'Jianna, please,' Samuel touched her hand.

'I'm not Jianna,' she said, 'I'm Jiddy.'

'Jiddy, I'm on your side.'

'Nobody's accusing you of anything,' Lord Ryethorpe said.

'She is.' Jiddy glared at Signora Vardarelli. She hadn't felt fire throbbing in her head since she'd left Robin Hood's Bay and it felt good to have it back. She wanted to let out the flames, heat these cold-blooded people until they burned with her anger.

'I will not be spoken to like this,' said Signora Vardarelli. 'Not by anyone.'

Lord Ryethorpe stepped between them. 'Let us sit down and talk about this,' he said. 'Maria,' he gestured to one of the two sofas but Signora Vardarelli didn't move.

Jiddy looked at Samuel and he nodded, his eyes pleading.

'Don't worry, I'm here,' he said.

She looked again at Signora Vardarelli, dangling the chain from her small hand and making the deep-red garnet swing.

'I loved visiting your beautiful shop,' she said. 'I've never, ever been treated like that, or been to such a place. And you hardly know me. I am very grateful. Mrs Farsyde let me unpick dresses and re-make her old gowns, but otherwise I've never have worn anything but what all girls wear in Bay.'

'Please, sit down,' Lord Ryethorpe gestured again. 'All this is your right Jianna, you don't need to be grateful.'

'The dress suits you,' said Signora Vardarelli. 'I am glad you like it.'

'Good,' said Lord Ryethorpe, 'now let's get to the bottom of this.'

Without saying a word, they settled onto the two sofas, Samuel close by Jiddy's side. She knew they were waiting for her to speak and for a moment she determined to keep silent, but she couldn't bear the pretence of politeness for long.

'Mrs Farsyde gave me the necklaces but I didn't know they belonged to you,' she said in a rush, 'I don't think Mrs Farsyde would have known either, she'd have bought them in a shop or Squire Farsyde could have given them to her, but it's all right. I understand why you don't want me to have them or for me even to be here.'

'You're upset,' Lord Ryethorpe spoke. 'Your mother does want you here.'

'Does she? I don't think so,' Jiddy interrupted. 'I'd like to go home now. Will someone take me or should I catch a stagecoach on my own?'

Lord Ryethorpe looked at Signora Vardarelli but she didn't say a word.

'No, no, Jiddy, have you forgotten? We have news ...' Samuel cut in.

'I will try and arrange it myself then.' Jiddy rose to her feet, the red and ochre skirt crackling as she stood.

'Wait,' Samuel said, 'Jiddy, wait.'

'Samuel is right,' said Lord Ryethorpe, 'please wait.

You haven't been long in London, please, give the city a chance. Give us a chance. You and Signora Vardarelli need time. You will give us time, won't you, Jianna?'

Jiddy felt her chest would burst. She wanted to scream that her name was Jiddy, not Jianna. The room was too big. She wanted the cottage with the cooking pots on the fire and the table they used for eating and sewing, for everything that they did. Most of all, she wanted the woman who'd acted as her mother all her life. Most of all, she wanted Mary.

Lord Ryethorpe kept talking. 'Maybe you're owed an explanation about what happened. What do you think Maria?' he said, indicating for everyone to sit again. 'Come Jianna, it's all right. Samuel?'

'Yes, stay, please.' Samuel moved closer.

'It's not my fault, all this, you know,' Signora Vardarelli interrupted.

'It is nobody's fault,' said Lord Ryethorpe. 'Jianna? What are you thinking?'

She had dreamed about living with her real family her whole life and here it was, in this beautiful house and yet, looking out of the window behind Signora Vardarelli's head, she yearned to be outside, feeling a breeze cooling her cheeks. But you're not outside, a voice in her head said, you're not out there, you're in here.

'I don't know,' she said.

Samuel remained close, too close by her side. 'Jiddy, you do know,' he said.

'Your mother was the same age as you are now when you were born,' Captain Ryethorpe cut in.

'My travelling companion died a little after we left France,' Signora Vardarelli said. She looked like a little girl now, fidgeting on the sofa, unable to sit still.

'Imagine how that must have felt,' he continued, 'sixteen, unmarried and the only female on board ship.'

'They threw me into the sea, but not before I took what was mine. I pushed as many jewels as I could into the pockets of Gregory's jacket.' Signora Vardarelli was shaking. Lord Ryethorpe tried to take her hand but she brushed him away. 'I put on his jacket. This huge man grabbed me and squeezed my wrists so tight they were bruised for months afterwards, but I had something in my pockets that he didn't know about.' She turned to Lord Ryethorpe, her eyes wide and frightened.

'He pushed us both overboard,' he said, taking her hand and this time, Signora Vardarelli let him. 'He was a pirate, or a smuggler who took ships by slaughtering the crew and disposing of any who stood in his way.'

'I used the jewels and I set up my business. If I hadn't done that, I would have had nothing. Isn't that true, John? When Gregory's parents didn't want to know, I didn't have to rely on you, did I? Or anyone. I had my own money and I built up the Vardarelli Emporium. It's wonderful, isn't it? You like it, don't you? You said you did.'

Jiddy nodded. 'You took some of your jewels with you?'

'Wasn't I clever to think of it when any other woman would have been too terrified?'

'Where was I?' Jiddy asked.

'What do you mean?'

'Your father hid you in a cupboard,' said Lord Ryethorpe.

'We had to keep you safe,' said Signora Vardarelli. 'You were so tiny and new. You were only a few hours old.'

'If that. We thought this captain – that's what the others called him, but God knows, he didn't look like any other captain I'd seen before – we thought he would take your mother's jewels and what else he wanted on the ship and go.'

'But he didn't take them and go.' Jiddy found her voice again.

'No, he didn't,' said Lord Ryethorpe. 'This captain wanted the ship.'

'I prayed you wouldn't cry and you didn't, so I thought you were safe. I didn't expect them to take me on deck away from you.'

'Nobody planned to leave you behind,' said Lord Ryethorpe. 'It wasn't anyone's fault.'

Leave you behind. The words echoed in Jiddy's head. 'But it must have been someone's fault,' she said.

'Luckily, we were near the coast. Those jewels were heavy, it's a miracle they didn't pull your mother under. She has tremendous will power. We made it to the shore, with the help of a barrel. You remember that barrel, Maria?'

He turned to Signora Vardarelli. 'Yes, yes,' she said, 'you told me to find something to hold onto, and I did.'

'And luck was with us again when we reached land. We didn't have to walk far to find help once we reached the shore.'

'Walk?' interrupted Maria. 'We staggered half dead, we were exhausted and soaking wet. If it wasn't for finding that terrible inn on a clifftop, I don't think we'd have survived.'

'It was Robin Hood's Bay, wasn't it?' said Jiddy.

'That's right. Robin Hood's Bay,' Captain Ryethorpe said.

'I hope that wicked captain got caught and was hanged for everyone to see.'

'I would have been dead if it wasn't for him,' said Jiddy.

'I remember his name,' said Lord Ryethorpe, 'Pinkney. They called him Captain Pinkney. Davey, Captain David Pinkney.'

Samuel jumped to his feet. 'I've heard of him,' he said, 'I've met him.'

'You know him?' Lord Ryethorpe was on his feet too. 'You've met that murderer?'

Murderer. The word battered inside Jiddy's head. This was the same Captain Pinkney who had taught her to love the sea as much as he did, who'd taught her how to stand in a line on the beach and pass packets and bags of cinnamon or tea from hand to hand. The man who'd turned her into a smuggler and shown her how to load a pistol, he was the man who had thought her as important if not more, than her mother's jewels.

'Let me understand this,' Lord Ryethorpe said. 'You know him, Samuel? This man is alive and walking about free as you please?'

'But he rescued me.' Jiddy said.

'Rescued you? This Captain Pinkney probably hoped

to sell you.' Lord Ryethorpe began pacing up and down. 'Samuel? Do you know if there was a price paid for Jianna? Did the Farsyde's pay or what about this couple?'

'Nobody in Bay has any money,' Jiddy said, 'Mary and Thomas couldn't have paid anything for me.'

'These Farsydes' then. They are in it up to their necks accepting stolen goods.'

Jiddy rose slowly. 'I'm not stolen goods. You abandoned me and he saved me. The Farsydes were going to have their own children so they gave me freely to a couple who didn't have children. I was precious to them. I am more precious to them than any diamonds or garnets. I don't understand why you never came to look for me. How could you abandon me and never come back?'

They were staring at her as if she'd spoken in a different language.

'I was sixteen,' Signora Vardarelli cried out, rising to her feet. Her entire body trembled. 'I knew no-one except John and I hardly knew him. I was in a strange country and I was frightened.'

'I'm sixteen too!' said Jiddy. 'I've lived all my life feeling I was in a strange country where no-one understood me. You should have come to find me!'

'I was weak from giving birth, never mind from the terrible ordeal in the sea.'

Lord Ryethorpe stood beside her mother, anguish flashing across his face.

'Jianna, I am sorry, it was my responsibility, please accept my sincere apologies for being lacking. I should have returned. It is not your mother's fault.'

Maria continued to tremble. Jiddy realised she was too fragile a woman to have ever taken care of her, wherever they had lived.

'It makes me sad, that's all,' she said.

'Thank you,' Lord Ryethorpe said, his face softening. 'Jianna is a thoughtful girl, isn't she, Maria?' Maria nodded, holding her emotion tight as a locked box. 'Captain Pinkney saved you from the ship and we're grateful for that, but he is still a smuggler, Jianna and whichever way you look at it, he is breaking the law of the land.'

Samuel marched to the door. 'I'll head back to Robin Hood's Bay immediately and see this man pays for his crimes. He can't get away with what he's done to you both.'

'Yes, arrest him. Thank you, Samuel, thank you,' Signora Vardarelli said, the words she'd held in bursting out. 'Go, go now. And bring back my other jewels and arrest those other people too while you're at it for accepting stolen goods when they must have known he'd killed people for them. In fact, arrest everyone in Robin Hood's Bay, I bet they are all in on this ship stealing and killing of innocent people. They're all thieves and murderers. Arrest them all.'

Samuel strained to leave, fired up like an avenging angel with the law and righteousness on his side. Jiddy's tongue dried to the top of her mouth. She could see him riding into Robin Hood's Bay with a pack of soldiers on horseback, swords and pistols ready to cut anyone down who obstructed their mission. He would find Captain

Pinkney and in doing so, he'd find out the truth about the real Jiddy Vardy. What was even worse, he'd find out that they were all smugglers in Robin Hood's Bay and wouldn't hesitate to throw every one of them on a prison ship bound for Australia.

CHAPTER FIFTY-TWO

The entire way North, Samuel tried to convince Jiddy to change her mind but Jiddy would not be swayed.

'But you don't need to be there when I arrest him,' said Samuel, 'I will do it in your name.'

'No, no, I have to be there,' said Jiddy. 'You heard what he did. I have to look him in the eye and, oh, I don't know, but I have to see him.'

Samuel tried hard, reasoning and cajoling but it made her more determined. She didn't know how she'd manage it but she couldn't let everyone in the Bay be punished, even if she had to risk her life to keep them safe.

At the inn in York, she waited impatiently for their horses to be saddled up. The inn bustled with activity, wagons and carriages arriving and leaving, trunks and bags being strapped and unstrapped. The innkeeper calling out. Travellers milling about. Several lamps had been lit around the yard and candles showed from the inn's windows, glowing orange in the dimming light. No-one took any notice of them and Jiddy, for the first time in over six days, felt she could see an end to the journey even though she still didn't know what to do.

They stood by the wall of the stable waiting for the call that they too were leaving, watching the comings and goings of the yard.

'Jianna?' Samuel interrupted her thoughts.

She watched a man help a child into a carriage. 'Mmm?'

'You haven't said anything about my proposal?'

Proposal? What did he mean? She jolted away from the wall and he took hold of her hand.

'About you becoming Jianna Ryethorpe?'

Jianna Ryethorpe, of course. She'd agreed to be Samuel's wife. That was something to hold onto. Nellie would do it in a trice. Betsie and Annie would leap at the chance and Jonas wouldn't care what she did. Jonas had never said a word about marriage. Ever.

'I love you,' he said.

That was it. She would be Jianna Ryethorpe whether they stayed in the North or returned to London.

'Then you need to kiss me.'

Pressing the palms of both hands into his back, she tipped her head back. Her hood slipped and he caught it with one hand. Closing her eyes, she held her lips against his. He didn't move and she realised he was waiting for her. She let her breath escape between his lips. That was all it took. His grip tightened and they were kissing, his mouth opening and his tongue moving. At last, thank God, at last. She tried to work out the taste. His tongue spread over her lips, wobbly and formless. She tried to shift away but his tongue coated her mouth with saliva and then it was inside, all flapping and flopping. No, no. She pulled back but he held her tighter, gripping his other arm around her shoulders. He wanted this kiss now, more than she did. His tongue felt huge and wet, wet everywhere but what did it taste of? What did he taste of? She couldn't work it out, his tongue moved so fast. There. She almost had it. She tried to touch it, feel it, but it was so wet. Like the sea? No, not a trace of salt. Like a fresh cold stream? Like sunshine? Night? What was it? She pulled his jacket. Stay still, she urged, slow down. She tried to calm the tongue that whipped faster than a dodging rabbit. Ah. She caught it, her tongue in his mouth shocking him to a standstill. He waited. Any minute and he'd be licking her mouth and chin and she wouldn't know. What was it? What was it? There. She'd never tasted anything like it before. For all his wealth and being above the law, she felt the full impact of him.

She didn't know what to say when they were called to their horses. Samuel acted as if a pact had been sealed. He strode confidently across the yard, ordering a stable hand to help her mount a chestnut mare. It was a relief to leave the noisy inn and taste of that kiss and start out on the Salt Road. The skin around her mouth felt sore and she dreaded to think what it looked like. How could someone who looked so perfect kiss so badly?

As they crossed the moors, clouds lifted with a strong breeze and the sky brightened, so they kept their lanterns dangling unlit from their saddles. She wondered if he was planning his strategy as the reality of their destination grew nearer. What if the Baytowners still wanted her dead, traitor or not? She still rode alongside Captain Ryethorpe, as she had when she left. What would Jonas do? After all, last thing he'd seen was Samuel and her kissing and here she was returning and what really was so different now?

You're going to be married to him. It was a mess. A complete mess. Only the taste of Samuel made her sure.

Thankfully, he remained silent, keeping a little ahead. Nearing the Buttercross, they saw a body hanging from the gibbet and they slowed to pass.

'It's a woman,' said Samuel, 'don't look.'

Jiddy pulled her mare to a standstill. The girl's open mouth showed a dark wizened tongue and her bulging eyes dropped from bruised sockets. Her cracked feet were swollen and black.

'I know her,' Jiddy said.

'Not all the people we know are good, Jiddy. Let's go on.'

'Jonas was right,' she said.

'Who is Jonas?'

'He doesn't believe in hanging or stoning.'

The torn skirt flapped and the girl's mousy brown hair fluttered strands across the ashen face.

'If she was caught stealing, then she had to pay the consequences,' Samuel said.

'She didn't have anything,' said Jiddy, 'like that little boy.'

'What little boy?'

The rope creaked, making the body move. 'He was hungry,' Jiddy said. 'You'd say anything if you were starving. It's not right to be punished for having nothing.'

'Let's move on,' Samuel said, 'we have somewhere to be and it's growing dark.'

'Her name is Nellie,' Jiddy said, 'Nellie Ashner. The girl in the church. Remember?'

She flipped the reins so that the horse walked on. It was finally real coming back to Robin Hood's Bay. The moors stretched either side, on and on as far as they could see. A grouse rose up, a flurry of wings, startled by their approach. At last, catching sight of the sea, glittering in a strand of pink sunset, she knew the journey was at an end. Golden fields rippled with long grass on either side of the track and trees clustered thick where the land nestled in hollows before cresting over the next hill and silhouetting against the sky. This was Jonas' country. Everywhere she looked reminded her of him. She couldn't believe she'd ever wanted to leave. The horses walked slowly down the hill through Fylingthorpe, their hooves making the only noise. By the time they rode through the entrance way to Thorpe Hall, night had fallen, bats were swooping between trees and light glowed from the lower windows.

'They've waited up,' said Samuel, dismounting by the side door of the house.

Jiddy slid off her horse and walked to the rear door while Samuel tied the horses' reins to a metal ring on the wall.

'You can't leave them there,' she said, 'stable's round back.'

'I'll ask Squire Farsyde to call a stable hand for your horse,' he said, following her inside. 'I will probably head straight off.'

There was no-one in the kitchen or the corridor leading to the main house. Immediately she saw the signs. There was a run on. Squire Farsyde was waiting up for that, not for her, and if Samuel headed straight off he could collide with Jonas or whoever was carrying goods inland.

'What do you want me to do about Mrs Farsyde and the jewels?' Samuel said as they crossed the hall. 'She does have part of your inheritance in her closet.'

'You don't need to do anything,' Jiddy said. 'I'm too tired, I don't want to think of that right now.'

A light shone under the library door. Jiddy touched her mouth. The skin felt raw. Shaking her hair across her face, she opened it and walked into the room. Straight away, Squire and Mrs Farsyde stood.

'Come in,' Squire Farsyde said, 'have some bread and wine. You're later than we expected.' He strode to meet Samuel while Mrs Farsyde reached out to take Jiddy's hands.

'You must be cold and tired,' Mrs Farsyde said. 'Sit by the fire. I'll pour you some wine.'

'Thank you but I'm not staying,' Jiddy said, hoping they'd get the hint. 'I want to know if it's safe for me to go down to Bay. I want to see Mary.'

'It would be best to wait until tomorrow,' the squire said. 'It's too late now, she'll be asleep and best not to wake her. But don't worry, you can go tomorrow, everyone realises you're no informer. Jonas Chaplow got the truth out of that girl, Nellie Ashner.'

'We saw the gibbet,' Samuel said.

'Jonas weren't for having that,' said Squire Farsyde, 'but Bay folk have their way of doing things.'

'Your deputy wasn't happy about it,' said Mrs Farsyde.

The squire shook his head. 'It wasn't a good day.'

'If you'll excuse me interrupting,' said Samuel, 'I need to see Clifton. I'll spend the night at the Musgrave Inn and will be back tomorrow and we will talk about it then. If Jiddy could stay the night with you, ma'am?'

'Of course, of course,

It wasn't working. The squire never caught on quickly. Jiddy tapped Samuel's arm. 'Samuel,' she said, 'why don't you tell them why you are really here?'

Samuel straightened his belt. He looked from Jiddy to Squire Farsyde. 'I have come to arrest Captain David Pinkney,' he said. 'He not only stole a ship and all its contents but he murdered a titled gentleman from London and attempted to kill not only my own father, but also Jiddy's mother, Signora Vardarelli.'

Jiddy knew they were all looking at her but she kept her eyes down. She needed to form a plan.

'Are you sure you have the right man?' Squire Farsyde said. 'That doesn't sound like the captain.'

'They heard the crew call him by name,' Samuel said. 'There is no mistake.'

Mrs Farsyde looked at her husband and for once, the squire was lost for words.

'He committed a crime and he has to pay for it,' Samuel said. 'I believe this is the way of Baytowners too.'

The way of Baytowners. Jiddy couldn't get that out of her head. They stoned people, they'd hanged Nellie.

They stole from innocent travellers. But Jonas didn't. And they shouldn't have to. Baytowners didn't have to live like this.

'Squire Farsyde, you'll tell me where Captain Pinkney lives, won't you?' said Samuel.

Now they were in trouble. Jiddy wondered if Squire Farsyde would be clever enough to get out of this.

The squire cleared his throat. 'I'm not sure,' he said. 'Captain Pinkney is often at sea for months at a time. He's never on land for long.'

'Is he on land or at sea right now?'

'He's probably at sea,' said the squire. 'I'm not party to his movements.'

'Is he a friend of yours?'

'No, he's not a friend,' said the squire. 'I know him of course, everyone knows everyone in the Bay, but he's not a friend, no, definitely not.'

'Do you know where he lives when he is on land in Robin Hood's Bay?' Samuel persisted.

Squire Farsyde licked his lips.

'He lives at High Normanby back the way we came, heading north,' said Jiddy before he could answer, 'and he's always on land at this time of year.'

'Right,' Samuel said. 'Thank you, Squire Farsyde, I will collect my men from Musgrave's, make the arrest and be back here tomorrow, bright and early.'

'No, go straight to High Normanby,' Jiddy said, touching his arm again. 'Catch him unawares while he's asleep. You don't need to trek over to Musgrave's. That'll be such a waste of precious time.'

'Jiddy's right,' said the squire, stepping in. 'Pinkney rises early and you could be in danger of missing him, if you make a detour over moor in the opposite direction.'

Samuel looked at them both, trying to make a decision. 'No,' he said eventually, 'I need Clifton and a few others. It won't take long if I make a short cut.'

Jiddy looked at the squire. It didn't seem as if there was more they could do and not arouse suspicion. Squire Farsyde looked like a rabbit caught in a trap.

'Well, good luck,' he said.

'You must stay here,' Samuel said to Jiddy. 'Don't risk going to see anyone tonight. Please,' he addressed the squire and his wife, 'take care of her. It's been a hard journey up from London and we've not taken any rests. And Mrs Farsyde?'

'Yes?'

'Those jewels you prize, I believe they were taken from the ship Captain Pinkney commandeered.'

Mrs Farsyde looked at Jiddy.

'He means the diamonds and the garnet you gave me,' said Jiddy.

Samuel took hold of Jiddy's hands. 'We'll sort this later,' he said. 'Go to bed and get a good night's sleep.'

'Why don't you stay here as well?' she said. 'It's been a long journey for both of us. You need a good night's sleep. You can fetch Deputy Clifton in the morning and arrest Captain Pinkney then. That's a better idea, don't you think so Squire Farsyde?'

'Absolutely, stay here, captain, I'll have you woken

early. Jiddy's right, that's definitely the best plan. My dear? We have the rooms ready, don't we?'

'Yes, they're always ready,' Mrs Farsyde said, making for the door.

'Please don't trouble yourself,' Samuel said. 'As you say, who knows where Pinkney will be by tomorrow. No, my mind's made up. You stay here, Jiddy, and I'll see you all tomorrow, with justice done.'

He was at the door and they listened to his fading footsteps and then the horse's hooves clatter over the pavestones and fade as he galloped into the night.

'I didn't know Captain Pinkney lived at High Normanby,' said Mrs Farsyde, breaking the silence.

'He doesn't. He's always lived at Fisherhead,' said the squire. 'High Normanby would have taken him in the opposite direction to Pinkney and tonight's run.'

'I tried, but I didn't know what else to do,' Jiddy said.

'We'll just have to hope Captain Ryethorpe and his men don't go too near Mill Beck or run into any of carts heading back over the moor.'

'I have to do something,' Jiddy said. 'I can't come back to Robin Hood's Bay and let everyone on the run be caught by the captain of the dragoons. I have to go to Mill Beck and warn everyone.'

Silence pricked the room but outside a wind was getting up and branches murmured under the strain. Mrs Farsyde's shoes tapped up the stairs to the floor above as she went to fetch Signora Vardarelli's jewels.

Knowing she wouldn't have long, Jiddy opened the top drawer of the squire's desk and uncovered the wooden box inside. The floorboards from the room above creaked. She lifted out the pistol that Captain Pinkney had shown her how to use.

'Preparation is the key,' he had said. 'You can't turn up and think you're ready.'

She would definitely turn up ready.

Taking the bag of metal ballbearings and small wooden container of gunpowder, Jiddy held up each item she'd need to use before slipping them into the pocket of her cloak.

'Thank you,' she said. Clutching the pistol, she headed for the door.

'Jiddy?'

She paused.

'Best take a lantern,' he said. 'It's dark when the moon goes in.'

The sky lightened to charcoal grey around a large waxing moon pressing brown and mauve through the clouds. With the lantern's help, she could clearly see the field and woods with high branches creaking in the wind. Feeling the cold bite of an East wind on her cheeks, Jiddy headed across the front lawn. Scrambling over the wall, she jumped down awkwardly on the other side, holding the lantern in one hand, pistol in the other.

A distant noise made her turn her head. There, coming at an angle from across the fields. She knew that sound; hooves interspersed with metal. The dragoons were heading towards the coast and they were riding hard. Jonas would be a sitting duck on the clifftop.

Think, think, she forced herself. Captain Pinkney would sail off as soon as he saw a hint of trouble, but if he thought he had plenty of time he'd linger. She knew him too well. The dragoons would be looking out for wagons trailing inland. They were always on the lookout for lights wending their way across the moors. Trouble was, if any local carts were coming across from Boggle Hole or Mill Beck they'd be spotted. She had an idea. White Moor. She'd lead the dragoons onto the treacherous marshes at White Moor.

She moved swiftly, swinging the light at intervals, and listening carefully for the sound of horses. Soon the moorland grass interspersed with reeds and her boots began to squelch in the wet ground. She daren't go any further, or she too would be dragged into the deadly bog. Desperate to run, she swung the bright lantern, and holding her nerve waited for them to come to her. She swung it again. The lamp's wick wouldn't last much longer. She listened. That could be horses' hooves on the peat. Yes, the noise came closer. Thank heavens. There came the shouts and she dropped the lantern. The light went out. Shouts, yells, horses whinnying, thuds as men hit the ground. She could imagine the horses' panic, their eyes wild in the dark and men sprawling, terrified as they sank deeper into the marsh. She looked around, wondering if she could make out any wagons from the smuggling train, but a large cloud obscured the moon. If she couldn't see, the dragoons wouldn't be able to see either and that was something.

'Gregory.'

'Harris?'

Names. She hadn't expected them to call out names but she couldn't stay and hear more, she had to get word. And then she heard it.

'Captain Ryethorpe!'

She took a step towards the shout.

'Help the men.'

That was Samuel's voice but she couldn't wait. There were so many of them, calling out, shouting to each other, checking others were all right. Clutching the pistol, she gathered her skirt and cloak in her free hand and ran. Tufts of grass and heather made the going difficult. Out of breath, she paused, listening for sounds that anyone had followed. A horse whinnied and there was what sounded like a voice, but it could have been the wind.

'Please let him be all right,' she whispered, before kicking through the grass towards the rise of hill and the Musgrave Inn. She smelled the sea. She kept running. Her throat parched dry. Sweat beaded her skin. Not much further; she forced herself to keep moving and it wasn't long before a building loomed dark against the sky. Pushing open the heavy front door, Jiddy staggered into the bar of the inn.

'I led dragoons onto marshes. They need help,' she panted.

'Isn't that …?' Someone said.

'Jiddy Vardy.'

'By Gad, Jiddy!' Jane Bell, the landlady, strode across the room to meet her. 'We thought we'd lost you to big city for good.'

'Please,' Jiddy said, 'can some of you help out with ropes?' Jiddy looked around the room at the men sitting at the tables, mugs of ale in their hands. She knew them all. 'Dragoons' horses are sinking on White Moor,' she said. 'It's wetter than I thought. Fred, Tom, can't you fetch some long branches? Oars? Anything! I know there's a run on and I only wanted to hold them up. We don't want them to drown in bog, do we? It'll only bring more trouble. Please say we're better than that.'

The men remained silent. She was asking them to rescue dragoons, soldiers that would have them behind bars if they gave them cause. These weren't the preventives that could be bargained with, these men were ruthless.

Suddenly, someone laughed. It caught on, a couple more were chuckling.

'Aye, we can do that,' Fred pushed back his chair, gesturing to others. 'Come on lads, let's *rescue* them soldiers stuck with their nags in marshes. Got some tackle, Bill? I feel like milking this one. Welcome back, Jiddy Vardy.'

The men were off, pushing aside their chairs, slurping back the last of their beer and knocking back cups of rum.

'Sit down,' said Jane Bell, 'you must be starving.'

'No thanks,' Jiddy said, 'I've got to find Jonas.'

Jiddy was glad to feel the wind's bite on her cheeks. She could smell mud and damp grass mingling with salty air. The sea shimmered in the moonlight. It was almost in around the promontory. Soon, the beaches would be cut off. Out at sea, a schooner floated ghost-like on the water. The run was nearly over but still a rowing boat nestled close to the cliff. Captain Pinkney must still be on the shore.

A whinny caught her attention. A horse and cart stood a short way from the cliff edge. It was definitely Boy. She looked around. A scraping sound crackled across the grass. Jonas was still there; he hadn't left. She'd recognise the shape of his shoulders and the way he bent his head, anywhere.

CHAPTER FIFTY-FOUR

'Jonas?' she said.

He looked up, fists raised. And then a look of recognition flashed across his face. 'Hell's bells,' he said, 'don't go creeping up on folk. I could have knocked you off cliff.'

Desperate to touch him, she stepped closer.

'Dragoons are out on moor. I didn't want you getting caught,' she said.

'You came back from London for that?'

Hostility clouded his voice.

'I led them onto marshes.' She reached out her hand but he didn't take it. 'At least say something. We saw Nellie ...'

'We?'

'Can't we talk later? They may still come and boat's down there and you're still loading barrels.'

'You telling me how to do my job now?'

'We can't wait around, Jonas. I want to help, let me help you.'

'As you said, let's talk about it later.' Jonas bent down and began rolling a barrel towards the cart.

'I've missed you,' she said, but he didn't hear. The wind whipped her hair and her cloak. She shifted her feet again and the pistol bumped against her leg. Down on the beach, Captain Pinkney, in his familiar tricorn hat and long cloak, was climbing into a rowing boat alongside two other men.

Further out to sea, the schooner rocked on the water, its sails caught in the moonlight looking like pale sheets. blown taut to dry. In a very short time, it would be sailing away with Captain Pinkney on board. Jonas hurried back and he followed her gaze.

'It's time we were off too,' he said. 'Help me with this last barrel and come back to the farm and we can talk.

His eyes were the same as they'd always been, probing and thoughtful.

'You load the barrel up,' she said, 'I'll tidy away the ropes.'

He nodded, rolling the last barrel over the grass.

She hadn't planned this. She hadn't known exactly what she'd thought she'd do, but seeing Captain Pinkney on the beach, readying to sail away and leave them to whatever fate happened if they were caught, flared up the anger she'd felt before.

Dropping to her knees, she pulled out the rod running down the side of the pistol. Hands trembling, she took out the box of gunpowder and bag of flint rocks from her pocket. The drawstring resisted. 'Come on, come on.' Wriggling the cord, she looked up again.

'What are you doing?' Jonas said, walking towards her across the grass.

The bag opened. She drew out a metal ball.

'Jiddy, what are you doing?'

'Captain Pinkney,' she said, shaking the bag so the

metal balls dropped onto her lap, 'I have to get him before he sails off. I won't let him leave me.' She grabbed the box and shook powder down the barrel.

Crouching down, Jonas grasped her hand, but pushing him away she dropped a bullet down the barrel and began feeling around in the grass.

'Is this what you're looking for?' Jonas said, holding out the metal rod. Grasping it from him she poked the rod after the bullet. 'You're going to shoot Captain Pinkney?' he said.

'Yes, now where's the powder?' Jonas held out the box. 'You don't need to stay,' she said, shaking powder into the pan and half over her knees. 'Load up cart and I'll come after you when I'm done.'

'When I'm done? Can you hear yourself?' Jonas said. 'Did you leave your brain behind in London?'

She looked up. Jonas was staring hard.

'You don't understand,' she said, glancing down at the boat. 'I learned things when I was away. I won't let him leave. I won't.' She reached out her hand but standing, Jonas stepped back. Rising to her feet, she half-cocked the pistol.

'Stop it. No. No, Jiddy.' Jonas put his hand on the pistol but she snatched it away and aimed at the rowing boat.

'What has Captain Pinkney done to you?' he said.

All she had to do was not flinch and pray that the flint sparked and the black powder ignited. Splaying her feet for balance, she slowly squeezed the trigger.

'Jiddy? What happened to you in London?' Jonas said. 'This isn't you. What the hell has he done to deserve this?'

Gusts of wind blew her cloak around her legs and tendrils of hair across her face but she didn't take her eye off the captain. If she didn't pull the trigger right now her hands would begin to shake with the weight of the pistol and her chance would be gone.

She'd have to pull the trigger fully back, hold still, wait for the pistol to fire and then tell Jonas what the captain had done.

'Think about Mary,' he said. 'All of Baytown. Captain's one of us. Are you seriously going to shoot one of your own?'

'I'm not letting him go,' she said.

Jonas looked down at the rowing boat then back at Jiddy. Waves sent spray that misted up the cliff face.

'Jiddy? Are you listening? Put down that gun.'

'No!'

'Whatever he's done, don't let it change you. You have me, you have Mary and your friends. Annie will be over moon to see you. Come on, come home with me, you don't want to end up swinging from a gibbet like Nellie, do you?'

If she answered she'd lose concentration and then she'd lose her aim and Captain Pinkney would be gone without knowing that she knew what he'd done. The wind was picking up. Waves were beating the cliff and dragging back. It was her last chance but Jonas' words trickled through. She wanted to scream. Damn it. Damn it. No, she didn't want to end up like Nellie. She never wanted to be like her. She could see herself as a little girl. That eight-year-old, all over again, angry and fighting and desperate to explore beyond the Bay.

'He threw my mother overboard. He killed my father. He's not a good man.' Her arms began to shake. 'Leave me alone, let me do this.'

Jonas didn't say anything straight away and she narrowed her eyes, keeping her aim on the big triangle of a hat.

'Mother?' Jonas' voice sounded mocking. 'When did you start using words like that?'

'Mam!' she shouted over her shoulder. 'He threw my mam into that freezing sea. He's a murderer. He killed my da and I could have died too!'

'But you're here. Did he save you?'

'He's lied to me.'

'Give me pistol.'

'No.'

'Well, seems to me, he's tried to make up for whatever he's done, hasn't he? Why else d'you think he's paid you all that attention all your life?'

'Stop it. Stop talking. He's not a good man.'

'None of us are, Jiddy. We do what we can for each other and to keep going, that's all.'

'Go away. You can't stop me.'

She could barely hold the gun still. Captain Pinkney had tried to make it up over the years, ever since she'd first seen him. He'd talked to her, shown her how to get extras to help Mary. He'd tried to be a sort of father when Thomas had gone. But he'd killed her real father. Blast him. She wanted to hate him but she couldn't. He'd made her who she was. He'd given her that very first bag of salt. He'd made her into Jiddy Vardy.

'Think about it, Jiddy,' said Jonas. 'If Captain hadn't save you, I could be marrying Nellie. Seems to me you should be thanking him, not trying to kill him. I'm certainly grateful.'

The wind gusted, rocking her feet and steadying her arm again, she took aim.

'Jiddy, put it down,' Jonas said. 'You'll never hit him from here.'

'I damn well will.' She re-aimed the gun. 'Captain Pinkney?' she shouted as loud as she could.

Squeezing the trigger all the way back, she waited for the flint to spark and ignite the powder, forcing the bullet from the barrel.

'Captain Pinkney!'

This time he heard. He looked up and his tricorn hat slipped. Any minute and the gun would fire. He stared up at her, his look of surprise turning to understanding. She held his gaze. He'd seen her. He knew what she intended. He was looking. He'd seen her and she'd seen him. Raising the barrel high towards the stars twinkling above them, she fired the gun into the air.

The gunpowder blasted, numbing her ears. Burning sparks and splinters of flint billowed up and she screwed her eyes closed, falling to the ground as the body of the gun pushed into her hands. Dropping the pistol, she rubbed her eyes to clear grains of powder. Jonas lay a short distance away, shaking his head and tapping his ears. Shouts from below filtered upwards. Looking around, she saw the pistol smoking on the grass. Jonas was rising to his feet but the earth was shaking. He stumbled. She caught a look of horror on his face. The ground was vibrating, sending tremors up her arms and then the cliff gave way with a loud rumble. Along with the grass, soil and rocks, Jiddy fell, grasping and clutching at the crumbling ground.

CHAPTER FIFTY-FIVE

The cold water took her breath away. Waves crashed against the cliff, sucking back and surging forward, filling her ears. Disorientated, she paddled to stay afloat. Waves surged again, lifting her on their crest then lowering her into a trough. Clumps of turf fell, splashing into the water and she looked up at the jagged gash of cliff. She couldn't see Jonas. Another wave took her by surprise and she swallowed a mouthful of water, spluttering as she tried to orientate herself. A distance away, she made out Captain Pinkney and the two men in the rowing boat.

The captain was standing and shouting something, but he was too far away to hear and a rising wave soon hid him from view. Besides, the tide was dragging her in the opposite direction and her ears dulled with the weight of water and foaming sound as it hit the cliff. A wave smashed over her head and she resurfaced, gasping for breath. Spray filled the air. She went under again, gulping in water, and she pushed up, head back to gulp in air again. The sash around her throat pulled taut. Kicking, she untangled the cloak from around her legs and sliding her fingers under the sash, loosened it. Rising on another peak and down into a dip, she struggled to push it away. The boat was further off, moving out to sea, and the captain had sat down, his back a cloud of black against the dark sky and his head a round bullet without the tricorn hat. She mustn't panic. She knew she should keep still, try to splay herself out flat and float.

Something fell into the water, a few feet away. It bobbed to the surface, rising and falling on the next wave and she looked up at the cliff, wary of being hit. It floated. It was the barrel that Jonas should have loaded on the cart. Something else rose to the surface nearby. It looked like another barrel but smaller. Round and dark. A face turned towards her then disappeared.

'Jonas!' she shouted.

He appeared again to her left before disappearing under a round of swell. Dark water rose and fell deeper than she had imagined. She couldn't see him. There. She caught sight of his head again. Waves dragged him towards her, another wave and he'd be there. He raised his arms, mouth open, lifting on the crest then dipping again. One more wave and he glided into her arms. Clutching him tightly, she brought him around to face her. His chestnut hair had turned black with wet, his jacket, thick and heavy with sea. Shivering, she bent her head to rest her forehead against his.

'We have to swim,' she said.

At the next wave, he slipped from her arms and they plunged under, until, snatching at the water, she resurfaced. Grasping his sleeve, they bobbed on the surface. She caught sight of the barrel again.

'Kick your legs,' she shouted above the roar.

He looked at her blankly and she shook him as hard as she could, drawing his face to hers. 'Kick!'

He kicked, limply at first then harder. They couldn't survive much longer in the freezing water and Captain Pinkney and the boat had gone. Another wave and a sharp crack as the barrel hit the rocks and broke apart, sending pieces flying in the spray. Their chance of a buoy to hold them afloat had gone. Further along, still intact, a path straggled up the cliff. It was their only chance against the tide pushing them towards the hard, jagged cliff face. Another wave and they rose over its peak.

'Kick,' she shouted and in the dip before the next wave broke, they edged towards the path. 'Again,' she said, water streaming from her mouth.

Eyes half closed against the spray, he nodded, and pulling him she felt his legs kick against hers as they floated forward. Swallowing another mouthful, she spat out water. He kicked but his sodden jacket was pulling him down.

'Help me, Jonas,' she said. 'Lie out as much as you can and paddle.'

He was sinking. The crown of his head showed above the surface, but each time a wave lifted them he recovered less. Her strength ebbing, she held his arm and used her other to sweep forward. They were so close. She kicked but it hardly moved them. Her limbs were tiring, she couldn't do it alone.

Another wave and she put her hand out. Touching rock, she opened her eyes. They dipped again.

'Jonas, grab something.'

Shouldering him sideways, she held onto a protruding bush. The path sloped into the water and the next wave lifted them. Nearest, Jonas landed on the rough slope, his legs floating behind. The tide pulled back and he slipped with it, plunging underwater. Letting go of the bush, she seized his shoulder and, pressing him against the rock, readied to heave as hard as she could when the wave lifted them.

'Grab hold,' she shouted as they rose up and Jonas reached out one hand and caught the twisted stem of a stunted broom.

The swell sucked back and letting go, Jiddy splashed into the water, submerging into the eddy of a whirlpool. Scraping hands against the rock, she scrabbled upwards, surfacing and grasping whatever she could reach, kicking her toes into crevices and heaving herself out of the water. It dragged at her skirt but she pulled harder, scuffing her knees and shoes, clambering, climbing, panting to hold on. She couldn't believe it. Not again. Not dragging at her life again. She pressed herself into the path, her cheeks imprinting with gravel but she didn't care. She clung on.

Her dress clung shivering wet to her skin and her hair stuck to her scalp and cheeks. Jonas sat, forehead on his arms, clutching his legs on a short, level stretch of path a little way above. Holding the twisted bush, she balanced herself before taking another step.

Stones slipped under her feet and trickling soil cascaded in gravelly rivulets, forcing Jiddy to stop. A few steps more and she passed Jonas, touching his head to balance again. Taking careful steps, she reached the top and waited. The edge zig-zagged unrecognisably with straggling bushes and grass clinging to exposed earth. Jonas appeared and walking unsteadily towards her.

'There he is,' Jiddy pointed at the shadowy shape of Captain Pinkney's schooner.

Jonas looked exhausted. 'Don't ever fire a gun up here again,' he said. 'I'm half wishing you'd stayed in London.'

She looked at him. 'I'm cold,' she said. 'Aren't you cold?'

'Freezing.'

They strode through the grass to Boy and the cart and climbed up. Pulling a blanket around Jiddy's shoulders, Jonas spoke to the horse. 'It's all right Boy, it's all right, let's hope she's done all damage she can for one night.'

'You're not funny,' Jiddy said.

'Hell, Jiddy, we could have drowned.'

'I know, but we didn't.'

He pulled a blanket around himself, and sitting down lifted Boy's reins. The wind picked up. He flicked the reins and the cart jolted, making them rock against each other.

'Have you seen Mary yet?' he said.

'I came straight here.'

'To see me or Captain Pinkney?'

She pulled the blanket closer under her chin. 'You,' she said.

Knocking her arm he gave her a brief smile. 'So you're happy you let Captain Pinkney go then?' he said.

'I'll catch him next time.'

'Oh, you will, will you? You and your great aim will, hey?'

'I won't mind if I never see him again.'

'Think he'd be wise never to come back.'

Jiddy knocked his arm this time. She might never see Captain Pinkney again, but she knew she'd have to see Samuel again. Maybe he'd know after tonight that they were as different as silk from sacking. She hoped so. It was surely preferable to having to tell him that when they kissed, he had tasted of nothing. That nothing taste of fresh water which had sat in a pan overnight and grown stale. Looking sideways at Jonas, the reins loose in his hands and his observant eyes scanning the moonlit grassland, she knew she'd done the right thing.

She snuggled closer. 'You love Bay, don't you?'

'Most of time.'

Most of time. Most of the time, she hadn't seen London for what it meant but she knew everything about the Bay now, the good and the bad.

'This smuggling can't go on, can it?' she said. 'None of this can go on.'

He looked at her. 'No, but it takes two sides to change things,' he said.

She kissed his cheek. 'You taste of salt,' she said.

He shook the reins again before looking at her. 'What?' he said. 'What are you smiling at?'

She looked at the dark moor ahead and the stars flickering high above them.

'You told me once, we'd die without salt,' she said. 'I don't want to die.'

The End